Homegrown Healer
Hillbilly Hijinks
Book 1

Janet Taylor-Perry

Homegrown Healer

Janet Taylor-Perry

Book 1
in the
Hillbilly Hijinks Series

Dragon Breath Press
Ridgeland, MS

ISBN: 978-0-9990692-3-3

Semifinalist, Faulkner Wisdom Competition

Other Books by Janet Taylor-Perry

The Raiford Chronicles:

Lucky Thirteen
http://amzn.to/1ld8grm
Heartless
http://amzn.to/1iWuYmP
Broken
http://goo.gl/6YTwyz
Whatever It Takes
http://goo.gl/1eLv66

The Legend of Draconis:

King Satin's Realm
http://goo.gl/wf7UbM
Spirits' Desire
Winner: Preditors and Editors Award
2017, Best "Other" Novel

goo.gl/H9St2K

April Chastain Intrigues:

Wilted Magnolias
https://goo.gl/2oJOjc

Disclaimer

All entities in the following story are fictional. Any resemblance to any person living or dead is coincidence.

Dedication

For my two homegrown healers and precious daughters-in-law, Bridgett and Taylor.

Acknowledgments

Thank you, Cathy, with Christ Covenant School for information regarding the set-up and beginning faculty for a small school. And a special nod goes to John DeBoer (books available on Amazon) for the lesson on lacerated versus severed femoral artery and other medical questions.

As always, my gratitude goes to Lottie Brent Boggan, my editor and dearest friend. Lottie's books are available on Amazon. And I will ever be grateful to Christopher Chambers for cover design. If you need an amazing cover, contact him at cchambers@juroddesigns.com.

I would also like to give a shout-out to all my friends at thenextbigwriter.com who read this story in its roughest form and to the Red Dog Writers who struggled through weeks of read-alouds.

Many thanks to my cover model, my youngest son, Samuel Perry.

...Healing all manner of sickness and all manner of disease among the people.

Matthew 4:23B

Table of Contents

Preface

In 1999, I saw a documentary about patches of population in Appalachia that still did not have running water and electricity. I could not believe what I was watching. A couple of years after that, a local television station had a report about pockets in Mississippi that did not have medical care closer than 50-100 miles. Again, I could not believe what I was hearing and seeing. I was struck by the necessity of letting the world know these horrible truths. Thus, the story of Possum Holler and four young men who put their small community on a map. Even in the face of hardship, it is paramount to have hope. My *Hillbilly Hijinks* series is all about having hope.

During the school year of 2008-2009, I worked in a district in Mississippi that was impoverished and very low performing. My assistant principal dared me to drive into Tchula proper. I took the challenge, and I thought I had driven into a third-world country. Ten miles either way of this small town was at least comfort, if not affluence. I could not believe I was witnessing firsthand such deplorable circumstances. It was another catalyst to tell the world this story of so much despair.

The original completion date of the first draft of *Homegrown Healer* was February 16, 2010. That summer, I also work for the Census Bureau. Imagine my shock when one of the areas I worked was only a step better that the abominable conditions described above. I drove down a small dip into a neighborhood where one house in particular broke my heart. One elderly lady lived there alone. My foot literally sank into a plank on her porch. When I was asked in by this sweet old woman, I walked into a three-room house, a semblance of a living room, a combined dining room and kitchen, and a bedroom where a box fan in July was the only comfort afforded the old woman. July in Mississippi is usually 95+ degrees with almost unbreathable humidity, cause a "real feel" of at least 115 degrees.

It has taken 9 years to bring this story to print, but it is a story that needs telling. America needs to be aware that these conditions still exist. We cannot rest on our laurels and turn a blind eye to the plight of our fellow man. We don't have to go to an actual third-world country to make a difference. We need to start at home. We must give these people hope!

Prologue

Five-year-old MacKenzie Reardon buried his face in his great-great-grandmother's apron. Hazel eyes squeezed tightly, he covered his ears to block out the screams from the other room. A man's low echo of sorrow replaced a woman's high-pitched wail.

Guiding Mac's father across the room lit by oil lamps to a cane-bottom chair, Preacher Leo Tomlin said, "Ander, I'm so sorry. May was a good woman." The boy burrowed brown hair deeper into the old woman's lap. An age-spotted hand caressed the child's head.

Leo comforted, "I've prayed for a doctor closer than a hundred miles. Grandma Newton did all she could. We'll bury May and the baby tomorrow. You *must* think of the boys."

"I gotta find 'em a momma. Mac ain't but five. Zeb's three, and Jack ain't even walkin' good." Ander Reardon shook his head. "I gotta go to the mine. I gotta work."

Leo sighed. *The new momma would die, too. Ander, only twenty-five, won't live long working in that mine.* "Ander, Tal Jones has survived alone since June's death." *Can I steer Ander away from condemning another woman to an early grave? Too many women in Possum Holler die in childbirth.*

"He ain't got three little boys, jest Gator. The other four run off. I gotta have help."

"I'm sure Ina Campbell will help. She was May's cousin and best friend. Talk to her."

"I'll think on it." Ander rubbed his face with calloused hands. "I'm too tired right now."

Leo patted Ander's shoulder. *Possum Holler, West Virginia, is a third world country in the middle of late twentieth-century America. I wouldn't have believed it if God hadn't called me here to minister. I love these people. I'll stay and guide them until I die. What else can I do to help?*

Leo picked up Mac, kissed his forehead, and held him close, whispering a prayer. "Dear God, watch over this little one and his brothers. Send us a doctor. Give me wisdom to help these people. Amen."

1

A Dream Come True

"Doctor MacKenzie Reardon" shook the dean's hand and held his diploma close to his chest, not hoisting it in the air or dancing a jig as some of the other graduates had. *This is far too valuable to treat with such disrespect.*

Mac sighed. *Is this a waking dream? I'm really a doctor.* His mortarboard sat crown-like on his short, light-brown hair. Soft hazel eyes found the only person watching him. *She understands how important this is to me—well, at least, professes to.*

Mac Reardon had a dream. *I'll go back to Possum Holler, be its doctor.* He would be one of a few people in town who had attended college. Only one person had ever returned—and that with reluctance. Most left, never looking back. *I want hope and health for my people, especially women—that they can give birth without dying, like my mother did.*

He glanced at his one supporter. *Felicia, my dear wife.* She threw him a kiss. *I'm worried about you. Do you understand my dream?* He sighed. *Five more years for post-graduate work and residency. I <u>will</u> return to Possum Holler. My people need me.*

Mac returned to his seat and looked over his shoulder. Unable to see his wife, he continued thinking. *I'll let Felicia celebrate. For now.*

His mind drifted to how they met at Marshall University:

"Stop gawking at that cute blonde." His roommate, Marvcus, prodded him with a sharp elbow. "Introduce yourself. I dare you, man. She's rich and popular. *I'm* betting she laughs in your face." Never one to run from a challenge, Mac took the dare. He introduced himself and asked the lovely Felicia Chambry out. *She taught me to salsa.* A different part of his anatomy tingled at that moment. *New subject.*

He let his mind wander back to his best friend, Tipper Campbell. Both Marvcus and Tipper had unusual names. There had been a few jokes about Tipper and booze, and now he was a moonshiner, although he rarely imbibed. And Mac himself had jested about his roommate's mother not knowing which name she wanted—Marvin or Marcus—so she combined the two. Yet, Mac's mind strayed back to his wife and what she might think of his friends, not just Tipper, but Gator and Alain. He sighed as he considered his own views of Alain Richter. His cousin, Gator Jones, was a simple man; Alain Richter, complicated beyond words. *Felicia, Felicia, Felicia, what will you think about them?*

He had tried to explain his dream to her, before and after their marriage. *Felicia still doesn't understand what <u>under-privileged Appalachia</u> really means. She doesn't realize we'll be off the grid—literally. She sees our future as a fantasy, that we'll transform Possum Holler into a picturesque mountain village.*

"We'll renovate your family home," she had said to him. "I'll look at the house and design something wonderful."

Her degree in architectural design will be useless in Possum Holler. Women there are expected to be barefoot and pregnant. Felicia's fancy notions won't fly. The only women who garner respect in Appalachia are teachers or healers and midwives like Grandma Newton. He smiled. *Grandma, what do you think of me now? I know Papa's kept you abreast of everything.* He grinned just thinking about the old woman's reaction. He visualized, for a moment, her dancing a jig and taking a swig of moonshine. If he had been anywhere else besides a solemn graduation ceremony, he would have laughed aloud.

What will you make of my wife, Grandma? His stomach knotted with worry. *Felicia and I are worlds apart. Opposites attract, they say, but Possum Holler just might prove too much for her. Unless...* Mac envisioned his bride obtaining a nursing degree while he did his internship at Cook Memorial Hospital. *Will she do it, if I ask her? But...she's pregnant. Couldn't be worse timing.*

Felicia met Mac in the auditorium lobby. "I'm so proud of you!" She locked perfectly manicured fingers around his neck. Five-inch stilettos put her nose-to-nose with him as they kissed. "Let's celebrate. We can't be out late because the movers will be coming early."

"Mm-hm," Mac murmured. He looked into her big blue eyes. "Love you, but you talk too much sometimes. I don't want anyone making dumb-blonde jokes tonight, okay?"

"You know it's just an act, right?" She fluffed her blonde curls and flashed him a seductive smile.

"Yeah, I know how *different* you are from the stereotype." Mac pushed Felicia's hair from her face. "Let's go home and cook spaghetti *after* we make love."

"MacKenzie Reardon!" She playfully popped his arm. "You have a one-track mind."

"It's not my fault you're so beautiful. My celebration, right? I get to do what I want, right?"

"Yes."

"I want to make love to you. Guess what."

"What?"

"There's no reason to use a condom, is there? I can truly *feel* you."

Felicia bit her lip. "I suppose so."

"Take me home, so I can celebrate my dream come true."

Felicia's frown turned upside down. "As the doctor prescribes."

Later at home, the lovers prepared spaghetti together.

Mac watched his beautiful wife in the negligee move around the kitchen and mentally pinched himself. *Mountain boy, you're out of your league—she comes from wealth and knows nothing of your impoverished world. How could she ever love you?*

As she stirred the sauce, Mac drained the pasta, stopping to kiss the back of his wife's neck. "Mm," he whispered. "Maybe I'll eat *you* instead."

She laughed and turned to give her husband a kiss, letting her red-tipped nails trail down his chest. "That could be arranged. Let's eat fast."

"Yes, ma'am. Then dessert in the bedroom, milady. There will be no more interruptions. Tipper called this morning and Papa called just as we got home." Mac announced, "He might come for a visit to Chicago—another dream. I need to see him."

"I'd like to meet him."

"Later." He wiggled mischievous eyebrows.

Cries of agony...laments of loss...silence of water-filled lungs...coppery lightning strike of deadly venom...labored breathing...rumbling cough—in a cold, clammy sweat, Mac bolted upright in bed and screamed.

Felicia sat up beside him and put her arm around his muscled shoulders. "Sh. Which nightmare was it this time?"

"All of them," Mac gasped. "Oh, Felicia, my people need me."

"You'll be there soon."

"I have to go. *Please* understand. I cannot let these dreams come true again." Mac kissed Felicia. "Make love to me again. Replace the nightmares with dreams of you."

Felicia made her husband's dream come true, if only for that one night.

2
Shepherd the Flock

The five hundred twenty-seven residents within Possum Holler,

West Virginia, did not refer to Leo Tomlin as "Reverend," "Brother," or "Pastor." Although he had a Doctor of Theology, nobody called him "Doctor" Tomlin. He was "Preacher" Tomlin. He was pastor, counselor, preacher; he performed weddings, funerals, baptisms; he played banjo and guitar, square danced, took occasional swigs of moonshine with members of his congregation. He did not shepherd his flock for money. His paltry salary from the mission board barely fed and clothed him, but he never went hungry. Most residents invited him to dine with them often. His housing was free. He was the religious shepherd in Possum Holler because he loved the people.

Leo lost himself in thought. *I'm glad to be hidden from the mainstream of religion. The ruling ministers of the mission board would never condescend to visit here. I know the way I conduct myself would fall under serious criticism of most evangelicals. Still, this is my congregation, and if the church authorities cut me off, I'll always have a home with these people.* He uttered a prayer of thanksgiving that his church remained non-denominational and accepted all who attended.

When Leo heeded God's call, he realized serving the Lord meant remaining a bachelor—leaving someone he loved dearly. "Being a missionary means going to remote places. I can't take you there, Lauren," he had said and waited for her reaction, breath held.

It did not go well. She screamed; she threw books, shoes, and knickknacks at him. "Get out, you coward! How dare you think so little of me?"

It was I thought so highly of you. Still do. He heaved a weighty sigh at the memory.

Nonetheless, after eulogizing five members of the same family in three years, he had taken on the additional shepherding responsibility of a child.

Once he arrived at age twenty-seven, Leo's wide-eyed ideal of saving souls and bodies changed almost overnight. By Possum Holler standards, he was middle-aged, though he saw himself as young, with an undergraduate degree in psychology, a Master of Christian Education and a Doctor of Theology.

Well, Lord, You called me here, instead of to an inner-city church or a third-world country. And I've been here for eighteen years. Leo meditated on those years as he read Scripture. "Bring up a child in the way he is to go, and when he is old he will not depart from it."

He flipped pages of his journal:

Population here is 589; middle income is $11,000; average household size—seven; median education level is eighth grade. Most popular jobs: coal mining, farming, and bootlegging. Life expectancy: 44—men, 40—women. Only homes within the corporate limits have running water and electricity. Outlying areas might have wells or pumps, but no indoor plumbing; some have outhouses; others don't.

Medical care is almost non-existent. Grandma Newton, midwife and herbalist, still delivers babies. The woman could be an ancient Druid. Some of her practices seem like witchcraft, but many of the herbal remedies work. Infant mortality rate is still sky-high, as are childbirth deaths.

"Things haven't improved much, since I first arrived." Leo sighed. "Girls are still married or pregnant by sixteen." He shook his head and read another entry: *The horror stories about inbreeding are real. Grandma does a good job when there are no complications.* "I can say *most* of the inbreeding has stopped."

He dog-eared the page. *Alain, Alain, Alain.* He bit his lip and tasted the bitterness of blood.

"Many of the people have simple, childlike faith," he said softly. "A few escape, but most never return. Others die, still believing, still loving, and still trying." Ander Reardon's face came to the front of his memory. "You were twenty-four when I met you, Ander, but looked forty, trying so hard to be a good father, husband, and friend." A tear rolled down his cheek. "I still miss him, Lord. I had to bury his wife, three of the children—and Ander." *Pneumonia took you, my dear friend.* "Nobody so young and healthy should die like that, Lord."

That night was frigid—single digits. Starless, pitch-black. Mac walked twelve miles from their cabin to this house. A seven-year-old. The preacher rubbed his face with both hands. "I'll never forget opening the door and hearing, 'Pa's not breathing.'" Leo wiped away another tear. "That day, Mac became the child of my heart, even if I never legally adopted him."

He sat pensively a few minutes longer. "My precious boy is now a doctor." He smiled. "Time to make a call."

Dr. MacKenzie Reardon snatched the receiver from the phone on the wall as he and his wife entered their apartment just after his graduation. "Hello?"

Felicia continued to their bedroom with a seductive lick to her lips and a wink that said, "Make it quick."

"Hello, Dr. Reardon!"

"Papa! I wish you were here." Mac closed the apartment door with his foot.

"Me, too. Congratulations. I won't keep you long. What's next?"

"We leave tomorrow for Chicago."

"That soon?"

"Yes, sir. Felicia has a job interview. Papa, I have news."

"What's that?"

Mac gusted a breath. "We're expecting a baby."

"Oh." The one word was weighted with shock. "I thought you were waiting."

"Me too."

"Well, it's a gift—just like you were. Congratulations a second time."

"Thanks."

"I'm so proud of you. Ander would be just as proud."

Strained silence followed. "Mac?" Leo prompted.

"Papa, why don't you come to Chicago for a short visit?"

"I have my flock here."

"They'll survive a couple of weeks without you. This little lamb could use a visit."

"I'll try. Call me when you get settled. I love you, Mac."

"I love you, too, Papa." Mac hung up the receiver.

The pink lace teddy Felicia wore as she ran her hands up her husband's back did not dilute her acerbic question. "Why do you call him 'Papa'? It sounds so childish. Why not 'Dad'?"

Prejudice? Judgment? "Where I'm from 'Dad' is strange. Sometimes 'Daddy', but never 'Dad.' Usually it's 'Pa'."

"You're so silly."

"No, I'm serious."

"You make it sound like *The Beverly Hillbillies*. Were you surprised by the cement ponds?" Felicia laughed.

Does she realize how awful that sounds? Mac scowled and shot back, "Felicia, *The Beverly Hillbillies* is a joke. If you want closer to the truth, watch *Deliverance*."

"Are you mad at me?" She nibbled her index finger.

"No, darling." He placed his hands on her shoulders. "Forget the stereotypes—just like you're not a dumb blonde. I just want you to understand."

"I do."

Doubtful. "Oh, I hope so."

She put on a pouty face. "I thought we were celebrating. I'm dressed for the occasion."

"We are, and you're gorgeous, breathtaking. No more depressing talk. Come here." Mac kissed Felicia and then swept her into his arms and took her to bed.

"Lord, Mac's troubled. What do I do?" At his desk in Possum Holler, Leo prayed, one hand still on the receiver. "Yes, I must visit my lamb—he's not lost, but in need. The father will travel, but the preacher must make plans."

Leo stood, stretched his thin seventy-four-inch frame and headed outside to find Royce Dent, a deacon and owner of the general store. "He'll take care of the Sunday Sing and dinner on the grounds." He took a deep breath. "Yes, my flock won't flounder for only one weekend without me." Preacher Tomlin walked down the dirt road to the general store.

3
His Father's Eyes

Mac and Felicia moved into a two-bedroom, furnished apartment near the hospital where housing was less expensive. Felicia snagged a job with an architectural firm.

Leo's plane landed two days later at O'Hare. As he had expected, nobody met his flight. Leo took a taxi to the apartment building, rode up the elevator, and knocked on the door. His heart thudded. *Will his bride be all Mac says? Is she more than beauty? She comes from privilege. Will she understand Mac and his people? I shouldn't worry,* Leo reminded himself. *I raised him right. Mac can hold his own.*

The door opened. *What a beautiful young woman. Mac was right. Is her spirit sweet as well?* "Hello, Felicia. I'm Leo Tomlin."

"You're *Papa*, according to Mac." She smiled. "Come in and sit, please."

After a cool glass of water, he perched on the plaid tweed sofa and listened to Felicia prattle about their wedding. "We decided on a simple wedding at a Methodist church." She showed Leo the photo album. "My parents like Mac," she said, "and don't mind he comes from humble beginnings. They paid for our honeymoon—two weeks in a Swiss chalet." She beamed. "After all, Mac *is* a doctor, the kind of man my father wanted me to marry." Her pretty mouth drooped. "But, they weren't happy about his wish to return to Possum Holler."

The pictures Mac sent had shown some disparity of social standing and had given Leo cause for concern, but he let his son make his choices. *Only a few fraternity brothers and Marvcus as best man for Mac—a packed side of the church for Felicia.*

"Are you close to your folks? Do you have siblings?"

"I'm an only child. I can't say we're close though." She scowled. "They *hated* when I dated a nightclub owner. They're politically conservative, but they think Mac is a good catch."

Good catch, indeed. "What do they say about going to Possum Holler?"

"They don't want me in such a backward place." Leo's arched eyebrows did not deter Felicia's chattering. "I didn't tell them about it until *after* the wedding." She smiled impishly. "Actually—when we returned from our honeymoon. Mother screeched, and Father glared. They moved from Mom's Trading Post, Pennsylvania, a small town, to a big city where they had more opportunities. Father's all about making the bucks." She shrugged. "They'll get over it."

Finally face to face, Leo appraised Felicia as if she were a precious gemstone. *She's smart, friendly, and appears to love my son, but something's missing. Such different backgrounds? She won't eat biscuits-with-gravy and hog souse. Mac would gag on caviar. The difference: Mac would eat caviar and be thankful he had food to stay alive; whereas, Felicia would go hungry rather than eat something she perceives as disgusting.*

Leo chided himself. *Am I being unfair? Can Felicia share Mac's love for the people of Possum Holler? Doubtful. There'll be contention in the end.* He held his tongue, listened, and learned. "I understand you're quite the architect."

"I'm just getting started. I have big dreams."

"No doubt you do."

Though Mac prodded, Felicia found hands-on care of the sick repulsive. He had to accept his wife did not possess the gift of empathy. "I hoped for a helper in my practice," Mac quietly confided to Leo. "It would've made things better in Possum Holler."

"Being a healer isn't for everyone," Leo said, with an attempt at diplomacy. "Nursing is a special calling. Felicia's on another path. Looks like you'll have your hands full, starting your rotations."

"Yes. I'm starting pediatrics in the morning. I might not be here every night."

The evenings he was home, Mac talked about the children he attended, usually run-of-the-mill cases expected among children—a broken bone, stitches, a stomach virus.

Felicia sat at the 1950s-style, aluminum-and-Formica dining table and sighed deeply after Mac sat down. "Dr. Tomlin, I apologize for spaghetti, but Mac would eat it every day." She pushed back the red-and-silver aluminum chair and put her napkin in her lap. "It must be his favorite meal. I can't fathom why he likes it so much."

Leo laughed. "Felicia, Mac had never tasted good spaghetti until he was seven years old." Leo waved a hand as if to erase something. "That stuff they serve in a school cafeteria doesn't count. It's an easy bachelor meal. I'm surprised his favorite's not pizza. You should've seen him devour *that* the first time I took him to the city."

"What do you eat in Possum Holler, honey?" Felicia chuckled. "Opossums?"

"Pork chops," said Leo quickly, knowing full-well some residents might eat opossum.

"That's not strange." She tilted her head and lifted an eyebrow.

"No, sweetheart." Mac smirked. "But you'd balk at hog brains scrambled with eggs."

"That's disgusting!" She grimaced.

"Any more than snails?" The young doctor smiled. "I ate escargot. Think of hog brains as a mountain delicacy."

"I'll remember that. Let's eat normal spaghetti now," Felicia asserted.

"And it's delicious." Mac kissed his wife's hand. "Thanks for making it."

Leo admitted, *Mac handled the food analogy well*. He asked, "Any unusual cases today?"

"No." Mac ate a large bite of spaghetti. "Well, yes," he said after he swallowed.

"So, tell us," Leo suggested. "I'm interested."

Mac eyed Felicia. "It was gross."

"It couldn't be that bad," she encouraged.

The doctor cocked an eyebrow. "Three-year-old partially eaten by rats."

"Ewww!" Her nose wrinkled.

"We had to amputate his leg and start rabies injections. His mother was arrested. She's a junkie. The child will go into foster care." He released a deep, sad sigh. "I wanted to bring him home with me."

"No way!" Felicia asserted.

"No, Mac," said Leo gently. "You can't bring them *all* home."

"You brought me home," Mac countered.

"You came to *me*." Leo grinned.

"You didn't have to keep me."

Nodding, Leo said, "But I haven't kept every child who lost parents in Possum Holler. Remember Alain Richter? You're special."

After swallowing a bite of spaghetti, Mac said, "Papa, we need more than a doctor in Possum Holler. We need a school, so children don't have to ride a bus fifty miles. And we could use an orphanage, for lack of a better term, for children like Alain Richter." He twirled more spaghetti onto his fork and held it up as he spoke. "I know kids like me are usually taken in by friends or family, but they don't get what I got from you. They don't get educated or even fed well. The Richters sure could've used some help."

"Who's Alain Richter?" asked Felicia.

"The eldest of fourteen children," Leo said. "He became the head of his family when he was fourteen after a family tragedy and took care of all his siblings. He's a year older than Mac."

Mac scowled. "We used to be friends," he said.

Leo hooded his eyes at the calloused comment. Unfazed, Mac continued his diatribe on the woes of Possum Holler society. "Papa, you know in the big city, foster care is available. It's regulated, and the kids are usually cared for. If social workers tried to come into Possum Holler, they would probably never be seen again. I remember the one who went to the Richter place." He wagged his head. "The poor woman probably resigned immediately. No more ever came. They were afraid of meeting a shotgun face-to-face."

He consumed the spaghetti he had been holding aloft. "But if we could get some of the locals to run a home for the children, we could oversee their care.

"I know the only way for change is education on all levels— mental development, physical education, nutrition, medical care, and safe sex. Spiritual guidance is your area. When I get back, I'll take care of the medical side." He chugged tea. "But we don't have the school."

"I keep applying for grants," assured Leo. "I'm tenacious. I'll write more letters when I get home. Focus on *your* job. Better health might lead to no need for an orphanage." Leo forked salad and pointed with the loaded utensil. "We need to talk."

Mac half-opened his mouth to speak. Leo shook his head slowly. "Not now."

Felicia's eyes flicked from father to son. "Possum Holler sounds like a third-world country."

Mac nodded. "In some ways, it's worse because the town sits in the middle of affluence. It's hidden and forgotten. I want the world to see it."

Leo admonished, "Just remember you can't make *everything* right. It'll take time, especially the *Richters*."

Mac sighed and nodded. "Sorry."

Felicia shivered. *My father would never have made a point by a mere facial expression. He'd have lectured me an hour.* A chill also ran the length of her spine. *Possum Holler hides real ugliness.*

Leo ate the salad on his fork.

Mac went to bed, and Felicia noticed Leo reading his Bible. *He's not Mac's biological father, but they share the same serene expression. Mac reads his Bible. Is that the key? They share something profound enough that a look is all they need to communicate.* She approached Leo. "Dr. Tomlin, why does Mac want to fix everything? Did he bring home stray puppies?"

Leo chuckled. "All dogs are strays in Possum Holler, except the hounds." He closed the book onto his index finger to mark his place and peered over his half-glasses with soulful brown eyes. "No, Mac is full of love. He sees everything with His Father's eyes."

"Was Ander like that?"

"Yes, Ander was a lot like Mac." Leo removed his glasses and held them by one arm, flipping them back and forth. "But I was referring to his Heavenly Father, Felicia."

"I see." She furrowed her brow. "Well, good night." She went to bed too.

Leo realized the underlying issue. *Felicia doesn't see. That lack of sight is the missing link. Not only are Mac and Felicia on different levels economically and socially, but also spiritually.* He prayed, *Lord, let her have complete understanding. Thank You Mac does see everything through Your eyes.*

4

Underhanded Means

The ninth day of Leo's visit, Mac went to the hospital, and Felicia got ready for her first day at her new job. "Will you be all right, Dr. Tomlin?" she asked.

"Yes, dear. I think I'll do some sightseeing and go to a museum. Since it's my last full day, maybe I'll surprise you and Mac with some mountain cooking for dinner."

"How sweet. I'll see you tonight, then. The spare key is on the hook by the door."

Before he did anything else, Leo grocery-shopped for the items he wanted to make for supper. He found ham steaks and sweet potatoes easily. Finding fresh turnip greens with the greens still attached was harder, and he whistled at the cost. *At least corn meal's cheap.* He took the groceries home, soaked the greens, and set the other items to the side.

"Time for a shower. What a luxury, after years of tub baths." He had forgotten how stimulating and relaxing the rhythmic pelting of steamy water could be. His back muscles had not felt so unknotted in years.

Looking in the medicine cabinet for shaving cream, he found a box of condoms, in plain view on the bottom shelf, open. The package on top looked strange to him. Out of curiosity, he picked it up. *Are those pin pricks?* He tore it open and filled the condom with water. Water dripped freely. *No!* He examined several more packets. All were the same.

"She didn't," he mumbled. "Mac wanted to wait."

Leo disposed of the open packages and went to the museum. Trying to decide if he should tell Mac the truth, he hardly paid attention to the guide. *It won't matter. Mac'll be a great father. However, the deception will hurt him. Why did Felicia feel the need to use underhanded means to get pregnant? Is she afraid of losing Mac? Does she think a child will hold them together, that*

Mac will hesitate to take his child back to the environment he came from? Does she hope a child will spur Mac to practice medicine for money, thus placating her parents?

When Leo returned to the apartment, someone was in the shower. *It's Mac. Their car's not here.* Leo prayed as he heated the oven and prepared to bake the sweet potatoes.

"Hey, Papa," Mac greeted, entering the kitchen in pajama pants and a gray undershirt. "Do you mind if I'm comfortable during supper?"

"No, not at all."

"What are you making?" He leaned on the bar separating the dining area from the small, functional kitchen.

"Ham steaks, turnip greens with the green, baked sweet potatoes, rice, and corn bread with red-eye cornmeal gravy." Leo rolled the potatoes in foil and placed them on the top oven rack.

"No dessert?" Mac asked in a childlike manner.

"Do you want one?"

"There are some frozen pie shells in the freezer." He jerked his thumb over his shoulder. "And some apple filling in the pantry." The pantry behind him was a ceiling-to-floor cupboard for canned goods.

"Hardly homemade," Leo observed with an uneasy grin.

"It's Felicia's idea of homemade. It's not bought already baked."

"*You* make it."

"All right. Is something the matter? You seem upset."

A weighty breath escaped Leo's chest. "Son, would you tell me if I'd been deceived by a person I love?" He snipped the first of the greens into a pot.

Mac sighed. "Are you trying to tell me something?"

"Yes, and I'm not sure how."

"You found the condoms."

Leo looked up from cutting the greens. "You knew?"

Mac nodded. "I discovered the condoms with holes as I unpacked," he admitted. "No matter, we're having a baby. I left them in the cabinet hoping she'd say something to me. I didn't expect *you* to find them."

"I wasn't snooping," Leo hastened. "It'd been so long since I last flew, I didn't know about all the new regulations. I had to take my shaving cream out of my carry-on at the airport. I haven't shaved since I got here. I figured you'd have some in the cabinet. You did, right next to an open box of condoms. The packages looked odd." He shrugged. "You know me—too curious."

"Should I tell her I know what she did?"

"I don't know, Mac. It worries me it's a sign of things to come."

"You don't like her, do you, Papa?"

"I don't *trust* her, Mac. I hardly know her, but something's amiss. She tricked you with this. She also deceived her parents about your future plans and feels no remorse for it. I'm sorry." He drew his mouth into a thin line. "I love you, and I would never lie to you again. Keeping one secret from you was enough, but it wasn't my secret to tell."

Mac interjected, "Pa and Miss Ina were happy. She shouldn't've been forced to have a secret."

"True, but things haven't changed much. Felicia will have a hard time."

"I'm afraid of that, too, but I know what I have to do." Mac tapped the countertop several times in rapid succession with the flat of his hand. "I keep praying she'll adjust. She says she understands, but I don't think she can without seeing it firsthand. I've tried to describe it. I won't deceive her. My family *will* go to Possum Holler. Having a baby won't change that. I love her, but I know my calling. I hope she loves me enough to support me."

"Me too, Mac."

The apartment door opened. Felicia came into the kitchen. "Something smells good."

Leo smiled. "I'm preparing a mountain meal fit for royalty."

"Great. I'm starving."

"I hope you enjoy it. It'll be ready in about an hour. Why don't you take a hot bath and get comfortable the way Mac has?"

"I think I will."

Mac nodded at Leo and followed his wife.

Felicia teased, "Do you want to join me?" as she slipped into a bubble bath.

Mac opened the medicine cabinet and set the condoms on the side of the tub. "Let's talk."

"Is something wrong?"

"Felicia, there are holes in *all* of them."

"Really?"

Mac gave her a cold, hard stare. "Baby, no matter what, we're having a baby. Why did you do this and lie?"

"I thought I threw those out."

"They got packed. Talk to me."

"I didn't want to wait five or six years. You're so stubborn. I knew you'd be happy if it happened, so I took matters into my own hands. I won't apologize."

"Why did you lie?" Mac dropped the box into the bathroom wastebasket. "*That* hurts. If you'd argued, told me how you felt, you could've persuaded me. Don't lie to me again. I love you, and I will love this child. Lying to me is one thing that will make me angry."

"I'm sorry. I do love you, Mac," she pleaded. "I just wanted a family." She leaned back in the tub and rubbed wet hands across her face.

"I just wanted everything to be settled first. However, what's done is done. We'll have a wonderful family. Just no more lies or deceit."

"I promise."

"Okay. I'm making apple pie for dessert. Don't rush." He took his wife's hand and kissed it. Before he went to the kitchen, he paused at the medicine cabinet. "And I'm growing a beard." He tossed the shaving cream next to the condoms.

Felicia sighed with relief. *Mac's satisfied. He has no idea just how underhanded I've been.*

Felicia joined the men as Leo placed dinner on the table. She had never eaten the leafy part of the turnip or had red-eye cornmeal gravy. "My compliments to the chef, Dr. Tomlin," she said. "This is good. I think Mac'll miss your cooking."

"Maybe. My flight leaves tomorrow afternoon. Call when the baby comes, or if you need anything."

Leo finished his visit. He prayed fervently on the flight back to West Virginia.

5
A Ray of Hope

Barred *windows and razor-wire fencing. The place looks like either maximum-security or about to be condemned.* Sunny Bankston pulled her Honda Accord into a parking space, stomach lurching. *Are children expected to learn under these conditions?*

The rookie teacher climbed concrete steps into the school building near Chicago's Jefferson Park. *I know the fence and windows are safety measures, but it's gloomy. Can it get more oppressive?* "Yep. Metal detectors," she groaned as she stepped through the doors.

Once in her classroom, Sunny felt better. *This flowerchild is about to create beauty.* She flipped strawberry-blonde, waist-length hair over her shoulder. *The principal said I can do whatever I please to the room. I'll make it conducive to learning.* She did a three-sixty. *I'll decorate with off-white walls two-thirds of the way down, soft blue the rest of the way; put curtains on the windows and place six round tables rather than desks, with five children at each table.* Sunny pointed to three corners. *Three rectangular tables—reading, technology, art.* She spoke aloud. "I want at least two bookshelves, a file cabinet, a storage cabinet and a metal desk with a comfortable chair for myself. I'll put my desk in the corner closest to the door." She sat at a worn student desk, drew the diagram, and made her list.

Principal Perry Knotts laughed when he saw the list. "How much of this do you plan to buy yourself?"

"Excuse me?"

"Miss Bankston, I see where you want to go. Commendable. I'd like to see us get there, but you're in the lowest-performing school in the city." He pointed to the sketch of the room layout she'd handed him. "What do you plan to put in this technology corner?"

"The two computers I saw in the room. Do they work?"

"Slowly, but they work."

"Do we have internet?"

"Yes."

"That's what goes in that corner. We'll call it our 'Funknowlogy Technology.'"

"Catchy." He tapped another section of her drawing. "What goes in your art corner?"

"Art supplies, of course: construction paper, art paper, crayons, et cetera." She rolled her hand upward.

He pursed thin lips. "What if only three or four of your students bring art supplies?"

"I'll figure it out." The five-foot-nothing woman clenched her jaw. "Somehow."

"Please, what's its name?" The corners of his mouth turned up in a teasing grin.

"I think 'Kreative Korner,' with K's not C's."

"Nice touch." The principal sat on the edge of his desk. "And the reading corner?"

"That's the 'Book Nook.' I have a lot of books I can use."

"Uh-huh. Be sure to put your name in all of them."

"I'll divide it into fiction and nonfiction. I'll label them 'Fiction Addiction' and 'The Real Deal.'"

"Okay." He laughed. "The office supplies, tables, chairs and desk I can get. You'll want to cover or paint them."

"Mr. Knotts, do we have textbooks?"

"Yes, they're new. Federal grant."

"Do you mind if I paint?"

"Not at all. I'll even buy the paint. When do you want it?"

"Tomorrow."

"Everything?" His almond-shaped eyes grew wide as his thin brows arched.

"I'll paint first."

"Miss Bankston, did your parents wait to name you after your terrible twos?"

"No." She blushed. "Why?"

"You're so...sunny. They must've named you *after* they got to know you."

She laughed. "No, my parents are sort of the hippie types. My two sisters are Starr and Skye, and my brother is River."

"Interesting."

"My childhood was different. The first time I ate a non-soy cheeseburger was as a college freshman—away from Mom. My parents were and remain strict vegetarians. Dad *will* eat fish or seafood on occasion, but not Mom." She shook her head.

"Tough on a kid."

She nodded. "Our friends thought we were strange."

"Is that why you're such a tiny thing?" His light-skinned hand laid Sunny's diagram on his desk.

"No, that's genetics. My mom is about the same size, and my dad is maybe five-six. My siblings are all short and small-framed, too."

"I hope your enthusiasm rubs off on both your students *and* the faculty. You're the little ray of hope this place needs." They meandered toward the door. "How would you feel about a cheeseburger with me?"

"I'd love to."

"We'll pick up the paint afterward."

Over cheeseburgers and fries, Mr. Knotts became Perry and Miss Bankston became Sunny. Buying paint at the nearest home improvement store proved to be fun.

Perry picked up small cans of rainbow colors, white, and gray.

"What's that for?" asked Sunny.

Arcing his hand, he said, "I see a mural of sun, clouds, and a rainbow on one wall. Bring your little ray of hope to the cinder blocks. Let's do it tonight—you and me—unless you're tired of my company."

"All right." Her bright-blue eyes danced with enthusiasm. "Grab little cans of gold, silver, and black. I'll add a pot of gold at the end of the rainbow and silver linings to the clouds. The gold will be in the shape of little books. After all, education *is* the pot of gold at the end of the rainbow."

"Oh, I like that."

They carried the painting supplies into Sunny's classroom and work began. She surveyed her boss. *Thirtyish, thin, slightly over six feet, short kinky hair. Light skin, almond-shaped eyes. An interesting mixed heritage.* She said, "Okay, you asked me about *my* genetics. Talk."

He blushed. "All right. I'm Amerasian. My biracial father met my Vietnamese mother while on active duty and got her out during the fall of Saigon. A priest had already married them. My white grandfather married a black lounge singer in Detroit. The rest of my family lives there. Two brothers work for car manufacturers, one is a minister, and one is in the military. We're all tall and skinny like my dad and granddad."

"Was the multi-racial thing difficult growing up?"

"Not so much in Detroit." Honey-brown eyes twinkled. "There's more, but we weren't vegetarians, and we didn't eat our dogs—three Labs."

Sunny chuckled. "Do tell."

"I'm the youngest of five boys, but that's not the most bizarre." His grin turned impish. "I'm only seven years old. *I* should be in your class."

"What?" She laughed out loud, holding her paint brush in the air.

"I was born on February 29th."

She stood back, slack-jawed. "For real?"

He nodded. "I'm one of a kind."

They painted until after midnight. Perry brushed a streak of red down Sunny's nose. "This is not face-painting!" she squealed.

Perry laughed merrily. "It was either paint you or kiss you."

"Oh!" She blushed and looked at the floor.

"Too much too soon." He handed her the handkerchief from his pocket. "I'll slow down, my little ray of hope."

6

Clouds on a Sunny Day

Sunny's was the brightest, happiest room on the third-grade hall. She had thirty-six students, not thirty, so she added a chair to each table. The seventeen boys and nineteen girls were racially diverse, but predominantly black. As Mr. Knotts warned, only half a dozen brought school supplies, including pencils and paper.

The poverty and lack of supplies was the first cloud on Sunny's day, but she looked for a silver lining, as in each cloud in the mural on the wall. She went to her church, sought donations, and came back with supplies to fill her cabinet for the year.

The next cloud was some students' personal hygiene. She found herself keeping a scented handkerchief inside her blouse. She talked to Mr. Knotts about the issue.

"Sunny, I promise to send paperwork through proper channels to investigate," he assured. "However, keep your handkerchief because I don't know how long it'll take."

He took Sunny's handkerchief and sniffed it. "Miss Bankston, I'd love to sit *very* close to you."

"Then, one of us would *have* to change schools. Keep that one. I have another."

"I wouldn't tell, so no clouds on *my* sunny day, *please*. I'll get paperwork rolling on this. Dinner tonight?"

"On the other side of town, or are you cooking?"

"Mexican. I'll pick you up at six."

"Okay."

"While I have your attention," Sunny said over fajitas, "only five of my kids read on third-grade level. *But,* I have one little girl who is far above third-grade reading level. I need to challenge her. I'd like to name her my reading assistant, so she can help tutor some of her classmates. What do you think?"

"Great idea." He swigged Corona. "Just be careful not to make the others think you're showing favoritism."

"I will. The ones who are really *far* below I'll work with one-on-one and in small groups to bridge the gap. Plus, I've sent the proper documents home and to the exceptional education department for those who definitely need greater assistance."

"Good. Sunny, I'd like to leave school behind now." He took her hand across the table. "I want to dine with my Sunshine."

"You're silly, Perry. What would you like to talk about?"

"Anything but school."

"As someone said, 'When it rains, it pours.' My room might *flood*," Sunny told herself. "Gang affiliations. Seriously?" Hostility spilled over even to eight-and nine-year-olds, forcing Sunny to break the class into two groups by gang loyalties—not gender as she would have expected at that age. Then she learned the cousin of one student had been killed in a drive-by shooting. *This is frightening.*

She fled to Perry's office on her off time when the physical education teacher took the children.

"A harsh reality of inner-city," he calmly informed her. "Sunny, that is why certain styles and color combinations are forbidden even at this level." He pulled a long list from his file. "This is a list of things to look for showing gang affiliation and which gang. If any of your students wear these things, send them to me immediately. It could be seriously dangerous."

"Is that why there are metal detectors?"

"One reason. We certainly don't want a Columbine on our hands."

"Perry, you're scaring me. These are elementary children."

"I'm just being realistic. Stay vigilant, okay?"

Perry stood, indicating he had another appointment. He walked with her toward his open door and peeked out for a second. He pulled her behind the door and kissed her softly. "I'll do everything I can to keep you safe," he promised before they went into the outer office.

The next turbulence came when a nine-year-old came to school with a bag of his brother's marijuana. "Holy smokes," Sunny murmured. "Another cloud with consequences." Confiscating a controlled substance from a third-grader meant drug testing among the faculty.

Perry knocked on Sunny's door. "Your turn, Sunshine."

Students always laughed when they heard Mr. Knotts call Miss Bankston "Sunshine," and they quickly spread their thoughts that Mr. Knotts was hot for Miss Bankston. A substitute teacher watched Sunny's class for a short time while she walked with Perry to be drug tested.

"First," she said, pinching his ribs.

"Ouch. What'd I do?"

"You really shouldn't call me *Sunshine* in front of the kids."

"Sorry." He sang, "'I'm just a little black rain cloud, hovering under the honey tree. Pay no attention to little me.'"

She giggled. "Silly-willy. You know I'm clean."

"I know, but *everybody* has to be tested, even *moi*. Just make dinner for me tonight. Be a little silver lining, okay?" He rubbed his temples. "I've had to let two teachers go because they weren't clean."

"Who?"

"You'll find out at the faculty meeting later. So, Sunshine, what's for dinner?" He put his hand on the doorknob.

"You know, if you keep calling me Sunshine around the kids, one of us *will* have to change schools."

"Sunshine, if anyone transfers, *I* will." The look in his eyes told her if they weren't in the hallway of the school, he'd gather her in his arms.

"All right." She gave him a mock scowl. "I'll make my famous tuna casserole."

"I'll bring a bottle of white wine. I'll need a drink after today, maybe two. Here you go." He opened the door. "Good luck." Perry left Sunny with health department officials.

Her heart raced, not for fear of drug testing, but for the feelings Perry stirred in her.

The next cloud proved the darkest—suspected sexual abuse of one of her female students. The girl climbed into Sunny's lap as she watched her group on the playground. The child laid her head on her teacher's shoulder.

"What is it, sweetheart? Hm?" Sunny felt shaking shoulders, then shifted the child. *Blood? From this little one? Oh, no!* Her white slacks were heavily stained. She called for help and rushed the little girl to the hospital. The mother's boyfriend was arrested as a result.

Distraught, Sunny entered Perry's office in tears. He closed the door and pulled her into his arms. "Sunny," he said, "you have to distance yourself or go crazy. How about a comedy with me on the other side of town?"

"I need a comedy." She sniffled. "Can we eat Thai afterward?"

"Anything you want." He dried her tears with his thumbs and kissed her. "We've done everything we can do for that child. It's in the hands of the proper authorities."

More clouds descended with flu season. Sunny's class had three or four different students absent every day for a month before she, herself, missed three consecutive days, during which Perry brought chicken soup and medicine every night.

When she returned to class, the sub had accomplished nothing except to allow chaos to ensue. "Three more wasted days to regain control of my students," Sunny grumbled.

"Now, the real storm," Sunny told herself after Easter break. "Spring testing." She'd done everything she knew to do in order to bring her students' performance level up. Now—she prayed.

With testing over, Sunny took a day to relax. They had read "The Knight Who Was Afraid of the Dark" in class. Sunny found an animated video of the story to watch. Then, they went online to find their family crests and designed their own shields on construction paper, which Sunny laminated, as if they were knights. Finally, each child had to write a paragraph on the topic, "If I were a knight, I would…"

"Oh, dear," Sunny muttered, once she read a paragraph from one of her boys:

If I were a knight, I would be able to chop off the heads of my enemies with my broadsword. I wouldn't have to worry about anybody being mean to me or hurting me. I would be the strong one, and I wouldn't

have to be afraid if I were I a knight.

"Flawless, but it describes a terrible truth," Sunny told herself. *Amir is being hurt and wants to get rid of the person hurting him. I have no choice. I'm required to turn this over to the school counselor.* "I had no idea this innocent, imaginative assignment could become a tempest," she whispered.

That night, Sunny went home and cried until she heard a knock at her door. Perry stood there with a sunshine-yellow rose, a bottle of pre-mixed Bahama Mama and *Finding Nemo* in his hands.

"May I come in?"

"Of course."

"Do you need to talk?"

"Perry, how could something so innocuous cause such uproar? I thought it was creative, and the children enjoyed it so much."

"It was a marvelous assignment. Don't let this dampen your enthusiasm. Try this on for a silver lining." He poured two glasses and brought them to the sofa, then sat beside her. "Wasn't that child far below grade-level when you got him?" He handed her a drink.

"Yes."

"Where is he now?"

Sunny thought as she sipped her drink. "Amir was on first-grade level when school started. Considering the fluidity of his paragraph, he has exceeded third-grade. I taught this child something, and he learned it."

"Very good, Sunshine. This one might have *two* silver linings. If he *is* being abused, something can be done."

Sunny and Perry stared into each other's eyes. Both knew they were breaking the rules, but rationalized they were each other's a silver lining. They were friends. Nothing beyond a kiss had happened. Yet, both knew one cloud too many on a sunny day might change that.

7

Little Reardon

Mac finished his rotation in pediatrics and psychiatry and began his time in obstetrics and gynecology. *Perfect timing* Mac thought when Felicia went into labor.

Mac exclaimed, "I can deliver my own child!"

"Have fun," the attending obstetrician joked. "Let me know when to attend divorce court."

"We'll be fine," Mac assured Dr. Castillo.

"Sure, you will. I'll check back on you." Castillo left Mac with Felicia.

For a while, things *were* fine. Then Felicia hit hard labor. Sharp cries and deep suffering groans triggered Mac's memories. *I can't do this, but I have to. Felicia's not dying. Not like my mother. Man up, Doctor. Get past the memory.* He tried not to show his anxiety as he coaxed, "Felicia, everything's fine, but it's not time to push yet."

She grabbed Mac's scrub top at the throat. "Give me something for pain, you stupid hillbilly!"

"You're not dilated enough yet," Mac said. *Women say cruel things while in labor. It's not personal.* "An epidural this early would only slow your progress."

"Give me some Demerol." White-knuckled, she grasped the bed rail.

"That's not good for the baby." He washed her face with a cool washcloth. "You can do this, honey. Breathe. Remember how we practiced."

She relaxed and took deep breaths until the next contraction. She pulled her knees up and released a piercing scream. "Damn you, Mac Reardon, for causing me to do this."

Dr. Castillo peeked in. "How is she?"

"I hurt!" she screamed. "He won't give me anything."

"Mrs. Reardon, pain killers would only make it take longer. Dr. Reardon, how dilated?"

"Five."

The obstetrician nodded. "He's treating you right. I'll be back. I have a C-section to perform. Mac should really be helping, but he can help with the next one." They saw the woman next to Felicia being wheeled to surgery.

Felicia grabbed Mac's hand. "What if *I* need a C-section?"

"You're progressing fine, darling." He squeezed her hand. "You don't have to worry."

She ground her teeth. "You sure?"

"Yes."

"*I'm* not, dumbass."

Whew—she's vicious. Remember—not personal. Not. Personal. Mac took a deep breath.

Hours went by. *How much longer? The insults are getting worse.* Mac's nerves were frayed.

Felicia snapped, "You jackass! Why won't you help me? You caused me to do this. This is your fault!"

Mac retorted, "*You* did this to you. *I* didn't sabotage the birth control."

She picked up her cup of ice chips and threw them at her husband as Dr. Castillo checked on their progress.

"Whoa!" he said. "It can't be *that* bad. Women have been doing this for thousands of years. Mac, check her."

"Don't touch me!" snapped Felicia.

"Oh, shut up!" Mac snapped back and checked her.

He announced, "Almost eight centimeters. You can have your epidural now, but this probably won't happen in the next hour."

The anesthesiologist came in and administered her epidural. Half an hour later, Felicia still screamed. "I thought that bitch gave me an epidural."

"She did. It's not working. Let's discuss who's a bitch."

"Give me something else!" She pounded Mac's arm.

"No. It's almost time." He moved back to deliver the baby. "Come on. You can do this. You wanted to do this."

"No, I didn't. I made a mistake. I didn't have a choice. I didn't know it would hurt this much. I don't ever want to do it again."

Yeah, yeah. The pain's talking. "Come on, now. You can start pushing."

"Just get it out!"

"Push."

After an episiotomy and several pushes, Mac announced, "It's a boy," as he clamped the cord. "We have a son."

"Thank God," moaned Felicia. "It's over."

"Almost," assured Mac, handing the baby to the nurse. "You have to push out the afterbirth. Come on. Let's finish."

A little later, the new mother held the baby. "Is he normal?" she asked. "He looks very pink."

"He's fine," Mac said. "You did great."

Felicia sighed. "Did I? I was mean to you."

"It was the pain. I'm sorry the epidural didn't work. You just had to be one in a million, didn't you?" The new father kissed his wife's forehead.

"I guess so. What shall we name him? We've never discussed it."

"Sorry I've been so busy here. We need to find time to spend with each other. What did you have in mind?"

"I am *never* doing this again, so I'd like to name him Chambry, my maiden name."

"Never?" asked Mac.

"Never!" said Felicia firmly.

Mac looked at her with a little concern. *Surely, she'll change her mind in time.* "Chambry is good," he agreed. "Do you think we could name him for my father, too?"

"Leo?"

"No, Ander. I know it was a hillbilly perversion of Andrew, or at least I think it was, but that's what they called him. Will you be all right with Chambry Ander Reardon?"

Felicia pursed her lips. She said. "Yes, it flows."

"Are you ready to start nursing Chambry, Momma?" Mac asked affectionately, rubbing the baby's down-soft head.

Her mouth twisted. She declared, "I'm not nursing. That's what formula is for. I already discussed that with my doctor."

"It's healthier for both of you," Mac argued.

"I survived just fine on a bottle and so will he. *Mother* is *not* nursing." She shook her head. "No, no. In six weeks, *Mother* is going back to work. Chambry will be going to daycare."

Eyes wide, color drained from his face, Mac said, "I assumed you'd take care of our son. You should be thinking about what's best for *him*."

"Mac, I turned out all right. Chambry will, too. Besides, we need *my* income to have a decent living right now."

It dawned on Mac: *Just as a little Reardon won't change my plans to return to Possum Holler, neither will it change Felicia's life. She has it planned. She won't survive Possum Holler. Now, I have to consider my son.* He took the baby from his mother as she was transported to a room.

Holding Chambry close to his chest, Mac called Leo. *I need Papa.*

Leo answered, "Possum Holler Community Church."

Unable to contain his joy, Mac proclaimed, "Papa, it's a boy, Chambry Ander Reardon."

"Congratulations!" Leo responded excitedly. "Papaw can't wait to meet him."

"Are you coming to visit soon?"

"I don't have plans to at this time, Mac. Trips to Chicago aren't cheap."

"I know." He swallowed hard. "I just need you." Pages sounded over the hospital system.

"What's wrong?" Leo asked.

"Felicia."

"What now?" Leo settled into his chair to hear the story. "Tell me everything."

"First, she refuses to nurse Chambry. I can't convince her it's best for both of them. Second, she's going back to work and putting him in daycare as soon as she can. *Daycare*—with *strangers. And* she insists on being called *'Mother.'* How unaffectionate is that?" His teeth grated over the line. "Besides, she says she's never having another baby."

In his mind's eye, Leo saw steam coming from his son's ears. He well remembered the school fights. *Rein in the temper.* "Relax, Mac. Give her time to recover. Was it a bad delivery?"

"Pretty bad. The epidural didn't work. She had natural childbirth."

"For a pampered city girl, that was tough. Let her heal. She'll want another one eventually. As for 'Mother,' what does she call her mother?"

"Mother."

"That's what I thought. It's what she knows."

"Yeah, I guess, but she made fun of me for calling you 'Papa.' She said it was childish."

"Oh?" Leo pictured Mac's frown. "And you're pouting."

"Papa!"

"Calm down." Leo sighed. "Don't worry about the official address. How she treats the baby is more important. What do you want Chambry to call *you*?"

"'Daddy.'"

"Your choice, just as 'Mother' is hers. It's not worth fretting."

"What about nursing and work?"

"Well, yes, nursing would be better, but many babies do just fine on formula. Polly Richter did."

"Humph! Do you call that fine?"

"I'm not talking about the family's choice of lifestyle. Back off." Mac heard Leo slap the top of his desk. "Polly is a healthy young woman. So are Betsy and Callie Campbell—formula babies. Don't fret work either. The hospital has a good daycare system, right?"

"Yes."

"Take Chambry to work with you. Pop in for visits when you can. It's how Felicia was raised. She said her family wasn't close or affectionate. It might fall to you to show the physical affection as well as create the emotional bond. You chose her. Deal with who she is." Leo's tone could have been delivered from the pulpit in a fire-and-brimstone sermon.

"Put me in my place, why don't you?"

"Did you call just for me to give you strokes, or for me to be your father?"

"No, I wanted your honest opinion *and* advice."

"And I've given you both. In addition, stop judging the Richters." Preacher Tomlin's tone brooked no argument.

"Sorry about what I said about the Richter clan," Mac muttered, duly chastised.

You should be. "Send me some pictures of my grandson. I want to show off your little Reardon."

"I will, Papa. Thanks. I love you."

"Love you too, Mac. Congratulations, again."

8

A Distant Rumble

Distant thunder rolled from the west as Mac carried his eight-month-old son into the daycare at Cook Memorial Hospital. "I'll be in emergency room rotation for a twelve-hour shift, so my wife will pick up our son," he told Mrs. Elliot, the daycare supervisor, then passed Chambry over. "Give Daddy a kiss." Chambry leaned forward and slobbered all over his father's cheek. Mac kissed him on the forehead.

Mrs. Elliot laughed. "He's such a smart little boy. You must be so proud of him, Dr. Reardon."

"I am," affirmed Mac. "Daddy'll see you later, buddy. I love you." Chambry opened and closed his hand in a crude baby wave but did not cry as Mac waved bye-bye going down the hall.

I hate rainy days in the ER. City people are dumber than inbred hillbillies. Mountainfolk know not to drive at excessive speeds in pouring rain.

As Mac pressed the call button for the elevator, the distant rumble morphed into a crackling bang. "I think I'll take the stairs," he mumbled to himself. "We're in for a long, hellacious day. I bet we have multiple wrecks in the next three hours."

The distant rumble of the freight train stopped abruptly and was followed instantaneously by grating, grinding, grenade-like explosions.

Felicia, along with hundreds of other commuters, sprang from her car to watch the fireworks in the dead-still evening rush-hour traffic. *Dear God! Propane tankers erupting.* She pulled out her cell phone and dialed her husband. He felt the vibration but was busy setting the arm of the latest traffic casualty in the ER and could not answer.

Mac checked his voice mail as soon as he could. Felicia's message said, "Hey. I can't get there anytime soon. Can Chambry stay for night care? It might be hours before I get out of here. You'd better get ready for lots of patients. I'm literally stuck in traffic. Some gas tankers have derailed and are exploding." A loud boom resounded in the background. "Did you hear that? I'm sure there are injuries, and I don't know when I'll be able to move. You might be there all night too."

Shit! Mac called Felicia back. "Are *you* all right?" was his first question, which she barely heard over explosions, sirens, and helicopters.

"I'm not in harm's way," she yelled into the phone. "I'm too far back, but I can't move this car an inch. Sorry."

"Not your fault. I'll zip down to the daycare and make arrangements until I can get free. Thanks for the warning. Be careful. Call when you get home."

"Will do."

"I love you." The phone had already clicked in Mac's ear. He sighed but sounded the alert.

Within half an hour, injuries related to the freight train derailment, along with other rush-hour traffic injuries, inundated the ER.

Mac attended a mother and her infant, both severely burned. They had been very close to the propane explosion. *Please, God, help me help them.* He tried hard but lost both. *I've never lost one, Lord. Help me.* He left the ER and cried.

The chief resident found Mac. "Suck it up, Reardon," Dr. Gillette said.

That's cold and unfeeling. "I just need a minute," said Mac. "The baby just..." He tensed and shook all over. "Chambry's upstairs in daycare because Felicia's stuck in traffic from this. It could've been my son."

"First loss?" asked Gillette.

"Yes." Sitting on a bench, he leaned elbows on his knees, his face in his hands, and sighed. He pushed up straight after a moment.

"It never gets easier," Dr. Gillette said more gently. "You just learn to suck it up better. I still cry sometimes at home in the shower. You got a really hard one, though, for your first. I really need you back out there. It's gonna be a long night. Don't count on going home. You'd just have to turn around and come back. You're good, Reardon. You'll learn to handle it. Have you ever lost a loved one?"

Mac snorted. "All of 'em."

"What?"

"My mother, my father, and three siblings by the time I was seven. I grew up in Appalachia—backwoods hillbilly."

"You're *really* good. I mean, you got out."

"Yeah, but I'm going back."

"Why?"

"They need a doctor. If we'd had one, I might not have been an orphan." He stood.

"Best of luck, man. Right now, we need a doctor out here." He handed Mac a chart. "Come on."

"I'm coming."

Mac didn't lose another patient that evening, but by midnight, he felt exhausted and was still on call. He decided to take Gillette's advice. *I might as well stay. Besides, the storm's not over.* He hadn't yet heard from Felicia. *Better catch a nap while I can.*

Just as he put his head on the pillow in the doctors' lounge, his phone rang. "Felicia?" he answered.

"Yes. I'm finally home. It was awful, Mac." She had her hand to her cheek. "There were dead bodies on the side of the road. Some were completely charred."

"I'm sorry you had to see that. It's been bad here, too. I lost my first patient today. It was a baby burned so badly. He was younger than Chambry. His mother died, too."

"Well, I'm tired. I wanted to let you know I was home."

"Thanks. I'm gonna take a nap, too, before someone else comes in. No reason to come home, since I'm on call anyway. Sweet dreams. I love you."

"Good night."

Mac looked at his phone. He breathed heavily. *How long has it been since Felicia's said she loves me? Couldn't she have shown sympathy for the loss I suffered today even if she was tired? Why am I such a selfish prick?*

The thunder rumbled again. Mac leaned back and dozed off from sheer exhaustion.

Mac's pager went off. His eyes popped open. He looked at his watch. *Ninety minutes—might have gotten two REM cycles. Glad I stayed, or I'd be running back in the deluge.* He rushed back to the ER. *Six-car pile-up and still raining.* He didn't have time to think about his personal life. There was too much carnage in front of him.

The next day dawned just as stormy as the last. Mac paid a visit to the daycare on the second floor. Chambry bounced up and down in the crib where he had slept. Mac picked him up and hugged him close for a few minutes.

"Dr. Reardon," said Mrs. Elliot, back for a new day. "He'll be fine. These things happen with interns' children. I've had to make arrangements many times."

"I'll be off at six tonight. I'll take him home then."

"I'm sure you will. We'll be waiting for you."

Mac kissed Chambry. "I'll see you later, buddy. I love you. I love you so much." He placed Chambry back in the crib and returned to the ER.

Thunder crashed in the distance. *The ER will be packed again very soon.*

The same thunder woke Sunny Bankston. She groaned. *I hope today's better than yesterday. Maybe the power won't blip off again.* The weather had kept thirty-two rambunctious third-graders inside all day. Then, they practiced a tornado drill. Convincing her students it was just a drill had been extremely difficult. She had stopped by Perry's office. Hands on hips, she chastised, "Of all days to have a tornado drill."

He brushed past her, kissed her on the neck just below her ear and whispered, "It was real."

She kicked off covers and sighed. "I *have* to go to school." Sunny made breakfast—eggs, sausage, toast, apple sauce, grape juice and coffee with cream and sugar. *Casual Friday. Yay!* She dressed in jeans, a fuzzy pastel-pink sweater and sneakers.

Gathering everything she would need for the day, Sunny dashed to her car and drove to work. *Things might be better if certain students I won't mention by name don't show up. I hope.* She instantly chided herself for the thought. *This year's group is much worse than my first one.* Sunny decided her first class had been fantastic. *If not for Perry, I would've quit this year. I wonder if we can keep things under control.* She tingled with joy, remembering his touch.

Although they were not sleeping together, their relationship was a big step more than casual. Dimples etched her face then she trembled. A transfer for either of them *would* change the nature of their involvement—certainly, it would deepen.

Oh, good. My biggest troublemaker isn't here today. I shouldn't be happy about it, but I am. And then there are the test scores. If this group can match my previous class scores, I'll be ecstatic. If she could pull off a miracle for *this* class, life would be tolerable. *But maybe not today.*

She waited with excitement to share last year's success with Perry at dinner. She smiled to herself.

The thunder rumbled closer and closer. The electricity went off as the thunderclap rattled windows. *Can't do book work in the dark.* Sunny tapped the dry-erase marker impatiently on her desk chair. She stood. "Everybody, get your chairs. Let's make a circle."

When the children had formed a circle, Sunny sat in a chair and held up the marker. "This is a story stick," she said. "We're going to tell a story as a group. You can only speak if you're holding the story stick. We'll pass it around the circle. I'll start. When it gets to you, add to the story. It can be serious or funny. When it gets back to me, I'll end the story. Okay?"

The children nodded.

"Once upon a time," Sunny began, "it was a stormy day. Bad weather made studying difficult for Miss Bankston's third-grade class. The electricity went off, and the thunder was so loud it made everybody jump." She jumped toward the child on her left. Some students squealed and then giggled. Sunny handed the story stick to the boy on her left. He looked a bit confused, but his teacher nodded encouragement.

The student said, "The storm made everything spooky because it was real dark. The thunder sounded like gunshots…"

Sunny listened. *Gunshots? That* does *sound like gunshots. I think. Never heard gunshots before, but it's not thunder.* Her eyes widened. *The electricity is off. The metal detectors aren't working! Neither are the intercom or bells or alarm system!* Sunny ran to her classroom door and locked it.

"Students!" she said trying not to alarm the children. "Move quickly but quietly. Get under the computer table, behind my desk and under my desk. Do not make any noise."

One little girl whispered, "Miss Bankston, are those really gunshots?"

"I think so," said Sunny. "But if we're quiet, nobody will know we're in here. Now, hide."

The little girl took Sunny's hand. "You, too."

"I'm coming, Markita. You go first."

"I'm scared."

Sunny hugged the little girl. "Me, too, but we have to be brave and quiet." She had never had this group obey her so completely. She thought, *Lord, this isn't how I wanted my miracle.*

When the children were as safe as possible, Sunny slid the orange caution card reserved for this kind of situation under her door and then sat down in front of the children, placing her chair in front of her. *This is the best I can do.* She hoped the children could not hear her heart thumping or read the terror on her face. She forced a smile at the students closest to her.

The shots got closer. Markita clutched Sunny's hand. Someone rattled the doorknob. The lock splintered—the door burst open. Hands popped over mouths, but nobody screamed.

A lone gunman slung Sunny's chair across the room. Heart hammering, she put herself between the pupils and the crazy man. "You will not hurt these children," she said firmly, fighting tears.

The man growled, "I ain't come to hurt them kids. I'm looking for Miss Bankston. Tell me where she is, and this'll all be over."

Me? Why me? "I'm Miss Bankston. What do you want with me?"

"I want you to die."

"Why?" *Keep him talking. Help will come. Perry will come. Perry promised to keep me safe. Perry. Where are you, Perry? Come on. I need you.* She gulped. *I love you.*

"You took my family away from me." He pointed a nine-millimeter handgun at her. "I only tried to teach Amir to do right. If I had to whoop him to do it, so be it."

"Whoop?" She placed her arms away from her body to form a cross as she felt the children press against her. "You're *Amir's* father? You didn't *spank* him. You *beat* him. He had broken bones! He wanted to cut your head off with a broadsword."

"I can't even see my boy 'cause of you. Him and his momma have disappeared. Some women's group helped 'em hide."

You were arrested. "Why aren't you in jail?"

The skeletal face grinned like the Grim Reaper. "Bail. Now, I can get a little revenge."

"And you'll go away *forever.* Is that what you want to do to Amir?"

"No. I just want *you* to die."

BOOM! BOOM! BOOM!

Students screaming...

Searing pain…
The man's head exploding…
A distant rumble of thunder…
Perry…
Blackness…

9

Thirty-Six Straight

Three fractured collar bones, dozens of lacerations from shattered windshields, two labor and deliveries brought on by the drastic drop in barometric pressure, a knifing from the jail, all before ten A.M. christened Dr. Reardon's second shift in the ER, although he had been on call all night, managing less than two hours' sleep. The admissions and triage station constantly monitored the police scanner, so they would know when to expect a massive influx of patients. Delores Davis, the triage nurse on duty hollered out the door down the hall, "Dr. Reardon, there's been a school shooting with casualties and fatalities. Get ready!"

Oh, Lord! thought Mac. *Emergency medicine is bad enough, but without sleep it's ridiculous. And, now, a lunatic has struck.* He yelled back to Delores, "Page Omarkhail. He's in the cafeteria. I'm gonna need help."

Just as Mac spoke, paramedics wheeled Perry Knotts into the ER. He had been shot in the abdomen and had internal bleeding. Mac shipped him off to surgery.

Mrs. Dotson, the school counselor; Mrs. Granell, the attendance clerk; Officer Diaz, the truant officer and security; and Mr. Dykes, the physical education teacher came in and were sent to surgery, but Diaz was DOA.

Dr. Gillette rushed in. "I got here as fast as I could. Reardon, what have we got?"

"School shooting. We've seen six, five in surgery, one DOA. I hope that's it."

"No such luck!" yelled Delores. "Here comes another one. Three shots to the torso, and she's conscious. One more after her, DOA, apparently the shooter."

Another paramedic team rushed Sunny Bankston into the ER. "Type and cross!" yelled Mac.

"A positive," spoke a voice from the petite strawberry-blonde on the gurney.

Mac Reardon looked down at her. "You're coherent," he said, surprised. "Are you sure you're A positive?"

"Yes."

"Allergies?"

"Not that I know of."

"How are you having a conversation with this woman?" asked Dr. Gillette.

"No idea," replied Mac. "With this blood loss, she should be unconscious."

"Name?" asked Gillette

"Sunny."

"What?"

"Sunny Bankston."

"Well, Miss Bankston, we've got to get you to surgery. You're gonna have to trust Dr. Reardon and me. Everybody else is tied up."

"Me?" asked Mac. *I've only observed, monitored, and assisted with minor operations, never major surgery. Done sutures and set bones, but nothing to the extent of removing bullets. Even the appendectomy and C-sections I helped with don't compare to removing bullets.*

"Yep," replied Gillette. "Let's go."

"You'll do fine, Dr. Reardon," said Sunny calmly.

Mac Reardon looked down into crystal-clear blue eyes, despite massive blood loss. Sunny clutched the doctor's hand. The ER nurse started Sunny's first unit of blood, and the anesthetist injected Sunny's I.V. with anesthesia. The last thing Sunny heard was Mac Reardon saying, "So will you, Miss Bankston."

Several hours later, thunder still rumbled in the east, but the rain had finally stopped, and patches of blue dotted the west. Mac stopped in the room where Sunny had been moved before he left the hospital after thirty-six straight hours of overwhelming emergencies on an hour and a half of sleep, since he never got to go home.

As Mac checked Sunny's vital signs, she opened her eyes. "Dr. Reardon?"

"I'm surprised you remember me. You're a miracle, lady. How do you take three bullets to the chest and live? Not one of them hit a vital organ." He thought, *Thank God, they weren't hollow points.* He replaced the chart and rubbed his own eyes.

"Providence," whispered Sunny in a weak voice.

"Yes," agreed Mac. "Do you believe in Providence, Miss Bankston?" He stifled a yawn.

"I do. Dr. Reardon, how are my students?"

"Unharmed. It seems the S.W.A.T team killed Sayid Bashir almost as he shot you."

"Oh, I wish…"

"I know, but you're alive. Your students need you. In a few weeks, you'll be able to go back."

"Is anyone else dead?"

The young doctor did not respond right away. His patient said, "Don't lie to me."

"Unfortunately, Mr. Knotts and Officer Diaz did not survive."

"Oh, *Perry*!" Tears trickled down Sunny's cheeks. She bit her lip to try to stop a torrent of tears. "He was a good man and a great principal. Honestly, I'm not sure I can stay at this school without him."

"He must have been special to you."

"Very."

"Pray about it." He soothed her hair from her forehead. "It's all right to cry. I'll pray for you."

"Thank you, Dr. Reardon."

"Rest now. That's what I'm gonna to do. Just finished an extended ER shift, thirty-six straight. I'd expected to go home last night, but no such luck. I'm glad I didn't fall asleep during your surgery."

"You did a great job. Will you come to see me before I leave?"

"Sure. I'll be gone the next two days. Then, I'll have a week of twelve-hour shifts, not on call. I'll drop in."

"I'll probably sleep most of that time."

"Well, sweet dreams, Miss Bankston."

"You, too, Dr. Reardon."

Dr. MacKenzie Reardon picked up Chambry and went home to sleep.

Sunny Bankston asked God to guide her in her decision of where to teach and cried herself to sleep as she mourned alone for Perry Knotts.

10

A Safer Challenge

Sunny only got one quick visit from Dr. Reardon before Dr. Gillette released her from the hospital. Her family rushed to her side. Her father fumed that she should have ever been put in harm's way. Her mother hovered and almost confiscated the sausage on her breakfast tray before Sunny snatched her plate away and turned her big blue eyes imploringly toward her dad. He smiled with relief as he saw she would recover and forced his wife to go home. River and Starr, two of Sunny's siblings left with their parents. Her sister, Skye, stayed to take care of her for a short time.

Skye tucked her into her own car to take the youngest Bankston home. Once safe in her own apartment, the teacher confided in her sister she was apprehensive about going back to the school. "I know it's silly, Skye, but without Perry, I don't want to be there."

"Sunny, were you in love with your principal?"

"There was no relationship. That would have been inappropriate." She sighed. "Well, there were kisses and holding, nothing much more physical."

"But you fell for him and didn't even realize it."

"Maybe. Yes. Oh, I miss him." Sunny started to cry. "Mr. Brenner will be a fine principal, but we don't have any kind of relationship. I want *Perry*. I didn't even get to say good-bye." She released heartbreaking sobs.

"Oh, baby." Skye stroked her sibling's hair as the younger woman lay curled into a ball on her bed. "What will you do?"

"Oh, I'll finish the year, but I'd like to go somewhere else. It would be nice not to have to have metal detectors as I walk in."

"Well, pray and go ahead and look while you're recovering. I know you want to teach. Put out feelers."

"I'll do that, but right now I just want to sleep."

"Of course, you do." The big sister kissed her baby sister on the head.

Sunny recovered and went back to work, but she did not feel safe or comfortable. On the other hand, her students clung to her in fear of losing her. Nonetheless, Sunny continued to seek another position. She was not happy in Chicago anymore.

As Sunny looked for another position, Dr. Reardon moved to a different rotation in oncology, and then to neurology, and after that, cardiology. Mac was like a sponge, absorbing everything he could, so he could help his people. He recognized symptoms of many kinds of cancer and knew which treatments were best. He performed numerous neurological procedures and a dozen open-heart surgeries. Both the neurosurgeon and the cardiac surgeon encouraged the man toward one of those specialties rather than general surgery.

During this time, Chambry celebrated his first birthday, but when Mac suggested giving Chambry a brother or a sister, Felicia put his pillow on the sofa.

Mac took his pillow back to bed. "I get it," he snarled. "You really *don't* want any more children, do you?"

"No, Mac. I told you that."

"Felicia, mountain families are usually large. One child is almost unheard of. My friend, Tipper doesn't count because his father died when he was a baby. Amy Dent doesn't count—period."

Felicia glared at him. He growled, "I'd like at least one more. Not now. After I finish my residency." He huffed, "Please think about it."

He lay down with his back to Felicia and went to sleep.

Sunny went to church the week after school let out. She had not signed a contract to go back to the school for another year. She could not see herself there again without Perry. The teacher had finally admitted to herself she had loved her principal. The fact she had not even been able to attend his funeral devastated her.

Sunny decided to keep looking for a position and resigned herself to the fact if she did not find one, she could go home and work for her parents, as much as she dreaded that possibility. She concluded Illinois was not the only state where she would or could work. She was open to drastic relocation if necessary. Taking a test for another state would not be a challenge for her, and some states accepted licenses from other states.

After church, the youth minister approached her. "Sunny! I understand you'd like to leave Chicago after your incident."

"Yes, Chip, I would. There's too much pain there, not just physical."

"I met Perry when he came to church with you. I'm really sorry for your loss."

"Thanks."

"I received something that might interest you."

"What?"

"I got this email from a friend. I thought you might be interested, so I printed it out." He handed her a sheet of paper. "It might be almost like time travel. You could go back to the nineteenth century and a one-room school." The young man smirked.

Sunny read the communication. "This could be a real challenge," she said excitedly.

"You've got the number of the guy. Give him a call."

"Thanks, Chip."

After she ate a BLT alone, Sunny took a chance and called the number on the paper Chip had given her. A pleasant baritone voice answered, "Possum Holler Community Church."

"Good afternoon. My name is Sunny Bankston. May I speak to Dr. Leo Tomlin, please? I'm calling regarding the charter school."

"This is Dr. Tomlin; however, around here, I'm Preacher Tomlin. What can I do for you, Miss Bankston?"

"I'm interested in helping you set up your charter school. A friend of mine gave me your number."

"Have you ever taught, Miss Bankston?"

"Yes, two years in Chicago."

"Why are you leaving?"

"Honestly?"

"No other way."

"I was shot this year. The Lord spared me for some reason, but I don't feel led to be there anymore." Sunny heard muffled voices as if the mouthpiece of Leo's phone was covered.

After a moment, the preacher asked, "What do you know about Appalachia?"

"Very little, but could it be any worse than inner-city Chicago?"

"Not worse, just different. The people here are poor and uneducated. The few who receive an education usually leave. I've been given a government grant for a charter school because the children here have to ride a bus fifty miles one way. In the winter, they don't go, so they often fail. If there's a school close enough, maybe the people will be better educated, which would raise the standard of living.

"No, Miss Bankston, I don't think you have to worry about getting shot here, but it would still be a challenge, maybe just a safer challenge.

"I've sent information to many of my fellow pastors, hoping to get a response. You're the first call I've had."

"Preacher Tomlin, you said 'first,' not only. So, I'm the beginning. There will be more. Would it be possible for me to come there and meet you?"

Leo laughed. "You have the same enthusiasm, optimism, and idealism as my adopted son. Miss Bankston, which hospital did you go to?"

"Cook Memorial. Why?"

"I was wondering if it could be possible you met my son. He's a doctor, an intern, at Cook Memorial."

"I didn't have any Tomlins as doctors."

"Oh, his name is Reardon, Mac Reardon."

"Are you serious?" she trilled.

"Yes. Why?"

"Dr. Reardon did my surgery. He told me he'd pray about my future. Now, you *must* hire me. This has God's hand all over it." Sunny tightened her grip on her phone. *There must be a spiritual connection to the situation.*

Leo leaned back in his chair and put his feet on his desk. He laughed again. "So, I should hire you sight unseen and without references?"

"Absolutely. Your son saved my life and, apparently, put a bug in God's ear."

Leo laughed even louder. "And you had the audacity to break the Sabbath to get the job."

"I followed the guidance of the Holy Spirit. He was telling me to get His children out of a rut."

"Oh, good one. You're hired. When can you come?"

"The first of June. Should I come prepared to stay?"

"Yes. There's a small house here in town where you can live. Classes will be held temporarily in the Sunday school rooms at the church because that's the only place with enough room. You won't be making a large salary—base salary for two years' experience is $33,000. That's twice the median income here in Possum Holler, which is probably why I've had so little response."

"I have some ideas on how to get response. Preacher Tomlin…"

"Leo, please."

"Leo, I don't teach for the money. Can you promise I won't starve?"

"I've been here twenty-three years, and I haven't starved yet. As a matter of fact, a member of my congregation was just summoning mc to come out to the dinner on the grounds."

"That's good enough for me. I don't have much to bring with me. What's the plan?" She changed the phone to her other ear.

"Do you have a car?"

"Yes."

"Hm. It might be easier for me to come to Chicago and help you load a U-haul. I'll drive it back, and you follow in your car. We'll have to take the U-haul back to a bigger city."

"All right. When?"

"I think I'll call Mac and arrange a little visit. I've never seen Chambry."

"Who's Chambry?"

"His son."

"I didn't know he had a child. I did notice his wedding ring."

"Noticed my son, did you?" Leo swung his feet down and leaned forward.

"Not like that, although he is a very handsome man."

"Don't apologize. He looks like his father. He did turn out very handsome. Felicia is pretty, too, so I imagine Chambry is adorable, and his pictures don't do him justice.

"Anyway. I'll make arrangements to get there for Memorial Day. We'll pack you up and move you out the last day of May. We might have to stop overnight. We'll pull in here sometime on June second. How does that sound?"

"Fine."

"Hold on." Sunny could hear the voices distinctly this time.

Leo answered the tap at the door. "Come in."

"Preacher Tomlin, my dumplin's were goin' fast, and I know how much you like 'em. I made you a plate."

"Thank you, Ina. Set it on my desk. I'll be out in a minute. I'm talking to our first teacher."

"Praise the Lord!"

Sunny heard the door close. Leo said, "Sorry about that."

"It sounds as if you're well cared for."

"I am. Maybe you can get together with me at Mac's. You should meet the whole family since they'll be coming back here when Mac finishes his residency."

"That would be nice."

"Sunny? Is that your real name?"

"Yes. I know it's strange."

"Not really. You should hear some of the ones we have here, such as, Panther Matlock and Gator Jones. Maybe the strangest would be Tipper Campbell who happens to be a bootlegger."

"Seriously?"

"I'm afraid so. That was his mother just now."

Sunny laughed. "Then, I'll fit right in. My sisters are Starr and Skye, and my brother is River. I'm the baby. I can't wait for you to get here. Take down my number for when you get to town."

Mac was excited to have Leo visit. He had not seen him in two years. He took Chambry with him to the airport to meet Papaw.

"Papa!" Mac unceremoniously hugged Leo in the airport. Leo took Chambry from Mac.

"So, this is my grandson. He's beautiful. Where's Felicia?"

"At work," Mac answered shortly.

"Mac?"

"Papa, don't ask." He held up his hand and ticked off an enumeration. "These are her priorities: Felicia, work, Chambry, Mac." Running a cupped hand back and forth across the raised digits on the other hand, he said, "Sometimes, I think there's another man in there somewhere."

"Mac?"

"It's okay, Papa. I married a city girl. Now, you said you had another surprise."

"Impatient."

"Come on!"

"All right. I got a grant for a charter school. I'm here to move our first teacher to Possum Holler."

"Wow! Terrific! Who is he?"

"She. I think you've met her."

"Who?"

"Sunny Bankston."

"Really?" Mac said with a laugh. "She's tough. She can handle it."

"How much time did you spend with this woman, Mac?"

"Other than the ER and surgery? Maybe a total of half an hour. She makes a good impression."

"Tell me more."

"Like what?"

"I don't know. Whatever comes to mind."

Mac and Leo retrieved Leo's luggage, strapped Chambry into the baby seat in Mac's new Cobalt, and talked as they drove.

"Let's see," said Mac, rolling his lips together in thought. "Miss Bankston was coherent enough to know her blood type when she came into the ER. When we talked, she came across as a believer. She's this tiny little thing, but I don't think I'd want to make her mad. She's strawberry blonde. You know, that's a shade of red. I'd bet she has a temper even though her name suits her personality."

Leo looked at Mac, deep lines of concern etching his brow. "Mac, how bad is it with Felicia?"

"There's nothing there, Papa. We sleep in the same bed— that's it, sleep. I take Chambry to the hospital with me." Mac maneuvered through the traffic. "Sometimes, Felicia's home for supper. Sometimes, she's not. She says she never wants another baby, but she says she still wants to be married and go to Possum Holler with me. Why do you ask? Do I show my feelings that obviously?"

"You just seemed to notice a whole lot about Miss Bankston in a very short time."

"Papa! I would never be unfaithful to Felicia."

"Keep the faith, Mac. You should know I've invited Miss Bankston to dine with us, all of us, *once* while I'm here."

"Felicia will be there." Mac laughed. "Maybe I *should* flirt with Miss Bankston. Felicia might get jealous."

"Don't play with fire."

Felicia acted the same as she had the last time Leo had visited. She graciously invited Sunny for a Memorial Day cookout. Mac had just begun his rotation in orthopedics, but he was home by six. When he got home, Sunny was already there, in the kitchen making her potato salad. She and Felicia chatted as if they had known each other forever.

Mac and Leo looked at each other and both shrugged. "Maybe she just needed a break," the son whispered.

"I hope so."

The cookout proved pleasant, and a few days later, Leo and Sunny left for Possum Holler. As Mac flipped through the television channels, Felicia slipped her arms around him. "I like Sunny. I'm glad she's going to Possum Holler. I'll have a friend there."

Mac kissed Felicia's hand and whispered, "Felicia, I love you. Are we all right?"

"I love you, too, Mac. We're fine. Maybe when Chambry is five, we can have another baby. Come and make love to me."

Sunny's first week in Possum Holler proved a little overwhelming. Leo asked after her first hog-rendering at which she met, not only the prominent citizens, but also the rejects of Possum Holler, "Can you handle it, Sunny?"

"Yes, but I don't think anyone can be prepared for what is actually here. Leo, I'm worried about Felicia."

"Me, too, Sunny."

"The Matlocks have invited me to supper Friday, and the Joneses have me for Wednesday. Is that a good sign?"

"Very good. Once you get an invitation from Grandma Newton, you're in like Flynn."

"Tipper Campbell and Gator Jones already signed their children up for school. What's the whole story on the Richters?"

Leo told her a story that had her in tears, a story of child abuse, murder, suicide, and incest. Sunny could hardly believe her ears, but she determined to convince Alain Richter, the patriarch of the family, to allow the children to attend school. She vowed to get him past his fear of the children being ridiculed because they were inbred.

The next day, Leo and Sunny fell to planning for the school. They decided they would need eighteen teachers to have a successful K-12 school: one for kindergarten through sixth grade, each; two each for secondary math, English, science, and social studies; and two elective teachers, which would entail music, physical education, and whatever else might be needed eventually; and one special education and gifted teacher. Sunny felt sure she could fill the gifted slot in the beginning and worried the special education teacher might have the most students from her observations.

Both Leo and Sunny sent letters to organizations and individuals offering the challenge to come and start a school. They listed a truthful picture of the situation. Sunny drove to the county library where she created a website and checked it every week. Then, they waited and prayed.

After several weeks, responses trickled in. They called three dozen men and women to come to Possum Holler. Several of them changed their minds and left quickly. By the middle of July, they had seventeen positions filled.

"We need one more English teacher," said the preacher.

"Leo, exactly what am I doing?"

"Other than the few gifted we'll have? Head mistress."

"Principal?" Sunny's big blue eyes stretched wide.

"Yep, and filling in when somebody gets sick. You and I will be the only two subs."

"Some classes will be as small as three or four."

"For now. You'll probably only have one—Betsy Campbell. She's already been tested and labeled gifted at the county school."

Sunny looked at the list of students who were planning to come. "And, we might not even have any seniors, maybe no juniors."

"Yeah, I know. So, the extras can pick up slack where it's needed."

"Leo, you seem melancholy."

He held up a response letter and résumé. "She'd make a great senior English teacher, even if we don't have one this year."

Sunny read the letter and résumé. "So, call her."

Leo sighed.

"Talk," commanded Sunny.

"Lauren Langston was my sweetheart. I sort of left her behind to come here." He rubbed his cheekbone as he remembered the figurine that hit him the last time he saw the woman. "She was a lot younger than me, and it appears she never married."

"Were you lovers?"

"What? No." He shook his head in denial.

"Leo?" Sunny turned her head to the side and gave him a cockeyed look.

"Well, yes, a couple of times—a lot of times." He dog-eared the résumé she had placed back on his desk. "Even men of God have urges and needs. And we sin. Lord, Sunny! I haven't been with anybody since I left Lauren behind. I don't know if I can face her."

"Leo, maybe this is God's way of putting you back together."

"You think?" His eyebrows shot to his hairline.

"Call her."

"You call her." He pushed the paper across his desk.

"Chicken?"

"You bet. She throws things with force."

Sunny called Lauren Langston who came to Possum Holler two days later. Lauren walked into a room to meet with a girl young enough to be her daughter and a man she had not seen in twenty-three years.

The tall, lanky, dark, salt-and-pepper-haired, brown-eyed Leo Tomlin stood to greet the tall, blonde-haired, brown-eyed woman who had hardly changed in twenty-three years. Lauren shook hands with both her interviewers. Then, she said, "Well, Leo, do you think I can handle it now?"

"Please, Lauren, cut to the chase."

"I just did. You can see I have the qualifications it takes to teach. I've taught some of these Possum Holler hillbillies before at the county school."

Leo interrupted, "Why didn't you come on in?"

"I was hesitant to come where I wasn't wanted. Now, do you think I can handle Possum Holler?"

"Maybe the question is, 'Can you handle being around me?'"

"Ask *yourself* that question."

"Maybe I should leave the room," said Sunny. "I vote to keep her."

Sunny walked out. "Sunny!" Leo called, panicky at being left alone with his former flame.

Outside the door, Sunny laughed out loud. "Oh, she'll keep you in line, Preacher Tomlin."

Leo took a deep breath and looked at Lauren. "I never thought I'd see you again."

"Is it a good thing or a bad thing?"

"Lauren."

"Is there a Mrs. Tomlin?"

"No."

"Why?"

The preacher rubbed his head. Through the open window, the cooing of turtledoves could be heard. He mumbled, "I never stopped loving you."

"Hm. Well, do I get the job?"

"Why do you want it?" He indicated with his hand for her to sit as he sat behind his desk.

She took a seat. "You need me."

"And?"

"Did you not notice the last name is still Langston?"

"And?"

"Maybe it's my way of haunting you." She set her jaw in a hard line.

"Haunting?"

"Maybe I need to prove to you I'm strong." She crossed her legs and swung her foot.

Leo noted her still-shapely calves as she wore a navy-blue linen skirt and white blouse. "I believe you. I wish I had twenty-three years ago."

"Me, too."

"I still love you, Lauren," Leo confessed barely above a whisper.

"That's good to know."

He put his head back on the chair and closed his eyes. "Lauren, you're making this hard."

"I guess I'm still a little angry." She held up her thumb and index finger to measure about an inch.

"I'm sorry." He opened his eyes and looked directly into hers. "I wish I had brought you with me as Mrs. Tomlin."

"Me, too."

"I still feel the sting of that angel you threw at me." He rubbed his cheek. "You get the job. I need you."

"Thank you."

"Will you have a problem sharing a house with Sunny?"

"I'd rather share one with you."

"What?" Leo leaned forward.

"You said you still love me. Ask me."

"You want to marry me after all these years?"

"Yes. I still love you. And..." She hesitated.

"Yes?" He furrowed his eyebrows deeply.

"I think Jessica should get to know her father."

"What did you say?" Leo shouted, standing quickly and banging his knee on his desk.

"She's at William Carey University. She'll be graduating in a couple of weeks."

"Why didn't you tell me?" Total disbelief clouded the man's face.

"Preacher Tomlin didn't need a family."

"Leo Tomlin *did*." A hint of anger tinted his voice. "God sent me a son. I sort of became his guardian."

"I know. Mac."

"Yes. You're Mac's Miss Langston?"

"Did you *look* at my employment history?" She jabbed a finger onto the résumé lying on the desk.

"Briefly." Leo stared at the woman he had left behind for a long moment. He leaned across his desk, fisted hands resting on top. "Lauren, I was wrong. Yes, I think we should get married. We'll make up for lost time. Sunny was right. This was God's way of putting us back together."

"So, you're really up for the challenge?"

"Absolutely, but first I'd like to meet my daughter." He straightened up, squaring his shoulders.

"That's easily arranged, and I'd like to see Mac again."

"That's easily arranged, too."

Leo called Sunny to come back in. "She's hired. Now, we have something to tell you."

Sunny remained speechless after their story.

Leo flew to Mississippi and met Jessica. Leo's daughter acted as stunned as he had been at meeting her father. She cried, and he got his first chance to hug his child. "I wish I had known," he whispered into her hair.

Then, Leo, Lauren, and Jessica flew to Chicago after Jessica graduated and visited with Mac and his family. Mac consented to be Leo's best man and sounded more like the father in their conversation. "Big surprise, Papa. Who was it that told me to keep it covered one way or another?"

"Hush."

Leo and Lauren exchanged vows before they went back to Possum Holler and a big wedding party planned by Sunny and thrown by Leo's congregation while Jessica went to Sudan as a journeyman missionary for the next two years. Lauren saw Tipper and Gator and asked about Alain and Amy, to shocking and disturbing news. Then, Leo and Sunny opened a school with seventy-one total students.

Leo thought, *Sunny might have found a safer challenge, but mine might have become a lot more dangerous.*

11

General Medicine

After three years of rotating through every medical department at Cook Memorial Hospital, with even a side stint in veterinary medicine after having worked for a veterinarian while at Marshall and knowing he might have to attend some of the prize animals in Possum Holler, Dr. MacKenzie Reardon refused to choose a specialty. He insisted general surgery should be its own specialty. The chief of staff, Dr. Morgenstern, talked with Mac. Sitting in his office, he sounded almost like Leo in the way he handled the situation.

"Dr. Reardon, the closest thing I can give you to a general medicine residency would be a residency in our family practice clinic. Either that, or the ER, and next year you would most likely be attending resident, which would mean a bit more money. The ER is probably general surgery on steroids. You do a little bit of everything there."

Mac asked, "Do the ER residents have to be on call thirty-six straight?"

"Sometimes."

"Honestly, that practice is absurd. Doctors should know better than anybody the human body needs rest. The incident with the train derailment pushed all of us beyond our limits."

"I happen to agree, but there is method to the madness. Tell me, Dr. Reardon, what do you plan to do with general medicine?" The seasoned doctor leaned back in his plush leather executive chair and laced his fingers across his still-firm middle.

"Dr. Morgenstern, I'm from a very small town called Possum Holler. My entire family died because there was no doctor readily available. The closest hospital is a hundred miles away. You won't find Possum Holler on a map, and you would pass right by it if you weren't looking for the turn-off. We're hidden deep in Appalachia. Basically, nobody much cares what becomes of a little band of poor, mostly illiterate, often inbred, hillbillies." He tensed all over at the thought. "But I do. I plan to go home and be a general practitioner. I won't get rich, but maybe I can save lives and improve the standard of living."

"Very commendable." The man in his early fifties propped his feet on his desk. "What happens if you've worked all day and you're tired when suddenly you have a catastrophe—say a mine cave-in or explosion? How do you handle it if you don't train your body to deal with extended hours? That's why we do the thirty-six straight on-calls. Let's face it; when an emergency like that hits, our adrenaline kicks in and we run on empty."

"I never thought of it like that. I understand. And you're right; we do function on pure adrenaline sometimes."

"Dr. Reardon, do you have basic equipment in Possum Holler?"

"No, we have nothing." Mac shook his head.

"When you finish your residency and go home, let me know. I'll help you apply for a grant, and I'll see what I can do to help otherwise."

"I've already signed papers to have all my loans paid off by setting up a practice and staying a minimum of five years."

Morgenstern gave a hearty laugh. "Sounds as if you might've pulled the wool over somebody's eyes."

"I guess. I didn't tell them I would be going *home*, just I knew of a community needing my services."

The chief of staff clapped his hands in praise. "I like the way you think. Now, do you want my suggestion?"

"Yes, please." Mac's pager went off. He fidgeted when he checked it.

"Important?" asked Morgenstern.

"Wife. I'll call her when we're done. So, tell me, what do you suggest?"

"ER. It'll push you to your limit. I can almost guarantee attending. Save the extra money for some of the things you'll need in Possum Holler your little arrangement won't cover."

"I do have a wife and child." He held up his pager.

"This is a tough time for a family man, peanut-butter-and-jelly days. Spend as much time as you can with them. Two years is not an eternity. You can do this. Dr. Reardon, Mac, there are only six residencies open for the next year. Most of your fellow interns will not be here. It's my pleasure and dreaded task to say who stays and who goes. I'd like you to stay. I'm offering you one of the two ER residencies."

"Appreciate your vote of confidence. Yes, I'll stay. And if I get attending next year, your ER will dance with precision. Dr. Gillette is good. I learned a lot from him during my ER rotation."

"Yes, he's good. I'm proud to say he's the one resident coming on staff."

"I look forward to working with him again."

"He's going into cardiac surgery, so you just might. He speaks highly of you, too. He thinks you have surgeon's hands. Dr. Petrovsky also said that."

"I'll try to remember that if I have to do emergency surgery. General surgery must be my calling."

"Well, you have two weeks off. What are you going do?"

"I don't know." The younger doctor shrugged.

"Go home."

"I don't think my wife is ready for that."

"So, go without her."

"I hadn't thought about that. Maybe we do need a break from each other."

"Trouble?"

"No. I can't put a finger on it. I guess I don't want her to feel neglected."

"Hm. Ask her to go, but don't let her stop you from going." Morgenstern's pager sounded. He looked at it. "I still practice medicine." He stood. "When was the last time you were home?"

"Ten years."

"Go home."

Mac took Dr. Morgenstern's advice, but he could not convince Felicia to put her project on hold and go with him. Nonetheless, Mac packed Chambry into his Chevy Cobalt and made the fifteen-hour drive home. He decided to surprise Leo and not call ahead of time. It had been only two months since he had seen his father and served as his best man for an impromptu wedding.

Navigating the mountain roads came back to Mac as if riding a bike again after ten years. He maneuvered the curves with precision, yet his lungs could feel the lightness of the air with each mile he climbed. Finally parking outside the manse, he woke Chambry and carried him up the steps with a finger to his lips. The little boy nodded with eagerness.

The knock on the door as Lauren and Leo prepared for bed scared the couple. His past experiences with late-night knocking had always been bad. Memories of Mac knocking and telling him Ander was dead, of Tal knocking to tell him about the incident at the Richter home, of Gator Jones knocking to tell him Tal was dead flooded his mind. Leo just knew there was an emergency, and he didn't want to leave Lauren who had been sick for days. Preacher Tomlin opened the door with great trepidation.

"Mac!" he shouted.

"Hey, Papa! Surprise!"

"Papaw, spise!" Chambry chimed in.

"This is a wonderful surprise! Come in."

"Mac," said Lauren coming to the door. "Hey, little man. Come see Mamaw." Lauren picked up Chambry. "Why didn't you call? Where's Felicia?"

"Felicia couldn't get away, and I wanted to surprise you. We're only here for five days."

"Well," said Leo, "I'll have to get word out for dinner on the grounds Sunday so everyone, especially Ina, can make your favorites. Tipper needs to see you. This will be so good for him. Sunny will be terribly disappointed she missed you."

"Where is she?"

"On a mission to raise more money to build an actual school."

"I didn't come to see her anyway. I came to see you, but, of course, I'll visit with Tipper."

"I'm so glad you did. I need a free doctor."

"Is something wrong, Papa?"

"Not with me. Lauren has been sick for days."

Mac glanced at Lauren Tomlin. "You don't look sick. What seems to be the matter?"

"Nothing. I'm just queasy and tired. It'll pass."

Mac started laughing.

"What's so funny?" asked Leo.

"Never fear. Dr. Reardon is here," joked Mac. "Lauren, how old are you?"

"Forty-four. Why?"

"Do you still have regular cycles? You're not quite old enough for menopause."

"Mac, what are you thinking?" Lauren asked, hand to her chest.

"I think you're pregnant."

"Oh, my Lord! Leo!" She placed a protective hand on her abdomen. "He could be right."

"How do we know for sure?" asked Leo.

"We'll have to go into a drug store unless Dent's General Store has started carrying home pregnancy tests. I didn't bring my little black bag. I didn't think I'd need it for a short visit home."

Lauren was, indeed, pregnant. She glowed with excitement, even at forty-four. Mac assured her she was not in a high-risk category for complications even if she was a little older. Lauren was healthy and had given birth to a child without complications. Still, Mac insisted she see a doctor in the city and go to the hospital at the first contraction. He said, "I love Grandma Newton, but she's getting long in the tooth. Her eyesight is failing, and she can't do emergency surgery should you need it." Lauren agreed to find a doctor in the city. Mac was delighted his first case in Possum Holler was a happy one.

However, seeing his old friends did not bring him joy. Mac paid a visit to Gator Jones and met Sherry, Gator's wife. Mac's eyes bulged. *Is Sherry the child I <u>know</u> Miss Ina had when she disappeared just after Pa died? Can she possibly be my sister?* Of course, Gator said Sherry was only a couple of years younger than he was. *The resemblance to Tipper and Miss Ina must be coincidence. If the two of them are lying about Sherry's age, Gator is a criminal, the marriage is illegal, and the five children they have are illegitimate.* Other than that, Gator was fine. He was happy, and that made Mac happy.

Mac gathered the courage to drive to Richter Farms with Tipper. The laden fruit trees lining the long drive to the Richter home belied the picture at the end of the dirt road. The man who greeted him did not resemble the person he once knew. Alain Richter looked old and drawn. Gray streaked his shaggy brown beard, if not his hair. He had neglected himself miserably. He obviously drank frequently and smelled awful. He was barely civil to Mac although he seemed touched Mac had even considered visiting him. Mac regarded the yard full of children and knew they were inbred. He felt nauseated and repulsed, and he could not hide it from Alain. Alain was miserable, and that made Mac miserable.

Mac's visit with Tipper was not much better. Tipper was despondent. Mac knew from the letters Tipper wrote him Amy's desertion of him and their three daughters had broken the doctor's best friend. Still he tried to function. He worked and cared for his family the best he could, but the joy was gone from him. He did not laugh with Mac. The two men talked, and Tipper bared his soul as they sat beneath trees whose leaves had already begun to change. Mac had almost forgotten how beautiful autumn was in the mountains. Gray skies and gray buildings clouded his memories.

On Sunday, Mac savored one of Ina Campbell's deviled eggs. His face looked rapt. "It ain't that good," laughed the woman who had almost been Mac's stepmother.

Mac nodded. "Better than sex."

"MacKenzie Reardon!" The woman blushed and left Mac to find her son.

After the meal, Mac forced a banjo into Tipper's hand. "No, Mac. I can't," said Tipper, shaking his sandy-blond lion's mane of hair.

"Oh, yeah, you can. This is Mac and Tipper, pickin' and grinnin'. I know you can pick. I expect to see some form of grin."

Mac began to play and sing, "Bring Back the Springtime." Tipper could not help but sing and play with his friend. It felt natural, something they had done since childhood. After the song Tipper said, "Thanks. I needed that. 'Take away the cold and dark of sin.' You know how to pick 'em. Those words were exactly what I needed to hear. I've been feeling Amy is the only one who sinned." Tipper, who was much taller than Mac's five-eleven, engulfed his friend in a bear hug, lifting the doctor off the ground. His blue eyes misted as he set Mac down. "No, my bitterness is sin, too. Yes, Mac, I feel the springtime coming back. I can't wait 'til you get back permanently. I need you. You're good medicine."

"I'm always here for you. Just pick up the telephone either at the church or the store or Papa's house. Neither Papa nor Royce will care if you make a long-distance call to me, or call collect. I'll accept the charges."

Tipper grinned. "Will do. Hurry home."

"Now, that's my Tipper. Come on. Let's liven up this party." Tipper and Mac began a banjo duel. Mac was ready to come home. *Two more years does seem like an eternity.*

Feeling deep homesickness, Mac returned to Chicago happy and refreshed, but anxious for the time to fly by. He began a two-year residency in the ER, first as resident, followed by attending resident.

Although Mac seemed rejuvenated, Felicia seemed to be in a worse mood than ever. After a short time, following Leo's visit when she had seemed her old self, she became increasingly cold and distant. She did not talk about anything with Mac anymore.

The doctor slipped his arms around his wife as she stared out the window. He whispered, "I have a prescription for you. You need a vacation. Why don't you take Chambry for a week with your folks? They haven't seen him since he was a week old. It did miracles for me to go home."

"My home isn't as warm and loving as yours, but you're right. I've got to get away, but I won't be going home. Mac, I have to go to Paris for a while."

"Why?"

"The partners want me to supervise the building of the shopping mall we designed."

"How long?"

"Three months, there about."

He turned her to face him. "Do you want to go?"

"Yes. It'll be good for my career."

"Career?" He took a step back. "What about your family?"

"You and Chambry will be just fine for a little while."

"Felicia, what about when it comes time to go to Possum Holler?"

"We'll see."

"What's changed, Felicia?"

"Oh, Mac. Stop whining. I still plan to go to that God-forsaken place with you. But for now, I'll be leaving for Paris on Saturday. If I only get this short time to live in the twenty-first century and be my own person, I'm going to seize the moment. Don't begrudge me that."

He took her by the shoulders and glared at her. She splayed her fingers against his chest. Mac said barely above a whisper, "A bad word for you is coming to my mind, but I won't say it in front of my son."

She shrugged away from him and stomped to their bedroom. Saturday, she kissed Chambry and barely looked at her husband when she took a taxi to the airport.

Three months became six, and Mac and Chambry celebrated a third birthday. Mac's phone rang as he cut the small cake he had picked up at the nearby bakery. Mac answered, his voice heavy with anger. "You finally decided to call?"

Felicia said, "Let me speak to Chambry."

"You need to talk to me. When the hell will you be home? A rented apartment; no calls; no return calls; no mail; not even an email," he said through clenched teeth as he walked away from the table where Chambry sat. "Who are you with?"

"Mac, there were complications with the builders. This is my job."

"And this is your *family*! Chambry asks about you every day. If you don't love me, for God sake, at least talk to your son."

"That's what I'm trying to do. Put him on."

With a deep sigh, Mac gave the phone to the child. The little boy talked to his mother several minutes, ending with, "When are you coming home, Mother? Okay."

Mac took the phone the child held up. A buzz greeted him. The phone sailed through the air and hit the glass of the eight-by-ten family portrait hanging on the wall, shattering glass. "Damn you!"

Chambry jumped at his father's outburst. "Daddy!"

Angry tears on his cheeks, Mac gulped, "I'm sorry." He held out his arms. "Come here." He hugged his son in an embrace that almost crushed the boy. Once the child was in bed, Mac cleaned up his mess. He dialed Felicia's number. It went straight to voice mail. He clutched the phone so hard his knuckles turned white. *Nope, not calling Papa. I have to handle this on my own.*

Mac worked almost every day. He was tired. Yet, he spent time with his son every day. The two were joined at the hip. The father knew he would be lost without his child.

One evening as they came home at a reasonable hour, they were surprised to find Felicia with a spaghetti dinner waiting as if nothing had ever changed and she had only been on a day's jaunt into Canada. *Is she bipolar?* Mac had to wonder. *I never know what to expect.*

Felicia kissed his cheek. "I'm home."

"For how long?"

She sighed. "I'm home."

For several months, life seemed normal with Felicia. Mac finished his residency and prepared to return to Possum Holler.

12

Culture Shock

The U-Haul truck Dr. MacKenzie Reardon drove bumped and rattled down the narrow gravel road that could easily have been mistaken for a private driveway. The moving van towed his Cobalt. Mac drove slowly rather than zipping along as he would have in his car since Felicia followed him. Ancient trees formed a canopy over much of the road and offered coolness from the summer heat. Several low-hanging limbs brushed the top of the van.

Far enough behind the moving truck not to be hit by flying rocks, but close enough to keep the truck in sight, Felicia, with her son in the back seat of her Volvo, jolted carefully along. She fumed silently about the condition of the road. As they pulled to a stop in front of the parsonage where Leo and Lauren Tomlin, and now their nineteen-month-old son, Rushton, Rush for short, lived, Felicia jumped from her car and examined it for damage. Other than being coated in dust, it seemed unharmed.

"Mac Reardon," she chided, "you didn't say there were no roads." She punched his shoulder.

"I told you it was hidden." He rubbed his arm. "Ow!"

"It's in the middle of nowhere." Her voice became shrill. "Where's the grocery store? Where do you shop?"

"There's the general store." Mac pointed down another totally dirt road. "It's attached to the post office. As you can see, the church is next door. We grow most of our own food, and we make most of our own clothes. You can order store-bought clothes and household goods through the Sears catalog in the general store."

On the wooden porch of the store, sat a decrepit-looking old man, bald and sporting a long, yellowed beard. He wore overalls with no shirt beneath. A stream of tobacco juice hit the dust over the rail, landing only a foot from the one gas pump in town.

Felicia gawked at the pump. One side held diesel and the other, regular gas, but it was so old, the counter was still dial rather than digital.

"I can't believe this. *Dog Patch, USA*." Felicia pulled out her cell phone.

Mac shook his head. "It won't do you any good here. There's no reception from any carrier. There is no television. Cable doesn't come way out here, and satellite is blocked by the mountains. There are now six phones: the store, the post office, the jail, the slaughterhouse, the church, and the parsonage. Lauren insisted on a phone. I'll get one as soon as I get a clinic set up, and I'm sure when the school gets built, it'll have one.

"Families spend time together here, and there are community and church activities for socializing. We can pick up a couple of radio stations, country and bluegrass. So, if you want that old-time rock-and-roll, which I now do, pull out your CDs. I warned you it's like a third-world country."

As they talked, Leo and Lauren came out, as did several neighbors, including Sunny Bankston. Seeing Sunny, Felicia ran to her. "How do you stand it here?" she wailed. "This place is barbaric."

Sunny laughed. "A little backward, but not barbaric. The people are wonderful, the salt-of-the-earth kind."

"I'm just glad someone civilized is here."

"You'll be fine, Felicia. Let's get you unpacked. Grab Chambry."

"Who's that scary old man?" She inclined her head.

"The Elder Farmer Maddox. He's a sweetheart. He's eighty and very revered. He's Possum Holler's mayor. Come on." She turned to Lauren. "Do you have any tea? I'm sure everybody is parched."

Mac and Felicia sank into chairs at Lauren's dining table. Chambry scarfed down a sandwich and a glass of milk and immediately started playing with Rush.

"That's nice," voiced Lauren serving iced tea and ham sandwiches to all the adults at the table.

"Yes, it is," agreed Felicia. She took Mac's hand. "Mac, where are we going to live?"

"Here for now."

"Mac! We can't impose on Dr. and Mrs. Tomlin."

"It won't be forever, Felicia. Papa, are any of the houses vacant?"

"Yeah, the old Bustin place, but it needs a lot of fixin'."

"Is it solid enough to store our stuff?"

"Yeah. Felicia, you're very welcome here. Jessica will be here in a few weeks. The house will be full finally. We'll fix up the Bustin place. It was pretty nice once."

"How much do they want for it?" asked Felicia.

"Nothing. It's just sitting there," replied Leo.

"We'd just move in?" Felicia's voice rose an octave in shock.

The preacher nodded. "Yeah."

As Leo and Felicia talked, Mac inhaled the food in front of him. Sunny and Lauren carried on their own conversation about the upcoming school year.

Felicia went on, "Who owns it?"

"Nobody. It's deserted," Leo informed.

"What about property taxes?" Felicia's face looked dubious, her mouth slightly ajar and eyes wide open.

"One advantage to being hidden is the county doesn't really know we exist. We might be hurting ourselves by bringing civilization here." A playful grin crossed the preacher's face.

"You don't pay taxes?" Felicia's question came out in a whisper.

Leo laughed. "Yes, we pay taxes. The taxes on the old place were about fifty dollars last year. However, the outlying places don't exist to the government. Why don't you take a look at the house and design your renovations? Tell the men what you want, and they'll do it."

"You're sure?" she asked once more.

"Yes, Felicia." assured Leo. "I know this is a culture shock for you, and I hate to tell you this, but you ain't seen nothin' yet!"

Felicia examined the old house. She had to admit it had some measure of charm and quaintness, especially the lion-claw bathtub with wrap-around shower curtain, although it did not have a shower. She ran her hand over the antique. "I like this." She nodded. "This house has lots of potential."

She took a couple of days to sketch the plans to make the house livable. Leo looked them over. "I can get these done. It'll take a little time because we won't be using a construction company. We'll do everything except the plumbing and electrical rewiring ourselves. We do almost everything around here ourselves, Felicia, but give us until Christmas at the latest, sooner if we get more hands to work. First, we'll build Mac a clinic. Can you design that?"

Mac smiled at the way Leo tried to use Felicia's talent to help her fit in.

"Yes, I can," the architect said brightly. "How large do you want it, Mac?"

"Look at where we are, Felicia," her husband replied looking back and forth.

"Well, what do you need?" she prodded.

After a moment's thought, the doctor gave her a rundown. "A reception/waiting room, a couple of exam rooms, an x-ray room, a surgery, a pharmaceutical and supply pantry."

"Mac, you need an office." She gave a decisive nod.

"Okay, and, maybe a couple of overnight rooms," Mac agreed.

With her eyes wide, Felicia asked, "You mean like a small hospital?"

"I guess." Mac nodded.

"Where?" She looked around her.

Leo said, "You see that cleared area?" as he pointed catty-cornered, slightly down the road from the church.

"Yes."

"We did that for Mac."

"Okay. I can do this." The architect nodded with enthusiasm, finding a niche for herself. "Thank you for making me feel as if I'm a part of this."

"You're welcome. You know, it's for free." Leo flashed a teasing grin.

"Yeah. I don't usually come cheap." She smiled.

"I'm sure."

Felicia drew a blueprint for Mac's clinic on Saturday and went to a country church meeting on Sunday with a potluck dinner on the church grounds afterward. She had never experienced anything like it.

Sunny knocked on the door, and Felicia opened it since Leo and Lauren had gone early for Sunday school. Each woman surveyed the other. Sunny wore a long, cotton Bohemian skirt of brown and turquoise paisley with a matching turquoise peasant blouse and flip-flops. Felicia had on an expensive tailored navy-blue linen suit with a white silk blouse and high-heeled navy-blue pumps.

Carrying his son, Mac came down the stairs in a pair of Levis and a plain white button-down oxford shirt and cowboy boots. He had Chambry dressed just like him.

"Oh, my God!" exclaimed Felicia. "What do you have on?"

Mac scowled. "Something nicer than most of the people at church will have on. You're overdressed for country church, but you look stunning." He set down the child in his arms.

Felicia looked at the other woman. "Sunny?"

Sunny nodded. "Do you have something a bit more casual?"

"I don't know."

Sunny held out her hand. "Come on. Let's look."

They found a sleeveless flowered jumper Felicia had worn when she was pregnant. She slipped it on. "It's hideous," said Felicia. "I wore it once. Besides, it's a maternity smock."

"Not if you put a belt with it." Sunny looked through Lauren's sewing kit and found a piece of ribbon that matched some of the flowers. She tied a bow around Felicia's waist. "There. It's cute," she declared.

"Do you really think so?"

"Yes. The people here will love it."

"Oh, all right. What about shoes?"

"Do you have any sandals?"

"A pair I wear at the beach."

"Get them."

The shoes were simple white, sling-back sandals. "They're perfect," assured Sunny.

When they came downstairs, Mac nodded. "Nice. Very nice, except."

"Now what?" snapped Felicia.

"Lighten the make-up."

"No. Sunny even has on make-up."

"Not that dark. Just take off the eye shadow. Leave the rest." He waved his hand. "You could help the ladies around here learn how to apply make-up. Either they don't wear any or they wear so much they look like they've been slapped and in the most garish shades of red."

Felicia stared angrily at her husband. "No. I refuse to be that plain," she said curtly.

"You could never be plain. You could wear a croaker sack and no make-up at all and be beautiful."

"I think that was a compliment."

"Of course, it was. You're gorgeous. Suit yourself. Let's go."

Church was different, too. The Reardon family, along with Sunny Bankston, eased into a pew. There was no choir or music director or orchestra. The church did not have even a pipe organ, like Felicia's home church. There was an old upright spinet Lauren could play well, which she did softly as the people entered the sanctuary. Several banjos and guitars were visible in the congregation. Felicia noticed a couple of washboards and tambourines and gasped when she saw a sprinkling of whiskey jugs. If she had looked closely, she would have seen several harmonicas in some of the men's pockets.

There was no air conditioning, and many fans moved in the churchgoers' hands. The windows were open to allow cross ventilation. A crow's "caw" startled Felicia. Mac squeezed her hand. She said, "Okay. I get why you don't dress up for church. It's hot as hell in here."

The service began with Leo at the pulpit as plainly dressed as Mac. Everyone stood when he lifted his hands.

Without a microphone, Leo said loudly, "He is risen!"

The congregation responded, "He is risen, indeed!"

Leo announced, "'Glory to His Name.'"

As if on cue, the instruments began an up-tempo rendition of an antiquated hymn. The people seemed to know the words by heart because there were no hymnals or projection screens, and they sang every word.

Next, Leo asked, "People of God what do you believe?"

The people responded by reciting *The Apostle's Creed.*

Once again, Leo announced an old hymn, "'When We All Get to Heaven;'" the musicians started up; and the congregation sang every word. It was followed immediately by "When the Roll Is Called up Yonder." The congregation had not sat down in the hard, wooden pews since they had stood the moment Leo moved behind the podium.

A few men went forward after the third hymn and Leo said a prayer. Finally, they sat. However, they never knelt, which was unusual to Felicia. The men passed the offering plates as a young girl sang "Our God Reigns." Felicia thought: *Ah, something a little more modern.*

Then, the people began to put their hands in the air and sing along. Felicia had never known that song had so many stanzas. Moreover, she was shocked Mac knew everyone of them and felt comfortable raising his hands in praise. Felicia looked around for a wooden box. *I'm leaving if I see one snake being handled.* There were no snakes, but Felicia had read West Virginia was the only state in which snake handling in church had not been outlawed.

At last, Leo stood to preach. Felicia listened intently, curious about what he would say. He chose John 3:16, from the King James Bible as his one Scripture reference. He read it and bowed his head to pray. He began his sermon, "When we all get to

Heaven. Who is 'we all'? Does that mean everybody will go to Heaven? Let's examine what the Bible teaches."

During his sermon, Leo did refer to other passages of Scripture. Felicia gathered he believed those who trusted in Jesus would go to Heaven. He emphasized it was not man's place to know another's heart, but each person was responsible for his own spiritual relationship. Then, he asked each person to consider if he or she had trusted in Jesus, so when the roll was called up Yonder he or she would be there.

Felicia thought, *Yes, I believe in Jesus*, and put her uncomfortable feeling to the side.

Leo asked the congregation if any would like to speak with him regarding their place in Heaven. They sang another song, "Just as I Am," to give anyone who wanted to go forward time to do so.

Finally, Leo announced the dinner following church and asked the congregation to stand. He held his hands up and out toward the congregation as he spoke. "May the Grace of the Lord Jesus Christ, and the love of God, and the fellowship of the Holy Spirit be with you all."

The congregation milled around and talked while many of the women, including Lauren and Sunny, left to set out the food.

After church, the people shared a potluck meal as they did every Sunday. Tables were spread beneath shady oaks. Felicia whispered to Mac, "Are there any hog brains and scrambled eggs here?"

Mac looked over the tables. "No. Try the souse." He put a small piece on Felicia's plate.

"The what?" she asked.

"Souse."

"What is it?"

"It's related to sausage. Just try it."

"All right. What's this? It looks like little chicken leg quarters."

"Try it."

"What is it?"

"Just try it. It's wild game." Mac refused to tell Felicia she ate fried squirrel.

Many of the people met Felicia. They were warm and friendly. She noted some were truly shabbily dressed, but they were nice. A somewhat short, stocky, balding man and a tall, pretty blonde woman with luminous blue eyes, approached Mac and Felicia. The two men looked as if they could be related. Mac and the man embraced each other warmly. Mac turned to Felicia, "Honey, I want you to meet my friend and cousin, Gator Jones. Gator this is my Felicia."

"Nice to meet ya, finally," said Gator. "This is my wife, Sherry. Mac, you remember Sherry?"

"She's hard to forget. She looks so much like..." Mac let his thought trail off. "She looks wonderful. Sherry, it's hard to believe you have six children and one on the way."

"Six children?" Felicia said in bewilderment. "You don't look old enough to have six children."

"I do," Sherry replied with a smile as she introduced each one of them: Fox, Rooster, Lily, Rabbit, Buck, and Rose.

Felicia laughed slightly. "Those are some unusual names, at least the boys' names."

"I suppose." Sherry rubbed her abdomen. "This is either Iris or Tiger. Chambry ain't real common."

"No, it was my maiden name."

"Mine wouldn't do for a name."

"What was it?"

"Fields."

Mac's first medical emergency occurred almost at that moment when he had to perform the Heimlich maneuver on Ina Campbell.

After the excitement, Sherry and Felicia talked a little more as the music started. Then, Sherry went to dance with Gator. Felicia looked flabbergasted. "Mac," she said, "I refuse to even consider having six children."

"I won't ask, but I told you mountain families are large. Tipper has three children. Alain. Well, I have no idea how many of them are his and how many belong to his brothers. They're inbred."

"Oh, my Lord! This man is your friend?"

"Once. Now, I don't know." The doctor shrugged. "He's rather pathetic. Never mind that. Today is for fun."

"Is he here?"

"No. He hasn't come to church in ages. Let's dance."

"No. I don't know how. Dance with your friends, and I'll watch."

After the musicians began to play and a man about Mac's age and who Felicia thought very handsome began to call a square dance, an ancient woman approached Mac and received a warm hug. Mac introduced her. "Grandma Newton, this is my wife, Felicia. Felicia, my actual great-great-grandmother, Miriam Newton. Listen to whatever she tells you, honey. She will never give you bad advice."

The old woman hugged Felicia who stiffly returned the hug.

"Relax, dear. I'm harmless," said the old woman.

"I'm just a little overwhelmed," admitted Felicia.

"Of course, you are. You a city girl. But you got a good man."

"It would seem so."

Grandma Newton turned to Mac. "You gonna sing it for me?"

"It's been a long time, Grandma."

"You ain't forgot it, have you?"

"No, ma'am, but my partner's gone."

"Git yo wife to sing it with you."

"No," said Felicia firmly. "I probably don't know it anyway, and I'm not much of a singer."

"Humph! All you gotta do is make a joyful noise," scoffed Grandma Newton.

"No, Grandma. I don't feel comfortable with that."

"Suit yoself. Mac, I bet little Sunny knows it. Ask her. This might be the last time I ever git to hear it."

He shook his head and grinned at the guilt trip the old matriarch tried to pull. "Yes, ma'am."

Mac approached Sunny. "Excuse me. Do you by any chance know 'Sing Hosanna'?"

"You mean that silly little song?"

"Yes."

"Yeah. We used to do it at RUF retreats."

Mac laughed. "Strange. You aren't your average Presbyterian to be a part of Reformed University Fellowship, but, yes, that's the song. Grandma Newton wants me to sing it, but my partner left these hills. Felicia doesn't know it and wouldn't sing if she did. Will you sing the high part with me? You know Grandma gets what she wants."

"Sure. It'll be fun. Can you pick the banjo? I can play the guitar."

"Yes, I can. This will thrill her."

Mac retrieved the two instruments and he and Sunny flanked Grandma Newton. Everybody else encircled them. Felicia watched from near Lauren's side. The old lady bounced with excitement just like a child. Mac began:

> *Sing hosanna; sing hosanna; sing hosanna to the King of kings.*
> *Sing hosanna; sing hosanna; sing hosanna to the King.*

As he sang that part, Sunny sang a high descant:

> *Sing...Sing...Sing... King of Kings.*
> *Sing...Sing...Sing hosanna to the King.*

Then, they launched into the first stanza followed by the chorus each time:

> *Give me oil for my lamp; keep me burning.*
> *Give me oil for my lamp, I pray.*
> *Give me oil lamp; keep me burning, burning, burning.*
> *Keep me burning 'til the break of day.*

Give me hay for my mule; help me get to Sunday school.
Give me hay for my mule, I pray.
Give me hay for my mule; help me get to Sunday school.
Give me hay 'til the break of day.

Give me gas for my Ford; keep me trucking for the Lord.
Give me gas for my Ford, I pray.
Give me gas for my Ford; keep me trucking for the Lord.
Give my gas 'til the break of day.

Sunny sang and Mac laughed because he had never heard the verse she sang. It was sillier than the rest of them.

Give me umption for my gumption; help me function, function, function.
Give me umption for my gumption, I pray.
Give me umption for my gumption; help me function, function, function.
Help me function 'til the break of day.

After the last chorus, Mac flipped the banjo in the air and shouted, "That's it, Grandma!"

The crowd applauded raucously and laughed voluminously. The fellowship continued until nearly three o'clock. Then, the people began to trickle home. There was no night church or mid-week service for the hardship of it, but there was dinner on the grounds every Sunday and fellowship afterward.

As the women who lived in the town cleaned up, Felicia helped. She talked to Sunny and Lauren.

"What's souse?" she asked.

"Mary Lou's was very good today, wasn't it?" said Sunny.

"Yes. It was spicy. What is it though?"

Sunny explained. "Some people call it hog head cheese because it's molded like cheese. It's made from the meat peeled off the boiled hog head and ground like sausage, making sure to include the gristly part of the ears for consistency. It has seasonings like hot peppers and sage added. Then, it's set in a mold to take shape and sliced. It's really good with saltines."

Felicia looked repulsed. "No wonder Mac didn't tell me what it was! What were the little leg quarters? Mac wouldn't tell me that either."

"Squirrel."

"I ate a big rodent?"

"It was well fried, not too tough."

"I think I'm going be sick."

"Felicia, those are the kinds of things people eat here. You'll get used to it. Some of it's tasty. Can you imagine these people eating, say caviar and escargot? Fish eggs and snails would be just as big a culture shock to them as what you ate today, although they have been known to fry the eggs inside a female fish." The teacher placed plastic tablecloths in a drawer of the church kitchen. She laughed. "I guess that would be mountain caviar."

"You've adjusted well, Sunny."

"I've never run from a challenge or an adventure. Inner city was a culture shock to me, too." Sunny laughed again. "Having been raised a vegetarian, even a cheeseburger was a culture shock to me. Up here, they grind their own ground beef."

"Are you serious?"

"Yes. They kill and process their own animals, both wild and domestic, as well as grow their own crops; make their own butter, real butter, not margarine; milk their own cows, not pasteurized and homogenized milk; gather their own eggs; make their own cider, hard cider; and make their own moonshine. Wait 'til you try that."

"I might run away before then."

"No. You'll love Tipper's moonshine."

"Somebody is seriously named Tipper? He's Mac's friend, I think."

"Yes, his name is actually Tipper, not a nickname. He was the one calling the square dances. I'm surprised he didn't meet you today, but he did have to break up Callie's fight. She's a real scrapper."

Felicia's face still looked flabbergasted.

Sunny laughed and shook her head. "I know it's a culture shock, Felicia, but the people will grow on you. These are Mac's people. Try to remember that."

Felicia stared at Sunny in disgust, fear, and amazement. *This might be a little too much culture shock* raced through her head.

13

Hog-Rendering

Before the sun came up the next morning, Felicia started from her sleep as squealing and grunting and human voices shouting, "Sooie!" scared the living daylights out of her.

"Mac!" she screamed. "What's going on?" She hit her sleeping husband in the back with force.

"What?" Mac snapped as he sat up.

"Don't you hear that?"

"Oh, that. Yeah. I forgot to tell you they're having a hog-rendering today at the end of town at the slaughterhouse." He lay back down and propped his head on his fist as he reclined on his bent elbow. "It's sort of a holiday in Possum Holler. People bring the hogs in for slaughter and have 'em cut into various things like hams, chops, roasts, ribs, et cetera." He yawned. "Most families still have their own smoke houses for smoked meats, but they keep a cooling locker at the slaughterhouse. They come in periodically to get what they want. Some of the hogs being brought in will be shipped to market. My friend, Gator, is a hog farmer. Just be glad the hog farmers are out in the sticks, or you couldn't stand the smell." He wrinkled his nose. "In addition to slaughtering, there will be a big cookout of a sort tonight in town. The parts the government won't approve will be cooked and eaten this evening, as will some other things. This is one of the social events I told you about."

"The things the government won't approve? Like the brains?" Felicia asked between gags.

"Yes, and others. One of the best things is called the lights."

"What exactly is that?"

"Lungs. They're great boiled with rice made in the broth."

"Do you expect me to eat this?"

"Absolutely."

"Mac, I ate hog head cheese and squirrel yesterday. Is there anything you people don't eat?"

"Us people?"

"Hillbillies!"

"Yeah, snails!" He pushed himself up a bit.

"Oh, Mac!"

"I don't guess you'll be up for mountain oysters either."

"I love oysters."

Mac guffawed. "They're not really oysters although they're supposed to be an aphrodisiac and instill virility."

"What are they?"

"Bull balls. I can't wait to see you wring a chicken's neck."

"I will not!"

"Suit yourself. You might go hungry when the only way a patient can pay is with a food offering, whatever it might be."

Several loud pops made Felicia scream. "What was that?"

"The first dead pigs. Felicia, this goes on in big cities, too. You just don't see it or hear it."

"This is hog-rendering day, huh?"

"Yes."

"Do they have cow day?" The frightened woman narrowed her eyes to slits.

"Not exactly. There aren't really any ranchers. The few cattle killed and processed are for personal use. They don't ship cattle. The slaughterhouse is one of the few businesses where the people of Possum Holler actually earn an income. The farmers will get market price for their crops, produce or animals. The miners make more money than anybody else, but they also get sicker even with all the safety measures mining companies must have in place today. Believe it or not, there are still bootleggers here."

"I have gone back in time. I want to go home." She lay back and covered her face with her hands momentarily. Then, she dropped them to her sides and sighed.

"Felicia, you know, this place isn't so bad. People don't kill one another. We have no Hatfields and McCoys here. Teachers don't get shot." Mac laughed. "Social workers, maybe, but not teachers. The last murder we had occurred when I was thirteen. Alain Richter's father killed his wife and then himself. There is very little actual crime. There's an occasional fight and public drunks. We have a constable—just one. There are two cells in the back of the post office just in case the brawlers need to be separated. The people here are poor; eighty percent are below poverty level. They're relatively uneducated and a little old-fashioned and backward, but they're good people. Give my people a chance. Please?"

"What about rape, Mac? Is that a crime around here?"

"Yes. Why?"

"Well, a lot of your good men were leering at me yesterday."

"I'm sure they were. You're beautiful. Of course, they were looking. However, nobody would dare touch my wife. Infidelity is practically unheard of. Although some of the men might visit a brothel, they don't consider that infidelity." Holding up a hand to ward off her comment, he went on, "I do, but they don't. There is an occasional sex crime. The perpetrators are shipped off to county jail. Contrary to popular myth, mountain men do not 'take' women or abuse women very often. On the contrary, women are placed on pedestals. We mountain men love our women passionately."

He pinned her onto the bed. "May I show you?"

Sufficiently chastised, Felicia laughed. "Please do. And if I happen to scream, nobody will hear me over all the screaming outside."

Mac and Felicia came to breakfast. Chambry climbed onto Mac's lap. "Daddy," he said, "why are the pigs so unhappy? They're screaming."

"Yes, they are. Chambry, this is the day we call Hog-Rendering. It's sort of a holiday here. It's the day the pigs become pork."

"Do you mean food?"

"Yes. Does that bother you?"

"No, sir. We have to eat, and I like bacon." To prove his point, the boy ate a piece. "Mamaw has cooked a big batch. We have eggs and biscuits with honey. There's a lady who lives out from town that has beehives. Will you take me to see the bees make honey?"

"If you'd like."

"Yes, sir, I would. Mother, will you come?"

"When?" asked Felicia.

"I don't know. When can we go, Daddy?"

"Tomorrow. We have Hog-Rendering today."

"Mac!" objected Felicia. "You're not taking him to the slaughterhouse."

"Yes, I am."

"No! He does *not* need to see that."

Mac rolled his eyes. "I won't take him into the kill room at this age, but he can see how different things are made. You, my dear, can learn to cook some of these things. You know, I was hunting with a .22 rifle at eight."

Felicia looked horrified. "Very well," she relented. "We'll go, but you had better give me something for nausea before we go."

Mac laughed. "You'll be fine."

Chambry tugged his father's arm. "When can I get a hunting rifle?"

"Not before you're eight." The father tousled the child's hair.

After breakfast, of which Felicia ate very little, the household walked to the end of town. Outside tables were set up and several large cauldron-like pots already boiled hog heads while the aroma of baking and frying pig skins and cracklings came from clay ovens and deep fryers. At the tables, the women ground peppers and sage, as well as the cooked meat from the boiled hog heads. Others strained the grease to make lard and separated the cracklings.

Felicia had to admit the aromas were appetizing; the smell was much like bacon and ham. Her stomach growled, and her mouth watered. Sunny came from one of the tables and grabbed Felicia by the hand. "Come on. I'm going to teach you how to make souse."

"Is it disgusting?"

"No, but you'll have to get your hands dirty." Sunny laughed. "I was just thinking my parents would love living here for the feeling of its almost being like a commune. They were hippies. Of course, my mother would get sick because she's a strict vegetarian. There's such a feeling of family here. Actually"—She looked around—"almost everybody around here is distantly related if not close kin."

Sunny shuddered. "Leo told me one of the hardest things he had to drive home was close kin cannot marry. He said a few folks got angry enough he ended up with cracked ribs and black eyes."

"Good grief!" Felicia exclaimed.

"Couples have to prove to him they're no closer than third cousins."

"That's sick."

"Disquieting, for sure. It's one reason there have been many genetic illnesses and disabilities."

"Such as?"

"Mentally handicapped."

"Mac must not be from a set of cousins. He told me about some man he used to be friends with."

"The Richters?"

"His name was Alain."

"The Richters." Sunny nodded. "They're a breed apart, but, no, Mac isn't inbred. Leo told me Mac's mother's family came here from another town to start up the slaughterhouse. They were the Newtons from Lilo. They came six generations ago. Grandma Newton was a little girl. She's ancient, but very progressive. She never changed her name when she got married." Sunny lowered her voice. "Rumor is she never married, but had common-law relationships, all of whom died. That's why her offspring had the last name of Newton. She swears her longevity is due in part to 'a glass o' moonshine ever'day and satisfyin' six husbands.'" Sunny affected a hillbilly accent to sound like Grandma Newton.

Their conversation was momentarily interrupted as they heard piglets squealing and Chambry shouting, "Mother! Mother!" The child ran up, covered in mud and carrying a baby pig. "I caught him, Mother! He's mine."

"Oh, my God!" Felicia looked around for Mac, who trotted up with Gator Jones. She pointed toward their son, her mouth opening and closing without sound before she managed, "He's filthy!"

Mac laughed. "I'll run him home to change."

Chambry squeezed the piglet in a hug.

Felicia inhaled sharply. She mouthed, "What happens when it becomes pork?"

"Don't worry about that," Gator said. "Chambry, what's his name?"

"Babe."

Gator smiled. "Babe will go in a special pen at my place where you can come visit him. When he grows up, he'll help make some more baby pigs. He won't *ever* become pork. I had a special hog once named Wilbur."

Mac said, "Babe is another famous storybook pig, Gator."

Gator nodded. "Let's go get Babe tagged on his ear so nobody else can claim him."

"Then, let's run home and get you cleaned up," Mac said nudging Chambry and winking at Felicia.

Sunny laughed at the look on Felicia's face. "Gator Jones in one of the nicest people you'll ever meet. His mother was a Newton too. Grandma Newton is proud of her great-great-grands."

Felicia laughed. "She sounds like a hoot!"

"She is. On the other hand, she says just what she thinks, even if it hurts your feelings."

"I wonder what she thinks of me."

"Don't ask her if you don't want to know. She's coming over here. Get your hands in the pan quick."

Felicia slipped her wedding ring into the pocket of her jeans and began to knead the sage and peppers into the meat in the bowl before her. She sniffed. "It smells like sausage."

"Good," encouraged Sunny. "It's just like sausage. The spicier you like it, the more pepper you add."

"Ugh. This is nastier than mud pies the way it oozes through my fingers. There's a lot of fat in this," observed Felicia. "It can't be healthy."

"Not in large quantities," agreed Sunny, "but it does taste good. You liked what you ate yesterday."

"It was flavorful."

"Yes, it was."

"Good morning, Felicia," greeted Grandma Newton.

"Good morning, Grandma Newton."

"Whatcha doin'?"

"Learning to make souse."

"Nothin' to it."

"It appears easy."

"Well, you won't have to do much of it. Folks'll make sure Mac's family gits fed."

"That's nice."

Grandma Newton scrutinized Felicia. "You don't think much o' us mountain folk, do ya, little miss high-falootin', Felicia?"

"Why would you say that?"

"You don't think we as good as you."

"Not so. It's just I grew up in the big city. This takes a lot of adjustment."

"I imagine it do, at that. Mac's a good man. He'll treat you right if you let 'im. Jest because he wants a simple life don't mean he don't love ya. Just remember that when ya git ready to pack yo bags and run off."

Grandma Newton moved on. Felicia looked at Sunny. "Sunny, she's just downright mean and nasty."

Sunny whispered, "You could've won her over if you had sung a chorus or two yesterday with Mac."

"I can't carry a tune in a bucket."

"It doesn't matter. Just do it. Then, when she tells you that you can't sing, agree and say, 'No, but I can make a joyful noise.' That'll get her goat, and she'll leave you alone."

"What if I don't know the song?"

"Mac can teach you."

"I sound like a man when I sing."

"So? You're a contralto. Can you harmonize?"

"I wouldn't know how. Why?"

Sunny wiped her hands on a dishtowel and handed it to Felicia. "I was thinking we could do a duet."

"I also hate country music."

"How about Bob Dylan?"

"He's old."

"I think I can teach you 'Blowin' in the Wind' easily though. Or we could try John Denver's 'Country Roads.'"

"I'd rather try Dylan. He always sounds a little flat anyway. I do know the words."

"We'll work on it. They'll start picking and singing really soon."

More and more old pickup trucks arrived with a hog or two. The people snacked on cracklings, roasted corn and potatoes, and boiled peanuts for a long time. A large livestock truck pulled out loaded with hogs for market around four o'clock, and the residents began their Hog Fest. There were ribs marinated in whiskey and done over the pit barbeque. The hog liver and lights were prepared with the rice and the broth, and there were the dreaded hog brains and scrambled eggs. That was topped off by the chitterlings.

Felicia had no problem with the ribs. They were messy, but tasty. She tried the liver and lights with rice rationalizing it had to be the same as liver and onions. She had to agree with Mac— the lights were to die for. She scooped one spoonful of the brains. Mac prodded her. "Don't push," she warned.

The combination was interesting, but one bite of the chitterlings was all Felicia could handle. She gagged so hard she almost threw up what she had eaten.

She looked at Mac in horror and shouted, "They won't sell the lungs for general consumption, but they'll let people eat the guts? Why, for God's sake? That's the nastiest thing I've ever tasted. The lights were delicious."

"Trichinosis," stated Mac.

"What?"

"If you don't cook the lights thoroughly, you *could* get trichinosis, just like undercooked hamburger *could* result in e-coli or undercooked chicken or fish *could* result in salmonella. So far, the government has only banned pork lung. They just require the other three to be fully cooked unless you count sushi."

"Well, I will not eat, what did you call it, 'chitlins,' again!"

"You don't have to. Just the fact you tried it is enough. Come on the party's started." Mac took Felicia's hand. "Dance with me."

The square dance caller began to encourage the gents to find their partners. Felicia hesitated. "Mac, I've never square danced before."

"I had never salsa danced before." Mac grinned impishly. "You watched yesterday. Just listen to what Tipper says and watch the others. If you mess up, laugh about it. Everybody knows you're new to this. They'll laugh with you."

"Don't you mean at me?"

"No. Try it. Please?"

"Tipper? The one that wrote you?"

"Yes. Will you do it? It's a lot more fun than chitlins."

Several squares formed. Felicia noticed Lauren with Leo, Gator and Sherry Jones, and Sunny with the man from the store, Royce Dent. "Only if you get us in Sunny's square."

"Come on."

Tipper started, "Bow to your partners. Bow to your corners. Forward and back. Now, swing your partners round and round.

Do-si-do. Allemande left. Swing your partners, and promenade the ladies back home."

Tipper seemed to realize Felicia was dancing for the first time and kept the steps simple. He repeated the sequence three times before stopping and calling for a drink.

Felicia approached Tipper Campbell who was Mac's age. He was extremely good-looking. He was quite tall at six-foot-four, lean and muscled, about a hundred ninety pounds. He had sandy-blond hair and pale-blue eyes. Felicia said, "Thank you for keeping it simple. I guess I need a book on square dancing for dummies."

"You did fine, Mrs. Reardon, but if you'd like, I could teach you some more steps."

"That would be nice."

"Of course, Mac's a real good dancer, and he'd have to give his permission."

"For you to teach me to dance?"

"Yes, ma'am. It wouldn't be seemly for me to teach a married woman to dance without her husband's permission."

"How quaint."

"My permission for what?" asked Mac as he brought three tin cups of moonshine.

Felicia took a sip and coughed uncontrollably before she gasped, "What is that?"

Tipper laughed. "My homemade distillation. You ain't used to something so stout. I'm tryin' to make it legit. I wanna bottle it and sell it to city folk."

Mac took a swig. "Whoa! That's good. You've improved it. It's smoother."

"Smooth?" questioned Felicia.

Tipper said deferentially, "It ain't French wine, but it's pretty good moonshine."

Felicia sipped the beverage again. "I guess I could get used to it."

"Have a couple o' cups and you won't care if you dance bad," laughed Tipper.

Felicia slipped her arm around Mac's. "Yes, dear. Tipper has offered to teach me to square dance if it's all right with you."

"It's a great idea," agreed Mac.

"Then, I'll come to Preacher Tomlin's tomorrow afternoon, Mrs. Reardon."

"Only if you call me Felicia."

Tipper raised his eyebrow. "Mac?"

"Of course, you may use her first name."

"If you say so. Felicia, I'll see you tomorrow. Mac, you ready to do some singin'? I've missed my partner."

"I thought your partner was a girl," teased Felicia.

"Only for that one song," explained Mac. "Tipper and I have been picking and singing since grade school." The doctor smirked. "But Tipper could take the descant in falsetto."

"So, you went to school with Mac?"

"Yes, ma'am. We graduated together."

"Why didn't you go to college? You could've gotten a marketing degree for that moonshine."

"We didn't have the money for me to go off to the city, ma'am. I had to take care of my ma."

"Where's your father?"

"Dead, ma'am. Coal mine accident."

"I'm sorry."

"It's the way things are around here, ma'am."

"Can we stop with the ma'ams?" She put her hands in front of her as if to make a shield.

Tipper looked at Mac. Mac nodded.

"All right," agreed Tipper.

Mac said, "Yes, Felicia, Tipper was almost my brother. My pa was engaged to his ma when he died."

"Poor woman," said Felicia.

"Yes," said Tipper. "It was a hard time for her."

"Well," observed Felicia, "you seem to have done well despite hardship."

"I reckon."

She puckered her lips in thought. "Tipper, I have a friend who might be able to help you market your beverage. Would you be interested?"

Tipper looked at his friend for approval. Mac nodded discreetly.

"I would much appreciate it," Tipper said. "Maybe we could call it payment for dance lessons."

"It's a deal." Felicia extended her hand. Tipper timidly shook it.

Tipper took up a banjo as did Mac, and they began a duel after jumping onto the makeshift stage. After several minutes, Mac raised his hands in surrender. "Whew! I'm rusty."

He laid the banjo in its case and picked up a guitar. He began to croon, "'Hear that lonesome whippoorwill...'"

"He's good," said Sunny behind Felicia.

"Yeah. Maybe too good."

"What does that mean?"

"Nothing. I know the words to Dylan. Will you play the guitar? Do you think these people would like a flute? I can play the flute."

"They would love it. Do you have it here?"

"Yes."

"Go get it. Hurry."

Felicia jogged toward the Tomlins' home and ran smack dab into the stereotypical hillbilly: a tall, but not quite as tall as Tipper, rather thin man with long caramel-brown hair pulled into a ponytail at the nape of his neck with a rubber band, a long unkempt beard, and sparkling green eyes. The man who wore a plaid shirt in browns and greens and ragged overalls smelled as if he had bathed in Tipper's moonshine.

Felicia gasped. "Pardon me, ma'am," said the man.

"No harm done," said Felicia nervously.

"You Mac'sh wife?"

"Yes."

"I ain't shurprised he didn't introdushe you to me. I'm a dishgrashe." The man swayed, obviously quite drunk.

"I'm Felicia." She didn't quite know why she introduced herself, but the man was pitiable.

"Nishe to meet ya. I'm Alain Richter."

"Oh."

"Oh, ish right. I can tell from your expression Mac mushta told ya shomethin' about me. Obvioushly, it wudn't good."

"He said you and he used to be friends."

"Ushed to be. Yeah. Ushed to be." He nodded slowly and sadly. "I guessh that meansh we ain't no more."

"I'm not sure. I'm sorry I bumped your shoulder. I was in a hurry to get my flute. I'm going to play it."

"Don't let me keep ya. Run on."

Felicia started on but turned back. There was something both frightening and endearing about this pathetic creature. She said, "Be sure to listen. I'm sort of a disgrace, too."

Alain inclined his head and Felicia ran on.

14

A New Step

Felicia got back with her flute ready to play. "I don't know any bluegrass or country," she whispered to Sunny.

"Do you know 'Amazing Grace'?"

"Yes, I can play that."

"We are about to knock Grandma Newton's socks off," laughed Sunny as she held up a violin. "Come on, Mrs. Reardon."

Sunny and Felicia jumped onto the little makeshift platform. Mac tried to speak, but no words found him. He was dumbstruck with shock.

"Time for a quartet," announced Sunny. She played a few bars of "Amazing Grace."

Mac nodded. "You got it." He gave a count in, and they played a stanza of the song with Mac on guitar, Tipper on banjo, Sunny on violin, and Felicia on flute. Then, Mac and Tipper harmonized perfectly as they sang the first stanza á cappella, with Tipper singing tenor and Mac baritone. When they started the second, Sunny and Felicia played softly through it and the third. They cranked up the volume for the fourth, and the men added instrument to voice. The mesmerized crowd exploded with applause.

After the song concluded, Sunny said, "Take a break, gents. It's our turn." She nodded encouragement to Felicia. "You said you know the words."

"I do."

"When we finish that, we'll go right into 'This Land Is Your Land.' Do you know it?"

"Yeah. Every school child knows that one."

"You get the first stanza alone. We'll duet the second. You just carry the melody. I'll do the harmony."

Sunny picked up the guitar and began to strum. Felicia nervously sang, "'How many roads…'"

The one face that caught her attention in the crowd had his green eyes glistening with tears as it seemed every word sung, he took to heart. Felicia had heard bits and pieces about him. She wondered just how many lonely, deserted roads he had traveled. The expression on his face told her it had been many. Alain Richter disappeared from sight.

When the song finished, Sunny changed immediately to the other tune and the ladies sang a duet. Then, Sunny indicated another flute piece.

"What?" mouthed Felicia.

"'Ode to Joy'?"

Felicia nodded. They finished with a stirring impromptu rendition of "Ode to Joy."

"Next!" announced Sunny as they left the makeshift stage of packing crates.

"Very nice, ladies!" Mac said over the clapping.

"Indeed," agreed Tipper. "But it's gettin' late. I have to work. Until tomorrow, Felicia. Miss Bankston, good night. Mac, good to have you home."

Tipper rounded up three little girls between the ages of eleven and three and an older woman who looked like Tipper (*And Sherry Jones*, thought Felicia.). They loaded into a pickup and left.

"Whose children?" asked the city girl, trying hard to fit in.

"His. I told you he had three," Mac answered.

"Yes, but one of them looked like a teenager."

"Not quite. Betsy's eleven."

"Where's his wife?"

"Ran off with a salesman. He got his divorce papers when I was last here. She was my other singing partner, Amy. She insisted. I didn't like her much." He snorted. "Actually, it was more her ma. Lucille Dent made everyone's life miserable. I'm sure she had something to do with Amy running off. Amy is an artist. She went to make her fame. Tipper's hurt."

"Tipper Campbell is the one who wrote you all the time, the one you sent two boxes of condoms."

"He's the one. Good thing I sent them. He obviously used them, or he'd have a dozen kids to bring up alone."

"Maybe he'll meet somebody else. Sunny, don't you think he's cute?" Felecia turned to the schoolteacher.

Sunny waved both hands in the air. "Mr. Campbell is a nice man and the father of two of my students. There's no spark there, Felicia. I'll meet the right man someday. Hey! Jessica Langston will be coming here soon. Now, that might work."

Mac looked around. "It seems the party's over. Let's go home, too. Chambry!" Mac called his son.

Lauren informed him, "He went home with Papaw and Rush. They were all about to fall asleep."

"Me, too," admitted Mac. "Sunny, good night."

Mac took Felicia's hand. As they started away, Grandma Newton came up on her way home, too. "Good night, Grandma," said Mac, kissing her on the cheek.

"Good night, my boy. Good night, Felicia. Stick to tootin' that horn. It was real purty. Leave the singin' to Mac."

"Good night, Grandma," said Felicia, but she thought, *Bitch*.

A truck arrived the next day with cement and lumber, along with other building supplies. Felicia went with Mac to the clinic site. "Will the men be insulted I came?" she asked.

"You're with me because I want you here. You designed the structure, and if they have questions, you're the one who knows the answers." He put his arm around her. "You're a talented architect, my darling. I'm grateful to have you on my team."

"It's what I can offer, Mac. I'm not a nurse."

"I know."

The men who did not have to work away from their homes made sure the foundation for what they saw as their hospital was poured. Rather than the usual raised foundation, the hospital would be slab. They also cut and stacked the framing timbers.

With so many determined hands working, a great deal was accomplished that day.

Close to dark, Tipper pulled up. He was filthy, smudged with coal dust. The dark black powder made his eyes bluer, and Felicia noticed that among a people with horrendous teeth, Tipper's were perfectly straight and white just like Mac's.

Tipper shook hands with Mac and dipped his head toward Felicia. "Looks like I'm too late to help with the building today."

"It's all right," assured Mac.

"Mac, do you think Mrs. Tomlin will let me wash up at her house?" He looked at Felicia. "Felicia, I can't give you dance lessons lookin' and smellin' like this. I get filthy even when I don't actually go into the mine, which I did have to do today."

Mac nodded. "I'm sure Mamaw will be fine with it. She made Papa install a shower. Let's go to the house."

"You're not a miner?" Felicia asked for clarification.

"Shift foreman. Some days I just stay in the air-conditioned trailer." Tipper grinned.

"Ah, big boss man," Felicia teased.

Tipper grabbed a bag from his truck. Felicia looked at it. The tall man smirked. "Like my fancy suitcase? It's a change of clothes."

"It works" said Felicia, "but you need a gym bag."

Mac shook his head, and he and Tipper laughed.

Tipper showered and changed clothes while Mac cleared a place for dancing. Mac kissed Felicia as Tipper came in. "I'm going to write some letters to solicit supplies for our little hospital. You can show me what you learn later."

First, Tipper handed Felicia a list of written commands. "I wrote this down for you. I'll demonstrate the moves, and, then, you can try 'em."

"You're so organized," laughed Felicia. "Next time you come, bring a few bottles of your distillation. I'll send them to my friend for sampling."

"Yes, ma'am. You ready?"

"Show me."

Tipper pronounced each call and showed Felicia what to do. Then, she did the step. Finally, Tipper took her list away.

"Let's see what you learned," he teased good-naturedly. He gave a call and made Felicia do it. She missed one.

"Not too bad for your first lesson," laughed Tipper. "Now I need to get home to my girls. Tuesday is the best day for me. Next week?"

"Yes. Thank you. How old are your girls? What are their names?"

"Well, my first girl's my ma, Ina. My pa died when I was just a baby. She never married again, but she was engaged to marry Mac's pa." He held the door open with his hand resting atop it. "Ander died from pneumonia the night before their wedding. He always got me to town to catch the bus for school. Even after he died, Ma insisted I go to school. She wanted me to have book learning. She would have given anything to send me off with Mac."

"You should have gone."

"Maybe so, but I stayed and married Amy Dent, my second girl. I loved her. Amy was an artist. She was very talented." He looked out toward the stars that had begun to twinkle. Only a silver sliver of a moon hung among the glittering diamonds. Felicia followed his gaze and noted how bright the sky was without city lights. Tipper heaved a breath and continued. "One day we were in the general store her pa owns. This book salesman came in. He saw some of her paintings and said they were good. He became Amy's agent and got her a show in Philadelphia. He came back every few months.

"Lucille, Amy's ma, hated me for some reason. When she died, Amy grew cold and distant from me. One day when Laurie was just walkin', she left with the salesman and sent me the divorce papers in the mail."

"You need to meet somebody else."

"Maybe someday. I ain't afraid to be alone. Maybe when I'm a whiskey entrepreneur." Tipper laughed.

"Anyway, about my girls. Laurie's three. She's the baby. Amy's been gone two years. Callie is almost six. She'll be in first grade, but she can already read. She's a scrapper. I had to break up a fight with her Sunday. That's why I couldn't meet you. Betsy is too grown up. She's eleven. She hopes one day a handsome prince will come and take her to live in a castle. Oh! I wish I could make that happen."

"How old were you when Betsy was born?"

"Nineteen."

"Tipper, did you marry Amy because she was pregnant?"

"No. I married Amy because I loved her." He blushed. "She married me because she was pregnant. Mac warned me. He never trusted our relationship. He always felt something was off."

"I understand. I think my friend really can market your moonshine. Tell me something. Do your girls sing as well as you?"

"You think I can sing?"

"Very well. If the girls are as good as you, take them to the city and get exposure."

Tipper was quiet as they listened to the crickets chirping. "That's a thought. I don't sing to make money. It brings me joy to sing. Betsy draws just like her momma." Tipper sighed and rapped his hand on top of the door. "Well, Felicia, good night. I'll see you Sunday at church."

"Good night, Tipper."

"Tell Mac I said good night."

"I will." As he drove away, Felicia felt Mac's hand on her shoulder. She patted it. "Maybe you can help his spirit heal. I like him, Mac. I see why you're friends."

Felicia strove to fit in. She kept hoping Grandma Newton would be pleasant. She asked Leo if she could play her flute for the offertory in church, and he thought it a wonderful idea. So, on Sunday, Felicia played a rousing medley of "Stand up, Stand up for Jesus," "Onward Christian Soldiers," and "Victory in Jesus."

As they ate dinner again, Felicia thought when Grandma Newton came up to her: *If this old bat doesn't say something totally positive to me, I'm going to hit her with my flute.*

Grandma Newton asked, "Whatcha call that little whistle you blow?"

"A flute," answered Felicia.

"Well, you blow it real good. I bet it sounds real sweet if you play slow."

"Yes, it does."

"Well, next Sunday is my ninety-seventh birthday. Sunny plays her fiddle haunting like when she plays slow. I want you two girls to play me somethin' real purty, a duet, for my birthday."

"We'll do that, Grandma."

The old lady wandered on to speak to others.

"I heard," Sunny said as she cut a piece of apple pie. "What do you want to do?"

"Something very mellow and haunting. Something to make her cry."

The next day, Felicia drafted a blueprint for a two-story, three-wing school, which would eventually house two hundred students, kindergarten through twelfth grade, and gave it to Leo.

"Nice," he commented. "You're planning big."

"Dr. Tomlin, if all the school-age children from Possum Holler actually went to school, how many would it be?"

"Maybe a hundred thirty."

"So, I'm leaving room for growth. I mean, what if Tipper's distillery takes off? You could have a real business here."

"I like your thinking. After the clinic, we'll start on this. Although if Tipper's business takes off, other moonshiners might not like it." He rolled the blueprint and put it in the cylinder Felicia provided.

"It could offer them legitimate work helping him make his whiskey."

"You seem to have found a new step to dance."

"I'm trying."

"Yes, you are." The surrogate father-in-law patted the woman's shoulder.

The next day Tipper came for dance lessons and brought six bottles of "Tipper's Authentic Mountain Moonshine." Betsy had made labels for the bottles and glued them on.

Tipper said, "I brought special ones. They're fruit flavored. They have fruit in the bottom. See?" Tipper held the bottle up to the light. "I thought city folk would like that. I got peach, apple, blackberry, watermelon, pear, and one plain."

"I'll package them and ship them to my friend, Ron Norton, tomorrow."

"Thank you, Felicia."

"What are you going to teach me tonight?"

"We're gonna review the steps. You know what to do. You need to practice now. Can you pretend there are three other couples? I'll call a dance and we'll pretend we're dancin' with other people. You can put your lessons to use at Grandma Newton's birthday party after church Sunday."

They practiced for forty-five minutes before Tipper went home. Felicia noted he was clean when he arrived. He had apparently gone home before he came.

Felicia went to the room she and Mac were using and wrote a long letter to her friend, Ron, who owned several night clubs. The next morning, she used a packing crate and straw for the moonshine and drove into a large post office where she shipped the cargo overnight express. She included the phone number at the church for contact information for Tipper.

On Friday, Felicia was summoned to the phone at the church.

"Felicia, this is Ron. Where the hell are you?"

"Possum Holler, West Virginia."

"You actually moved there with that hillbilly doctor?"

"Yes, I did."

"Good job. You've discovered a bestselling alcoholic beverage, and I love the name—Tipper's. It's great! The people I shared this with are begging for more. Is this bootleg whiskey?"

"It's Tipper's moonshine."

"Don't tell me Tipper is a real person."

"All six feet, four inches of him. Hey, our former second lady was named Tipper." She switched the phone to her other ear and nodded at Leo.

"True," said Ron to her comment. "Can this guy get this done on a large scale?"

"A couple hundred bottles. His facility is in his backyard. Can you really market this for him?"

"You bet. Get him to file all the paperwork to be a legal distillery and a trademark for his brand. When that's done, get back in touch with me. We'll get the ball rolling. I can help him build a future. I need two hundred bottles ASAP."

"This is great news, Ron! I can't wait to tell Tipper." She hung up the receiver.

"I heard!" Leo clapped his hands. "Your friend can make him legit."

"And rich, too, probably."

"You can drive out and tell him."

"Would it be proper for me as a woman to go alone?" she asked with great skepticism.

"No. Drag Mac."

"He's supervising the clinic building."

"I can't go right now. I have a meeting with Alain Richter."

"He's coming to the church? Mac said..."

Leo shook his head. "No, I'm meeting him. Just wait until Sunday to tell Tipper."

"No," she said in a little frustration. "Would it be all right if two women went?"

"I guess. Take Sunny. A visit from the school principal wouldn't be inappropriate."

Felicia wagged her head.

"I know," sighed Leo. "It's a bit ridiculous, but the people here are a tad old-fashioned. Tipper is very old-fashioned."

"Really? I think he just needs a little push. He did get his girlfriend pregnant."

"True, but that will never happen again. He learned from his mistake."

"He's sweet."

"Yeah. He would be mortified if you came out there alone though to give him this news."

"I wouldn't want to hurt Tipper. He's a very nice person. I can see why he and Mac are friends. They're almost two of a kind."

"You sound so sad, Felicia." Leo stood.

The woman shrugged. "Grandma Newton said I thought I was better than the people here. That's not true. Sometimes I think I'm not good enough for Mac, not the other way around."

"Nonsense! Don't let Grandma Newton get to you. She's old and cantankerous."

"Thanks, Dr. Tomlin."

"Felicia, you can call me Leo."

"How about 'Papa'?"

"If you want to."

Felicia shook her head. "No, it doesn't feel right to me, but I guess I can handle Leo. Of course, you're Papaw for Chambry. That's very appropriate."

"That's fine. And make it Lauren, and, of course, Mamaw."

"Okay. Well, I'm going to find Sunny. I want to deliver this news to Tipper."

"And I'm going to see one of my little lost lambs about a rattling noise in my car. There's not much that man can't fix on a car." The two walked out together.

Sunny happily accompanied Felicia. As they drove down the dirt road to the Campbell shack, for it was little more than a shack, Felicia said, "Oh, my God! Do they really live in that?"

"Yes. It's solid."

"It's so small."

"It has four rooms. There is one big open kitchen, dining, living area. Tipper turned the one other room into three small ones. He has a room, Miss Ina has a room, and the girls share a room."

"Where's the bathroom?"

Sunny pointed to the outhouse. "There."

Felicia gasped.

"They don't have running water or electricity," Sunny continued. "They do have a pump to the kitchen sink Ander Reardon installed. They bathe in a washtub in the kitchen at night. Miss Ina has a curtained-off section. And Tipper made their stove propane. They have it better than some others out here." She indicated several other small buildings. "Smokehouse, chicken coop, barn, corn crib, storage shed."

"How does he run a still?"

"By hand with firewood."

Tipper came onto the porch with a lantern since twilight had begun to fall, and the two women got out of the car. "Is something wrong?" he asked.

A lot, thought Felicia, but she said, "No. I came to tell you I heard from my friend, Ron."

"What did he say?" asked Tipper, coming to the car.

"He said for you to file all the proper paperwork to have a legitimate distillery, and a trademark, and get him two hundred bottles as soon as possible."

Tipper whooped and hugged Felicia. He stood back quickly, embarrassed by his action.

"Congratulations, Mr. Campbell," said Sunny.

"Thank you." He looked back at the house. "I can build a real house and make sure my girls go to college."

"Ron is willing to help build a real distillery. Maybe you could build it in town. You might get some of the other entrepreneurs to work for you," suggested Felicia.

"That's a good idea, but the process has to stay the same or it won't taste the same."

"That's your area, but I could draw the plans for you. You'll have to tell me what you need."

"Okay. How about instead of dance lessons, you help me make sure I have the right papers, and I can tell you what I need?"

"That's good. I guess we need to get back now. We'll see you Sunday."

"Good night."

Sunday came and Felicia and Sunny's duet of Tchaikovsky's "Sleeping Beauty" did indeed, bring tears to Grandma Newton's eyes. As soon as they saw their desired effect, they changed to "One Tin Soldier" with flute accompaniment and Sunny's singing. Mac thought the way they turned the tables on the old woman was marvelous, especially when he saw how much she appreciated it.

When Tuesday came, Mac went into the city to purchase medicines from a pharmaceutical representative that would not drive into Possum Holler. The clinic would be ready soon with so many helping.

Tipper came earlier than expected. "Where's Mac?" he asked. "I had hoped to visit with him."

"I'm sorry," said Felicia. "He went into the city. I expect him back soon."

"Perhaps he'll get here before I leave." Tipper produced two envelopes. "Yesterday and today I also went to the city. Felicia, are these all the papers I need?" He handed her the larger envelope.

Felicia looked over the papers. "I think so," she informed. "We need to get copies to send to Ron."

"Those are his. I asked the lady to make a copy for him and a copy for me."

"Good forethought. What's in the other envelope?"

"A list of things I'll need for a distillery. It's for you, so you can draw the plans."

Felicia smiled at Tipper's innocent, child-like exuberance. She teased, "Didn't you bring a bottle, so we could celebrate?"

"I'm sorry. I didn't think."

"I'm teasing, Tipper. Come here. Sit down." Felicia patted the couch beside her. "Let's look over this list."

Tipper sat down shyly, hands on his knees. She looked at the list and hastily sketched a building. "How's this?"

"Yes. It has everything I asked for," the new businessman remarked after looking at the sketch.

"Where will you build it?"

"I thought in the space just beyond the slaughterhouse. I filed the papers to own that area. It's mine now. Felicia, this has to succeed. I used the money I had saved since childhood to purchase the land."

"It will." She patted his leg.

He stood. "I should go now."

"How about a dance lesson?"

"You know how to square dance now. You were great at Grandma Newton's birthday celebration."

"No. I'll teach you to salsa."

"What's that?"

"A dance they do in the big city for when you go there."

"Show me."

The city girl showed Tipper some salsa moves. He stared at her with his mouth agape. "Felicia, that is very inappropriate dancing."

"Why?"

"It's very…" He blinked and shook his head.

"Sexy?"

"Yes."

"I suppose. However, it's what they do in the city."

"Then, perhaps, I won't go to the city."

"You'll have to if you want to market your product. Believe me, this is how they dance in Ron's clubs."

"Very well. I'll try."

Tipper attempted the steps with stiff accuracy.

"Loosen up," encouraged Felicia. "Like this." She put her hands on Tipper's hips and pulled him closer, so he could feel the movement. "That's it. You're feeling the sway," she encouraged.

"Hold on a second." She found a CD and started some music on her laptop she had little other use for.

For a brief moment, Tipper put his hands on Felicia's shoulders and moved fluidly with the rhythm. Just as quickly, he jumped away, stating, "I have to go."

"Tipper, what's wrong?"

"You're Mac's wife. I *cannot* dance like this with you."

"Tipper, you didn't do anything wrong."

"Yes, I did."

Felicia realized the physical closeness had affected Tipper. She whispered, "Oh. It's all right. You didn't do anything wrong. I'm sorry. I should've realized."

"I have to go, Felicia. This is very wrong. You're my best friend's wife. I can't risk something like this happening again. I'm sorry."

"Don't apologize. You didn't do anything wrong." She reached out to touch his arm. He jumped farther from her. "Nothing happened, Tipper. You didn't even kiss me."

"But I wanted to," he admitted barely above a whisper. "Therein, lies the wrong. I won't be alone with you again."

Tipper went out the door as Mac drove up.

"Hello!" Mac called.

"I have to go home now," Tipper said.

"Tipper, what's wrong?" asked Mac.

"Nothing," said Felicia quickly. "Nothing at all. Tipper, I'll draw the plans in detail and leave them at the post office for you. Let me know if you want to make changes. I'll see you Sunday."

Tipper nodded. "Thank you, Felicia. Good night. Good night, Mac." He hardly looked at his friend as he left. *That new step is not for me.* He was so upset by his arousal he cried all the way home.

15

Hospital Privileges

Wednesday morning, Dr. MacKenzie Reardon and his wife entered Possum Holler Health Facility, as the sign above the door read. The building was ready in short time since so many Possum Hollerites worked feverishly, reminiscent of an old-time barn-raising. It smelled of fresh paint, and voices echoed in its emptiness.

Mac put his arm around Felicia. "It's great. Thank you. I guess I can put the medications I got in the pharmaceutical pantry. I don't have anything else yet. However, I do have hospital privileges with the county hospital. That way, if any of my people have to go, I can take care of them."

"You'll do great work, Mac. Your presence has already caused change. The house is almost ready, the school foundation has been poured, and, now, Tipper will have a real business."

"What was wrong with him last night?"

"He was embarrassed. Since he'll have to go to the city, maybe even to Ron's clubs, I was teaching him to salsa. Mac, he's so innocent. Don't you dare think anything bad about him." Her face took on a look of chastisement before her husband could react. "His body responded to the salsa movements. He got an erection. He thinks he did something wrong to you."

"Oh. He would. He would think he needed to have control of himself. I'll talk to him."

"Mac, nothing inappropriate happened."

"I believe you. Tipper would never do that to me. He was almost my brother. Miss Ina, his ma, was to marry my pa. Pa died the night before their wedding."

"And there's never been anyone else for her?"

"No. She went into a serious depression after that. She said she would never fall in love again because it hurt too much to lose the man."

"Were they lovers, Mac?"

He was quiet. "Mac?" prompted Felicia.

"Yes. Please, don't mention that. People around here at the time would have crucified her for sleeping with my father without being married."

"I'm sorry." She patted her husband's deeply muscled chest. "You love her."

"I do."

"Tipper slept with Amy before they got married. Have things changed since Miss Ina's time?"

"Not much. Tipper married Amy. Amy's mother was the biggest gossip and would've caused Miss Ina to be disgraced, especially if there had been a child, like Tipper and Amy."

"Was there?"

"Why do you ask?"

She bit her lip. "Sherry Jones."

"I thought so, too, when I saw her, but Gator says she's too old. If she were younger, I'd say yes because Miss Ina disappeared and went to the city to get a barber's license. I find it ironic Lucille is the one who had to bear some shame. She hated Tipper."

"Like Grandma Newton hates me?"

"Grandma doesn't hate you. She's just opinionated."

"If you say so."

As Mac and Felicia talked, three large delivery trucks lumbered on the dirt road into Possum Holler. "What the devil?" asked Mac to no one in particular as they walked outside the clinic to swirling dust because the summer had been unusually dry.

The man in the lead truck got out with a clipboard. Royce Dent, who was hoping to be mayor, Leo Tomlin, and Mac Reardon approached the man from three different directions. The man announced, "I'm looking for Dr. MacKenzie Reardon."

"I'm Dr. Reardon," said Mac.

"Dr. Reardon, we have a delivery for you. Will you, please, sign here?" The man indicated the blank for Mac to sign and continued, "There's a letter, too."

Mac took the form, which proved to be a bill of lading and an envelope. First, he opened the envelope. It contained a short note that read:

Good luck, Dr. Reardon!

If you need anything else, let me know. I'll call in some more favors.

Fondest regards,
Dr. Joseph Morgenstern

Mac reviewed the list. "Oh, my God!" he exclaimed.

The truck driver said, "We also have instructions to stay until we've helped you install the equipment."

"I can't believe this," stammered Mac. "Felicia, it's almost everything I need. When we get this installed, we can open."

"Honey, that's fantastic!" She hooked her arm through his.

"Let's get busy!" the doctor said excitedly.

As repayment of a sort, Mac flew back to Chicago a month later to speak at the request of Dr. Morgenstern.

Every available hand began unloading the trucks. Even the children carried small items. Mac supervised the installation and set-up of the medical equipment. He caressed each piece with love. By the weekend, everything was in place. The only thing Mac still needed was chairs for the waiting room.

"This is amazing," Mac said late Saturday as tears welled in his eyes.

"Well, I think you need your first patient, Dr. Reardon," laughed Felicia. "Get this damned splinter out of my finger. I'll figure out a way to pay you later."

Mac took Felicia's hand. "My, my, you're injured. Come this way."

Mac pulled the splinter out with sterilized tweezers and covered the small prick with a bandage that contained antibacterial ointment in the pad. Then, he kissed Felicia's finger.

The crowd, which had been helping unload and install equipment, applauded. In the back of the room, Tipper who had joined the frenzy on Saturday clapped, too, and started to back out the door, colliding with a thin, dark-haired and dark-eyed woman standing behind him.

"Pardon me," he said.

"No harm done." The woman smiled with perfect white teeth and dimples. "Hello, I'm Jessica Langston, Preacher Tomlin's daughter and Dr. Reardon's nurse. I just drove up and followed the crowd."

"Welcome." The tall man smiled back. "I'm Tipper Campbell, Dr. Reardon's friend. I was only able to help today because I work at the mine, but not for long. I'm building my own distillery."

"Congratulations!" laughed Jessica.

A sudden clanging drew the crowd to a laden table in front of the church where Lauren Tomlin and Sunny Bankston stood ready to serve food. Lauren announced, "We have ham sandwiches, roasted potatoes, and lemonade. Dig in."

Lauren looked up and saw her daughter. "Jessica!" she squealed and raced to hug her.

Tipper who still stood near Jessica began to drift away. Lauren slapped his hand. "Stay, silly boy."

She hugged Jessica. "Have you met Tipper?"

"Yes, ma'am," said Tipper, uncertainly. With some measure of hopefulness, he turned to Jessica. "Can I make you a plate, Miss Langston?"

"That would be sweet. I'll meet you on Momma's porch."

As Tipper went to the table, Lauren wiggled her eyebrows mischievously at Jessica. "He's cute, isn't he?"

"Momma! I just got here, but, yeah. Is he taken?"

"Nope. Divorced. Three little girls. They live with him."

"Wow. Don't push, Momma. That would be a lot to take on. Besides, I'm here to help Mac with the clinic. Where did all the equipment come from?"

"Dr. Morgenstern, Chief of Staff at Cook Memorial. Mac's sort of special to him."

"It's good to have friends in high places."

"Hey, Tipper's on the porch with two plates. Go!" Lauren popped Jessica affectionately on the behind.

Everybody ate and visited for a while. The children discovered balloons, and the faucet in the Tomlin home provided endless ammunition for water-balloon fights. Squeals of laughter epitomized the general feeling in town.

Finished with their work and another meal, the truckers indicated they were ready to leave. "I don't think so," chided Lauren. "You fellows will not leave until after church tomorrow. One more night here will be good for you." The men did not argue for they enjoyed the hospitality.

Lauren went to her front porch where Jessica and Tipper still chatted. "Tipper, do you have any moonshine here?"

"Yes, ma'am. There's some in the truck."

"Get it, all of it. We need to christen the clinic and have a toast. Where's Mac?"

Tipper blushed. "I think he and Felicia went into the clinic. I think he's, um, extracting payment."

Lauren laughed. "And you're blushing. They *are* married, Tipper."

"Yes, I know," said Tipper soberly. A shadow passed over his face. "I'll get the whiskey. I'll let you get Mac. Excuse me, Miss Langston."

Jessica held up her finger. "Uh-uh! Jessica, remember."

"Excuse me, Jessica."

Jessica winked at her mother as Tipper walked off. "Nice work," muttered Lauren.

Lauren knocked at the clinic door. Mac and Felicia had definitely been making payment arrangements. She cracked the door and called, "Dr. and Mrs. Reardon, we need you outside. Make it a quickie!"

Felicia giggled and Mac's body heaved with silent laughter. "Shall we go?" he whispered.

"Are we done?"

"For now. I might need a second payment later. Let's go."

Mac and Felicia went outside where everyone waited. Felicia turned deep crimson. She knew everybody present realized exactly what she and Mac had been doing. Lauren handed Mac a bottle of Tipper's apple moonshine. She shrugged. "No champagne available, and an apple a day keeps the doctor away."

Mac flicked his thumb toward the door. "Hospital privileges," he joked to cover Felicia's embarrassment. The crowd applauded and whooped with laughter.

Mac held up the bottle. "I hereby dedicate this facility to the people of Possum Holler and christen it Possum Holler Health Facility." Mac broke the bottle on a post. Everybody seemed to have a glass ready.

"Prost!" shouted Tipper in honor of his friend. Lauren handed Mac and Felicia a tin cup, and the crowd downed their beverage in unison. Then they began to disperse toward home.

Tipper came to Mac. "Mac," he said with downcast eyes, "I…"

"Not a problem, Tipper. Let it go." Mac cut him off. "Felicia told me everything. You didn't do anything wrong. Neither did she. She was trying to help you by teaching you city things. I'll tell you a secret." He put his hand on his friend's shoulder and leaned closer. "The same thing happened to me the first time I danced salsa with her. I had just met her. Don't worry about it. Just meet somebody else."

"I think I have."

Mac raised an eyebrow in question.

Tipper smiled. "Your nurse. She just arrived." Tipper grinned the naughty grin Mac had often seen when he was younger. "Does she have hospital privileges, too?"

16
A Place of Their Own

The clinic began to see patients on a daily basis, and Jessica proved to be an excellent nurse. Many of the people's complaints and ailments she could handle without Mac.

Jessica's arrival did fill the Tomlin residence to overflowing. In addition to family, it also seemed Tipper found a reason to drop by frequently. He appeared to have recovered from his incident with Felicia and talked to her about the plans for Tipper's Bottling as he had decided to call his distillery. The entrepreneur's eleven-year-old daughter even designed an ad and label. It read in twisting letters:

Tipper's
Authentic Mountain Moonshine
With a Twist

The next item was whichever fruit was in the bottle or a little brown jug for unflavored whiskey.

Distilled and Bottled by Hand
Tipper's Bottling

An opossum with its mouth open as if screaming came next. It looked as if the animal was saying:

"*Possum Holler, West Virginia.*"

With all the activity, Jessica ran the clinic, and Mac worked extra hours renovating the old Bustin place while most of the townsfolk worked toward having the school ready to open after Labor Day.

While this building was going on, Felicia sent the ad/bottle labels to Ron. The New York businessman did not send a reply.

A week later, Ron Norton pulled into Possum Holler in a delivery truck.

"Oh, my God! Ron!" Felicia greeted her friend with a hug and a kiss. The townsfolk peering from windows and standing on porches looked appalled at the greeting.

Ron held Felicia at arms' length. "You look fine, but I still don't think you belong here. However, if you hadn't come, I wouldn't have my new business venture. Where's Tipper? I've brought him something, and I'm dying to meet him."

"He's working at the mine right now, but he'll come by on his way home. He always does these days. He's, um, 'smitten' with Jessica, the preacher's daughter and Mac's nurse."

"Jealous?"

"Don't be absurd. I like Tipper. He *is* gorgeous and a very nice person, but he's more of a hillbilly than Mac."

"Speaking of, when do I get to meet your husband?"

"Seeing as how you rudely left our wedding reception without meeting him, now's as good a time as any. He's working on our house. Follow me."

"You don't want me to meet Mac, do you?" The businessman followed Mac's wife down the road.

"It's awkward."

"Afraid, he'll know?"

"A little." Ron fell into step with her.

"That's why I came to your frigging wedding. I wanted to make sure he knew."

"I know. Drop it please. The people around here see and hear *everything*. Their tongues are already wagging about the way I greeted you."

"Good," said Ron snidely.

"Stop!" said Felicia as she opened the door to her house.

"Nice house," commented Ron honestly.

"Yes, it is. Too nice for me."

"Don't be silly. I apologize for putting you in an awkward situation."

Felicia shrugged and called, "Mac?"

"I'm in the kitchen," came the reply.

Felicia led the way to the kitchen where Mac and another man laid the last of the tile. The house would be ready to move into in a day or so.

"Mac," said Felicia. "Mr. Matlock, how are you today?"

"Jest fine, Mrs. Reardon, and you?"

"Excellent. Mac, this is my friend, Ron Norton. He just drove in with a truckload of something to meet Tipper."

"Nice to meet you," said Mac, wiping his hands the best he could on his old jeans. When he looked at Ron, he felt nauseous. Ron was about his size with light brown hair and blue eyes. He looked more like Chambry than either Mac or Felicia.

Ron shook Mac's hand firmly. "Dr. Reardon, it's a pleasure to meet the man that stole Felicia."

Mac knew there was more to the comment than flattering his wife, but he tried to recover from the awful feeling in the pit of his stomach. *This is the man who showed up at the wedding and danced one dance with Felicia before leaving abruptly.* Mac sputtered, "Please call me Mac."

"Of course, and I'm Ron. Your house is wonderful. Did you do it all yourself?"

"It was built a long time ago. With the help of my friends, we've got it livable again. I think we'll have a housewarming after church Sunday. I've done the last bit by myself with Panther's help. Everybody else, who can, has been working to get the school ready to open. Ron, this is Panther Matlock."

Ron shook the man's hand. "Good to meet you."

"Well," said Mac. "Is it lunchtime? We could use a break."

"Almost," Felicia said. "Come to the house. Lauren's whipping something up."

Panther said, "I'll finish these here last few tiles 'fore I come up."

"All right. Thanks," said Mac

As Mac, Felicia, and Ron walked toward the Tomlin home down the dirt road, Mac asked, "What did you bring Tipper?"

"I think I'll surprise him, if you don't mind," replied Ron.

"Of course not."

"Where's he building the distillery?"

Mac indicated with his hand, "About a mile that way, just around that bend."

"Where does he live?"

"Out in the sticks," informed Felicia.

"He should be closer. Are there any more houses to fix up?"

"Not right now," replied Mac. "The teachers took most of them."

"Well, is the land ready to build?"

"Yes. We'll pour the foundation as soon as the school is ready."

Ron nodded. "How long do you think it'll take?"

"It depends on how soon winter comes." The doctor gave a little shrug.

"So, I guess Tipper's first batch for market will come from the still in his backyard." The businessman looked from his friend to her husband. "Is that a good assumption?"

"Yes. Why?" Mac responded.

"Well, my patrons are clamoring for the stuff." Ron smiled.

"Tipper will do as much as he can," Mac assured. "Hopefully, winter will come late. We hope to have him up and running by Christmas."

Excitement danced in the newcomer's eyes. "If I can have my first batch New Year's Eve, it would give the celebration some punch."

"Tipper's moonshine does pack some punch," agreed Mac.

Upon entering the house, Ron met the Tomlins as Chambry and Rush charged in. Ron appeared shocked at Chambry's appearance, too, but he did not have time to dwell on it as Jessica Langston and Panther Matlock came in. Lauren announced lunch was ready, and Ron joined the locals for a meal of pork loin, mashed potatoes, sautéed squash, and fresh baked bread. The guest complimented the meal and said if he stayed long in Possum Holler he'd get fat.

Ron visited the distillery building site with Leo and looked over the blueprints Felicia had drawn. "This will be a good facility," he commented to the preacher. "Dr. Tomlin, you don't disapprove of the liquor plant?"

"No. This is the way of life here. I focus on the soul."

"That's nice. You don't judge people, not even Felicia."

"What's there to judge? She's Mac's wife. I accept her."

"But you think she's a fish out of water." He looked at the ground.

The preacher hooked his thumbs on the back pockets of the jeans he wore. "She's trying hard to fit in."

"What if she fails?" Ron looked up.

Leo surveyed the man before he answered. "I think you'll be waiting to help her pick up the pieces."

"I didn't come here for that. She sent me a legitimate business opportunity. It will help your town."

"I believe you, but you have feelings for her. Am I right?"

"For a long time, but she's here. She wants to make it work."

"It was obvious she was miserable in Chicago. Is she trying for Chambry?"

"Yes, but she does love Mac in her own way."

"Does she love you?"

"I wish I could tell you she does. In her own way, I guess she might."

Plunging his hands all the way into his pockets, the preacher asked, "Why are you telling me these things?"

"Confession is good for the soul. You're a man of God." Ron looked to him like a little boy who needed a father.

"So, is this in confidence?"

"Please keep it so. I just need to talk to somebody." Ron rolled the blueprint up and looked Leo in the eye. "I'll only be here long enough to meet Tipper and get a few things in place, maybe two nights. I didn't come here to disturb Mac and Felicia's life."

"One more question."

"Of course." Ron put the architectural cylinder under his arm.

"Is Chambry your son?"

"Why?"

"He resembles you."

"No."

"Could he be? I'm not going to tell Mac." The pastor placed a hand on the shoulder of the disturbed businessman.

Ron sighed. "Chambry is Mac's son even if he were to have my genes. Do you understand?"

"I do."

Leo and Ron returned to the house just as Tipper drove up. The moonshiner looked curiously at the large truck. "Tipper!" Leo called. "Come here!" He waved his hand in beckoning.

The tall blond man ran up. "Preacher Tomlin, what's that?" He pointed over his shoulder.

"Ask this man. Tipper, this is Ron Norton. Ron, Tipper Campbell."

"It's a pleasure," said Ron genuinely, grasping Tipper's hand. "Come see what I have for you."

When everyone realized Tipper had arrived, they poured out to see what the truck held. Ron opened it. Inside were numerous packing crates. He took a crowbar from a hook inside the truck and pried off a lid. He pulled out a short, squatty, smoked-brown, glass jug with a handle. It would hold a fifth of liquor. The one he displayed had Betsy's label with an apple emblazoned on it.

Tipper's
Authentic Mountain Moonshine
With a Twist

Distilled and Bottled by Hand
Tipper's Bottling
Possum Holler, West Virginia

Ron explained, "For your beverages. There are fifty of each kind." He looked at the bottle. "Who's your ad man? Your logo is amazing."

Tipper took the jug. "Thank you." He examined the jug. "My daughter, Betsy, drew the labels."

"How old is she?"

"Eleven."

"She definitely needs to go into advertising. She's gifted."

"These are great, Ron. Did you say there are three hundred?"

"I did. If possible, I'd like them filled and shipped to my four clubs by New Year's Eve."

"That'll take a lot of work on a backyard still."

"Get what you can. Also," Ron handed Tipper a sheet of paper. "Here's a requisition for building supplies. They should start arriving next week. Get your distillery up and running. Next year, you become a rich man." The city man clapped the country boy's shoulder. "I also have some contracts to go over with you."

Ron rode to the Campbell place where he met Tipper's family, and he encouraged Betsy to go into advertising. He borrowed Tipper's bed that night and the next. Tipper sent Laurie to sleep with her grandmother and used her bed. The next day, Ron unloaded the jugs into a rickety storage shed with the help of Ina Campbell and the Campbell girls. The native New Yorker enjoyed the company of the Campbell family.

The few people of Possum Holler he had met garnered deep respect from him. He really liked these people and felt exceedingly guilty for liking the wife of one more than he should. However, he could not help his feelings. Consequently, Ron left Possum Holler with ambivalent emotions, but he knew this business venture would be a good thing for a lot of people.

After Ron left, Felicia grew distant again; nevertheless, she and Mac moved into the renovated house. It felt both good and strange to have a place of their own.

The after-church fellowship migrated to the Reardon home as a housewarming of a kind. It turned into a pounding. The couple was honored with home-canned goods, smoked meats, and other food stores, along with quilts, needle point, and down pillows.

Felicia walked into the house with an armload of gifts. When she came out, Grandma Newton stood there with her arms folded and a deep scowl on her face.

"Grandma, is something wrong?" Felicia asked.

"Did MacKenzie Reardon carry you across that threshold?"

"What?"

"Did yo husband carry his bride across the threshold into yo new house?"

"No. Why?"

"Good Lord Almighty!" Grandma Newton screamed. "MacKenzie Charles Reardon!"

"What's the matter, Grandma?" Mac asked anxiously when he ran up to the old woman as the other people looked on.

"Are you atemptin' fate? You didn't carry yo bride across the threshold! You're bringin' bad luck down on yo own head, boy! Are you tryin' to condemn yo marriage?"

"Grandma, we've been married six years. This is not our first home."

"An apartment ain't a home! It's temporary!" shrieked the old woman. "This be yo first house!"

Felicia grabbed Mac's arm. "Mac, just carry me over the threshold."

"It be too late," said the old woman near tears. "He was supposed to do it when you first moved into a place of yo own."

Mac assured, "It's all right, Grandma." Mac scooped Felicia up and carried her through the doorway. He put her down inside the house and kissed her. "It'll be all right. I know it will," he said.

Grandma Newton sighed, "You both had good intentions. I hope you ain't jinxed yoself, Mac. This girl's been tryin' real hard. Sometimes, love jest ain't enough." Grandma Newton went home.

Felicia looked up at Mac. "Does that mean she finally accepts me and is now afraid of losing me?"

"She's just superstitious, baby. I carried you across the threshold on our honeymoon."

"That definitely wasn't permanent. It was only rented for two weeks." Felicia fled to their bedroom and cried.

After the Reardons' housewarming, the builders focused on finishing the school. The two outside contractors Leo brought in were a plumber and an electrician. The mountain folk did not have the expertise for those two essentials.

A week after Ron's visit, two more trucks and a cement truck rattled into Possum Holler. Half a dozen men took a day off from the school to help Tipper pour the foundation for his distillery while the plumber and electrician were there and could lay their groundwork. While the foundation set, Tipper took his turn putting shingles on the roof of the school. Even the women and children painted the inside, finishing in record time.

The last week of August, desks, tables, chairs, and books were moved into the brand-new school building from their temporary home in the Sunday school rooms. Labor Day served as a day to dedicate the new school, and the community threw a barbeque to celebrate. Sunny joyfully broke a bottle of Tipper's apple flavored moonshine to christen the facility saying it was an apple for the teachers. The next day, school began, and teachers and students alike started a journey of learning in a place of their own.

17
A Perfect Match

Tipper got up every weekday morning at four, so he could get to the mine by six. He worked in the mining office from six until two without a lunch break. He picked up Betsy and Callie at school at three o'clock. While he drove from the mine to the school, he ate a bite of lunch. After he got the girls home and started on their homework, he worked to get the whiskey for Ron bottled until dark.

After Tipper shut down the still for the day, he bathed, tucked his girls into bed, and came back into town. Every evening, he had supper with Jessica. Some evenings they ate with the Tomlins. Sometimes Jessica packed a picnic, and they ate at Tipper's building site by candlelight. Tipper and Jessica spent only an hour to an hour and a half together every evening before he went home to sleep a few hours.

He worked sunup until sundown on Saturdays to finish the whiskey shipment while the townspeople built his distillery under Felicia's watchful eye. Sundays were the Lord's. Tipper refused to distill whiskey on Sunday.

It quickly became common knowledge in Possum Holler Tipper Campbell was courting Jessica Langston. The townsfolk agreed it was a perfect match.

Jessica seemed to concur with general opinion. She spent her days with Dr. Reardon at the clinic attending to minor illnesses and injuries. So far, the clinic had not had a major crisis. The nastiest injury they had seen was a compound fracture when one of the builders fell from a beam while working on the distillery. The worst illness had been a case of appendicitis. They had performed an appendectomy and had an overnight patient for two nights.

One afternoon, Mac found Jessica doodling, "*Jessica Campbell...Jessica Langston Campbell...Mrs. Tipper Campbell.*" Mac guffawed and teased her mercilessly as he leaned over the reception desk where she usually sat when they were not busy.

"Stop it!" she snapped. "Do you disapprove? I admit it—I'm head over heels in love. I just wish Tipper would say, 'I love you, Jess.' Mac, he doesn't even kiss me. He just holds my hand. Do you think he actually cares about me?"

"Would you like me to ask him?"

"No. That's childish."

"And doodling 'Jessica-n-Tipper' isn't?"

The nurse glowered at the doctor.

Mac laughed. "I think he's totally besotted, but Tipper's afraid of being hurt again. He also wants to be financially able to support you. You're not a poor mountain girl. He wants the distillery to be up and running, and he wants to build a house here in town."

"Did he tell you these things?"

"No, but I've known Tipper my whole life."

"I just want him to tell me he loves me. I can wait for the rest. Except a kiss. If that man doesn't kiss me on our next date, I'm going to kiss him."

"Do it. That will *definitely* get his attention. That will be tonight, right?"

"Yes. Why?"

"I want to have a camera ready."

Mac could hear the grinding of his quasi-sister's teeth. He laughed so hard tears streamed down his cheeks. Sobering, he said, "Have supper with Felicia and me. I'll plant the seed in his brain."

"Would you really, big brother?"

He laughed again. "Yes, I would, little sister. I agree you two are a great couple."

"Really? I'm surprised you didn't fix him up with Sunny."

"Felicia suggested that. Sunny was against it."

"I can't believe it. Does she have a special man?"

"No."

"I'm glad she didn't want Tipper. So, we'll join you for supper tonight. What's for supper?"

"I'm having my favorite meal—spaghetti. You know, this is the first time I've had spaghetti since coming home."

"What else?"

"I guess it's sort of city cooking. We're having Caesar salad, garlic bread, cheesecake, and a nice Merlot I picked up in the city."

"It'll be about seven before we can get there. That's earlier than normal because it's getting dark sooner. I'm actually looking forward to ending daylight-saving time this year, when I usually dread it. Tipper will have to shut down earlier."

Mac looked at his watch. "It's five. Let's go home. You get all prettied up."

"Am I ugly?"

"No. You know what I mean. Hey, does Mamaw have any of those big mushrooms?"

"Yeah, why?"

He opened the door for her. "Can you do some of that ham and cream cheese stuffing and bring them for appetizers?"

"Yeah, sure. Is that all?"

"That's it. We'll be waiting. Hey, it's Friday. Maybe Tipper can stay longer than an hour."

"Help me with that."

"Yes, ma'am."

Tipper knocked on the Tomlins' door about a quarter to seven. Jessica answered wearing a tight-fitting, low-cut forest green sweater, a clinging black cotton skirt, and black pumps. Tipper's eyes almost jumped from their sockets.

"Hi," said Jessica. "Mac and Felicia have invited us to eat with them. I just need to get the appetizers to take down there. Come in a minute."

Tipper stepped inside while Jessica got the stuffed mushrooms. He stared at her as if in a trance.

"Is something wrong?" she asked.

"No. You're..."

"Yes?"

"Did you wear that for me?"

"Do you like it?" She twirled around.

"Very much. You're beautiful."

"Thank you. Yes, I wore it for you. Who else would I wear it for? Shall we go?"

Jessica put her arm around Tipper's as they walked to the Reardon home. The man rolled his eyes heavenward and peered at the brilliant twinkling stars before he whispered, "Jessica, do you know what clothes like that do to a man?"

"Make him appreciate his woman?"

"I appreciate you."

"Does that mean I'm your woman?"

"Do you want to be mine?"

She stopped walking just before they reached their destination. In the deafening silence of voices, tree frogs and crickets sang a symphony. Taking a deep breath, she said, "Tipper Campbell, I know you're a little old-fashioned. And I know I grew up in the city, but that does not make me a Jezebel. Are you going to make me take matters into my hands?"

"What do you mean?"

"Tipper!" Jessica stomped her foot. "What *does* this outfit do to you? Anything?"

"Yes. It makes me..."

"What?"

"Jessica, I've only ever been with one woman." He fidgeted. "I'm not sure how to act. Do you really want to know what that outfit does to me?"

"Yes."

"Really?" he asked, his voice higher than normal.

"Yes!"

Tipper tapped his foot nervously and ran his fingers through his longish blond hair before he finally grabbed Jessica's free hand and put it against his crotch. "That's what it does," he said through clenched teeth.

"Oh, Tipper!" Jessica jerked her hand away and reached for his face. "That's not what I intended, not yet. I just wanted you to kiss me. Yes, I want to be your woman. We've been going out two months. I wanted to know you felt the same things I feel. Tipper, I love you. Please, just tell me how you feel."

He breathed a sigh of relief. Then, he took Jessica's face in his hands and kissed her soundly. "I love you, Jessica, and I'm scared to death."

"Don't be afraid. I won't leave you. I'm exactly where I want to be."

He kissed her again. Suddenly, they heard Mac's voice. "Hey! Supper's getting cold. Save that for Papa's front-porch swing."

Tipper put his forehead against Jessica's. "That porch swing sounds really good."

"Yeah, it does. Let's have supper and get back."

Rather than taking Jessica's hand, Tipper put his arm around her, and they went into Mac's house where they had a pleasant meal.

Felicia did seem a little distant, but she played a good hostess. After dinner, Felicia suggested a game of Spades once Chambry was in bed. "I don't know how to play," Tipper said.

"It's easy," assured Felicia. "I taught Mac. Do you play, Jess?"

"It's been a while, but, yes."

"Tipper, it's up to you. You might rather hit that porch swing," Mac teased.

Tipper looked at Jessica and winked. "I *will* hit that porch swing come Hell or high water, but not until I've learned to play Spades and beaten you soundly."

After a couple of practice hands, Tipper said, "I think I've got it."

A real game got under way, and Tipper and Jessica won. Felicia joked, "You two are well-suited for this game. Are you cheating or communicating telepathically?"

"Neither," said Tipper, playing footsie with Jessica under the table. "We're just right for each other."

"Oh, Lord!" laughed Mac. "I think I hear that front-porch swing calling."

"Indeed," agreed Tipper. "But first, I'd like to talk to you a minute."

"What's up?"

"Privately."

Mac looked at Felicia and shrugged. "Would anybody like another slice of dessert? Tipper and I are serving."

Both ladies agreed they would. "Bring a nice glass of milk to go with it," ordered Felicia.

"Yes, ma'am," Mac said as he kissed her cheek. The men disappeared into the kitchen.

"Okay, what's up?" asked Mac, pulling out the cheesecake.

"Tell me what to do."

"About what?"

"Jess."

"What do you want to do?"

"Marry her. I'm crazy about her, but I need to have something to offer her."

"Buddy, all she wants is you. How about this?" The surgeon's hands sliced into the dessert. "Ask her to marry you and get engaged. When everything's going smoothly with the business and you've got your house here, tie the knot. I'll be your best man. But for God's sake, carry her over the threshold before you ever step foot into your house as husband and wife. You don't wanna give Grandma Newton a stroke. Just for the record, I think you two jive."

The tall man leaned on the counter with both hands. "How do I get her a ring? She'll expect a ring. City girls want more than a plain gold band."

"Hm. Not sure about that assumption, but are you up for a drive into the city tomorrow?"

"I've got a lot of distilling to do."

"Girl or whiskey? Your choice." Mac licked his finger where the cheesecake had touched it and put the remainder of the sweet back in the refrigerator.

"Girl," Tipper replied without hesitation. "Okay. Seven?"

"Eight. Sleep in. We'll even have breakfast in the city, my treat."

After a second dessert, Tipper took Jessica home and spent time in the front-porch swing.

The next day, Tipper and Mac went into Wilmington where they had breakfast before they went to a jewelry store.

Tipper said to Mac, "These things are expensive."

"Which one do you like? I have the money. You can pay me back."

"Mac, that's too much."

"Nonsense. Pick one."

Tipper picked up a quarter-carat square setting in white gold. "I like this one. It has matching wedding rings. But what if she says, 'No'?"

"She won't."

The clerk said, "If she does, you can bring it back."

"She won't," Mac reiterated. "We'll take the set." The set consisted of the engagement ring with matching wedding bands with three diamonds each. Not extravagant, but it was elegant.

On the way out of the city, Mac stopped at a Kentucky Fried Chicken and got chicken, biscuits, mashed potatoes, corn on the cob, and fried okra.

"What are you doing?" asked Tipper.

"Helping."

Then, he stopped at a Family Dollar Store where he found a picnic basket set. Finally, he got a bottle of white wine. He packed the picnic basket and grinned. "You are gonna surprise your lady with a picnic. Don't go to the building site."

Saturday morning, Jessica noticed Tipper's truck in front of Mac's house. Felicia told her the men had gone into the city.

Around three while Lauren prepared the evening meal, Tipper knocked at the door. "What a surprise!" Jessica said happily.

"How about a picnic?" He held up the basket.

"How sweet. Are we going courting in broad daylight?"

"Yes, and not at the building site. I thought we'd go down by the creek."

"I'd love to." Jessica hollered back over her shoulder, "Momma, I won't be here for supper. Tipper and I are going on a picnic."

Tipper spread the picnic after they hiked a little way to a clearing by the creek. Jessica laughed. "You could've cooked. You didn't have to go into the city just to get a picnic. Your company would've been enough."

"I did get something besides the picnic."

"What?"

"Eat first."

"Whatever."

They ate and drank wine. "Where's the dessert?" teased Jessica.

"Right here." He kissed her passionately.

"Mm. Nice dessert," breathed Jessica.

"There's more."

"What?"

He reached into the basket and pulled out a black box. "A lifetime with me if you say, 'Yes.' I love you, Jess. I'm ready to take a chance with you. Will you marry me?" He opened the box.

"Oh, my!" Jessica exclaimed.

"Is that all you can say?"

"No."

"No?" The man's face fell, and his heart raced.

"I mean that's not all I can say. Yes, Tipper. Yes, I'll marry you. I love you. When?"

"Once the business takes off and I get a house in town."

"You'd better work fast."

"I'll try. Can it wait for a little while? I'd like to spend time with you right now." He slipped the engagement ring on her hand. "I love you." He kissed his fiancée.

When Tipper brought Jessica home, he came into the parlor where Leo worked on his sermon. The preacher took off his glasses and asked, "Did you two have a pleasant afternoon?"

"Yes, sir," replied Tipper. "May I talk to you a minute?"

"Of course. Is something wrong?"

"No, sir. Everything is right. Preacher Tomlin, I'm in love with Jessica. I've asked her to marry me, and she said, 'Yes.' I'd like your permission and blessing."

Leo clapped his hands. "You have both. I knew this would be an ideal match. I'm proud to have you as part of my family, Tipper."

18

Panic

Once the autumnal equinox passed, it turned cold quickly, and darkness fell fast in Possum Holler once daylight-saving time ended. Tipper began to panic because he only had about half the bottles Ron wanted. He was so anxious he began to work by lantern light and cut his trips to see Jessica.

Jessica, in turn, became frantic because she feared for Tipper's safety. In an act unheard of in Possum Holler, she made a trip to the Campbell home alone after dark.

Tipper stopped work at the sight of Jessica's car. "What are you doing here?" he demanded as she got out. His three girls and his mother stared at Jessica in disbelief.

Undaunted, she declared, "I'm making sure you're safe. I don't like the idea of your running this still in the dark."

"Why didn't you at least bring Mac with you?"

"For what? He's as stubborn and pigheaded as you are. And look at this!" She swept her hand around. "Your girls are lugging jugs to the shed. No! You're better than this, Tipper Campbell. If Ron Norton doesn't get all the jugs he wanted by New Year's Eve, big deal! He can get some more by Valentine's Day when the distillery will be operational."

Jessica stomped to the still. "I don't want a rich dead man. I want a live Tipper Campbell! I couldn't care less if we sleep on a straw mat in a cave, as long as it's with you."

"What spunk!" exclaimed Ina Campbell. She turned to her granddaughters. "Girls, put those jugs with the others. Tipper, shut this thing off. The girls will not be helpin' you anymore. Bring this woman in the house. I like her."

"The fire's dead anyway," Tipper mumbled. "I guess we're done for today."

Jessica came up to Tipper and pulled his face to hers. She kissed him passionately.

"I smell awful, Jess," he apologized.

"I don't care. Have y'all had supper?"

"No. We'll scramble up some eggs."

"No. I brought some hotdogs for the girls and you, too. And marshmallows. Build us a little bonfire."

Tipper took a break, and his family roasted wieners and marshmallows with their future stepmother and daughter-in-law. After they ate, Tipper got out his banjo and the girls danced with Jessica.

Ina Campbell watched her son's face. There was happiness in his eyes. It had been a long time since she had seen that. Yet, she also saw the stubbornness Jessica knew was there. *This woman Tipper's found is strong. She'll keep him focused on his priorities as soon as he gets over this first hurdle.* Ina knew he felt he had to prove himself. She knew, too, Jessica would straighten him out. There was real love in her eyes and her words. The laughter Ina heard from her granddaughters thrilled her. For the first time in twenty-two years, Ina felt genuinely happy.

After a while, Laurie reached up for Jessica who picked up the child. "What's the matter?" Jessica asked.

"Are you gonna be our momma?"

"Yes, I am. Is that all right with you?"

"Are you gonna leave?"

"No." Jessica choked back tears. "No, baby, I'm not leaving. I love your papa. I love you. As soon as your papa and I are married, I'll be your momma forever."

"I'm glad. I love you." Laurie yawned.

"Ah. Someone's sleepy. May I help you girls get ready for bed?"

"Papa, can she?" asked Callie.

"Please?" encouraged Betsy.

"Yes, of course," Tipper permitted.

The girls and Ina heated several buckets of water and filled the large washtub in the kitchen. The girls piled in together. The lack of privacy disturbed Jessica. She asked, "Miss Ina, how do you and Tipper bathe?"

"I bathe after the girls. Tipper makes his own bath after ever'one has gone to sleep. Jessica, I'd like runnin' water and a real bathroom."

"I'm sure you would. May I come back out to visit as inappropriate as it may seem?"

"Please do. Ain't nobody gonna say nothin'. Lucille Dent is dead."

Jessica caught Ina's bitterness in the comment but did not ask questions. She tucked the girls into bed. Callie and Betsy had a bunk bed, and Laurie had a small cot. On a table between the beds Jessica saw a little book called *Love You Forever.*

Betsy said, "Papa reads it to us every night."

Jessica started reading the little story. By the time she got to the last page, she sobbed out every word.

Tipper came to the door and heard Jessica trying to finish the story. He took the book from her and closed it. He finished the story from memory:

> *"'And while he rocked he sang,*
> *"I'll love you forever.*
> *I'll like you for always.*
> *As long as I'm living,*
> *my baby you'll be.'"*

The devoted father laid the book back on the table. "All right, girls, prayers." Each little girl said a prayer, not rote, but from the heart. Each one prayed for their papa and that his business would be successful. Then, Laurie thanked God for her new momma, and Jessica sobbed harder. Tipper prayed for his girls and kissed each of them good night.

Afterward, he picked Jessica up and carried her outside where he promised not to work the still at night. They talked a long time before she told him she was going shopping for the girls and would be back the next night before they went to Harvest Fest. They set a wedding date for Valentine's Day, and Jessica promised to take Tipper to the beach in Miami for a honeymoon.

Tipper got up before dawn and stoked the still. He heard the pitter-patter of little feet. Looking over his shoulder, he gave Betsy a look of rebuke. "Get back inside and get dressed. It's too cold to be out here barefoot."

"Do you need my help, Papa?"

"Not until I start bottling. How about you scramblin' me some eggs? I'll come in and eat in a minute. I just need to get the fire going."

"Okay, Papa." Betsy ran back inside after she stopped to get some bacon from the smokehouse and some eggs from the henhouse. Tipper smiled at his little sweetheart. It wasn't long before he smelled coffee and bacon. Tipper left the fire for a little while. He really wanted a cup of coffee.

Jessica got up early and dragged her mother out of bed. "What are you doing, Jess?" asked Lauren sleepily.

"We're going to the city early, so we can get back for Harvest Fest. I want to buy some things for Tipper's girls. I'm their momma now, and I want to get them some girly stuff."

"Can't you order it?"

"I could, but, then, I wouldn't have it tonight when I go back out there."

"People are going to talk, Jess."

"Let 'em. Miss Ina is there, and we're engaged. We set a date—Valentine's Day. We can find a wedding dress while we're in the city."

"How can I quell such enthusiasm? Let's have breakfast and get ready to go."

They breakfasted of grits, ham, and eggs. Leo and Rush dragged into the kitchen. "The food's on the stove," Lauren informed them. "You'll have to do a man lunch. We're going shopping in the city. Love you." Lauren kissed her husband and her son.

Rush chirped, "Hab fun, Mommy." Leo Tomlin's ladies drove out of Possum Holler.

Mac woke up slowly. He had been up late delivering Gator Jones's seventh child. He rolled over and kissed Felicia on the back of the neck.

"Morning," she said groggily.

"Morning. Chambry's still asleep. Want to take advantage of the quiet?"

Felicia chuckled. "I might not be quiet, and, then, we'll wake Chambry up."

"Does that mean no?"

"Convince me."

"Mm. That has possibilities." Mac kissed Felicia's neck and shoulder and caressed her thigh.

"Mm, Dr. Reardon. You could be just what the doctor ordered." Felicia turned over into her husband's embrace.

Lauren and Jessica drove along leisurely the two hours it took to get into the city. The stores were just opening. Lauren asked, "What did you have in mind, Jess?"

"Cute PJs, a pretty dress for church, barrettes for their hair, and smell-good bath gel. Oh, and some good under garments."

"What happened last night, Jess?"

"I saw how much Tipper loves those girls. I saw the desire to give them the world in his eyes. I also saw what they have right now. The big t-shirts they slept in and their little panties were clean but worn. I've seen what they wear to church. I'm sure Miss Ina made them, and they're fine, but I just want them to have something nice. I want to see the pride in Tipper's eyes. I love him so much, Momma." She glanced at her mother in the passenger's seat. "I can't believe I fell for a real hillbilly, a moonshiner even. Tipper has a heart of gold. Momma, I never talk about this with you because of you and Daddy. I've waited. I've waited for Tipper."

Lauren stroked her daughter's hair. "I'm proud of you. Daddy's the only man I've ever been with. Yeah, we put the cart before the horse a long time ago. I got you for that. But I never loved anybody else. You and Tipper will be great. Get Ina something, too, and Tipper."

"What?"

"Oh, get her a pretty nightgown and some perfume."

"What do I get Tipper—silk boxers?"

"Save those for your wedding night. Get him some cologne, just a little happy."

"He wants me to get a wedding dress, and I'm taking him to the beach for a honeymoon."

"Well, let's get to shopping. I don't want your wedding day to be chaotic."

Tipper ate the scrambled eggs, bacon, and biscuits with molasses his eleven-year-old daughter had made as she talked about the kind of room she wanted when they moved to town. Tipper laughed. "How big do you think that room will be?"

"Big enough to hold us."

"Us? Don't you want your own room by yourself?"

"I don't know what I would do by myself."

"I see. Well, maybe you should describe what you want to Aunt Felicia."

"Papa, she's not my aunt."

"No, but Mac is like my brother, and she's his wife. And when Jess and I marry, Mac *will* be your uncle, and his wife will be your aunt."

Betsy puckered her lips. "Papa, can you picture Aunt Felicia dancing with us, helping us bathe, and reading a story that makes her cry?"

Tipper laughed. "No, she is a bit more materialistic, but she can draw us a nice house."

"Okay. I'll tell her, if I ever get a chance to talk to her. She sort of avoids us dirty little urchins."

"You're not an urchin, and right now you're clean."

Betsy laughed. "I won't be after I help you put jugs in the shed."

Tipper ruffled Betsy's hair. "No, you won't. Should we roust the rest of the gang?"

"I guess so. The sun is up now. They can wash all the dishes because they were a bunch of lazy bones."

"That sounds like a plan. You can keep me company until I start bottling."

"I'll get 'em and meet you outside."

Betsy started into the bedroom. Tipper stopped her. "Betsy."

"Yes, Papa?"

"Give me a hug." She put her arms around her father's neck. Tipper kissed her on the cheek. "I love you. Get dressed before you come outside."

Tipper laughed as he heard Betsy telling her younger sisters how lazy they were. He wished he could have been lazy, but he had a lot to do to be able to give Betsy the room she wanted.

Tipper checked the fire under the still and stoked it. Then, he checked the coils and tightened a few bolts. He grunted as he checked the valves that were rusting fast with the constant production. Tipper heard the screen door slam and knew Betsy was ready to work.

The proud father turned toward his daughter and called, "You know your new momma will not like you helping with this."

"Papa!" Betsy screamed. "Look out!"

With only the warning of a loud pop, one of the valve handles flew off and struck the inside of Tipper's right thigh with such force it ripped through his jeans and flesh. Blood spurted like a geyser. Tipper crumpled to the ground.

"Papa!" Betsy screamed in alarm as she dropped to her knees beside him.

Tipper grabbed her arm. "Don't panic. I need your shoestrings. Quick!"

Betsy ripped her shoestrings out as fast as she could. "Now, what, Papa?"

"Tie 'em together. Tie that around my leg above the wound. Tie it tight."

Betsy worked fast, but her shrieks brought Ina and the other two girls out.

"Oh, dear God!" Ina cried.

Tipper said weakly, "Ma, get me to Mac."

"I don't know how to drive, Tipper."

"I can do it," said Betsy firmly.

"You're not old enough," wept Ina.

Stubbornly, Betsy said, "I can do it. Help me get him in the back of the truck."

"All right." Ina nodded. "Callie, get Papa a blanket."

Tipper helped as much as he could to get himself in the truck bed. Ina climbed in beside him and covered him with the blanket Callie brought.

Laurie handed Betsy the truck key, and the three girls piled into the cab, Callie and Laurie still in nightshirts and barefoot.

Betsy cranked the truck and said, "Callie, look out the back window. Anything behind me?"

Callie got on her knees and looked out. "No."

Betsy put the truck in reverse and backed up several feet. She shifted to drive and pulled to the dirt drive, which lead to a dirt road. Betsy was tall for eleven. It was obvious she would grow up to be tall like her father. Even so, she sat on the edge of the seat to reach the pedals.

Every time Betsy hit a rut or a bump, and there were many, Tipper cried out. Ina kept her hand pressed against the wound. Betsy blinked back tears.

"Don't cry, Betsy," ordered Callie. "I can't drive. If you cry, you can't see. You can cry when we get to Uncle Mac's."

Betsy pulled onto the dirt road and drove as fast as she dared. The little girl thought her heart would burst from her chest it beat so hard.

Betsy swung and fishtailed onto the gravel road that would bring them right in front of the clinic. Callie and Laurie screamed, but Betsy pressed the accelerator, having finally gotten onto a straightaway.

Betsy screeched to a stop in front of the clinic. "He's not here on Saturday!" cried Callie.

"You and Laurie go get him and run!" commanded Betsy.

Mac and Felicia lounged in bed after an early-morning romantic interlude. They were surprised Chambry had not woken up yet. The sudden pounding on their front door startled them from the bed.

"What the devil?" wondered Mac as he hastily dressed. He headed to the door.

"Maybe a medical emergency," said Felicia, dressing rapidly.

Chambry lumbered into the hall, rubbing his eyes. "Daddy, what's wrong?"

"I don't know yet. Get dressed."

Mac opened the door to find Callie and Laurie who both started telling him what had happened.

"Stop!" Mac commanded. "Callie, who's hurt?"

"Papa. He's bleedin' real bad."

"Where is he?"

"At the clinic."

"How?"

Laurie piped up, "Betsy drove."

"Oh, my God! She's Tipper made over!" exclaimed Mac. "Let's go." He called over his shoulder. "Felicia, I need your help." To Callie he said, "Go get Jessica."

"She's not home. Her car is gone."

"Felicia!" Mac shouted. "I need you! Get to the clinic. Drop Chambry with Papaw and see if Jessica is there. If she's gone, I *really* need you." Mac ran to the clinic.

The desperate and panicking friend flung down the tailgate of the truck. Weakly, Tipper said, "It's bad, Mac."

Felicia got there and gasped when she saw all the blood. "Jess went to the city with Lauren," she informed Mac.

"Help me get him inside. Get in the truck."

"What?"

"You might get dirty and bloody, but get in the fucking truck!" Mac snapped.

"MacKenzie Reardon!" Ina shouted. "Watch your mouth!"

Felicia obeyed. Mac said anxiously, "Ladies, support his shoulders. I'm gonna get his legs." He handed Betsy the clinic key. "Unlock quick!"

Betsy scrambled out of the truck and unlocked the door. Mac, Felicia, and Ina laboriously carried Tipper into the clinic.

"Take him to the surgery," Mac instructed.

As they hoisted Tipper onto the bed, he let out a yelp. Mac first filled a syringe with morphine. "This will help the pain," he told Tipper.

Tipper nodded, too weak to speak. Then, Mac started an I.V. and drew some blood. Tipper had lost so much blood it was hard to get any. Mac got enough to get a blood type. "AB positive. That's good," he said. "Felicia, what's your blood type?"

"I don't know."

"It really doesn't matter so long as your iron is high enough. Give me your arm."

"Why?"

"Tipper needs blood. If you can do the surgery, I'll give him the blood. I'm B positive. He can take that. He can take anything."

Felicia offered Mac her arm. "How much?"

"Not enough to kill you." The look on Mac's face seemed mixed with rage and disgust. His wife met his glare with one of her own. The doctor said brusquely, "But I need more donors. I need this now, so you can recover quickly. I need you to help with the surgery. Jess isn't here."

"What will I have to do?" The woman's voice quivered.

"Whatever I tell you."

"I don't even know a scalpel from sutures."

Mac said nothing but took some of Felicia's blood. He typed it. "O positive, and your iron is normal."

Mac turned to Ina. "I need yours, too." Ina nodded. Mac drew her blood. "AB positive, the same as Tipper's. Betsy!"

"You're going take her blood?" asked Felicia in a panic.

"No. She's too young."

"Yes, sir?" Betsy asked, completely willing to give her blood.

"Go get Preacher Tomlin and Miss Bankston. Tell them to bring any juice they have with them. You'll need to stay at Preacher Tomlin's house and be the babysitter. Take Callie and Laurie with you. Can you do all that?"

"Yes, sir." Betsy took off.

"Betsy!" Mac called. "Get your grandfather, too."

He talked to Felecia and Ina. "Leo and Sunny will give us four units, and Royce Dent will make five. Hopefully that will be enough. Sunny is A positive. I remember that from when she came into the ER. If her iron is high enough, she'll be fine. See, AB positive is great. It's the universal recipient. O negative is horrible if you need blood. It's the universal donor. It's good in the respect."

Both Sunny and Leo came immediately and brought juice. Royce came as soon as he closed the store and brought more juice. Mac typed Leo and checked Sunny's iron.

"I'm afraid it'll be low. It always is," said Sunny apologetically. "If it's low, how can I help?"

"With the surgery," said Felicia.

"I can use both of you," assured Mac. "Sunny, can you read a BP gauge?"

"Yes."

"Then, I definitely need you." The doctor turned to his wife. "Baby, you just hand me what I ask for." His tone less hostile, Mac checked the blood readings. "Papa, you're A positive. Sunny you're normal, barely."

"That's a first."

"Okay, I've got to get this blood quickly. Felicia and Sunny first."

"I'll have tell my mother it's because I've been eating meat," Sunny said, trying to lighten the situation and alleviate some of the dread rolling off Mac. One look at his face told her she had failed miserably.

Mac started drawing blood into two I.V. bags. As he checked on Tipper, Royce Dent came in. Mac explained what he needed, and Royce was more than willing to help the man he still considered his son-in-law. Royce was O negative.

The morphine had put Tipper out. As Mac started back to the donors, Tipper grabbed his hand.

"Relax," assured Mac. "I'm getting blood. Then, I'll do surgery."

"Surgery? Are you takin' my leg?"

"Not if I can help it."

"Mac if the worst happens, I want my girls to live with Jess. Ma is great, but she needs help."

"I'm not gonna let you die, Tipper, but I hear you. Rest."

"I can't get three hundred bottles."

"Is that how this happened?"

"Valve handle flew off."

"Don't worry about the damned moonshine. Ron'll get what he gets. Then, he'll want more. By then, the distillery will be ready. Now, you have to heal. Don't argue with me, or I'll knock your ass out before surgery."

"Yes, doctor."

"I gotta check on your blood donors."

Mac clipped the two bags and gave Felicia and Sunny juice and told them to sit for a while. Then he started Ina, Leo, and Royce. When he got their blood, he roused Felicia and Sunny.

"Time for surgery. Let's get you scrubbed and suited."

Felicia shook like a leaf in a gale. Mac took her hand. "I need you. Tipper needs you. I *cannot* do this alone."

Sunny took Felicia's hand. "We can do this. We have to for Tipper."

Felicia said nothing. She did what she was told.

Mac stroked Tipper's forehead. Blue eyes fluttered open. "It's time," said the doctor. "I'm gonna put something in your I.V. You won't wake up for a while." Mac injected the anesthesia into his best friend's I.V. and handed a second syringe to Sunny. "If he starts to wake up before I'm done, put that in the I.V. just like I did."

Sunny nodded.

The doctor said, "Tipper, count backward from a hundred." He got to ninety-eight.

Mac turned to Felicia. "Scissors. I'm gonna cut off his jeans and take off the tourniquet. I'm pretty sure it's his femoral artery. If he starts bleeding, give me that clamp." Mac pointed to the clamp.

"Sunny, turn that little knob on the blood bag." Sunny turned it. "A little more. Good. Now, watch that BP monitor—above one eighty on top or one hundred on bottom, we've got a problem; below fifty on top or thirty on bottom, we've got a serious problem. Keep a check on the heart monitor. Tipper's a big man. If that gets over one hundred, we've got a problem. Neither should it get below thirty. It's at forty-eight. That's excellent. His heart is in good shape. I'd like to keep the heart rate ten points high or low. BP is? You tell me."

Sunny said, "BP is one hundred ten over seventy-four. That's really good, right?"

"Yes. We don't really want anything above one thirty or below fifty. Announce his reading from time to time, especially if there's a change. And if he wiggles or moans, inject."

"Gotcha."

"Let's go." Mac cut Tipper's jeans off. When he snipped the tourniquet, blood gushed.

"Clamp!" Mac ordered. Felicia handed Mac a clamp. He clamped one side. "Clamp!" Felicia handed Mac another clamp, and he clamped the other side.

Mac washed the wound and made an incision above and below the actual injury.

Sunny said, "BP and heart are steady."

Mac examined the wound. "It could be worse. Lacerated, but not severed. It's deep, and I'll have to repair the artery, but I can do it."

Jessica bought more than she intended, and she found the perfect wedding dress. The drive home felt so relaxed and right. As she drove up to her house, she threw her car into park. "Oh, my God! Something's happened at Tipper's!" she shrieked in panic. Without cutting the engine, she bounded from the vehicle and flew into the clinic.

Ina, Leo, and Royce waited, holding hands in a circle of prayer.

"Momma Ina, what happened?" demanded Jessica.

"I don't rightly know. Mac's jest took him outta surgery."

"How did you get here?"

"Betsy drove the truck."

"Oh, God! Which room?"

"One."

Jessica went through the door.

"Jess!" exclaimed Mac.

"How bad is it?"

"It was bad, but he's still with us. Lacerated femoral artery. I fixed it. You can change the blood bag."

"Where'd you get the blood?"

"Donors."

"Wow! Thank God you were here. If you hadn't been here, they could never have gotten Tipper to a hospital in time."

"Well, I couldn't let you be a widow before you were a wife."

"Thanks. How much blood have you used?"

"Four units. That's the fifth."

"Whose and what type?"

"Tipper's AB positive. He got lucky there. Ina is AB positive. Papa and Sunny are A positive. Felicia is O positive, and Royce is O negative."

"I'm surprised nobody panicked."

"Maybe we just didn't show it." The best friend ran his fingers through his dark wavy hair. "He'll survive. He'll have an ugly scar, but I guess you're the only one who'll see it often. Jess, I don't think you'll care."

The terrified fiancée rubbed her face with both hands. "I'm just glad to still have Tipper."

Felicia and Sunny waited for Mac's instructions. He smiled at them. "Ladies, you were great. Thank you. I'll take it from here. Tipper'll be here a few nights. You two get yourselves cleaned up."

Sunny patted Mac's arm and squeezed Jess's hand as she dragged out, completely exhausted.

Felicia breathed deeply and started after Sunny. Mac caught her hand. "You see why this is where I need to be, don't you?"

"Yes, I see this is where you need to be. I need a shower now."

Felicia trudged home without talking to anyone. She got into the shower and leaned against the wall. She sobbed, "Yes, Mac, you belong here, but I don't."

19

Love Is Not Enough

Felicia got out of the shower, a luxury she had demanded be installed. She dressed in jeans, a heavy sweater, and fur lined boots. She looked at the unmade bed and ran her hand across Mac's pillow. She opened the closet and pulled out her luggage into which she packed everything she owned.

She picked up the phone by the bed. The phone was another luxury she had demanded. She dialed a number. "Hey," she said when the party answered.

Ron Norton asked, "Is something wrong, Felicia?"

"Yes. Tipper had a serious accident. You won't be getting three hundred bottles. I don't know how many he got ready, but I'm sure they'll ship what they have."

"Is *he* all right? What happened?"

"He'll survive. A valve handle flew off the still and lacerated his femoral artery. Mac performed surgery, but Tipper will be out of commission for quite some time."

"Thank God Mac was there."

"Yes. This is where Mac belongs, but I don't." The distraught woman sat on the side of the bed and stifled a sob.

"Felicia, what are you saying?"

"Do you still have room for me?"

"Felicia, you love Mac."

"Love is not always enough. I can't stay here, Ron. I'll die."

"Felicia, you know I want you here. You know I love you. If love isn't enough for you and Mac, how can I be sure it'll be enough for me, especially if it's only me?"

"Ron, you know I love you, too. I've always been torn between you and Mac."

"You married Mac."

"And I slept with you." For a long time neither said a word. Felicia changed the phone to her other ear. "If you don't want me anymore, just say so."

"Felicia, I could never stop wanting you. What are you going to do?"

"Go where I belong. I'll see you late tomorrow."

She hung up and took out stationery.

Felicia loaded her luggage into the trunk and backseat of her car. She put the booster seat for Chambry on the porch and made one stop.

When Felicia entered the Tomlin home, the four older children were playing Monopoly. "Where is everybody?" she asked.

"Still at the clinic, Mother," replied her son.

"Chambry, come on the porch with me for a minute."

The child went on the porch with her. "What's wrong, Mother?" he asked.

"First, I think I'd like Momma if you don't mind." Felicia pulled Chambry into her arms as she squatted. She kissed him on the head. "Chambry, I have to go away for a while. I'll be back to see you, I promise. And you can come to the city to see me."

"What city?"

"New York."

"Why?"

Her voice strangled by tears, Felicia said, "Momma can't stay here. If I stay here, I'll die, baby. You be good for your daddy. He loves you so much. I would never take you from him. I'll call you tomorrow night. Now, go back inside."

The distressed mother got into her car and drove away. Chambry came back inside. He looked at Tipper's girls. Betsy took the little boy's hand. "Come on. It'll be all right. Our momma left us, too. At least yours said good-bye and told you where she was going. Maybe God will send you another momma like He did us."

Royce reopened the store while Mac, Jessica, Ina, Leo, and Lauren anxiously waited at the clinic for Tipper to wake up. Mac worried most about the massive blood loss and the lack of oxygen to the brain. The longer Tipper slept, the more Mac worried.

Jessica sat by the bed where they had moved Tipper. He was only the second patient who had stayed in the small five-bed hospital. Jessica worried, too. She knew the loss of blood was the biggest obstacle.

Mac took the time to clean and sterilize his small surgery before he came back into the tiny room. "Any change?" he asked.

"No," said Jessica sadly.

"If the jackass doesn't wake up soon, I'm gonna transport him to the city," Mac threatened.

"Uh!" Tipper grunted. "No city."

Jessica looked up at Mac. "How did you know?"

"That little rumble that must be the wimpiest snore I've ever heard stopped."

Tipper opened his eyes. "I was having a wonderful dream. I didn't wanna leave it."

Mac popped a thermometer into Tipper's mouth. "Don't talk." While he waited for the thermometer to register, Mac gave Tipper a tetanus shot.

"Ow!" Tipper whined around the thermometer.

Mac took the thermometer. "No fever. That's good."

"Couldn't you have given the shot while I was out? That hurt."

"Baby."

"What was it?"

"Tetanus. We don't want you getting lockjaw. I have penicillin in the I.V. We can't risk infection. What happened?"

"Too much pressure. Valve handle flew off. Needed a new one. Rust, you know. Jess, I can't get the rest of the order."

"Damn that order!" snarled Jessica.

"Jess, *please*, ship what I have. Tell Ron what happened. I wasn't workin' in the dark. It was broad daylight. Betsy wasn't workin', just keeping me company. She did make breakfast."

"And drove you here," said Jessica. "How does an eleven-year-old know how to drive?"

"Tipper drove at ten," Mac informed.

"What?"

"Make him tell you about it. It was when he first started delivering moonshine."

Jessica frowned at Tipper.

"I did what I had to do, like Betsy did." Tipper shrugged. "She watched me. She's smart."

"Yes, she is," Jessica admitted. "And brave."

"Mac, how long am I down?"

"Six weeks."

"Too long."

"That's how it is."

"I'll lose my job at the mine."

"You'll be fine." Mac made notations on Tipper's chart. "The distillery is almost ready. You can tell your employees what to do. And I'm pretty sure you have sick leave. Take it."

"I won't be able to get my girls anything for Christmas."

"Yes, you will," said Jessica, starting to cry. "I bought a lot more things today than I meant to. We'll use that."

"Jess, I can't let you do that."

"Why? I thought I was their momma now. You're not taking that back, are you?"

Tipper locked eyes with Jessica. He submitted. "I think we'd have a fight if I tried."

"I love you, Tipper. We're a team now."

"What if love isn't enough, Jess?"

"We have more. We have understanding, trust, respect, and commitment."

"Yes, ma'am. Mac, I hurt. Bad."

"I don't have those wonderful little pumps. I'll have to give you an injection."

Tipper scowled. "Is this like that movie Preacher Tomlin took us to see? What was it called?"

"*Major Payne.* This little trick won't hurt. I'll inject it into your I.V. It's morphine, just like I gave you when you came in. It might burn a little when it hits your vein. Tipper, I won't give you but a couple more of these. This stuff's bad news if you get addicted."

"I understand."

Mac injected the morphine into the I.V. Tipper moaned slightly at the burning sensation. Then, he looked up at Mac and grinned. "I see why it's so addictive. Is it gonna knock me out?"

"Probably. That's okay though. You need to rest."

Tipper fell asleep, and Mac and Jessica stepped out. Ina looked up with dark circles beneath her eyes.

Mac nodded. "He'll be fine. Y'all go home. Miss Ina, go to Papa's and get some rest. Jessica, you go, too. Check on the girls. They need their new momma and their grandma right now."

"You go get some rest, too, Mac," Lauren insisted. "I'm not too tired to sit with Tipper for a while. If I need you, I'll call the house. I do know how to use a phone."

"I think I will. He'll sleep a while after the morphine. The BP cuff is automated for every fifteen minutes. If his blood pressure goes up or down, get me. Take his temperature in four hours. If he has a fever, get me. A fever is anything over ninety-nine. He has a catheter. Check the bag and empty it if it needs it. There's a valve at the bottom." Mac sighed.

"Mac, I can handle it," assured Lauren.

"I'm sure you can. I'll be back about midnight."

"No," said Jessica. "I'll come tonight. You come in the morning."

"Yes, Nurse Langston. Felicia must've gone home and passed out. I should check on her. So much for Harvest Fest. I thought she would enjoy it, but I'm just too tired." He rubbed his eyes. "Today I was rough on her, and I might've been harsh. I need to tell her I'm sorry, that I panicked at the thought of losing Tipper. I'll see both of you tomorrow."

Mac entered his house to total quiet. Expecting to find Felicia asleep, he found the bed just as they had left it. He thought, perhaps, she had gone to the Tomlins' because Chambry was there. Then, he noticed an envelope on his pillow.

"Oh, God!" he breathed as apprehension set in. Before he opened the envelope, he opened the closet with trepidation. His heart told him she was gone.

Mac set on the edge of the bed and cried. "Baby, I'm sorry. I pushed too hard." Again, panic overtook him. "Chambry!" he bellowed.

Mac ran as fast as he could to the Tomlin home and burst through the door without knocking. Chambry sprang from the floor where the children were playing Go Fish and rushed to his father.

"Daddy!" the little boy cried.

Mac pulled him close and wept. "I couldn't live without you," he choked.

"I'm right here, Daddy. Mother left. Betsy says we'll be all right."

Mac wept harder as he realized Felicia had stopped to say good-bye to her son. "We will," he assured the little boy. The father pushed away a little and composed himself. "Have you had supper?"

"Yes, sir. Betsy made fried ham, mashed potatoes, and sliced tomatoes."

"Well, Betsy seems to be a little Jacqueline-of-all-trades."

"What's that, Uncle Mac?" asked Betsy.

"Have you ever heard of a Jack-of-all-trades?"

"Yes, sir."

"Are you a Jack?"

"No, sir. That's a boy. Oh, I get it. Jacqueline because I'm a girl."

"Exactly. Thank you for everything you did today."

"Is Papa really all right?"

"Yes. You may see him tomorrow." Mac turned to Chambry. "Buddy, would you mind much spending the night here?"

"Are you sure you want to be alone?"

"I don't want to be alone, but I have to process what's happened."

"Mother said she would call me and come back to see me, and I'm supposed to go and see her. Will that be all right?"

"Yes. Mother and I will work out the details." He soothed the child's hair back. "Don't worry about it. I'm gonna take a shower now. I love you. I'll talk to you tomorrow."

"I love you, too, Daddy. Don't be sad. Maybe like Betsy said—God will send us someone else."

"We'll see, Buddy. We'll see."

Mac went home and took a long hot shower. He let the steamy water beat on his face. He adjusted the shower massage nozzle and allowed the water to take the aching from his back muscles. He was glad Felicia had demanded the shower. After his shower, Mac picked up the envelope from the bed. He dreaded reading it, but the time had come. The distressed man opened and read:

Dear Mac,

Yes, today I saw without a doubt you are where you belong; however, it is not where I belong. Never doubt I love you, but it is as Grandma Newton said. Love is not enough. Rest assured I know you love me, too. But love is not enough.

Mac, I cannot stay in Possum Holler. I'll die there. Even if my body lives, my spirit and the person I am would die. As a physician, you took an oath to do no harm. It would do great harm to me to stay; so, please release me.

I'm leaving Chambry with you for I want him to see through His Father's eyes, just as you do. You're an amazing man, and I can't think of anyone better to mold Chambry. I'll visit him, and I'll want him to visit me. I'll send you the details.

I'm sure the residents of Possum Holler will despise me now, but there are those there I admire. Tipper is one of them. I pray he recovers fully for you would be incomplete without his friendship.

Believe it or not, the one person who will best understand what I've done is Grandma Newton. Tell her I'm sorry.

I'll tell you now, I'll be in New York with Ron. I think you already knew there was something there, but I truly wanted our marriage to work. That is why I came back from Paris.

Yes, Ron was with me in Paris. I also saw the question in your eyes when you met Ron. You wondered if Chambry is yours. Yet, you didn't ask. Is it because you didn't want to hear the truth? Does Chambry have your genes? You're the doctor. You can figure that out. Are you Chambry's father? Yes! Would you love him any less if you discovered he did not share your DNA? I don't think so. That's why I'm leaving him with you.

I once told Leo I didn't think I was better than the people of Possum Holler. No, I'm not. As a *matter of fact, I'm not as good. I'm definitely not good enough for you. I'm sorry for hurting you, for I know you are hurt. I will always love you. I'm certain you'll find love that fits you. I think I'm going to the love that fits me. I only ask that you not hate me (or Ron) for I could never hate you. No, I love you, but, again, love is not enough.*

Please, forgive me and understand.

Felicia

Mac lay down on the bed and cried himself to sleep.

20

Birth Control—Not!

Mac and Jessica went to Tipper's place and transported the bottled moonshine to town. They divided it as equally as possible and shipped it to Ron's four clubs. Jessica included a note in the shipment that would go to Ron's base club. As they packed the bottles, Jessica asked, "Mac, do you want to talk about it?"

"No."

"Keeping it bottled inside hurts more."

"Jess, I'm hurt. But, you know, I *do* understand. She was drawn to me because I was different. I was drawn to her because she was gorgeous. She was a real city girl who paid attention to me, a hillbilly. I don't hate her, and I don't hate Ron." The man sealed the crate with force. "They're a much better match than we were. I hope it works. I'm more worried about Chambry."

"Did she call him?"

"Just like she said she would. Jess, should I run a DNA test? Should Chambry ever know if Ron is his father?"

"No and no. Just love him."

"What if he should someday need Ron?"

"If you must know, run the test, but *never* tell Chambry unless it becomes necessary. That child idolizes you." She pulled a strip of tape to close the packing crate. "Don't shatter his illusion. That's selfish. And *do not* make him think anything negative about his mother."

"Whoa! Tipper has a tiger by the tail."

"You asked."

"And I'm listening. I love him no matter what."

"Now, that's the Mac I love."

"You know, Jess, it does bother me the lengths she went to. I mean, she made it look like she sabotaged our birth control. She made sure I found it."

"She was terrified. Does Ron know?"

"From the expression on his face when I met him, no. He does now, I'm sure. What do I do if they come to visit?"

"Be cordial."

"Where will they stay?"

Jessica grinned mischievously. "Tipper's place. Hopefully by then, we'll have a house in town."

"I can go for that."

They packed the last jug and shipped them.

Mac forced Tipper to stay in town at his place for several weeks. Miss Ina stayed in town with Grandma Newton, and the girls crashed at Mac's with their father.

The girls discovered the shower and bubble bath. Chambry discovered what it was like to have other children in the house, prompting him to ask, "Daddy, am I ever gonna have brothers and sisters?"

Mac answered, "Well, I don't know. I don't have a wife, and I don't know if Mother and Ron are gonna have children or not."

"What should I call Ron?"

"Ron."

"Are you angry?"

"Yes and no."

"Well, I'm angry." The little boy put his hands on his hips, reminding Mac so much of Grandma Newton he doubted the DNA results.

"It's understandable," he assured.

"Are you and Mother gonna get a divorce?"

"Yes. I'm waiting for her to send me some papers. I've sent her some."

"Do you hate her?"

"No. Your mother is a good lady. She'll be happier with Ron."

"Daddy, I miss her."

"Me, too, sometimes." The father put his hand on the child's head. "Would you like to call her?"

"May I?"

"Anytime you want. The number is on the pad by the phone. Can you dial it?"

"Yes, sir."

"Then, call. I'm going to the clinic. If Uncle Tipper tries to sneak out, come and get me."

After a few more days, Mac allowed Tipper to go home, but Jessica went to supervise his activity. Time went on, and Mac coped the best he could with losing Felicia.

Mac went to the clinic. Sherry Jones was scheduled to come in for her checkup after her seventh child in ten years. Gator dropped her and five of their children at the clinic at eight and left for the city to negotiate new contracts for the next year and to meet Alain Richter about a joint account they had. Fox and Rooster, the oldest children, he dropped at the school. They usually caught the bus that Leo drove every morning and every afternoon. School ran from eight until three for all ages.

When Sherry and her passel came in, Mac groaned silently, but he took the opportunity to take care of the kids, too. He knew Gator wouldn't bring them in unless they were almost dead, and Sherry was either too uneducated or too plain naïve to know the difference. Gator's four older brothers had run off to Detroit or joined the military to leave Gator alone with a farm he resented. Mac did not know where Gator had found Sherry because she was not from Possum Holler, but her resemblance to Tipper astounded Mac. He often wondered if Sherry was Ina and Ander's child, but she claimed to be only a couple of years younger than Gator, making her too old to be the child Mac knew Ina had delivered and placed for adoption.

Mac looked all of them over and asked, "Sherry, have any of them had their vaccinations?"

"Only them two at the school. They couldn't go to school without 'em. Gator took 'em to the county health department."

"Well, you don't have to go that far anymore. I can do it here."

"Can you do it today? Gator ain't gonna wanna drag us all back here if'n we ain't sick."

"Yes, I'll take care of them before I check you. I have to wait for Jess to be here to take care of you anyway."

Mac cleaned a place on each child's arm and leg and vaccinated them. As they all bellowed at once, Mac wanted a shot of Tipper's moonshine. Then, he noticed Sherry crying, too.

"Quiet!" Mac snapped angrily. All the children except the baby stopped crying. "Come over here," Mac commanded. There was a little play area with blocks and toys Felicia had foreseen as a need. Mac was suddenly grateful for her foresight, and a wave of loneliness swept over him. "Play here while I check your momma," he said more gently. Then he gave each one of then a lollipop from a jar on the counter.

He turned to Sherry. "Go in exam one. I'll get Jess."

Jessica was just sending Billy Maddox back to school. She had taken out a pencil lead from his hand where Callie Campbell had stabbed him when he pulled her hair. Sunny had paddled both of them and sent him to the clinic.

Mac requested, "Jess, I need you in here. I'm about to examine Sherry Jones."

"I'm coming."

When they walked in, Sherry nursed the baby. She looked up apologetically. "She was hungry, Dr. Mac."

"It's okay. Let's talk while you feed her. Are you still taking those vitamins I gave you?"

"Yeah. They make my milk good and rich."

"Yes, they help. Have your periods started back?"

"No, unless I'm pregnant again," she huffed.

"Why would you be pregnant? I told you and Gator not to have sex until after your exam."

"That man's hornier than a dog smellin' a bitch in heat. He wudn't listenin' when I said no."

In total disbelief of what he had just heard, Mac said, "Sherry, did Gator rape you?"

"A husband cain't rape his wife." Her voice sounded shrill.

"Yes, he can. It's a crime. Did he force you to have sex?"

"I done said too much." She shook her head.

"Sherry, what you say to me stays here. It's a crime for me to tell anybody else. Same goes for Jess. She can't say anything either unless you give your permission for either of us."

"He did wait 'til I stopped bleedin'. Yeah, he made me. He broke his promise to me, and I'm right mad."

"Did he hit you?"

Sherry glared at her doctor. "Now, he ain't one for beatin' me. Gator wouldn't *never* hit me. No, he jest held me down and told me it was my duty and his right. You sure he done wrong?"

"Yes, on more than one level."

"Dr. Mac, if'n I tell you somethin' you ain't gonna tell nobody else, right?"

"That's right."

"I don't wanna have no more babies. Grandma Newton done told us some things to do so's I can pleasure him. We tried 'em, and we like 'em jest fine, but he likes dippin' that wick. Still, I don't want no more babies."

"Of course, you don't."

"I cain't tell him no. Wouldn't no policeman listen to a backwoods hillbilly like me if'n I's a mind to tell. But I ain't, so don't ask me to do that to Gator. I cain't tell nobody but you."

"Sherry, you have options." Mac got a book from a shelf. "I'm gonna show you two things. First, I'm gonna draw some blood to make sure you're not pregnant."

Jessica drew a vile of blood and ran a pregnancy test. "She came back negative," said Jessica in relief.

"That mean I ain't pregnant?" asked Sherry.

"You are not pregnant," assured Jessica.

"Okay. Dr. Mac, show me them pictures."

"Well, you actually have a lot of options. Choice one would be condoms."

"Them rubber things?"

"Yes."

"We used 'em a couple of times. Gator don't like 'em."

"Okay. Another possibility that would be tiresome for you would be to take birth control pills."

"Would I have to take 'em ev'ry day?"

"Yes."

"I cain't do that. I don't want Gator to know."

"Okay," he said skeptically. As Gator's cousin, he doubted this woman would be able to lie to her husband. "Another option is Depo-Provera. It's medicine in a shot. It'll keep you from getting pregnant, but you'll have to take a shot every three months. That would mean me coming out or you coming in."

"I don't know 'bout that. Is there somethin' Gator don't have to know about?"

"Are you gonna lie to him?"

"You cain't tell him, so, yeah."

Mac cut her a look.

"What's that look for? You look like Gator when you do that."

Mac shook off the feeling Ina Campbell was talking to him. Sherry looked and sounded just like her. He said, "He might get mad if he finds out."

"I'll take my chances. Gator ain't mean. He's real lovin'. That's the problem. He's too lovin'."

The doctor had to stifle a chuckle. He realized this woman liked Gator's loving streak even if she feared having another baby.

"What else?" asked Sherry

"Well, a Norplant is out because that would go under your skin and Gator would see it. You look at this. Jess, show her the IUD and explain while I get one."

Mac retrieved an IUD from the pharmaceutical pantry. He came back in and asked, "Okay, did Jess explain this goes inside you?"

"Yeah. It don't let the fertilized egg implant. Does that mean if I get pregnant, it just goes on out with my flow?"

"Yes," Mac said, amazed at her actual understanding.

"Is that a sin?"

He dropped his eyes to the floor to consider the moral dilemma. "What do you think?"

"I wouldn't never know I's pregnant?"

"No."

"Gator couldn't tell it was there?"

"No."

Sherry thought for a while. Then, she said, "It's a sin I can live with. Put it in."

"All right, after I examine you. Is the baby finished eating?"

"Yeah."

"Give her to Jess and get undressed. Put the sheet over you. Jess'll get me when you're ready."

Jessica got Mac after Sherry covered herself with the sheet. He examined her breasts and found nothing unusual. Then, he did a pelvic and uterine exam and a pap test. He commented, "Sherry, you're very bruised down here. When did you and Gator have sex?"

"Night before last. Gator was real rough like he ain't never been before. Can you still put the thing in?"

"Yes, but, Sherry, if he forces you again, come to me. That's not like Gator. I'll talk to him."

"Okay, Dr. Mac."

"There'll be a little prick, and you might bleed a couple of days."

"That'll be good. Gator don't like to do it when I'm bleedin'."

"Are you ready?"

"Yeah."

Mac implanted the IUD and told Sherry he wanted to talk to her a few more minutes after she got dressed. When she was dressed, Mac came back in.

"Whatcha wanna talk about, Dr. Mac?"

"Hygiene."

"What's that?"

"Staying clean. Sherry, how often do y'all bathe?"

"We sponge off ev'ry night, but we git a tub bath ever Saturday before we come to church. I got an extry tub bath last night 'cause I's comin' to see you."

"Sherry, y'all need a tub bath every day. It'll keep you and the kids from getting sick."

"We ain't got no runnin' water. It's kindly hard with this many young'uns."

"I know. Even a bath where all the boys bathe together and all the girls bathe together would be better than none. That's what Tipper's girls do."

"I'll see to it."

"Now, if you have pain or any unusual bleeding or start running a fever, get back in here fast. We'll need to take the IUD out."

"Can it make me sick?"

"It doesn't usually make people sick. If you have no problems, I don't need to see you as your doctor for a whole year."

"Thank you. Dr. Mac, what if I do get pregnant?"

"That rarely happens. We'll deal with it if it should."

"Okay. If I ain't scairt of gettin' pregnant, I won't tell Gator no."

"That's because you love him. I understand."

"I do love him. Gator's my musketeer."

Mac smiled at the thought. He well remembered the musketeers. Then, he wondered what Gator had rescued Sherry from. Her words brought him back to reality. "We brung you a ham and Nurse Jess a slab o' bacon, but I didn't know you was gonna take care o' the young'uns."

"Don't worry about it. What are you gonna do about getting home?"

"I guess we can walk or wait for the school bus. Gator'll be late gettin' back."

Mac shook his head. "No. Jess, will you give them a ride?"

"Sure. Let's get loaded. My car's at Preacher Tomlin's." Jessica looked back at Mac and mouthed, "Thanks a lot."

Mac grinned back at her.

Mac had allowed Tipper to go home with orders not to touch the still. Jessica stayed several days to make sure Tipper obeyed doctor's orders, which kept her out of the clinic a lot. She did not come back the day of Sherry's visit after she took her and the children home.

Nobody came into the clinic after Jessica left until Mac readied to close. Gator stormed into the clinic and threw Mac across the room. Mac landed hard on his back on the tiled floor. Before he could get up, Gator straddled Mac and pummeled him across the face. Mac felt the skin around his left eye socket split and blood flowed freely to the floor.

In all the years he had known him, Mac had never seen Gator so angry. Gator screamed in fury, punctuating each irate question with a punch. "I raped my wife? What did the city do to you? What the hell did you put inside her? You call it birth control? You made it so she cain't have babies? And we dirty now, huh? Gotta have a tub bath ever' day?"

"Get off me, Gator!" Mac punched back, catching Gator with a cuff across the ear. "You moron!"

"Moron? Now, you callin' me retarded!" Gator slammed Mac's head into the floor.

"You're a fool!" shouted Mac. "You need to listen to me!" Mac punched Gator hard underneath the ribs.

"Listen to yo city notions? I don't think so. I seen what city notions done to Sherry. Birth control—not!"

"Listen to me, Gator. If you love Sherry, you won't make her have any more children. It's gonna kill her. Give her time to heal completely. Yes, she can have more children when she's ready. All we have to do is take it out. She doesn't want anymore. If you love her, you'll think of *her*." Mac bucked to dislodge his first cousin to no avail.

"Like you loved yo wife? Like you thought o' *her*? She left you. Was it because you wouldn't give her another baby?"

"You son-of-a-bitch!" shouted Mac as he came across with a right hook to Gator's jaw. "What I'm saying to you has nothing to do with Felicia!" A left caught Gator in the gut, but Gator did not loosen his grip on his cousin. "It has everything to do with

Sherry and your family. Did you rape her? *Yes!* If you forced or coerced her, that's rape. The law says even a husband can rape his wife. If you love her, you won't force her. She was bruised very badly, Gator. If you love her, you won't oppose the birth control, and she won't say no because she won't be scared of getting pregnant." Mac squirmed to get free, but Gator maintain his pressure, keeping Mac pinned by leaning in with his forearms against the doctor's chest.

Mac continued to bellow loudly enough to be heard outside. "Do you need to bathe every day? *Yes!* It'll keep you healthier. Gator, like it or not, you stink! For God's sake! Tipper doesn't have running water. They bathe every day. You can too, even if all the boys bathe together and all the girls bathe together. Hell! You can bathe with your wife. Sex in the bathtub is very nice!

"Now, get off of me!" Mac shoved backward with his feet. "Go home and make love to your wife."

"She's bleedin' because of you."

"For a day or two. Give this birth control a chance. See how much that woman will love you when she's not scared."

Gator punched Mac one more time and let him up. "I do love Sherry," he said defensively. "You ain't got a clue how much I love Sherry. You wudn't here."

"Then, show her. Protect her. Gator, can you afford to care for more children?"

"We make do." The wind seemed gone from the bluster of Gator's anger.

"Gator, you're a hog farmer. I think you have enough help. Do you want Sherry to die from bone cancer or leukemia like your mother because having so many children without good prenatal care has depleted her calcium or iron? She's a pretty woman, but she'll get old fast if you don't take care of her. Is that what you want?"

"I ain't never meant to hurt her."

"Have you really tried some of Grandma Newton's suggestions?" Mac pressed his hand to the injury near his eye.

Gator scowled. "Maybe a real bath ever'day ain't so bad."

Mac sniggered as he realized what some of Grandma Newton's suggestions must have been.

Gator looked at Mac. "Sorry I hit you. I was real mad 'cause I felt you were thinking I was bad. I ain't mean to my womarn. I love her. I love her more'n anything. You think this is the best thing for both of us?"

"I do."

"Do you think I raped Sherry?"

"I don't think that was your intention. What were you thinking?"

"I was feelin' down, and I needed her comfort. I was bein' selfish." He heaved a great sigh. "To be honest, I don't want no more kids neither. I'll give this birth control a shot. No hard feelin's?"

"No."

Gator stood and held his hand out; Mac shook it. Gator winced at the doctor's grip and then laughed and continued to help his first cousin to his feet. "We ain't never scrapped against each other. We always fought together. You gonna need a few stitches, Mac. Where's yo nurse?"

"Takin' care of Tipper at home. I'll use a mirror."

"Sorry."

"Forgiven."

Gator left without more words once Mac handed him a finger splint. Mac looked in the mirror in the bathroom. Blood ran down his left cheek. "A few?" he mumbled. "I'd say about ten."

21

Physician, Heal Thyself

As Sunny locked the school for the day, she saw Gator come out of the clinic, shaking his hand as if in pain. She approached the man carefully and asked, "Mr. Jones, is everything all right?"

"I reckon so, Miss Bankston. I had a misunderstandin' with Mac 'bout him puttin' somethin' inside Sherry so she couldn't have babies. I thought he was judgin' us and thinkin' bad, but he was jest tryin' to help."

Sunny saw the bruise and swelling around Gator's chin bone and under his eye. "Did you come to blows?"

"'Fraid so. Mac ain't no pansy. He can take a lick and give a purty good one, too. Least the city didn't take that out of him. He's still a scrapper." Gator laughed. "We jest never scrapped against each other, always with each other, and usually Tipper and Alain, too. The city boys didn't much like us Possum Holler kids at school."

Sunny drew her brow into a scowl. "Do I need to get the constable?"

"No, ma'am. Mac ain't got no hard feelin's. We shook on it."

"Do you need a hand?"

"No, ma'am. I'm goin' home to Sherry. She'll patch me up. A little lovin' is all I need. Mac might need some help though. He said he'd use the mirror. That might be a mite hard if'n his eye's swellin' like mine. Nurse Jess is at Tipper's. Mac ain't got no help. 'Bye, now."

"Good night, Mr. Jones."

With a cut in his left eyebrow and his left cheekbone, Mac's eye swelled shut fast. He filled a syringe with Novocain and dropped it three times as he tried to inject himself around the swelling and the continuous flow of blood.

"Damn it!" he muttered as he heard the door open. "Unless you're dying, come back tomorrow," he called from the bathroom where he attempted to stitch himself up.

Sunny opened the bathroom door that was slightly ajar. "Physician, heal thyself," she said sarcastically. Then she added, "Need a hand?"

"Please," admitted Mac.

"Go to an exam room and get on the table."

Mac took the suture kit to exam one and lay down on the table. Sunny looked him over. "Hm," she murmured. "Did you give Sherry Jones an IUD?"

"Why?"

"Gator said you put something inside her so she wouldn't have babies. That's the only thing I know of."

"Yes, and he was *not* happy."

"But you convinced him. He seemed satisfied you weren't judging him."

"I wasn't. I was helping Sherry."

"I know. Be still." Sunny injected the Novocain all around Mac's eye. "Do you have one of those cold metal thingies like they use in the boxing ring?"

"In the freezer."

Sunny retrieved the compress and rubbed it across Mac's eye numerous times, finally stemming the bleeding. She chuckled. "I was going to tell you to close your eye, but it looks closed."

"Funny."

Sunny gently washed Mac's eye with antibacterial soap. "Is this the suture kit you were planning to use?" she asked picking up the kit by the sink.

"Yes. It's not hard. You can do it. Make a stitch, tie it off, snip it, and do it again."

Sunny held up the needle. "It looks like a little upholstery needle."

"I suppose it does."

"Okay. Here I go." Sunny made the first stitch and kept talking. "What else did you say to Sherry?"

"Why do you ask?"

"I saw her getting cleaning supplies at the store when I ran over to get some more pencils. She also got a large supply of bath soap. I hope she uses it on Fox and Rooster because after Monday, I usually have to keep a scented hanky in my bosom, so I don't smell them."

"I told her they needed a real bath every day to help them stay healthy."

"Thank you."

"She obviously listened, but Gator thought I was judging them until I explained around punches."

"If it will make you feel better, I think his knuckles are broken."

"Good. Maybe next time he won't be such a hothead. I gave him a finger splint."

"I hope for your sake there's not a next time." The impromptu nurse wiped the disabled doctor's face with a clean gauze swab. "Well, Dr. Reardon, you have eighteen pretty little stitches."

"Eighteen? How small did you make them? I thought ten."

"Is small bad?"

"No, it actually makes the scar smaller. Let me see." Mac went to the mirror in the bathroom. "Nice work," he called. "Are you sure you're a teacher and not a nurse?"

"Who's trying to take my job, and what the devil is going on?" asked Jessica from the doorway. "I saw the light still on and knew something was up. Mac, what happened? There's blood on the floor."

"Apparently, Sherry found it necessary to tell Gator everything. He wasn't happy as you can see." He touched his new stitches. "We've come to an understanding after many blows. You weren't here to take care of me, and I was doing a terrible job on myself. Luckily, Sunny stepped in. What are you doing here?"

"I forgot something. I'm going back, but let me look at you while I'm here." Jessica looked over the wound. "Nice work,

Sunny. Mac, do you have a concussion? You have goose egg on the back of your head."

Sunny sniggered, "His head's too hard."

The doctor narrowed his one usable eye at his Good Samaritan. "No. I never lost consciousness. Just give me a couple of Vicodin for later. And will you clean up and close up before you go back to Tipper's?"

"Sure. Sunny, escort this lug home."

"I have to get Chambry first," protested Mac.

"Let him stay, or would you prefer to explain the way you look right now?" Jessica urged.

Mac grunted, "Fine. Let me call him."

Mac called his son at Leo's since Lauren had demanded a phone and told him to sleep over. Chambry asked, "Daddy, what's wrong?"

"I had to get a few stitches. I need to rest tonight. Is that all right?"

"Why did you get stitches?"

"I'll tell you when I see you. I love you. Good night."

"Good night, Daddy. I love you, too."

Sunny walked home with Mac where she stated, "I guess I should leave you here, or people will talk."

"Who?" argued Mac. "Everybody's in bed. The only lights on are at Papa's and the clinic. Do you know what time it is?"

Sunny pushed a little button on her watch to light up. "Half past ten."

"Have you had supper?"

"No, I was rather busy stitching you up, and I'm starving."

"Me, too. Eat with me."

"Does that mean I have to cook for you, too?"

"I hoped you would. I might burn whatever I try because I can't see very well." He fumbled with the key in the lock.

She took the key and unlocked the door. "Oh, play it up."

"I could use some company."

Sunny furrowed her brow.

"Please?" said Mac with his one good eye looking like a puppy dog.

"You're awful!" said Sunny, relenting. "All right. I'll make you something to eat. Then, it's off to bed, and I'm off to home."

Mac sat at his kitchen table and leaned his head on his hand. "Make something soft," he requested. "My eye is throbbing. My cheek is throbbing. I don't want to take the Vicodin on an empty stomach."

Sunny looked in the refrigerator. "Mac, what have you and Chambry been eating?"

"Whatever Mamaw cooks."

"Why?"

"It's hard to come home without Felicia."

"Mac, you have a lot more to heal than a black eye and a few stitches."

"I know." He became quiet.

Sunny found some eggs and some of Lauren's fresh baked bread. Lauren had time to bake since she only taught a one English class at the school. Sunny sliced and lightly toasted the bread and fried some eggs over easy for fried egg sandwiches. Mac had store-bought mayonnaise in the refrigerator. The teacher set two sandwiches in front of the doctor and one for her.

"Want to talk?" she asked gently.

Mac brushed a tear from his cheek. "Was I so awful? I really want to know what I did to drive her away."

"Mac, don't blame yourself. Felicia just did not belong here. She really tried, and she's not a bad person." She ate a few bites of her sandwich. "God asks us to give a tithe of money, talent, or time. Felicia is the type that will donate money in abundance. She will even give her talent as with the buildings here. Asking her to be in the midst of real suffering was too much. Don't hate her."

"I don't hate her. Sunny, are you aware she cheated on me with Ron?"

"No."

"Good. I don't want people to know."

"I don't blame you."

"Don't you want to know why?"

"Your reasons are your own, but you can tell me if you want to."

"Chambry's not mine."

"Are you sure?"

The doctor nodded. "I did a paternity test in case there's ever an emergency." Mac cried silently. "Sunny, I love him so much. I don't want anyone to tease him or do anything to hurt him. He's my son in the important ways just like I'm Leo's. It's crazy because I wonder how Ron feels or if he knows. I won't let him go if Felicia tries to take him. It hurts so much." He fisted his hand over his heart. "Seeing how much Gator loves his brood just brought all the pain to the surface."

Sunny squeezed Mac's hand. "Mac, if Felicia were going to take Chambry, she would've taken him with her. Hold on to your love for your son. Don't ever let him doubt it. Does anybody else know?"

"No, not even Papa or Jess. Jess knows I had doubts, but not that I did the test."

"No one will know from me. I think just telling me was the first step to healing yourself. You know you have a friend and a confidant. Physician, heal thyself. Finish eating and go to bed. You know where to find me if you need to talk. Good night." She put her dirty dishes in the sink.

22.

Grandma Newton

Sunday morning during the altar call, Grandma Newton hobbled forward. She and Leo carried on a lengthy conversation as the congregation sang "Only Trust Him" twice. Finally, Grandma Newton sat on the front pew while Leo got back into the pulpit.

"Please be seated," he said to the congregation. "Grandma Newton has something on her heart she would like to share with y'all. I think y'all should listen even if some of you might get offended. Grandma, do you want to come up here?"

She labored up the two steps to stand behind the pulpit. She flipped the pages of the Bible there and read Psalm 127:3-5:

> *³Lo, children are an heritage of the LORD: and the fruit of the womb is his reward. ⁴As arrows are in the hand of a mighty man; so are children of the youth. ⁵Happy is the man that hath his quiver full of them: they shall not be ashamed, but they shall speak with the enemies in the gate.*

"I want to talk to y'all today 'bout this newfangled birth control Mac's done brought to us. Some o' y'all got real upset. Look at his face." The old woman jutted her chin toward the young doctor.

A murmur started before Gator stood up. "Grandma Newton, me and Mac done worked out our differences. What happened between me and him ain't no concern of yourn."

"Sit down, Gator!" growled the old woman. "You ain't the only one actin' like a fool, though yo face sho 'nuff shows it, too."

Grandma Newton began her lecture. "Listen up, you men. The Bible tells us to be fruitful and multiply and children are gifts and blessin's. So, havin' a family is a good thang. Thang is, a family without a momma ain't a family."

She held tightly to the podium as she seemed unsteady on her feet. "I done delivered too many stillborns and buried too many young mommas. Mac's was one of 'em."

Grandma Newton held up her hand and shook her head. "I think some o' you men done misinterpreted God's Word. You women, too. Now, I know the Bible says for women to be subject to their husbands, but that don't make women doormats. We ain't slaves and we ain't whores for you men to be with at yo beck and call."

A slight murmur started up. "Hush up!" scolded Grandma Newton. "I ain't done." She slapped the podium.

Miriam Newton flipped the pages and read again from Ephesians 5:22-25:

> ²²*Wives, submit yourselves unto your own husbands, as unto the Lord.* ²³*For the husband is the head of the wife, even as Christ is the head of the church: and he is the saviour of the body.* ²⁴*Therefore as the church is subject unto Christ, so let the wives be to their own husbands in everything.* ²⁵*Husbands, love your wives, even as Christ also loved the church, and gave himself for it.*

"Men, as you can see, the same Bible says y'all supposed to love yo wives as Christ loved the church. You best be rememberin' Christ *died* for the church.

"What I'm sayin' is this. Mac ain't brought nothin' bad to you. He ain't tellin' you not to have children. What he is tellin' you is the same thang I've told ya for years. You ain't rabbits. Give yo women time to heal. Let yo young'uns have a little space between 'em.

"In years passed, I done told y'all things to do, but ya don't listen. You men don't seem to wanna sacrifice a little for yo wives. Jesus sho sacrificed a lot for the church."

She pointed around the sanctuary. "Remember this, too. The Bible says not to provoke yo children." Grandma Newton read another passage from Ephesians 6:4:

> *4And, ye fathers, provoke not your children to wrath: but bring them up in the nurture and admonition of the Lord.*

"Men, think about how much better off the ones you have would be if you could take care of 'em better.

"Now, I know not layin' with yo wife is a sacrifice, but I've told ya ways to ease the pain. Now, Mac's offerin' somethin' so ya won't have to have that pain and make that sacrifice. It's my understandin' there's more than one thang. I'm suggestin' y'all go as couples and ask Mac what's best for you. Don't make yo wife go behind yo back.

"Now, the Psalm I read says a man is happy if he has a quiver full of children. What's a full quiver? I drove to the library and read up on that. A hunter's quiver is five arrows. A warrior's quiver is thirteen arrows. That's the biggest I found. How many of y'all already got at least five young'uns? Raise yo hands, men."

Grandma Newton looked around. "That's more'n two-thirds of y'all. Now, how many of you men done had more'n one wife because the first one died due to childbirth, pregnancy, or somethin' related? Raise yo hand."

Grandma Newton looked around again. "That's nearly half. Now, I cain't say I'm right. I cain't say Mac's right. I jest know the safety and welfare of the women in Possum Holler has been weighin' on my old heart. The little ones without a momma weigh on my heart, too. You men that been left alone for whatever reason weigh on my heart. I jest ask that ya search yo hearts and recognize God might jest have sent ya a way to ease yo sufferin'."

She turned back to Leo who had taken his seat on the platform. "That's all I gotta say, Preacher Tomlin. My stomach's growlin'. Let's have dinner."

Over the next several days, many of the couples in Possum Holler must have taken Grandma Newton's words to heart. More than half of them visited Mac to learn their options to make informed decisions. Very few opted to take a pill every day or to have an IUD implanted. The most popular choices were condoms with spermicide and Depo-Provera shots. A few chose a five-year Norplant. The weight the old woman's words carried amazed Mac.

Grandma Newton also paid Mac a visit in his office. He jested, "To what do I owe this honor?"

"Ain't no honor. Sit down, shut up, and listen."

He obeyed like a naughty child. The old woman spoke her mind. "MacKenzie Reardon, I wanna talk to ya about Felicia. She was a precious girl, and she was thrown to the wolves here. I was 'bout the leader of the pack. Don't ya hate her 'cause she did the best thing for all o' y'all. Y'all woulda been miserable if she had stayed. If she comes back to see her boy, you be good to her. I know she'll come back with that Ron. He ain't a bad sort. They belong together. Now, I ain't gonna say who I think you belong with 'cause that would be interferin', but I think it'll come to you sooner or later. If'n it does, carry her over the damned threshold."

She pointed. "Now, call Felicia on the phone. I wanna talk to her."

Mac dialed. Felicia answered, "Mac, is something wrong?"

Mac assured, "Don't worry. Chambry's fine. Someone wants to talk to you." Mac handed the phone to Grandma Newton.

Felicia said, "Chambry?"

The old woman said, "No, Felicia. This is Grandma Newton."

"Grandma Newton, what?"

"Jest listen. First, I'm sorry for bein' mean to ya. You a *sweet* girl, and I miss yo flute. I ain't callin' to tell ya to come back to Mac. You done the best thing. I jest wanted to apologize and tell you I love ya."

Felicia sniffled. "Thank you."

"Sweetheart, you make sure that Ron carries ya over the threshold. 'Bye now." Grandma Newton hung up the receiver and left.

23

Legal Documents

On Christmas Eve, a UPS truck delivered half a dozen packages

to Chambry Reardon from his mother. Along with Chambry's packages came a large manila envelope for Mac.

"Merry Christmas, Felicia," Mac said to no one since he knew what the envelope held. He looked down at his son. "You open yours. I'm saving mine until after Christmas."

The little boy opened his gifts. The first one contained a durable fleece-lined, suede jacket, gloves, and boots. Mac nodded. "You'll need those when it really gets cold."

The second gift was a collection of classic children's books. "Very nice," commented Mac. "I read all of those."

The third box contained a comforter and bed set with a NASCAR theme, along with a book on the history of NASCAR and a note to Mac.

Mac,

> *I learned that NASCAR has its roots in hillbilly bootleggers, the Flock brothers. It's grown into a national sport. Share this book with Tipper. Show him what hillbilly bootleggers can accomplish.*

> *Felicia*

Mac laughed. "She really expects our friendship to stay intact."

"Can it, Daddy?" asked Chambry innocently. "Can you and Mother still be friends?"

"Huh?" Mac said, not realizing he had spoken aloud.

"Can you and Mother still be friends?"

"I don't know. Would you like that?"

"Yes. At least she hasn't deserted me like Betsy's momma. She still loves me."

"Then I'll try for you."

The child hugged his father around the legs. Mac caressed his head. "Open the rest," he said with a hitch in his voice.

An assortment of Christmas candies filled the fourth box. Mac winked at Chambry. "You have to share those."

The child laughed as he ripped opened the bag of bite-sized, fudge-filled Santas. "All right, Daddy." He handed his father one of the chocolates and popped one in his mouth. Mac ate his piece of candy and sat on the floor with his son just as if he were a little boy also.

The fifth box contained several pairs of jeans, shirts, underwear, and socks. "Useful," Mac said. "Now, the big one."

"I hope it's a bike."

"Did you ask her for that?"

"Yes, sir."

"I didn't know. What if Santa Claus is bringing one? He's already left the North Pole for the other side of the world."

"I didn't think of that. I could share one of them with the Jones boys."

"That's an idea. Well, let's see."

Chambry ripped off the paper. It was, indeed, a bike.

"So much for Santa Claus," muttered Mac.

The citizens of Possum Holler had a Christmas Eve service before sundown and sang Christmas carols. After the service, Tipper came up to Mac.

"You look good," said Mac.

"I feel great. Look what I got in the mail." Tipper showed Mac a passed-inspection permit to begin production, a contract with Ron as a silent partner, and a check for $150,000.00 to start up.

"Wow! Merry Christmas," Mac said.

"You okay with Ron as my partner?"

"Yeah. He's not a bad sort."

"He took your woman."

"No. She chose him. He's not to blame. To be honest, Felicia and I were wrong from the beginning. They belong together. I'll find love. You did."

"Yeah." Tipper smiled broadly. "I really love Jess. The girls adore her. Mac, when are you gonna get a divorce?"

"I think the papers are at home. I just have to sign 'em."

"So, sign 'em. Ask Little Miss Sunshine out."

"Who?"

"Miss Bankston. Sunny. We're on a first name basis now that I have some of her blood in me."

"Why would I do that?"

"You'd work."

"Don't start matchmaking."

"Okay. Oh, Jess says they have New Year's Eve celebrations in the city. We're gonna have a bonfire at my place, and she's going into Wilmington to by some fireworks. Bring Chambry out."

"Will do. That'll be fun. Do you want me to bring food?"

"If you want. Can you get some *real* champagne for toasting rather than using moonshine?"

"I can. What time?"

"Come for supper and stay."

"Okay. Merry Christmas."

The two men hugged in an affectionate, brotherly embrace.

Mac took Chambry home and tucked him in. He read "'Twas the Night before Christmas" to him and went downstairs. Mac picked up the envelope and sighed. He opened it and read the documents.

The papers were standard dissolution of their marriage on the grounds of irreconcilable differences. Felicia asked for no monetary settlement. She gave Mac physical custody of Chambry but asked for joint legal custody. Because of the distance between them, she asked for visitation at any time she should chose to drive in with prior notification, one month with her son in New York each summer with notification if they planned a vacation out of state or even the country, every spring break with Chambry in New York, and every other Christmas vacation with the boy in New York, as well as any special circumstances that might arise with notification. Under special circumstances, she stipulated Mac would be welcome to accompany the child. She volunteered monthly child support in the amount of $1000.00 each month for Mac to use for Chambry or to put in trust for college.

There was nothing underhanded or hidden in the papers. Before he signed them, Mac picked up the phone and called Felicia.

She answered, "Hello?"

Mac said, "Merry Christmas."

"Mac?"

"It's all right, Felicia. I just wanted to suggest we communicate about gifts."

"Did I do something wrong?"

"No. You had no idea Santa was bringing a bike, too. Chambry's amazing. I asked him what if Santa brought one, and he said he'd share one with the Jones boys."

"That's why I left him with you." She took a deep breath. "You see. He's already seeing through His Father's eyes."

"Yeah, but next time, let's talk. That way we can coordinate."

"All right. Are you okay?"

"I will be. I don't hate you, Felicia. You were right about Grandma. She has defended you to anyone who has had a harsh word. You were right about us, too. You belong with Ron, but a part of me will always love you."

"I know," said Felicia tearfully. "And a part of me will always love you. It's just for us, love was not enough."

"Well, listen." Mac put the phone receiver by the papers and signed. He picked up the receiver. "I'll mail them day after tomorrow. Question—do you want Chambry for this spring break since he's not in school?"

"No. I'll come there if it's all right."

"It'll be fine. Well, Merry Christmas."

"Merry Christmas, Mac."

The doctor held his head in his hands for brief moment after terminating the call. He released a long, sad sigh. "Well, all legal documents signed. Merry Christmas, MacKenzie Reardon. Let's hope next year ends better."

24
A New Year

On New Year's Eve, Mac and Chambry went into Wilmington where Mac purchased four bottles of champagne and took his son to lunch at a burger joint called Best Burger with a playground, after shopping to outfit his bike with lights and reflectors. Although it was below freezing, several children played in the play area. Chambry played well with children he had never met.

On the drive home, Chambry asked, "Is champagne as good as Uncle Tipper's moonshine?"

"They're totally different," Mac replied.

"Will you let me taste it?"

"You're four. I think not."

"How old were you when you tried moonshine?"

"Nine, and Papaw punished me when he found out."

"Was it good?" The child kicked his feet against the back of the front passenger's seat.

"I thought my throat would burn out. Don't kick the seat."

The boy pulled his feet in close to his body. "Good for killing germs, huh?"

"I could use it for an antiseptic."

"Then why drink it?"

Mac glanced over his shoulder to where the boy sat in the child safety seat in the back. "Well, a few glasses make you feel good. Too many make you sick."

"How many is too many?"

"Everybody's different, but I limit my glasses, especially Tipper's, to three."

"I don't guess I get to taste it either."

"No. You get cider. I'll tell you something that will make you very sick."

"What?"

"Tobacco. It's nasty."

"Did you try it?"

"I did with my friend Alain. I swallowed some of the juice and vomited everywhere."

"Yuck. What did your friend do?"

"Yes, it was yuck. Alain laughed at me." A sad smile flickered across Mac's face at the memory of a friend he never associated with anymore.

"Who is Alain, Daddy? Have I met him?"

"You've seen him. Alain Richter."

"The man Uncle Tipper gets fruit from?"

"Yes."

"He's scary to me."

"Me, too." Mac sighed. "I'm not afraid *of* him. I'm afraid *for* him."

"Do you miss him, Daddy? You sound sad. Why aren't you friends anymore?" The child kicked his feet against the back of the seat again.

"Chambry, stop," the father said more firmly. The kicking halted. "I can't explain why we're not close anymore to you, but, yes, Chambry, I miss him." Mac glanced at the sky. A lone raindrop hit the windshield. It felt like a single, isolated tear from Heaven to Mac. He whispered more to himself than his son, "Yes, I miss him."

"Did you have a fight?"

"We don't live the same way."

"Maybe you should make up."

Mac laughed. "Your mother was right."

"How?"

"You see everything through God's eyes." Another raindrop landed on the windshield.

Mac watched the barren trees whiz by as Chambry got quiet. Then the boy said, "Why doesn't Possum Holler have restaurants? I had fun at Best Burger."

"It's too little, I guess. Nobody has money to eat at restaurants."

"Why do we have more money than other folks?"

"Because I made a deal with the devil."

"What does that mean?"

Mac looked at his son in the review mirror. "My clinic is part of a grant from the government. After five years, the grant will be up. We might be poor."

"Daddy, you know, Uncle Tipper might bring money to Possum Holler."

"That's true. Another deal with the devil."

"Ron?"

Mac sniggered as he still felt angry. "No, booze, although Tipper's not a big drinker."

"Well, if we had a restaurant, they could serve some of his moonshine, but not too much."

Mac laughed. "I suppose."

"Mamaw makes good food. She could have a restaurant."

"Mamaw *does* make good food."

"Mother's not a very good cook."

Mac laughed again. Chambry was as opinionated and outspoken as Grandma Newton. "I guess she's not, but she tried."

"She did make good spaghetti. I miss her spaghetti."

"Me, too, Chambry."

"Daddy, will you make spaghetti for us soon?"

"I will. Chambry, did Mother tell you when she called on Christmas Day, she's coming to visit during the school's spring break?"

"No, sir."

"She must've wanted it to be a surprise. Sorry."

"Can I call her when we get home?"

"You may."

Chambry yawned.

"You need a nap because you get to stay up late tonight. We have an hour and a half left to drive. Snooze."

Chambry put his head back on the seat and went to sleep. Mac glanced over his shoulder. Chambry was a beautiful child, pretty enough to be mistaken for a girl if he had long hair. His light-brown, wavy hair and big blue eyes fringed with long lashes made him look cherubic. Mac whispered, "You're mine.

I'll love you forever, no matter what." He gripped the steering wheel as some hurt bubbled to the surface. A few more raindrops fell, punctuating the man's mood.

Chambry called Felicia to wish her a happy New Year before he and Mac left for Tipper's. As Mac buckled Chambry into the back seat, he noticed Sunny loading several trays of food into the trunk of her car. "I'll be right back," he told the boy.

Mac walked briskly down the road to the small house where Sunny lived. "Good evening, Miss Bankston."

"Miss Bankston? We've been on a first name basis since Chicago."

"True. I noticed you were loading your trunk, and I had the strangest thought. Are you, by any chance, going to Tipper's?"

"Yes, Jessica invited me. Why?"

"Tipper invited Chambry and me. I'm bringing *real* champagne."

"They must be having a *real* little party. Leo and Lauren are going, too. Grandma Newton went out with Royce Dent a little while ago. She still drives during the day, but she doesn't like to drive at night. I think the Joneses are invited, as well." Light auburn hair fell down her back as she looked at the sky. "It appears the rain might hold off."

"It might snow instead." Mac thought Tipper was just trying to be sneaky, but he didn't say so. Rather, he said, "Well, since we're both invited, why don't we use just one car?"

Sunny looked at the three platters in her trunk. "Yours or mine?" she asked.

"Chambry's already loaded, too. I'll drive down here and transfer the food. Agreeable?"

"Sure. Will you be too drunk to drive us back?"

"I doubt it. I don't normally get intoxicated."

"It doesn't take much of Tipper's moonshine to get one intoxicated."

"Three cups, max."

Sunny laughed. "One for me."

"If you think I'm too drunk, you can drive. And if we're both too drunk, Betsy can drive us home."

Both laughed. Sunny looked at the platters. "There's no reason for you to drive down here if you can carry a couple of platters."

"Pass 'em over."

Laden with food, they walked back to Mac's car and he stowed the platters in the trunk with the iced champagne. Sunny got into the passenger's seat and Chambry quipped, "Hey! Are you going to Uncle Tipper's, too?"

"I am. Your daddy suggested we take one car."

"That's a good idea." Chambry grinned. "I think that might have been Uncle Tipper's plan."

"What?"

"Never mind. My lips are sealed." He ran his fingers across his lips.

Mac got in. "Mac," said Sunny, "is Tipper trying to match us up?"

"Why?"

"He's devilish enough. Is it just coincidence we were leaving at the same time?"

"I didn't know you were going, but when I saw you packing food, I figured as much."

"Still, he couldn't have known we'd leave at the same time."

"No, he couldn't without a little help like *stalling*." Mac looked over his shoulder at Chambry. The child shrugged. Mac smirked at the boy. "Let's go have a good time."

Sunny agreed. "All right."

Tipper's small house was crowded even with the guests he invited spending much time outside. The bonfire he built offered both warmth and space. The ladies had prepared a feast of fried chicken, potato salad, roasted corn, boiled peanuts, deviled eggs, tuna sandwiches, hot biscuits, venison sausage, snickerdoodles, and fudge.

Tipper brought out six bottles of his moonshine and announced, "The first six bottles off the production line. I sent Ron the second six, but I told him they were the first. Shall we test my product?"

"Yes, we shall. I want peach," said Mac passing his cup. Cups were filled, and the tasting began.

"I have apple. Let me taste yours," Sunny said to Mac. They sipped each other's.

Leo said, "Tipper, the fruit was a great idea. It takes some of the burn out. This is good."

"Wait 'til you eat the fruit," joked Tipper.

They ate and drank, and Mac and Tipper picked and sang. Sunny and Jessica lent their voices to a few songs, and they got the children to sing. Shortly before midnight, Jessica and Tipper shot the fireworks she had bought. The children squealed with delight. It was the first time the Campbell children and the Jones children had experienced fireworks.

Mac asked discreetly, "No Alain?"

"I invited him," said Tipper.

As Jessica announced two minutes until midnight, Mac popped the cork on the champagne and filled each adult's cup. The children got cups of cider, although it was hard as well, just less hard.

At midnight, Tipper lit a round of Roman candles. They toasted the New Year and drank champagne. Leo kissed Lauren. Gator kissed Sherry. Tipper kissed Jessica. Laughingly, Royce Dent kissed Grandma Newton on the cheek. Chambry poked Mac.

"What?"

"Kiss Miss Bankston."

"What?" Sunny and Mac said simultaneously.

"Oh, come on! Just a little kiss. Not like Uncle Tipper or Uncle Gator. They haven't stopped yet. Ugh!"

Mac and Sunny could not help but laugh. Mac leaned down and pecked Sunny on the lips. "Happy New Year, Sunny." He chuckled before he gave Chambry a noogie.

Sunny returned the kiss softly. "Happy New Year, Mac."

25

Outbreak

School got back into swing the first Monday after the New Year. On Thursday, Sunny came into the clinic.

"Sunny," said Mac, "are you sick?"

"No, I'm fine. I have a favor to ask."

"What?"

"Abner Peacock hasn't come back to school since Christmas. He didn't miss a day before. I'm worried about him. Will you go with me to check on the family? You know, Ebenezer Peacock is one of those single fathers with several children under seven."

"Of course, I'll go with you. Do you want to go now? We're not busy. Jess can handle the clinic."

"I'd greatly appreciate it."

"Jess," Mac turned to his stepsister and nurse. "Hold down the fort."

"You got it, Mac. Go already."

The Peacocks lived even farther from town than either Tipper or the Joneses. Like Tipper, Ebenezer was a moonshiner, but he was hesitant to come to work with Tipper, unlike the other five who were comfortable with the assured income and lack of risk. Ebenezer's wife, Daisy, had been Grandma Newton's last delivery. The baby had lived, but Daisy had died. The baby girl was the youngest of six, five older brothers. Abner, the eldest, was seven.

There was no activity about the house as Mac and Sunny arrived. The still, visible to the side of the shack, did not rumble in production. Mac touched Sunny's hand. "Stay in the car."

"Why?"

"Trust me. If I need you, I'll call you."

Mac walked carefully up the steps that needed to be replaced. Pieces of an old catalogue flapped against his ankles as he approached the door. He knocked on the flimsy plywood, cracked and weathered gray. "Eb!" he called. "It's Mac Reardon. Let me in."

The door cracked. Ezekiel Peacock, three, sucking his thumb, reached up for Mac. Mac picked up the child. He was burning up with fever. Mac walked inside. He heard deep, rumbling coughing, so much like he had heard from his father the night he died, but in the higher pitch of a child. He shivered at the memory. He followed the sound. The three-room building smelled of filth. Mac wrinkled his nose. The stench stung his eyes.

Abner lay on a pallet near a dying fire. Mac knelt by the boy. He, too, had a high temperature. Mac set little Zeke beside his brother. "Sit right here," he told the child.

Mac walked through the house and found the other family members. Ebenezer was stiff. He had obviously been dead a few days. Baby Eve was also dead, as were the other three boys. "Oh, God!" Mac choked.

Dr. Reardon did not have time to weep. He had two very sick little boys to attend. He looked around the little three-room shack. Mac found the cleanest quilt he could find, bundled Zeke into it, and carried him to the car. He laid the little boy on the back seat.

"Mac?" Sunny asked.

"Zeke and Abner are alive but very sick."

"The others?"

"Dead several days, I think. I don't know what it is yet. Influenza maybe." He rubbed his furrowed brow. "Abner has a bad cough. Let me get him. We'll worry about the others after I make a call. Have any other students been out?"

"Several, but not the whole week."

"We'll check on them. What about the Joneses?"

"No. They've been there."

"I want to check on them anyway. Have they been clean?"

"Yes."

"Good. Let me get Abner." He stopped. "Do you have that scented hanky with you?"

"Is it that bad in there?"

Mac nodded, his face drawn into a grimace. Sunny fished her handkerchief from her purse and handed it to the man. He inhaled the fragrance of gardenias several times before returning to the house.

Back inside, Mac wrapped Abner in the quilt he lay on and placed him beside his brother. He drove them to the clinic.

When they got there, Sunny readily picked up the smaller boy to carry him in. "Sunny!" Mac scolded.

She shook her head at Mac. "I'm already exposed to whatever it is."

He nodded. "Thanks. Take him to one of the overnight rooms. I'll take Abner to the other. He's sicker than Zeke. I'll send Jess to you."

It was evident Abner had pneumonia, but it was a secondary infection. The doctor swabbed Abner's nasal passage and drew some blood and some fluid from the child's lungs. Mac prayed the pneumonia was bacterial because he could only treat the symptoms of viral pneumonia. He started an I.V. with antibiotics and gave the child an injection of ibuprofen. Through every procedure, Abner hardly flinched. As Mac started oxygen, Abner coughed and whispered, "Dr. Mac?"

"Yes, Abner. You're at the clinic."

"We all sick. Pa is real sick. He don't even move."

"I'm taking care of you now. Can you tell me who got sick first?"

"Pa. I stayed home from school to help when the other kids got sick. Everybody but Zeke was sick."

Mac stroked the boy's hair. "I've got you now. Zeke's next door."

"Is he sick?"

"Yeah."

"Dr. Mac, is Pa dead?"

"Yeah."

"Evie?"

"Yeah."

"She quit cryin'. Is it jest me and Zeke?"

"Yeah."

"I don't wanna die, Dr. Mac." Two silent tears spilled from the child's sapphire blue eyes.

"I'm doing my best. Don't cry. It'll make you feel worse."

"I'm scared."

"I know you are. You rest. The medicine should help. I need to check on Zeke."

Outside the door, the doctor drew a ragged breath to keep from crying himself. He stepped next door. Jessica had already swabbed, drawn blood, and started an I.V. while Sunny held the boy's hand. Jessica looked at Mac. "I gave him ibuprofen. Is it viral?"

"I don't know yet. I gotta check the blood. How high was his temp?"

"One-oh-three point nine."

"Abner's was one-oh-three point three. I went ahead and gave him penicillin."

Mac ran some tests. He came back in. "It appears to be related to the flu, but I've never seen this strain."

Mac called the county coroner. The bodies would have to be autopsied. Then, he called the closest hospital in Wilmington and learned there had been several cases of this new flu. Mac questioned Abner again and learned Eb had gone into the city just before Christmas and got sick New Year's.

When school let out for the day, Mac left the two boys with Jessica. He had to check on the Joneses. When he drove up, Gator greeted him, "I ain't too clean right now, Mac. I been workin', but I'll bathe before I go to bed."

"That's acceptable," said Mac. "I just wanted to check on y'all. The Peacocks have been really sick. Only Zeke and Abner are alive."

"What's the matter?"

"Some kind of new flu. Since y'all are so far out, I just wanted to check on you."

"Well, thank you. Come inside. It's cold out here."

Mac went in. He did not recognize the place. It smelled of bleach.

Gator said, "Things are diff'rent. Sherry, she figured if'n we were clean, ever'thing had to be clean."

"She was right. It looks great."

"I put new tickin' on the beds, too," bragged Sherry. "Gator's gonna add a room. We need more space."

"Let me know what I can do to help," Mac offered.

"What else do we need to do to stay healthy?" asked Gator. "I mean, what you told me outside, I don't want here."

"You're doing great. Keep it up. I'll let you know if you need to keep the kids home."

"What happened?" asked Sherry.

"Gator'll tell you." Mac turned to leave.

"Mac," said Gator.

"Yeah, Gator?"

"Thank you for carin'. You were right 'bout other things, too." Gator winked, and Sherry blushed.

"I'm glad. I gotta get back to two sick little boys. If any of y'all start getting sick, don't wait to come see me."

"Okay. Mac, did you check on Alain?"

Mac sighed. "Will you do that for me? You can even tell him I sent you."

"I will."

Mac got back to the clinic to find two teachers waiting for him. Both were suffering flu-like symptoms. They tested positive for influenza, so Mac gave them Tami-flu and a multi-symptom cold and flu medicine. They went home.

Not long after they left, the county coroner arrived. Mac rubbed his head. "Dr. Benson, it would be better if you picked up the bodies in the morning. There is no electricity out there, and it's pitch black. It'll be cold enough tonight the bodies won't be any worse than they are now."

"Where will I stay tonight?"

"My guest room, I suppose." Mac walked outside with the man and pointed out his house. "Last house on the right. It's not locked. There are sandwich makings in the refrigerator. The guest room is the only one downstairs."

Back inside, Mac sent Jessica home. "You get the graveyard shift. Come back about midnight. I'll be back at six. Tuck Chambry in for me."

"You sound worried."

"I am. I'm afraid this is just the beginning of an outbreak."

The next morning Mac's good news was Abner's pneumonia was bacterial. The bad news was Tipper brought Betsy and Ina into the clinic. Both were positive for the flu. Mac put them in two of the remaining beds and gave Tipper instructions. "Bring the other two girls into town and stay either at my house or at Papa's."

"How would that look?"

"Frankly, I don't give a damn. Leave the girls with Jess, and you stay with me. I want you close."

"Laurie's at Preacher Tomlin's now. Callie's at school."

"Go get some clothes and stay."

"Why are they sick, Mac?"

"Didn't they go to the city with Jess to get the fireworks?"

"Yeah."

"Eb went to the city. So, did the two teachers. It started in the city." Mac got a very worried look on his face.

"Mac, what's wrong?"

"Go. Do what I said. Talk to me when you get back."

Tipper nodded. Mac went into Abner's room. The little boy still coughed, but his temperature was lower. Mac took his hand, and the child woke up. "Dr. Mac?"

"Hey. You're doing better. Abner, where did your pa eat in the city? Why did he go?"

"A hamburger place. He brought us some hamburgers and some cardboard top hats and light-up bowties to play with. He went to get Christmas gifts. He bought us all some new clothes."

"Thank you. Rest. I'll be back."

Mac went to Betsy's room. The child looked scared. "Uncle Mac?"

"It's all right. Don't wiggle so much, or you'll pull your I.V. out." Mac took Betsy's temperature. "It's come down a little. Let the medicine work. Betsy, where did y'all eat when you were in the city?"

"The name was Best Burger."

"Thank you. Go to sleep." Mac kissed Betsy on the head.

The coroner came in. "Dr. Reardon, I have the bodies. I need you to sign this form."

"Of course." Mac signed. "Dr. Benson, will you stay here for a few minutes? I need to check on two patients at home, but my nurse won't be back until noon. It'll only take a few minutes. They live down the street."

"I suppose I can stay."

"Thank you."

Mac checked on Mrs. Gibbs and Mrs. Morris, both retired, widowed teachers who came to Possum Holler. They shared a house in town. They were resting and feeling better they said. They, too, told Mac they had shopped in the city before Christmas, but they had eaten in the food court at the mall.

Mac returned to the clinic and saw the coroner off. Then, he got the number for the customer service center at the mall and the Best Burger in Wilmington, the closest city where all his patients had either shopped and eaten or had a relative to shop and eat. He spoke with the managers at both places. They confirmed a number of employees with the flu. The manager at the Best Burger where he and Chambry had stopped when they purchased the champagne for Tipper's New Year's Eve party told him half his employees had been out with the flu during the last month and one of them had died.

"Good God!" exclaimed Mac. Then, he called the hospital in Wilmington. They had had massive numbers of a new strain of flu rather than just several as he had been told before, only a few cases requiring hospitalization. The cases had come from all around the city, and the surrounding areas. Mac informed them it had spread as far as Possum Holler.

"It won't spread from here because my clinic comes through a grant with the department of health. I can quarantine this place."

Mac hung up and called the department of health. They told him to keep them abreast of developments and if the situation worsened, he *might* be granted a quarantine.

Mac slammed the phone down. "If they volunteer to stay home, there's not a damned thing you can do about it. Why wait until hundreds die?"

Tipper got back to town for an extended stay. By Sunday, Mac was using both exam tables and the last bed. Grandma Newton was one of his new patients.

He cornered Sunny on the church steps. "I need to talk to you."

"What's wrong?"

"I have no more beds. This is just starting. I want you to cancel school until it passes."

"Is it that bad?"

He took her to the far end of the porch that stretched across the front of the church. "It will be. In addition, I might need to clear your cafeteria and make pallets to use as hospital beds."

"You're serious." She reached up and twirled her ponytail around her fingers.

"Yes."

"All right. I'll get Leo to announce it."

"I need to speak to the congregation, too. I need a voluntary quarantine."

"Oh, Mac! You're scaring me."

"What I'm seeing scares me."

Mac made his plea to the residents of Possum Holler from the pulpit. "I can't make you stay home yet. If it gets much worse, I can. I hope I don't have to take that action, but I will if I have to. Your voluntary cooperation would be better."

Leo dismissed church and the people ate quietly and talked among themselves. Mac caught Gator. "Mac, we all fine."

"I know you are. Stay home. Don't come into town unless somebody gets sick. Where did you eat the last time you went to the city?"

"I got a hamburger at the Best Burger. Are people gettin' sick from eatin' hamburgers, Mac?"

"No. Someone in the city had the flu. They exposed a lot of folks, maybe before they even realized they were actually sick. Everyone who's gotten sick either went to the city or was around someone who did."

"You sure?"

"Yes."

"We'll go home right now."

"You can eat first."

"Mac, why you so worried 'bout my fam'ly?"

Mac looked incredulous. "Gator, you're *my* family."

"That's the truth, ain't it?" He rubbed his hand across his balding pate. "I wudn't thinkin' 'bout our mas bein' sisters."

"I was."

"I'm glad. Mac, I ain't forgot The Three, well Four, Musketeers."

"Me either, Gator. Did you get out to Alain's place?"

"Yeah. They ain't been to the city since early December when I met Alain the day Sherry come to see you."

"Good. Let them know not to go."

"I'll do that, Mac."

Chambry came up and took Mac's hand. "Hey, buddy!" Mac picked him up. "I've missed you."

"I miss you. Daddy, I don't feel good."

Mac touched Chambry's face and looked terror-stricken.

"Is he sick, Mac?" asked Gator.

Mac nodded and almost started to cry. "Don't go home Gator. You've been exposed now. Just go stay at my house."

"I gotta get clothes."

"Then leave everybody and go. Yell at Alain from your truck. Don't breathe on any of them. Stay at my house. I think you'll figure out how to use the running water and appliances. You're smart."

"Jest not educated." Gator rubbed Chambry's head. "He'll be fine, Mac. Go take care of 'im. I'll tell Preacher Tomlin."

Mac took Chambry to the clinic and swabbed him. The doctor knew without the test, but he had to be sure. "Come here," he said to Chambry. "I need you to take this medicine."

"Am I gonna get real sick?"

"Hopefully not, if you take this medicine right now."

Chambry obediently took the Tami-flu. Mac picked up his son. "I don't know where to put you. All my beds are full."

"I'm not very big. I can sleep in a chair."

The door to the clinic opened as Sunny came in. "Mac, I saw you leave."

"He's sick. I have no more beds, Sunny."

"Give him here. I have a nice, comfy couch." To Chambry she said, "Guess what else I have."

"What?" asked Chambry.

"A TV and a DVD player with lots of movies."

"Are you sure?" asked Mac.

"I won't be in school. This is a way I can help."

"Chambry, will you go with Miss Bankston? I'll come down later."

"Yes, sir."

"Sunny, do you have Tylenol or ibuprofen he can take?"

"Liquid?"

"Yeah, or chewable."

"No."

"Daddy, I can swallow a pill."

"Can you?"

Chambry nodded.

"I have pills," assured Sunny.

"Okay. Do you have a thermometer?"

"Yes."

"If his fever goes up, bring him back. If he starts coughing, bring him back."

"I'll take care of him, Mac."

Sunny took Chambry on her hip as he laid his head on her shoulder. "Let's go, sweetie. I have ice cream, too, if you want some."

Mac sat down at his desk after Sunny left with Chambry. "I don't wana do this," he said aloud before he called Felicia.

"Do I need to come there?" Felicia asked in tears.

"No! Absolutely not! I don't want you to get sick, too."

"He caught this at a Best Burger?"

"Not necessarily. We shopped a little, but the manager at the restaurant said one of his employees died."

"You sound tired. How bad is it?"

"I gave him the Tami-flu immediately. Abner and Zeke are getting better, and they didn't have the Tami-flu. Betsy's better, too."

"Grandma Newton?"

"She's not responding as fast."

"Mac, I'm scared."

"Me, too, Felicia, and not just for Chambry."

"Call me every day."

"I promise."

By morning, five more cases came in. Those who lived in town, Mac treated and sent home. He made two pallets in the waiting room temporarily for the two who did not live close.

After his last talk with the department of health, Mac felt he would get little help. He picked up the phone and called a person he thought would help.

26
A Helping Hand

A friendly voice said, "Hello?"

"Dr. Morgenstern, this is Mac Reardon."

"Dr. Reardon, have you decided to come back to Chicago and work for me? I really appreciated your guest lecture."

"No, actually I was hoping either you or your emissary might come to Possum Holler."

"Mac, what's wrong?"

"Possum Holler is in the middle of an epidemic. Maybe a dozen illnesses and four deaths are not an epidemic in Chicago, but when the population is only around five hundred, that is epidemic proportion. The department of health doesn't seem predisposed to offer assistance, and my nurse and I are stressed to the breaking point. Joseph, Chambry is sick, too. Now, I'm a frightened father."

"Tell me everything, Mac. Exactly what do you need?"

"Manpower, beds, more medicine. I've arranged to use the school cafeteria as a makeshift hospital ward." Mac told Joseph the whole scenario.

Morgenstern listened to every word before he offered comment. "First, impose your quarantine. If you have to lie, do it. There have been a few cases of this new strain in Chicago, no deaths yet, that I've heard. Second, I'm sending you four interns and as many supplies as I can get. For beds, I'll send air mattresses and compressors. Third, don't send anyone else home. As a matter of fact, get those five back under one roof. As for Chambry, go ahead and start an I.V. just in case. If you want to let him stay with Miss Bankston, check on him regularly. I wish his mother was there for him, but she doesn't need to come in. Mac, is treatment working?"

"The kids seem to be responding. The older ladies, not so well." Mac sighed deeply. "I can't bring myself to tell Tipper Miss Ina has developed pneumonia."

"Okay. Put all your pneumonia cases together. When you have someone recover, set up a step-down center, just in case of relapse. Use the church. From what you've said, your people can sack out on the pews. To help the folks with pneumonia, give them a shot of Decadron."

"What about Menniere's as a possible side affect?"

"The benefits outweigh the risks. Mac, I wish I could come myself, but I have a huge hospital to run." The intercom alerted a code blue in the background as Morgenstern continued. "Expect four interns and supplies in forty-eight hours. It's the biggest helping hand I can give."

"It's more than anyone else has offered. I'm much obliged."

"Mac, keep nagging the department of health. Remember, 'the squeaky wheel gets the oil.'"

"Will do. Thanks again."

The doctor immediately called the department of health again. Officials told if he felt the quarantine necessary to put it in place but offered little more assistance.

Mac made the rounds of his in-house patients before he got the key for the school from Sunny. Chambry slept, but Mac woke him to start an I.V. Chambry cried, and Mac held him on his lap for a while. He whispered, "Go back to sleep. I have to go take care of some other people now. I love you."

Sunny took Chambry onto her lap. "We'll be fine, Mac," she assured. Chambry laid his head on her shoulder. "Go on. I've got him. I'll take care of him, Mac."

"Thank you, Sunny."

As the stressed doctor opened the school cafeteria, he felt a hand on each shoulder. Tipper and Gator flanked him. "You'll need help moving the furniture," said Tipper. "Actually, Gator and I can do this. You take care of the sick."

"Whatcha want us to do, Mac?" asked Gator.

"Push all the tables against the wall. Stack the chairs. Scrub everything down with bleach. I need to get the ones I sent home over here. We need to get blankets and pillows to make temporary beds. My friend, Dr. Morgenstern, is sending air mattresses and four doctors."

"You think there's gonna be more, don't ya?" asked Gator.

"Yes."

Tipper asked, "Mac, how are Ma and Betsy? Ma sounds bad, and she's got oxygen."

"She has pneumonia, Tipper. Betsy's getting better."

"Are we gonna lose Ma?"

The two men locked eyes, remembering Ander Reardon's untimely death.

"I'm doing everything I can." Mac swallowed hard.

"I know you are. Grandma Newton says you need to use a camphor poultice."

"It won't hurt." Mac rubbed his chin in thought. "As a matter of fact, Vicks VapoRub won't hurt either. Tipper and Gator, get your kids to get every bit Royce has in the store and knock on every door in town to collect more—Vicks, mentholatum, whatever."

"You got it. I'll get Callie on it," assured Tipper as he ran to the Tomlins' to get Callie to gather the children for a significant mission.

Mac grabbed one end of a table. "You go take care o' the sick folks," encouraged Gator. "I got this. Tipper'll be right back."

"You don't know how much I appreciate it," said Mac modestly.

Mac first checked on the three people he had sent home that day. He told them he wanted them to move to the school hospital when it was ready. They groaned but agreed to go and bring their own blankets and pillows.

He then checked on Mrs. Gibbs and Mrs. Morris. Although they were taking the medication Mac had given them, both older ladies had developed pneumonia. "Ladies," Mac said, "as soon as Tipper and Gator get the school ready, I'll be moving you to the clinic." Mac opened his bag. "Is either of you allergic to penicillin?"

Neither was allergic, so Mac gave them injections. He walked outside as snowflakes began to fall. "What now?" he muttered bitterly. His question was answered when he walked into the clinic.

Jess met Mac at the door in tears. He demanded, "What is it?"

"She's gone, Mac. She just closed her eyes and went to sleep."

"Miss Ina?"

"Grandma Newton."

"How? She didn't even have pneumonia." Mac rushed into her room. He took the old woman's hand as tears smarted his eyes. "Grandma, I need you."

Jessica squeezed his shoulder. "Mac, I'll get Papa. She was ninety-seven. Her body couldn't handle this illness. Her fever never came down. Put whatever you want on her death certificate.

"The coroner called while you were gone. Cause of death— asphyxiation due to pneumonia as a secondary infection stemming from influenza."

"But she didn't have pneumonia."

"Mac, I'm sure she had a stroke from the fever. She wouldn't have wanted to be an invalid."

"Oh, I know you're right, but I'm feeling my loss." He swiped the tears from his cheeks. "I'm so tired, Jess. I know you are, too. Joseph Morgenstern is sending supplies and four interns."

"That's good. We need a helping hand."

Mac rubbed his hands across his face. He had dark circles under his eyes. He breathed hard to cope with the loss of his great-great-grandmother. He informed, "Tipper and Gator are getting the school ready. Sunny has been amazing. I'm glad she's watching Chambry. She's good with kids."

"Mac, I'm worried I'll be giving the same news to Tipper." Jessica looked as tired as Mac. "Miss Ina isn't doing well."

"Give her an injection of Decadron. How are the kids?"

"Betsy's doing well. She responded fast to the Tami-flu. Zeke's temperature is down, one hundred-point-four. Abner's lungs sound better, and his white count is down. His temperature is down a little, one-oh-two point four. The McAdams twins are burning up even with ibuprofen and Tylenol alternating. They're so little."

Tipper came in shivering. "It's snowing," he informed

"I hope that doesn't delay the help," sighed the exhausted doctor.

"Mac, you're worn out. You need to rest," worried Tipper.

Stubbornly, Mac insisted, "I'll be fine. Is the school ready?"

"Yes."

"Okay. Jess, get Papa to take care of Grandma."

"What happened?" asked Tipper.

"She's gone."

"Oh!" Tipper's voice caught.

"We can mourn later. We need to move Zeke, Betsy, and the twins to the school." He started out and paused. "No, take Betsy to Sunny."

"Why?" asked Tipper.

"She's family. Sunny's taking care of my family."

"Okay."

"We need to bring Mrs. Gibbs and Mrs. Morris here."

"Gotcha. I'll take Betsy now."

Jess said, "I'll get Papa now. We need to move Grandma before we bring others in."

By nightfall, all the patients were situated, and Mac had arranged with Constable Hill to block the road—No one out, no one in, except the medical team when they arrived. Mail would be exchanged at the roadblock.

Six more cases came in the next day, and the twins were returned to the clinic when they developed pneumonia. Mac placed almost everyone under house quarantine. However, Tipper and Gator refused to leave.

Tipper insisted, "Show me what to do, Mac. You and Jess need some sleep, at least a few hours."

Mac nodded. "Jess, you go for four hours. Come back, and I'll go. I'll show Tipper and Gator everything to do."

"Okay," agreed Jessica without argument.

She went home for a short rest. While she was gone, Mac showed Tipper and Gator how to change I.V. bags, take temperatures, and inject medication into the I.V. He measured the medications for each person and told Tipper what time to administer each. Gator watched everything.

Gator said, "I can change them bags and take temperatures, but I don't wanna give nobody shots."

"You can give the oral medications," said Mac. "I know you can read."

"Yeah."

"I've written the time and the person's name on each cup with oral medication. I've already measured out what you need. All you have to do is give the person the pills and some juice or water."

"Okay. I can do that."

"Gator, you go to the school and stay with those patients. Take their medications with you. Tipper, you stay here with the pneumonia patients. They're the ones who have to have medication injected. Y'all will need to take breaks, too. We'll work to keep three people at all times, at least one trained medical person. Jess and I will go back and forth."

Jessica got back, and Mac went to Sunny's. He walked in without knocking. Sunny slept on the couch and jumped straight up when her door opened. "Mac, what's wrong?"

"I need to sleep. Where are the kids?"

"It worked great to have Betsy's I.V. in her right arm and Chambry's in his left. They're sharing my bed."

"Good idea. Grandma Newton passed."

Her hand flew to her throat, and tears flowed unbidden. "I'm so sorry."

"I'll cry later. May I sleep on your couch for four hours?"

She composed herself. "When did you last eat?"

"At the church."

"Mac, that's has been two full days. You can sleep after a sandwich. Don't argue, or I'll force feed you."

"I'm too tired to argue." He sank onto her sofa.

Sunny hurriedly made a peanut butter and jelly sandwich, grabbed a box of raisins, and poured a glass of milk.

Mac had his head back on the couch when she walked in. "Dr. Reardon?"

"I'm not asleep yet."

"Eat."

Mac ate the food gratefully before he passed out on the couch. "Four hours, no more," he mumbled.

Sunny woke Mac. "Wake up. It's been four hours."

Mac groaned, "Oh!"

"I have good news."

"Please give me some."

"Two kids have no fever."

"That *is* good news. Give them the medicine anyway for at least twenty-four more hours."

"Yes, doctor. They're sleeping tough."

"I need to get back."

"I've packed a basket of food for our healers."

"Thank you, Sunny. You are a little ray of sunshine, aren't you?"

A cloud passed over Sunny's face. "Just don't call me a ray of hope, okay?" Her voiced sounded choked.

"Okay, Sunshine."

Sunny smiled sadly and shook her head. "You okay?" he asked, reaching out to caress her arm.

"Yeah. Just both a good and bad memory."

"Let me know if anything changes with the kids."

"I will."

Mac took the basket of food and got back to work. On his return, he found five new cases. He began to watch the road. Luckily, Possum Holler had only received a light snow.

Finally, two delivery trucks rumbled into town. Possum Holler's homegrown healer rejoiced.

Doctors Bingham, Henley, Rockford, and Saik, along with two unexpected nurses, Mangum and Tarter, arrived with two trucks, one of supplies, and one of medicine.

For the next week, new cases came in. Twelve cases resulted in pneumonia in addition to the six Mac already had. Only two pneumonia cases survived, Abner Peacock and Ina Campbell.

The young doctors and nurses worked diligently with only short periods of rest. Dr. Rockford even accompanied Gator to visit families in the outlying areas, and the young intern seemed to not be able to take his eyes off Glenda Richter when they went to the Richter place. Not a single Richter became ill.

At long last, three days passed without a new case. Mac took the opportunity to go to Sunny's and sleep.

She came into the living room where he slept and mumbled in his sleep. She touched him to rouse him from an apparent nightmare.

"Oh, my God!" she exclaimed when her hand brushed his forehead.

Mac opened his eyes and moaned, "Oh, my head," and started to get up.

"Don't move!" ordered Sunny. "You're burning up, Mac. I'm going to take care of you. I'll be right back."

Sunny sprinted to the clinic and burst through the door. "Jessica! It's Mac. He's sick."

"Of course, he is. He's totally exhausted. He's made us rest and pushed himself too far."

"Bring whatever he needs to him. I'm not letting him move."

Jessica looked at Sunny but said nothing. She gathered the supplies she would need. Jessica swabbed Mac and started treatment. "Well," she jibed, "you got Sunny's attention. Was that your intent?"

"What?"

"She refuses to let you leave. She's going take care of you. Don't make her sick."

Sunny came in with chicken soup. "I'm not going to get sick, Jess. Maybe those flu vaccinations over the years have helped."

"Maybe. I'm not sick, but neither are a lot of others—none of the Richters."

"I've got this one under control, Jess. If I need you, I'll get you. You take care of the rest."

"I appreciate the assistance. Mac'll probably be a bigger pain than all the others put together."

"Leave me a sedative just in case I need it."

Jessica Langston left MacKenzie Reardon in the capable helping hands of Sunny Bankston.

27

Possum Holler, Population, 487

"**MacKenzie** Reardon!" snapped Sunny. "If you don't think I'll inject this sedative into your I.V., try to pull it out or get off that couch one more time, and you'll see. I might be five-foot-nothing, but I can be a formidable force if I have to be. Care to test me?"

Mac lay back and whined, "Sunny, I have patients."

"Right now, you *are* a patient. Now, hush. Open."

"You are *not* going to feed me."

"Then, here. Eat. It's chicken noodle soup. You probably couldn't swallow anything else or keep it down. You've been throwing up for two days, and your fever got up to one-oh-three. You were delirious. I've given you ibuprofen every six hours with Tylenol every six hours, one or the other every three hours. I've given you Phenergan and stuck your butt, literally, with penicillin. It's nice to see you're feeling better, but if you fight with me, I'll knock you out with this little guy right here." She held up a filled syringe. "Jess assures me it's strong enough to put a horse down."

Mac took the bowl. "Nurse Bankston, I'm thirsty."

"Don't get demanding either." Sunny went to the kitchen and returned with a glass of ginger ale. Mac shakily ate the soup.

"It's good," he said. "Did you make it?"

"Campbell's—from a can."

Mac tried to laugh and started coughing. When he recovered, he asked. "Do I have pneumonia?"

"No, bronchitis and strep. You'll live."

"Thanks a million. Where's Chambry?"

"Leo's. He was too worried about you. I made him go because he was too weak to be emotionally distressed. He was afraid you would die. I assured him I didn't let him die, and I wouldn't let you die. He trusted me. I'm glad to see I didn't let him down." She popped a hand to her hip.

"Me, too. I *am* feeling better."

"But you're not well. You still have a low-grade temp. Until it's gone, you're stuck here with me. It's just as well; there's a foot of snow on the ground."

"How are my patients?"

"No more have died, and no new cases have come in."

"What are we down to?"

"Four hundred eighty-seven."

"That's five less than my last count."

"Yes. Um. Leo went all the way out to the Springers'."

"All of them?"

"I'm afraid so."

He ate a few bites of soup before he asked, "The Richters?"

"Not a single illness."

"I guess that's what they get for isolating themselves."

"I suppose, but you should know, several of them came into town to help care for the sick and to help Leo bury the dead— Glenda has taken Dr. Rockford by storm."

He sipped ginger ale. "I don't even know what day it is."

"February twenty-third."

"Tipper missed his wedding."

"Well, at least they're still alive and can plan again."

"True."

"How's your throat?"

"I can swallow the soup."

"That's an improvement."

"Will you do me a favor?"

"Another one?" She arched her eyebrows, accentuating a few freckles on her nose.

Mac laughed softly. "Yes. Will you call Felicia? I promised to call her every day about Chambry's progress. I didn't count on getting sick myself. The number's on my rolodex in my office."

"Promise not to sneak out?"

"I promise." He ate another bite of soup.

Sunny went to Mac's office and dialed Felicia.

"Mac!" Felicia answered frantically. "I'm coming whether you like it or not!"

"It's Sunny, Felicia, but relax. Chambry's just fine. Mac got sick, too. That's why he couldn't call."

"Is *he* all right?"

"Yes. I took care of him, too."

"Thank you."

"You're welcome."

"Sunny, our divorce is final."

"And?"

"Well, you sound attached."

"Don't be ridiculous! Mac's a friend—end of story. New topic—Ron."

"What about him?"

"You're single."

"Not exactly."

Sunny sat on the edge of Mac's desk. "What does that mean?"

"We're married, but don't tell anybody. We'll break the news when we come. Grandma Newton will have a fit, but he did carry me over the threshold."

"Felicia, when was the last time you talked to Mac?"

"Days. I was worried sick. Our conversations were maybe five minutes. He just gave me updates on Chambry. Why?"

"Grandma Newton died."

"Oh! No!" There was a genuine catch in her voice. "What about Tipper's family?"

"They pulled through, but Tipper and Jess have postponed their wedding indefinitely."

"That's a shame."

"Yeah. Population is down to four hundred eighty-seven."

"Good grief!"

"I guess we could count the possums."

Both women laughed. "Sunny, let me know when it'll be safe to come."

"I will."

"Thank you for taking care of Chambry and Mac."

"Not a problem. Well, actually, Mac has been a pain in the butt."

Felicia laughed. "They say doctors make horrible patients."

Mac allowed himself to be "cared for" only a couple of more days. He insisted he had no fever, but he had a lot of work to do.

"You are one stubborn human being, Mac Reardon!" chastised Sunny.

"Look who's talking. I think you might be a little sadistic. I think you enjoyed jabbing me with needles."

"I only jabbed you once."

"And you enjoyed it."

"I'm gonna jab you with something else if you don't shut up." She held up her fist.

"Feisty, aren't you?"

"Absolutely. I have two older sisters and one older brother. I had to learn to defend myself."

"Well, Miss Ali, I'm going to work, but, first, I'm gonna see my son. We can fight another time." He waved and left.

Mac walked into the Tomlins', and Chambry dashed to him. "Daddy!"

Mac picked him up and held him close. "Oh, I've missed you."

"You got sick, too. Miss Bankston told you to shut up or she would slap you. You were talking nonsense."

"My fever was high. Did she slap me?"

"No, she put something in your I.V., and you went to sleep. That's when she made me come to Papaw's. I started to argue, but she put her finger in my face and said, 'You will not argue with me. You might be Mac Reardon's son, but I won't let you be as stubborn as he is.'"

Mac hooted. "I bet she did. I think Sunny can have solar flares."

"Are you well, Daddy?"

"Yes, but I need to check on the other patients."

"The other doctors and nurses have been doing a good job."

"I'm glad to hear it. Maybe this can count as one of their rotations."

When Mac checked on his patients, he found the school clear. The few remaining patients were at the clinic.

Mac talked with the doctors from Chicago. They were ready to head back. Young Dr. Jason Rockford who looked as if he were still in high school asked, "Dr. Reardon, how would you feel about a resident here?"

"It wouldn't pay a thing."

"I'm not looking for money. I like it here." He gave a mysterious smile.

Mac nodded. "Discuss it with Morgenstern and call me."

By Sunday, all patients were discharged. Leo used the service as a memorial to all those who had died. There had been no time for individual services. The dead had been buried quickly so the sick and living could be tended. There were fewer in the community, but many things were about to change.

28

Road to Recovery

Mac kept the quarantine in place for two more weeks while he checked with the hospital in Wilmington. After the initial outbreak, they had only seen a dozen cases. Therefore, Mac told Constable Hill to lift the quarantine.

The very next day, six dump trucks, a tar layer, a steamroller, and a paving crew rolled into town. The townsfolk came out to view the hoopla. The foreman of the crew got out with a clipboard and asked, "Is this Possum Holler?"

"Yes, it is," answered the mayor, Royce Dent, owner of the general store and Tipper's former father-in-law.

"We've been sent to pave Main Street, the intersecting streets, and as far out as we can. Where is Main Street?"

"You're standing on it. Who sent you?"

"Mr. Norton. I'm also supposed to find Mr. Campbell."

Still in town, Tipper stepped forward. "I'm Tipper Campbell."

"I'm supposed to give this to you. It's a wedding gift from Felicia." The man handed Tipper a long cylinder.

"What is it?" asked Tipper.

Mac put his hand on Tipper's shoulder. "House plans."

"She drew us a house?"

"*Designed* you a house."

"There's a difference?"

"Oh, yeah. It bet it's fabulous."

Royce busily discussed paving the roads. As mayor, he was eager to get the work done before the spring rains.

"How far out will you go?" he asked.

"We've been told to do the town and two miles out, more if we have materials."

Royce clapped his hands in delight. "This is wonderful!"

Tipper laughed. "Pa Dent, this is practical. Ron has invested a great deal in my business. Smooth roads equal less damage to the product."

"It *is* good, though," concurred Mac. "This will help us recover faster. Gentlemen, welcome and good luck."

School started back. They had lost several students, but the children were eager to learn. Abner Peacock came to school clean and in new clothes, a pleasant surprise for Sunny for Abner had been one of the children which caused her to keep her scented handkerchief in her bosom.

"You look wonderful, Abner," she greeted him.

"Dr. Mac done it."

"Did what?"

"Me and Zeke are livin' with him."

"Is that so?"

"We ain't got no fam'ly. He took us in like Preacher Tomlin took him in. He told us about when his pa died and how Preacher Tomlin became his papa."

"He's a good, kind man. Go to class."

Sunny marched to the clinic and straight into Mac's office without knocking. "MacKenzie Reardon!"

"What did I do this time?" he said standing from the chair behind his desk.

"Do you plan to take in every orphan that comes along?"

"Oh, Abner told you."

"Yes, he did. Mac, they're not stray puppies."

"No, they're two little boys without a home. What was I supposed to do—send 'em back to their place so they could become the new Richters? Maybe I should've shipped them off to a children's home where they wouldn't know anybody and might get separated." He crossed his arms over his chest. "Oh, wait. I know." He pointed toward her. "*You* wanted them."

Sunny sighed at Mac's anger. "Actually, I probably would've taken them."

"Sunny, they're not stray kittens. What are you gonna do—take in every orphan that comes along?"

"Touché. However, how are you going to bring up three little boys alone?"

"You can help." Mac grinned. "What was it the former First Lady said? 'It takes a village to raise a child.' This is a tight community. We'll pull together to recover."

"Oh, Mac, this might be a long road to recovery." She plopped into the chair where patients would sit to talk to their doctor. "The students missed so much time."

"So, go through the summer." He sat down and leaned back casually in the leather chair Leo had given him as a gift. He swiveled back and forth like a child with a new toy.

"That seems cruel."

"Okay. School now gets out at five until the time is made up."

"Extended hours?" She leaned forward and put her elbows on her knees with her chin on her hands. "Yes, that might work." She sat up. "Thank you. Thirty minutes added to each class in high school. Yes, good idea. We should argue more often."

Mac laughed. "That's very tempting."

"Seriously, how can I help with Abner and Zeke?"

"Preschool." He leaned forward and placed both arms on his desk. "Open a preschool. Use Grandma Newton's house. Get Miss Ina and Sherry Jones to run it. The Jones kids, Chambry, Zeke, Rush, and Laurie. You have a start right there."

"I'd want someone to actually do some instruction. I've lost two teachers as it is. Those left are giving up their planning time, and Leo and I are filling in."

"Miss Ina already has half those children at Papa's."

"You don't want the Joneses to go back to the boonies," she surmised from Mac's pushing Sherry Jones to work at the preschool.

"No, I don't. Gator goes out every day to tend the hogs. The house Mrs. Gibbs and Mrs. Morris shared is bigger than theirs."

"Then, let's give them Grandma Newton's house and use the other one for the preschool. She was Gator's great-great-grandmother also, wasn't she?"

"Yes. Our mothers were sisters. So? You'll do it?" He stood. "You'll open a preschool?"

"I will." She stood. "I'll talk to Miss Ina and Sherry. You talk to Gator."

"Yes, Ma'am." He walked her to the door.

She turned. "How can I help with Abner and Zeke in the meantime?"

Mac shrugged. "Not much way you can. Any ideas on how to get little Zeke to stop wetting the bed?"

"Does he have daytime problems with wetting himself?"

"No. Just night. There's nothing physically wrong with him except a little undernourishment. He looks two instead of three. He's very clingy. He likes to be held a lot."

"Abner likes hugs, too. Eb must have been affectionate."

"Yeah, he was."

"Zeke will grow into not wetting the bed. All I can do, I guess, is help you love them."

"That'll be a big help." Sunny went back to the school.

Mac went home that night to his overflowing residence.

"Mac," said Gator as the children squealed throughout the house, "is the danger past?"

"Yes."

"Then, we need to go home. There are too many people in this house."

"You're half right. There *are* too many people in this house, but don't go back to the sticks."

"My farm's there."

"So, do what you've been doing, but move into Grandma Newton's house. Stay in town."

Gator looked thoughtful. "Did you know Miss Bankston asked Sherry to stay and help Miss Ina with a preschool? What's a preschool?"

"A preschool is a place where children too young for school can go. Sherry and Miss Ina would be taking care of children whose parents can't be home to take care of them during the day, people like me."

"I see." Gator took Sherry's hand as she busily prepared supper. "Sherry, you wanna do it?"

"Would you mind, Gator? I do wanna stay in town. I like havin' a bathtub and a toilet."

"I don't mind. It can be our way to help Possum Holler recover."

Before spring, Possum Holler had paved roads with names, a preschool, a distillery in limited production, another house in progress, a store, the slaughterhouse, a school, a hospital, and another doctor due in the fall. Possum Holler was well on the road to recovery, but could it ever be ready for Felicia's return?

29

A Visit

On the Monday Possum Holler School was to have begun spring break, which was cancelled due to the massive outbreak of influenza and the need to make up time, Felicia and Ron drove into Possum Holler. Chambry bounced out the door, squealing, "Mother!"

For the first time Mac could remember, Felicia picked up Chambry in a real embrace. She soothed his hair back. "You look good. How are you feeling?"

"I'm fine, Mother. I'm not sick anymore. I have two new brothers. They were sick, too. Their whole family died. Grandma Newton died, too."

"Whoa! Whoa! Whoa! Two brothers?" She wheeled around. "Mac!"

"Hello, Felicia."

"Two brothers? Explain."

"Abner and Ezekiel Peacock are living with us."

"Those little urchins?"

"They're not urchins anymore." Mac called over his shoulder back into the house, "Zeke, Abner, come here,"

The two, little platinum-haired, crystal blue-eyed boys came out. Felicia could not deny they looked angelic. Mac said, "Boys, do you remember Chambry's mother?"

"I do," answered Abner. "Hello, Mrs..." Abner looked up at Mac.

Mac asked, "What do we call you these days, Felicia?"

"Miss Felicia will be fine. Mac, are you going to leave us standing on the road?"

The refrain came to Mac's mind. *You be good to her.*

He sighed. "Forgive my manners. Please come in."

Felicia continued to hold Chambry in her arms. Ron looked sheepish as he followed her.

The chant came to Mac's mind. *That Ron, he's not a bad sort.*

Mac caught Ron's arm. "We need to talk."

"Mac, I…"

"Don't apologize. You and Felicia are a better match. That's not what I wanna talk about. I want this said and *never* mentioned again unless it's an emergency. You need to know just in case. Biologically, Chambry is yours. It ends there. He's my son." There was no misunderstanding the resolutions and finality of Mac's tone.

"Agreed." Ron nodded discreetly. "I suspected when I saw him. I would never try to take him from you. You love him, and he loves you. I'll just be his stepfather."

"His what?"

"Felicia and I are married."

"Congratulations."

The sarcasm was not lost on the city man.

"I love her, Mac. I always have."

"I worry more about you, Ron. I hope it works. Honestly."

"Thanks."

"Let's go inside." He moved toward his door.

Ron said, "There's more."

"More?"

"She's pregnant."

"Yours or mine?" Annoyance exuded Mac's demeanor.

"She says mine."

"You think it's mine. What? Should we trade kids?"

Ron sighed. "When it comes, can you do the test? Just so we know. Can you let me raise it as mine just like you're doing Chambry?" Ron seemed so sad. "Mac, I want a child with Felicia. This could be my only chance."

"Some visit, huh?" The doctor plunged his hands into his pockets. He shivered in the cool wind.

"Yeah."

"Ron, I'll do the test. I hope it's yours."

"Mac, for what it's worth, nothing happened while I was here."

"I know. You're not a bad sort. I think we could eventually be friends. What you've done for Tipper is amazing."

"I'll get rich, too. It's not philanthropic."

"Yes, it is. You took a chance on a nobody. I'm sorry it's taking so long."

"Stuff happens." He shrugged. "It'll still pay off."

"Okay. I'm getting cold. Come in."

Inside, Felicia sat on the floor with the three boys, learning to play jacks. "What did you do to her?" whispered Mac.

"It was Possum Holler. Thank you."

The ball got away from her and bounced at Mac's feet. "Having fun?" he asked as she picked up the ball.

"Yes," answered Felicia. "Did Ron tell you our news?"

"He did. Did you tell Chambry?"

"I did."

"Both things?"

"Both things." She stretched her eyes wide to emphasize her stance.

"Well, congratulations on both. I wish you only happiness."

"Thank you, Mac. By the way, where are we going to stay?"

Mac laughed. "I had thought to send you to Tipper's house in the sticks, but his new house isn't ready. I could send you to the Joneses'. They're living in Grandma Newton's house. Maybe you could enjoy a stay in my old home, the one you planned to renovate."

"Mac!"

The chorus came to Mac. *You be good to her.*

Mac laughed again. "Yes, Grandma, I hear you."

"Mac?" said Felicia with a confused expression.

He said, "Chambry, can you sleep with Daddy for a few nights and let Mother and Ron have your room?"

"I suppose," teased Chambry.

"Thank you, sweetheart," said Felicia.

"It'll cost you," said Chambry seriously.

"How so?"

"You have to make spaghetti for me."

"Is that all?"

"Would you like me to think of more?"

"No. I'll make spaghetti for you. Would you like to invite anyone else to eat spaghetti?"

"Like who?" asked the boy.

"Sunny. I'd like to see Sunny. Tipper. I'd like to see them, too." She turned her blue eyes on her ex-husband. "Mac, may we invite them? I don't think they'll judge me harshly."

"Fine. If Papaw and Mamaw come, too," agreed Mac.

"Leo? H-h-he's a preacher, Mac." She squeezed the small rubber ball used for jacks.

"He won't judge you. Remember Jessica, his little skeleton in the closet."

"Just them?"

"No." The doctor crossed his arms over his chest. He enjoyed his ex-wife's discomfiture. "Gator and family."

"That's a crowd."

"Make a lot."

"Oh, all right. Mac, I'm sorry."

"No. You don't belong here. I'm so glad you weren't here for the flu, especially considering your condition."

"I wish Grandma could be here." She brushed hair from her face. "I can't believe I just said that."

"I wish she were here, too."

Mac turned to the boys. "Boys, you have errands. Chambry, go to the Joneses'. Abner, you get Miss Bankston at school where you should be going right now and stop at the clinic to tell Nurse Jess so she can get Tipper. Zeke, you can go to Papaw's. Hop to it!" The boys zipped to their assignments. "Felicia, you remember where the kitchen is, don't you? Ron, let's get your luggage."

Felicia made spaghetti for a crowd. Everyone came. She was as nervous as a cat in a room filled with rocking chairs, but nobody said anything unpleasant to either her or Ron. Mac announced to everyone Ron and Felicia were married and expecting a baby.

The house reverberated with laughter. Tipper and Mac pulled out their instruments and started picking and singing. Felicia shouted, "A square dance! We have to have a square dance! Tipper, you can't call it. You have to dance with Jess."

"I'll call it," volunteered Miss Ina. "Y'all couple up and make some squares. Betsy, play the banjo for me."

Ron protested, "I don't know how."

Two squares formed. Mac danced with Sunny while Tipper danced with Jessica and Gator danced with Sherry. Felicia dragged Ron into their square and laughed at the children's square in which Leo and Lauren participated. Refusing to dance with his sister, Fox Jones danced with Callie Campbell while Abner danced with Lily Jones but scowled the whole time because he wanted to dance with Callie. Chambry grabbed Laurie Campbell with a big grin on his face.

Ron learned quickly. They danced a while before the guests left because some of them had school the next day. On his way out the door, Leo took Felicia's hand. "All is forgiven," he said. "We love you." Felicia put her face in Leo's chest and cried. He held her like a father.

Chambry whined and wheedled and manipulated Felicia into staying for church. Ron loved the service. The meal afterward relocated in the school cafeteria because snow began to fall. Ron talked to Leo in depth about a real relationship with God, a subject which had haunted him since his first visit to Possum Holler. He left a changed man. Although his first visit had planted some seeds, he would never forget this visit. He looked forward to another and got Felicia to verbally agree to spring breaks in Possum Holler.

30

Graduation

April and May bustled with activity in Possum Holler. Sunny wanted the school to be as much like any other school as possible. Therefore, Possum Holler School had a prom in April.

There were only three seniors and five juniors, but Sunny allowed each person to invite a guest of his or her choice so long as the guest was at least ninth grade. She made sure each boy attending had a suit and tie, but not a tux because that would have been too outrageous for Possum Holler. On the other hand, she saw to it each girl had a formal evening dress even if they were sewn by the women of the community, specifically, Ina Campbell. Sunny encouraged the girls to choose a dress from a catalogue. Then, she purchased the materials, satin, taffeta, silk, chiffon, and velvet in the colors the girls wanted; and Ina made the garments. Sunny was amazed how beautifully Ina crafted eight outfits on an old pedal sewing machine.

The small prom was held in the school cafeteria. Some of the tables were pushed against a wall and laid with food prepared by the teachers. Six of the tables were arranged in a small dining area. Half the floor was cleared for a dance floor, and the town musicians, MacKenzie Reardon and Tipper Campbell, gladly played music for the occasion. The room was decorated with white linen tablecloths and heavy paper napkins, plates, cups, and cutlery, in blue and gray, the school colors, and fresh spring flowers.

Although the rain poured outside, the prom-goers arrived in style in the small white limousine Leo rented and drove. He delivered two couples at a time, and, thanks to the newly paved roads, the limo did not get stuck in the mud. As the couples arrived, Sunny took pictures.

For entertainment, Mac and Tipper tried their hand at music other than bluegrass and country. They mixed in a little southern rock from the likes of Lynard Skynard and Credence Clearwater Revival and a little rock and pop selected from among The Eagles, Journey, Foreigner, Styx, and others. Mac would have loved to have played a little hard rock, but he felt certain not even the young people of Possum Holler were ready for AC/DC or Led Zeppelin, although he did work in "Stairway to Heaven."

To spell the live music, Sunny played several CDs of classical music, jazz, and a salsa dance CD. Tipper's head jerked around at the sound and he almost jumped out of his skin when Jessica, who had volunteered to serve food, took his hand and said, "Dance with me."

"Do you want to embarrass me?" Tipper protested.

"No. When you get to New York in June, you'll need this."

"That's not what I mean." Tipper blushed.

"Pooh! Look. Sunny's getting Mac to dance with her. You won't be alone."

"But when I tried this with Felicia…"

"I can imagine. Just remember my father and sixteen kids are watching. That should keep you in line."

"A straight line is what I'm worried about," he snarled in her ear.

"Tipper Campbell! I don't believe you said that. Now, hush and dance."

Sunny tapped Mac on the shoulder. "Can you salsa?"

"Unfortunately. Felicia taught me."

"Dance with me. Tipper needs the moral support."

"Who's gonna babysit him in the big city?"

"We'll discuss that later. Dance now."

The students gathered around to watch the two couples boogie. They looked at one another as they observed the suggestiveness of the dance. When it was over, the students applauded. One called, "What was that, Miss Bankston?"

"City dancing," responded Sunny.

"Can you teach us?"

"You're too young."

"Yes, ma'am," agreed the boy. "It did look like something you should only do with your husband."

Sunny scowled and blushed. "I suppose it did. I apologize."

"No need. Just marry the man."

"Excuse me?"

"He don't have a wife no more."

"He *doesn't* have a wife *anymore*, but that makes no difference. Dr. Reardon is my friend."

"Whatever you say, Miss Bankston."

Sunny noticed a young man who was not a student. "Who are you?" she asked the boy near the punch table.

"Matthew Richter."

"Oh!"

"Betty Jo Maddox invited me."

"Welcome." Sunny talked with the boy for a while. She prayed this could spark Alain Richter to allow the children to attend school. All past attempts to convince the man had been unsuccessful.

All in all, Possum Holler School's first prom was a great success. Thoughts turned to their first graduation. Granted, there would be only three graduates, but the occasion would be a celebration.

The ceremony was held in the church. The entire community turned out, even the few who would not come to church for any other reason, such as, the Richter brothers who lived the farthest from town now that the Springers and Peacocks had succumbed to the flu epidemic.

The brothers ranged in age from twenty-two to thirty-one. They were all bachelors who lived as far from civilization as possible with their seven sisters who ranged in age from eighteen to thirty and several children from a baby to Matthew who was sixteen, all of which had been born from incestuous unions. Sunny had tried on more than one occasion to persuade the eldest brother and obvious leader of the clan to allow the children to come to school, without success. Lauren Tomlin had also visited

Alain Richter as an advocate for education and his former teacher.

The only days the Richters might come to town were Hog-Rendering and Harvest Fest, and the men usually got drunk and spent the night in jail if they did venture in. The few crimes in Possum Holler—mostly malicious mischief, nothing violent—were blamed on them, perhaps, unfairly; and it was rumored several women had been raped by them, but no one would confirm it for fear of retaliation. A number of young girls had delivered illegitimate children, and it was believed the Richter brothers were responsible. They both looked and smelled the part of the stereotypical hillbilly with long hair and beards, reminiscent of ZZ Top, and flannel shirts and overalls or jeans and cowboy boots. All the men were tall and thin.

When the seven Richter brothers and the eldest male child from the clan filed onto the back pew, more than a few eyebrows shot skyward. Sunny noticed and nodded acknowledgement of their presence to a nod back. Deep inside, she hoped this would sway Alain to send the children to school. Apparently, Matthew had reported on prom and convinced Alain to attend the graduation.

Although the presence of the Richter family caused a little stir, the baccalaureate service and graduation ceremony went forward as planned. As the first person from Possum Holler to have graduated college and returned, Dr. MacKenzie Reardon gave a speech:

"One of the Titles given to Jesus was Teacher. However, before He was a teacher, Jesus was a student. He spent time studying. Luke tells us Jesus went to Jerusalem and went missing. When Mary and Joseph realized He was missing, they went to look for Him. 'They found Him in the midst of the doctors, both hearing them and asking them questions...and all that heard Him were astonished at His understanding and answers.'

"I am so proud of this senior class. You have sat among teachers, hearing them and asking questions. I have talked to you. I am astonished at your understanding and answers.

"After Jesus became a teacher, He had students, His disciples and the multitudes. He gave instruction to twelve, His first graduating class, and to those who followed Him to His ascension. He said in Matthew 28:19, 'Go ye therefore and teach...'

"Now that you have been taught, you are supposed to teach. Does that mean you have to become a classroom teacher? No." The doctor shook his head. "It means to teach as you go, wherever you go.

"I would encourage you to continue your education. I would also encourage you to care for your own. Whatever you decide to do, bring it home. Never, *ever*, be ashamed of your roots." He rapped the podium. "How much more humble can your beginnings be than to be born in a barn? Remember Jesus took care of His own first.

"You are a first, but first means there will be more. Those after you will follow your example. Give them something to emulate. I salute you"—He tipped his fingertips of his right hand to his forehead—"the first graduating class of Possum Holler School. Go ye!" In a grand gesture, he pointed toward the door. "Show the world where you came from, who you are, and what you can be."

As the audience applauded, Sunny, wearing a gray cap and gown with a pale blue tassel, indicative of her degree in education, stood to call the names of the graduates as Mac sat down. Adorned in several colors, Leo rose to present the diplomas. He wore the gray gown of the school and a tassel in pale blue for his Master of Christian Education with an additional tassel of dark blue for his undergraduate degree in psychology on his mortar board. IIe was draped in a stole of scarlet for his Doctor of Theology.

Sunny said, "Graduates, please, stand and come forward to receive your diploma when I call your name."

The young people stood. They wore gray caps and gowns with tassels of mixed sky blue and white. The school colors, which the students had opted to have, were opossum gray, sky blue, and white. As Sunny read each name, the student walked onto the raised platform where the pulpit stood, shook her hand, continued to Leo, shook his hand, received his or her diploma, walked down the two steps on the other side, and went back to his or her seat to wait.

Sunny spoke clearly and could be heard in the back of the sanctuary. "Annie Mae Maddox...Beauregard James, 'Beau,' Matlock... Myrna Louise Wade."

Sunny backed away from the podium and Leo took her place. "Congratulations. I proudly present the first graduating class of Possum Holler School." As Leo moved his double tassel from one side to the other, the graduates followed his example.

The people applauded, and the three young graduates marched out to recorded music of "Pomp and Circumstance."

Afterwards, they enjoyed a typical Possum Holler shindig with mounds of food, including thinly sliced ham for sandwiches on Lauren Tomlin's fresh baked bread; Ina Campbell's deviled eggs; Sherry Jones's peach cobbler; and Sunny Bankston's stuffed portabella mushrooms, and bottles of Tipper's Authentic Mountain Moonshine. Of course, many drank too much, but the Richter men were herded off to spend the night with Constable Hill, rather unfairly, Sunny thought because they had done nothing worse than many others present and not as bad as some.

Sunny went home and started to get ready for bed. After much conviction and inner debate, she marched to the jail and demanded the Richter brothers be released. To Alain's surprise the constable gave in. Sunny's spunk elevated her to a level just below angel to him, and Sunny prayed the incident was not a setback in convincing Alain to allow the children to attend school.

31
Big City

Tipper prepared to accompany his first full shipment of moonshine to New York City. Actually, the beverage was shipped by truck while Tipper prepared to fly. He knew Jessica planned to fly with him, but he was terrified. The highest he had ever been off the ground was riding the Ferris wheel at the county fair, and Mac had dragged him onto that when Ander Reardon had taken all of them to the fair.

Ina came into her son's room. "Are you all packed?"

"Yes, ma'am. How about you and the girls? I insist you stay with Preacher Tomlin. The house will probably be ready by the time I get back."

"Yes, Tipper. When will you stop callin' Leo Preacher Tomlin? He's gonna be yo father-in-law."

"When he's my father-in-law."

"What then?"

"Papa like Jess."

"Tipper, what are yo sleeping arrangements in New York?"

"We each have a room, Ma." He lifted an eyebrow toward her.

"Very well. We should head into town. We already put our things in the GTO. We waitin' for you." Tipper's former whiskey-running car was a fully restored antique GTO Judge with a hollowed-out back seat.

"I'm comin'."

Tipper settled his family with his future family and transferred his new luggage, no longer a brown grocery sack, to Jessica's trunk. "Jess," he said, "did you bring enough clothes?"

"I don't know. I might buy something in New York."

"What?" The man's brows dipped in confusion. "There are a dozen suitcases here."

"There are not. There are nine, a dozen when you add yours. That's two suitcases and one carry-on for each person."

"Huh? I might be a hillbilly, but I can do math. Twelve divided by two equals six."

"Oh, I have a surprise for you. Mac and Sunny are going with us. Papa is taking Rush to Mac's. All the men will be at Mac's while the ladies are here."

"When did you decide this?"

"A long time ago. I just kept it a secret."

"Thank you." He planted a kiss on her cheek. "I love you, but I need Mac to hold my hand on that airplane."

"Wrong. That's my job. I was sort of hoping he'd hold Sunny's hand."

"Give it up. I already tried matchmaking." He arranged his luggage in the trunk.

"He did kiss her on New Year's Eve," Jess argued.

"To pacify Chambry."

"Ha! That's our new ally. We'll work on it after the big city."

"He's not new. He was helpin' me. Jess, we should leave it alone. Let it develop by itself."

"Whatever you say. Here they come. Sh."

Jessica parked her car in long-term parking, and the group from Possum Holler boarded a small shuttle flight in Wilmington to Charlotte, North Carolina. Jessica made sure Tipper got a window seat. She wanted him to enjoy flying, but rain poured at takeoff, and the small prop plane hit turbulence. Tipper's knuckles turned white from gripping the seat's armrests.

Jessica rubbed his arm gently. "Tipper, it's all right. Open your eyes."

He released a long sigh. "Is it just the weather?"

"Turbulence is rough. I hate you got that your first time out, but it's a short flight to Charlotte. We'll be there in about ten more minutes. Bigger planes handle turbulence better."

Tipper opened his eyes. He could see the rain hitting the windows, but the lightning flashed below them. They were in the clouds. Tipper watched the lightning for a minute. "It's actually pretty. I wish Betsy could see it. She would love to paint it. That's one beautiful thing she got from her mother—her art."

"She's very talented. We'll bring all of them to the city soon."

The captain announced their descent. "Now is the time to grip the armrest," whispered Jessica.

The descent was bumpy. Once safely inside the airport, Tipper asked, "Where are our things?"

Mac explained, "The airline will put our luggage on the next flight. We won't see it again until New York. Hopefully, they won't lose it."

"Lose it?" Tipper's voice squeaked. "That's all I have."

"It doesn't happen often, Tipper."

"I hope not."

By the time they boarded the flight to New York, the weather had cleared. Tipper watched out the window like an excited child. "Jess, what's that—those tiny worms?"

"Roads, rivers."

"Really?"

"Uh-hum."

"I like this without turbulence."

"I knew you would."

Darkness fell quickly. As they approached JFK Airport in New York, the city was ablaze. "Jess, look. It's beautiful," said Tipper in bewilderment.

Mac squeezed Sunny's hand. "You'd think he was a kid at Christmas."

"What were you like the first time you flew?"

"Just about as bad."

Sunny laughed. "Have you ever been to New York?"

"No, not to visit. Felicia and I flew out of La Guardia to go to Europe for our honeymoon, but it was a short layover, and it was daylight. I flew into O'Hare in Chicago to interview for my internship. It was daylight there, too." He chuckled. "It was even early morning when we got to Paris. We rented a car to drive to the chalet. Tipper's right. The city lights are beautiful." He stashed the medical journal he had been reading. "Have you been to New York?"

"Yes, in high school. Our choir came. We sang in Carnegie Hall." A shadow crossed her face. "The Twin Towers were still here."

"You know a few fellows from Possum Holler joined the army to go and fight. Even hidden away, we were affected. Panther Matlock went. Beau was ten. I thought about going, but Papa made me go to college."

"I'm glad he did. Without you, Possum Holler might not have any people now. I might be dead if you hadn't been in the ER."

"I guess you paid me back. You got me through the flu."

"That's what friends are for. I'm not keeping score."

"Yeah. And, now, we're here for Tipper."

"Jess has been here, too. We can't wait to show both of you the city."

Ron and Felicia met Tipper's flight. They were surprised to see the man's entourage. Ron quipped, "The more the merrier!"

Mac stared at Felicia. "Wow!" he said. "You're very pregnant."

"Yeah, I'm a lot bigger this time."

Mac whispered in her ear as he gave her a cordial kiss on the cheek, "Bigger or further along?"

"It's not yours, Mac," she whispered back. "I swear. I had a period just days after I left Possum Holler. Ron told me about Chambry. You still love him, don't you? Do you want me to take him?"

"No." His body stiffened, jaws clamped, teeth clenched. "Chambry is *my* son forever. I hope this one *is* Ron's—for Ron. He deserves it. The man loves you. You deserve a real marriage. Let him give it to you." A boarding call drowned out a few words.

"I'm telling the truth, Mac. I love Ron. I want this."

"Is it a boy or a girl?"

"I don't know. We decided to be surprised, so I didn't even have a sonogram. If it's a girl, I've decided to have one more to try and give Ron a son."

"You've changed a lot."

"I guess I grew up."

A late passenger bumped into the couple without apology. Mac brushed it off as Felicia scowled.

"I like it." The ex-husband put himself between the crowd and the woman he once loved. "Felicia, are we actually friends?"

"I guess we are."

"It's a good thing."

Ron came up. "Hey. We've claimed *all* the luggage." Ron laughed. "Tipper was scared they had lost it. Are you two going to talk all night?"

"We're coming," said Felicia.

Ron loaded everyone into the stretch limousine he had hired just for Tipper. "Well," he said, "do you have rooms at the hotel, Tipper?"

"Ask Jess. She made the reservations."

Jessica nodded. "We have reservations at the Excelsior."

"Nice," commented Felicia. "Good taste, Jess."

"Thanks."

"Okay, then," said Ron. "That's about a forty-minute drive." Ron gave the driver directions and turned back to his guests. "Let's get you checked in and go somewhere for a late dinner. Then, tomorrow, we'll pick you up about ten for a day of sightseeing. I'll get some more tickets for the things I have planned. I have a night at the opera, the ballet, and the symphony and a Broadway play. Sightseeing tomorrow. Several museums the day after and Coney Island the day after that. I have a baseball game. Oh, I have lots planned." He rubbed his hands together in his enthusiasm. "You won't get bored. The last night you're here, we'll go to my first and best club. We'll dance the night away."

"It sounds as if Tipper didn't need us," laughed Mac.

"Nonsense!" said Ron. "We'll have several packed days with a few lazy days thrown in. We'll take a day in the Hamptons, and you can meet my parents. We'll have a lot of fun."

They got to the hotel and Felicia accompanied Jessica and Sunny to their room. She laughed. "Jess, why aren't you staying with Tipper?"

"We're not married yet, Felicia."

"But you're totally in love with him."

"Felicia, I've waited my whole life for Tipper. A few more months won't kill me."

"Are you saying?"

"I'm a virgin, yes."

"Wow!" She plopped into one of the chairs in the room. Sunny took the one beside her.

"Strange, huh?" asked Jessica

"Not expected," admitted Felicia. "I mean, you're gorgeous. Surely, you've had boyfriends."

"I've dated." Jessica opened her luggage.

"Does Tipper know?" Felicia continued to pry.

"We've never discussed it. I guess we should." Jessica put her undergarments in a drawer.

Felicia looked at Sunny. "You, too?"

"That's a long story," said Sunny as a cloud crossed her brow.

"Sunny?" said Jessica with a little concern.

The teacher shivered. "Freshman year in college. It's called GHB."

Both women grabbed one of Sunny's hands.

Sunny shrugged. "I don't even remember what happened. I was at a fraternity party, and I was only drinking Coke. I don't know which one of them did it. I woke up the next day in pain. I went to a rape crisis center, and they took me to have a kit done. There was no evidence except I was no longer a virgin, some bruising, and my blood tested positive for GHB. I transferred to another university. I haven't been with anyone else, but I will admit I fell in love with my principal in Chicago. He was killed the day I was shot."

"It doesn't count!" Felicia snorted and set her jaw in a tight clench.

"What?" asked Sunny.

"You've never made love to a man you wanted to be with, so it doesn't count." Felicia stated firmly. "How long ago was it?"

"Nine years." Sunny answered.

Felicia squeezed her friend's hand. "When it happens, it'll be like the first time. Mac's very gentle."

"Why is everybody pushing Mac and me together?" Sunny's voice took on shrillness. "We're friends."

"Okay!" said Felicia hastily, raising her hands in surrender.

Jessica asked, "Felicia, Mac wasn't your first, was he?"

"No." The blonde in the group shook her head. "Third. Prom night, and I haven't seen him since graduation. Then, I met Ron. We drifted apart. I met Mac. Ron showed back up. Then, I wanted my marriage to work. Now, I would be lost without Ron. I belong with him. I love him." Felicia rubbed her abdomen. "This baby is his, not Mac's. Mac will always be very special to me. We're actually friends, but my future is with Ron."

Sunny laughed. "Can you believe we're having a real girl talk?"

"I wonder what they're talking about." Jessica jerked her thumb toward the room across the hall where Mac and Tipper would be.

"Well," said Felicia, "none of them are virgins."

A knock at the door startled the ladies. "We're starving," Ron called.

Felicia laughed. "I guess they were discussing food."

The group of friends who had come together from so many diverse walks of life found a pizzeria and had a relaxed late meal. The people were so different yet linked by one commonality—faith; and even *that* had been found through varying avenues.

They discussed their connections as they ate. "Dr. MacKenzie Reardon," Mac said. "I was so happy to hear the dean call my name. Here I was, an orphaned hillbilly who was raised by the missionary preacher who came to my hometown. Papa instilled in me the way out was through education. I don't feel worthy of any of the praise I've received." He smiled at his ex-wife. "I'm glad to say that even though Felicia and I aren't married anymore, we're still friends. There's never a time I can remember I haven't had faith. I joined the church early, before Pa died."

Tipper Campbell, Mac Reardon's oldest and best friend, nodded. "Yeah, we were baptized together. I told Mac in fourth grade I'd be an entrepreneur." He laughed out loud. "I showed him my still, and we sampled the product. We were so drunk. Preacher Tomlin made us sing the offertory in church the next day, but he had mercy and let us do it without instruments because we were hungover." He took Jessica's hand. "I married young, divorced, and am the father of three girls. I'm glad my bootleg whiskey tempted you city slickers, Ron. I guess I'm still naïve, and although my faith was tested when Amy left me alone with three little girls, I'm holding on to the faith of my childhood. And despite a broken heart, I've found love with this beautiful lady." He kissed Jessica's hand.

Tipper's business partner was the polar opposite of Tipper Campbell. Ronald Norton fidgeted a little before he shared his story. "I grew up a rich, spoiled brat. I come from old money, and I never lacked for anything except real love. I've made my own way, stepping out of my father's shadow." He put his arm around Felicia. "When I got a sample of Tipper's moonshine, I *knew* I had a winner. I have buyers lined up for the next five years, and the list is growing." He sighed. "I was very successful, but something was missing. This lady, for one. I love her with all my heart. Because of her, I visited Possum Holler, West Virginia, and came away with a newfound faith."

The ladies in the group were as diverse as the men. Sunny Bankston talked hesitantly. "I grew up in a home full of love, but with parents who encouraged their children to experience life and develop our own belief system. I guess I believe in giving everyone a second chance, including my mother who teeters on the precipice of losing touch with reality." The group laughed. "I'm serious," Sunny said. "I had a rough time in college, but that's where I found real faith. That's what kept me strong after Perry was killed and I was shot. I moved forward and went to Possum Holler. As a result, I met all of you. I think my faith has blossomed and grown deep roots."

"You're like sunshine," Mac said with a wink. Sunny rolled her eyes.

Jessica Langston laughed. "Well, I guess Papa never expected me. However, he accepts me and loves me. I have a whole family, including Mac, my sort-of brother, and Rush, my little sugar pie. Momma brought me up to have faith, which brought me to Possum Holler to be Mac's nurse. After two trying years as a journeyman missionary in Sudan, Possum Holler is a paradise." She blew out a breath. "I didn't come looking for love. Love is an unexpected blessing, and I can't wait to share my life with Tipper."

All eyes turned toward Felicia Chambry, formerly Reardon, now Norton. "I guess you guys expect me to talk, too." There were nods all around. "Okay. I never intended to be the liaison between two worlds, but it fell to me. Leo saw something in me and used my talents. I owe him. I came to the realization Mac and I didn't belong together. Despite my epiphany, I took seed faith from there and left development behind. I think what I've given will be terrific."

There were nods of agreement again. She took her husband's hand. "Ron and I are growing together."

"You're growing for sure," teased Tipper.

Not to be out done, she responded, "It makes it hard to salsa."

Mac and Jessica laughed loudly and pointed at the tall blushing man. Sunny looked at Ron for explanation. He shrugged.

The unlikely assortment of people formed an unbreakable alliance over pizza and beer or club soda for Felicia. The rest of the trip to New York was exciting. They visited the 9/11

Memorial, The Empire State Building, The Statue of Liberty, The Metropolitan Museum, Coney Island, The Hamptons where Ron's family lived, and Seventh Avenue, the garment district. They took in an opera, a symphony, a Broadway play, a ballet, a rock concert in Central Park, and a New York Mets baseball game. They made a trip to Atlantic City to the casinos where Tipper made a killing at the blackjack table. He confessed to Mac he had been able to remember which cards had been dealt. Mac told him not to tell anyone else because the casinos took great displeasure with the ability to count cards. Tipper felt he was choking in the tuxedo he had to wear for the formal productions, but he loved the productions themselves.

The dark cloud for Tipper's first visit to the big city proved to be the art museum.

32

Surprised in a New York Minute

The group spent a day visiting art galleries. Tipper loved the old masters and wished Betsy were there to see them. However, in the contemporary artists' section in which paintings were for sale, he stopped and stared at half a dozen as the others moved on.

Noticing Tipper lagging, Ron came back. "We don't want to lose you in the big city," he joked until he noticed the expression on Tipper's face. The businessman looked again at the painting that had drawn the whiskey entrepreneur's undivided attention. "How appropriate," murmured Ron. "Would you like to have it for the entrance to the distillery? It would be perfect."

Tipper glanced at Ron. Ron could not tell whether Tipper was mad or sad. Tipper barely whispered, "Amy did it."

"Excuse me?"

"The artist is my ex-wife."

"Are you sure?"

"Look at the picture, Ron. Look closely."

Ron examined the painting of a moonshine still with a lone man attending the fire, entitled "Mountain Moonshine."

"Good Lord!" Ron exclaimed. "That's you." Ron read the signature. "Amy DuBlane."

Tipper nodded. "The book salesman was Roscoe DuBlane. I never thought I'd ever see her again."

"You haven't. Only a painting, a very good painting."

Brushing his long sandy hair back Tipper declared, "Ron, I do want it, but I want to put cash in her hand. And I want to present her with a bottle of Tipper's Authentic Mountain Moonshine. Can you arrange a meeting with an anonymous buyer? Obviously, she hasn't left Possum Holler behind. Look at the other five she has here. They're all Possum Holler."

"You're right. I see it. Is this meeting going to be confrontational?"

"No. I just want to look her in the eye and thank her. If she had never left, I would never have had the courage to try this endeavor. I would have been too much of a coward to offer to teach Felicia to square dance if I'd had a wife to think about. I want her to meet my friends. I want her to see I am *not* an ignorant, good-for-nothing, bootlegging hillbilly." He took a deep breath to steady his nerves. "I want her to see I'm on my way to Easy Street, just as I promised."

The native New Yorker put a hand on Tipper's shoulder. "I'll arrange it."

Ron talked to the curator for a moment and came back to Tipper. "How much cash do you have on you?"

"Not a thousand dollars. That's the ticketed price."

Ron took out his wallet. "I have seven hundred right now."

Tipper checked his wallet. "Two fifty."

"Mac!" Ron called and motioned the others to come.

"What?" asked Mac.

"We're buying this painting. We need fifty more dollars to get it right now."

"I got it." Mac handed over a fifty.

Ron turned back to Tipper. "Okay, Tipper. She's in the back. The curator went to get her. Do you have one of those business cards we printed on you?"

"Several. Jess said I should carry them."

"Listen to Jess. Tell the curator to ship it to the address on the card."

"Who's in the back?" asked Mac.

"Read the name of the artist," instructed Tipper.

The curator approached the group with a fairly tall, slim woman with very short, dark-brown hair and bitter chocolate eyes. She stopped in her tracks. "Tipper?"

"Hello, Amy. I see you're doing quite well. Let me introduce you to my friends. You already know Mac, but it's *Doctor* MacKenzie Reardon now."

"Hello, Amy," said Mac.

Tipper took Jessica's hand, so Amy could see the engagement ring, something she had not had, flash. "This is my fiancée, Jessica Langston. Jess, this is my former wife, Amy."

"Hello," said Jessica stiffly. She now understood the tête-a-tête between Ron and Tipper.

Tipper continued, "This is Sunny Bankston, the principal at the school in Possum Holler."

Sunny cordially acknowledged the introduction. "Hello, Amy. It's nice to meet you. Your daughters are delightful."

Amy DuBlane was mortified. She had never wanted anyone to know where she came from, and she had never thought to see Tipper again. The curator watched with great interest. Amy stumbled over her words. "Thank you. They're good?"

"Very," said Sunny.

Last Tipper introduced Ron and Felicia. "Amy, meet Ron and Felicia Norton, good friends, and Ron is my business partner. When we saw this painting, we just *had* to have it for the entry to Tipper's Bottling." Tipper handed Amy the thousand dollars and his business card to the curator. "Please, ship my painting to that address."

The whiskey distiller turned again to the dark-haired beauty who stared at the floor. "You're very talented. I think you captured me quite well after so long a time and without a model. Yes, Ron, it's quite appropriate to show what humble beginnings and aspirations can accomplish.

"Amy, it's good to see you're doing well. How's Roscoe?"

"Dead."

"I'm sorry. The girls are great. Betsy designed my business logo." He handed her a card. "I'd like to send you a complimentary bottle. Do you have an address where I can send it?"

The curator blurted, "If she doesn't, I do. The watermelon is marvelous."

"You actually made it fruit flavored and started a business?" said Amy in disbelief, her eyes barely flitting upward.

"Yes."

"Where do you get the fruit?"

Tipper raised an eyebrow and smirked. "Alain. If you will recall, I promised to make him rich one day. Yes, thanks to you for setting me free to try my wings, I learned to fly. I'm sorry I don't have persimmon flavored." Tipper felt a not-so-gentle squeeze of his hand from Jessica. "What flavor would you like instead?"

"Whatever you deem appropriate. You can send it here."

"As you wish." Tipper turned again to the curator. "I'll be home this time next week. I expect my painting to be waiting for me, and I'll send you one of each. Amy, take care. Good day."

The group left. Outside, Mac asked, "What the hell was that?"

Jessica murmured, "Yes, what the hell *was* that?"

Tipper shrugged and grinned. "I was surprised in a New York minute."

"No more surprises," muttered Jessica.

"I wouldn't bet on it," Mac whispered to Sunny. "Tipper just humiliated Amy. The shit will hit the fan, and she has some major ammunition."

Sunny looked at the man with questions in her eyes. He whispered something in her ear. The woman's jaw dropped. "I don't know how or when, but it will," Mac said. "Not to mention my sister looks as if she wants to kill someone, and I think it's her fiancé."

Tipper thought the visit to New York would wrap up with a night at Ron's club. He danced with dozens of Ron's patrons until Jessica stepped in and sent Tipper's would-be harem packing.

Tipper pulled Jessica to the dance floor. "Thank you for rescuing me."

"You could have told them you were gay."

"What?"

"Homosexual."

"No. You're angry."

"Jealous. I already met your ex-wife today, and you flaunted me in her face."

"No need to be jealous. I love you. Let's dance."

"We'll dance, but if you ever pull a stunt like that again, I will dance you out the door." She stopped dead in her tracks. "I don't want to be your rebound."

"Oh, Jess, no. I'm sorry I made you feel like that. No. I love you."

"Kiss me."

Tipper grinned. "Yes, ma'am." He kissed Jessica passionately. "Let's dance."

"All right. Don't forget you're *my* fiancé. I love you, Tipper Campbell."

Mac tapped Sunny. "Let's dance."

"Okay. It appears the lovers' spat is over. I think we'll be safe on the same dance floor."

"What about us?" Felicia asked Ron.

"You feel up to it?"

"I'd love to dance with you."

"Come on."

Ron led Felicia carefully onto the dance floor. She was rather cumbersome, but Ron loved just the fact she wanted to dance with him. A little into the dance, Felicia's face went ashen and she gripped Ron's hand.

"What's wrong?" he asked.

"Contraction. Water broke. Ron, I'm scared. It's too soon."

Ron grabbed Mac's arm. "Felicia's in labor."

Mac looked concerned. "It's too soon."

"That's what she said."

"Let's get her to the hospital."

The three couples quickly changed locations.

33

Mass Production

By the time they got Felicia to the emergency room, she was in full-blown labor. The ER intern came in. "Dr. Epstein is in Jamaica. You're not due for six weeks."

"I know that, you moron!" screeched Felicia.

"Mrs. Norton, one of Dr. Epstein's colleagues will be here shortly."

"I don't want one of his colleagues! I want Mac!"

"Who's Mac?"

"Dr. MacKenzie Reardon. He's in the waiting room with my other friends."

"Mrs. Norton, he doesn't have hospital privileges here." The young man looked at her chart. Pages over the intercom drowned some of his words.

"I don't care! I want Mac! Ron, make them give me Mac." The scream was so shrill it scared her husband.

"Mrs. Norton, I can give you something for the pain," suggested the doctor.

"No! It's not good for the baby. I want Mac!"

Ron snapped, "Get Dr. Reardon in here!"

"Mr. Norton…"

"Now!"

"Sir, I can't do that."

"Dr. Pope, is it?" Ron narrowed his eyes to slits as he read the doctor's embroidered name on his lab coat. "My father is on the board here. Get Mac in here if you want a job. He'll have hospital privileges within the hour, but you won't."

Dr. Pope went into the waiting room. He called, "Who is Dr. Reardon?"

"I am," Mac said in some confusion.

"Dr. Reardon, Mrs. Norton is demanding for you to come in."

"Go!" Sunny said, pushing Mac up.

Mac came in. "Felicia, what do you want?"

"Help me. Something's wrong, Mac. I'm not due for six weeks. I'm scared. Please, take care of my baby."

Mac looked at Ron. "Ron?"

"Do what you can, Mac."

"Okay." Mac got a pair of gloves and examined Felicia.

"First," he said, "the baby is breech, but you are almost ready to deliver."

"What can you do?" Felicia gasped.

"I can try and turn the baby. Felicia, it'll hurt."

"Can she have an epidural?" asked Ron.

"It didn't work last time," grunted Felicia.

"Dr. Pope," said Mac. "Get an anesthesiologist in here stat. We want a spinal."

"Yes, sir."

"Felicia, if this doesn't work, you're gonna need a C-section. Your blood pressure is already spiking. I won't risk your life."

Felicia gripped Ron's arm.

The anesthesiologist entered. "You need a spinal?"

Mac said, "Yes, not an epidural."

"Got it."

The spinal worked, and Felicia breathed more easily. Her blood pressure decreased to a safe level. As Mac worked to get the baby to turn, Dr. Sandra Dijay entered.

"Who is this man?" she demanded.

"My friend!" answered Felicia huffily.

"Dr. Dijay," explained Ron, "this is Dr. Reardon. He's a friend of ours. He delivered Felicia's first child."

"I see. Well, Dr. Reardon, what's happening?"

"The baby is breech. She's fully dilated, but I can't get the baby to turn. I think it's time for a C-section."

"Let me look." Dr. Dijay's hands were smaller than Mac's. She got a strange look on her face. "Get me a sonogram, now!"

"What now?" asked Felicia. "Mac?"

Mac held up his hand. "I'm not sure. Dr. Dijay?" Mac held up two fingers.

"I think so. How could we have missed that?"

"What?" demanded Felicia.

A sonologist wheeled in a sonogram machine and began the procedure.

Dr. Dijay laughed. "No wonder we can't get the little monster to turn. We've been grabbing the wrong foot."

"Oh, my God!" blurted Ron. "No wonder you were so big."

"Is that what I think it is?" asked Felicia.

"Yes, it is," affirmed Dr. Dijay. "Dr. Reardon, can you tell which foot to grab?"

"No."

"Me either. Mr. and Mrs. Norton, it's time to go to surgery."

"Are you sure?" asked Ron.

"Yes. Dr. Reardon, care to assist me?"

"Please, Mac? I need you," begged Felicia.

Mac nodded. Dr. Dijay sent Ron to get suited and prepped Felicia for surgery. Then, she and Mac scrubbed and met the expectant parents in the operating room.

"Spinal is still strong and holding," announced the anesthesiologist.

"Let's get started," ordered Dr. Dijay. Three minutes later, Dr. Dijay handed Mac a baby boy.

"It's a boy," announced Mac. He weighed and measured the baby.

"It's a girl," announced Dr. Dijay.

Mac said, "Three pounds, three ounces, seventeen inches," and handed the baby to Ron who held him a moment before he passed him to Felicia.

Dr. Dijay announced, "She's a little smaller, two pounds, fifteen ounces, seventeen inches. They have healthy lungs." She handed the girl to Ron.

Ron blinked back tears as he held his daughter.

"Trade," said Felicia. Ron and Felicia traded babies. This time Felicia counted fingers and toes.

Mac smiled. He touched Ron's shoulder. "They're yours," he whispered. "Do you still want the tests?"

Ron shook his head. "No need. It wouldn't matter anyway, would it, Mac?"

"No. Congratulations."

"Thank you for everything."

Dr. Dijay said, "We need to get them to the preemie unit. They'll have to stay until they get to four pounds. Mrs. Norton, breast or bottle?"

Felicia looked at Ron. "It's up to you," he said.

"If I have trouble nursing, can we change?"

"Yes," said Dr. Dijay. "And if you only want to nurse until you go back to work, that's okay, too."

"I'm taking a year off," said Felicia decisively.

"That works. I'll have the breastfeeding nurse visit you in a couple of hours with the babies. They can stay with you long enough to eat, but, then, they have to get back. You're heading to a room as soon as we finish up here. You'll be here at least two nights."

"I need to call Chambry, and they need names, Ron."

"Well, I don't want a junior. I have an idea. How about Ronald MacKenzie?"

"What?" said Mac.

"Yes." Felicia nodded. "Mac, what was Grandma Newton's given name?"

"Miriam."

"Like Moses' sister. Ron, what do you think?"

"Miriam Amelia."

"That's good. Ken and Miri."

Mac found the rest of their party. "Well, we have Ronald MacKenzie Norton and Miriam Amelia Norton. They're calling the babies Ken and Miri. They're all fine. Felicia called Chambry. He thinks it's cool to have twins. They were six weeks premature to answer the question in your eyes. They're Ron's children, but I'm their godfather. Chambry doesn't have a godfather. Tipper, could you stand another one?"

"What about the other two you took?"

"Good point."

"Yeah, I could take 'em all if I had to. Let's hope I never have to."

"Yes, let's." He rubbed his face in fatigue. "Let's get some sleep. Our flight leaves at two. I suppose we'll visit here first."

They visited the next day, and Tipper teased Felicia about taking a shortcut to catch up with him rather than going into mass production.

Back in Possum Holler, Tipper's Bottling went into mass production. Tipper had twelve market areas baying for his product. The five other Possum Holler bootleggers happily gave up their illegal stills for guaranteed wages without risk of arrest. The product itself was still distilled and bottled by hand from a wood fire. Because of the time and care that went into each little brown jug, it fetched a good price. Even in poor areas, it sold for at least thirty dollars a bottle. In more affluent areas, it went for sixty to a hundred or more.

Tipper's house was ready to occupy. The week after he got back was a mass production to get moved in. He bought new furniture for the whole house and let Jessica and the girls decorate the way they wanted.

Tipper's company after Ron's twenty-five percent, the government's twenty-five percent, weekly expenses of about five thousand, and a payroll of about four thousand, was clearing around three thousand a week. After furnishing his home, Tipper's first act was to repay Mac for Jessica's engagement ring, prompting Mac to say, "Now, you need to marry the girl."

"Yep. First Saturday in October. You're still best man. Guess what I'm gonna do?"

"What?"

"Take night classes and get a business degree."

"Good idea."

"Mac, I think my company might put Possum Holler on the map."

"I think you're right."

"Will that be good or bad?"
"Time will tell, Tipper."

34

First Day of School

Just as the townspeople had done for Mac, they had a pounding for Tipper to help him settle into his new home. They celebrated late into the night. Miss Ina rejoiced in turning the faucet on and off as she gloried in having running water and an indoor toilet.

The residents of Possum Holler celebrated more than new homes. This year their Independence Day celebration included fireworks in addition to their annual barbeque. Early on July fifth, Mac flew to New York again, but on this trip, he accompanied his son, Chambry, so the child could spend a month of the summer with his mother. Chambry was excited to meet his new siblings who had just come home from the hospital. Felicia was still recovering and assured Mac this summer would be spent mostly at home with only one weekend planned with Ron's family in the Hamptons. She had no plans to go to Pittsburgh to see her parents although they might come in. Mac left his son with instructions to call anytime he wanted. Ron would bring him home in a month.

Back in Possum Holler, Mac spent the month getting to know two little boys he had taken into his home. Abner and Ezekiel Peacock could have been twins if there were not four years difference in their ages. Both had platinum-blond hair and vivid blue eyes, and both were small for their age. Mac took them fishing and taught Abner to ride the bike Santa had brought Chambry. With the outbreak of flu, it had never been delivered to the Joneses. Mac bought a smaller bike for Zeke. The boys hugged Mac tightly.

The month of July brought an influx of potential teachers to Possum Holler School. Sunny had to replace the two ladies who had died, and she needed a preschool teacher. In addition to teaching preschool, Sunny needed a teacher certified to teach gifted children. She had tested every child in Possum Holler School and had determined seven to fall in the gifted range, a small number, but a beginning; and new students would be coming in the fall. Besides the seven on the gifted end of the spectrum, Sunny had determined fifteen students to be in need of special services. She sought two teachers to teach exceptional and special needs, including speech therapy. Finding the right combination proved difficult. Sunny and Leo interviewed dozens of potential teachers before offering contracts to five, most notably and most highly qualified, Mattie Boone, a widow with three children of her own.

After the busy summer, the principal of the school cherished the week before school started to simply relax. Sunny went to the creek with a good book and dangled her feet in the water. She wore long, flowered walking shorts and a tank top in soft peach. She had her hair pulled back in a long ponytail. Her quiet time was suddenly broken as she heard children laughing and a man's voice coming through the thicket.

Armed with fishing poles, a blanket, and a picnic basket, Mac, accompanied by Chambry, Abner, and Zeke, intruded into Sunny's sanctuary. "Hello!" chirped the woman, barely affected by the intrusion.

"Well, hello," said Mac. "Are we interrupting you? This is our favorite fishing hole."

"Then, I've intruded. I come here to meditate."

"Do you mean be alone?"

Sunny laughed. "Sometimes."

"Then, we should move elsewhere."

"Nonsense. Just invite me to the picnic." She pointed toward the basket.

"You're invited. We're hoping to catch some fish to roast over a fire."

"Yum. I don't have anything to offer to the table."

"Your company is sufficient,"

Chambry grabbed Mac's hand. "Daddy, come on."

"You can bait your own hook." The father made a shooing motion with his hand. "Catch enough for Miss Bankston to eat with us."

Chambry shrugged and went back to the other two boys to fish. "May I?" Mac asked before he sat down.

"Of course."

"What are you reading?"

"*The Robe.*"

"Good book. Have you ever read *Christy*?"

"No."

The doctor sat beside the teacher and looked over her shoulder. "You should. It's about a young teacher who goes to Appalachia. She kept a scented hanky handy, too."

"I'll have to read it."

"Are you ready for the first day of school?" He leaned back resting his elbows on the lush grass.

"I suppose. Are you? Chambry will be in kindergarten."

"He's chomping at the bit."

"I'm sure he'll do just fine."

Zeke wandered up. "The fish not bitin', Daddy," he said with his big blue eyes looking sad.

"Darn!" laughed Mac, sitting up. "I guess we'll have to eat the tuna sandwiches I made. Maybe you boys should just go swimming."

Zeke scampered down the bank to tell the two older boys they could swim.

Mac laughed louder. "That's what they sent him up here for, you know," he confided to Sunny. "They think they've tricked me."

"Maybe you should join them. Zeke's mighty small to be down there swimming." She sat up straight. "Are they stripping to their underwear?"

"Oops. Sure you want me to join them?"

She chortled. "I dare you," she said, catching her breath.

Mac shrugged. "I will if you will." He took off his shirt, jeans and sneakers and left them by the picnic basket. Then, wearing just his boxers, he ran full speed and did a cannon ball into the creek, sending spray all over Sunny.

She screamed as water showered her.

"You might as well join us. You're all wet." Mac guffawed.

"It's a little different for me," said Sunny, indicating she was not dressed for swimming with her hands.

"I won't tell," teased Mac. "Will you boys tell?"

All three boys shook their heads and encouraged her. "Come on, Miss Bankston."

"It couldn't be any worse than some of the bikinis I've seen," Mac continued. "Probably less revealing."

Sunny blushed. The man kept goading her, "If you're embarrassed, just take off the shorts and keep the shirt on. We're not skinny dipping. We're all covered."

"What would people say?"

"They won't know. Come on, Sunny. I dare you."

Sunny scowled at all four taunters. "Turn around," she said. "And don't turn back around until I'm in the water."

"Yes, ma'am." They turned around.

Chambry whispered, "Are you gonna peek, Daddy?"

"No. I'm a man of honor."

"You wanna peek though."

"I do not!"

"I'd peek." The child nodded enthusiastically. "She's pretty."

"Chambry Ander Reardon!"

"I don't need a girlfriend. I already have one."

"Who?" The father glanced down at the boy.

Chambry pushed water back and forth with his hands, the gentle current washing past father and son. "Laurie. I kissed her, too."

"You did what?" Mac's eyebrows shot up, his voice an octave higher than normal

"Lily Jones is pretty, too."

"Chambry! She's your cousin."

"Third." The child shrugged. "Far enough Papaw would marry us."

Mac thought, *I'm not sure she's that far removed.* He could not shake the feeling Sherry Jones had secrets.

The next thing Mac knew, Sunny dunked him. He came up sputtering. "You're as big an imp as these boys."

They frolicked in the water for a while before Sunny told them to turn around again while she got out. "Are you hungry?" she called from the bank. "I could lay out the picnic."

"I'm starving," Mac yelled back over the splashing water.

Sunny took Mac's clothes to where the boys had laid theirs. She grinned. "Not that I didn't enjoy the view, but..."

"That's not fair," joked Mac. "You didn't give me a view."

"Uh!" Sunny gasped. "Mac Reardon! Get dressed." She went back to lay out the food.

"Way to go, Daddy," whispered Chambry.

"Chambry, I was teasing her."

"Whatever you say. Papaw says many a truth is said in jest."

After the picnic, they all walked back to town together. The boys ran ahead. After a few minutes, Zeke came back with a handful of dandelions for Sunny. She took them, and the little boy hugged her around the legs before he caught up with his brothers.

"What a sweetie!" said Sunny. "How's the bed wetting?"

"Better," Mac told her. "Not every night. Maybe once a week. He's waking up to use the bathroom now."

"He's grown a lot."

"Yes. I think it's the better nutrition and hygiene."

"You're probably right, doctor." Sunny waved to the boys as she turned toward her home.

Tuesday nights and Thursday nights Tipper drove to Wilmington to take classes at the community college. Mac asked, "When did you take the ACT?"

"April."

"You didn't tell me. What was your score?"

"Thirty-two."

"Seriously?" The doctor's eyes stretched in amazement.

"Yes. Why?"

"Why are you taking classes at a community college?"

"I can drive in and back."

"I see your logic, but what about a bachelor's degree?"

"I'll cross that bridge when I get to it."

"Well, how was the first class?"

"Slow. There are a lot of people about my age. Mac, I think some of them are dim."

"That's why you should be at a university. Tipper, you're extremely intelligent."

"Thanks. I'll get there, Mac. Let me get my feet wet."

"If that's what you want. I'm proud of you though." Mac clapped his friend on the shoulder.

"I want Jess to be proud of me. She has a college degree."

"It doesn't matter to her."

"It matters to me."

"Well, you're taking the right steps. Apparently, your first day of school was successful."

"Indeed."

As Tipper settled into being an adult college student, Possum Holler School began a new year. The number that showed up shocked Sunny. Some Possum Holler residents had continued to send their children to the county schools because they were uncertain of the new school's success, but after three school years, it seemed every student possible had chosen to come to Possum Holler, although Sunny noticed the conspicuous absence of the Richter children. Teachers who had taught five students had ten, still a small ratio, but double or triple from the year before. Only the new senior class remained unchanged; there were five.

The first day of school resulted in new enrollments and very little accomplishment in the actual classroom. It took several days to get everyone settled and in the right place. The first-year kindergarten teacher Sunny had hired to replace Mrs. Gibbs had expected four students, but she had eight, seven girls and one boy.

Chambry came home from his first day of school with a triumphant expression on his face. "I take it you had a good day," said Mac.

"Yes, sir. I have a harem."

"A what?" Mac laughed.

"I'm the only boy in class. There are seven girls. I can be like an Arabian knight and have a harem, like in the book we've been reading."

"You're not going to school to study girls."

"No, but it's a nice perk." The boy grinned.

Mac smiled slyly at the way Chambry picked up words and phrases, like Leo's saying many a truth was said in jest and Felicia having talked about perks on the job. He asked, "When did you develop an interest in girls?"

"When I kissed Laurie, but she won't be in kindergarten until next year."

"Kissed? Yes, you said that while we were swimming. Explain."

"Well"—the child tilted his head back and forth from shoulder to shoulder—"it was better than the one you gave Miss Bankston on New Year's Eve, but nothing like the one Uncle Tipper gave Aunt Jess. That was yucky."

"Show me," said Mac.

"If you bring Miss Bankston over, I'll give you pointers."

"Chambry!"

"Yes, Daddy, I would say this was a great first day of school." The child strutted off to tell his brothers all about his harem.

35
Bright Kid

Friday afternoon, Sunny entered the clinic walking straight to the doctor's office. "What now?" asked Mac. "The last time you came in like this, we had an epidemic."

"I would love an epidemic like this," laughed the school principal, holding up some files and a binder.

"Then, it's good. What's up?" He pointed to the chair in front of his desk. Sunny sat down.

"I want to test Chambry."

"For what?"

"Gifted. I'd like to test Abner again, too. Since he's been living with you and getting proper nutrition, he's made leaps and bounds. But I have to have your permission to do more than a cursory, unofficial, mental evaluation."

"Of course, test them. Do you usually test kindergartners?"

"No, but I have two who are amazing. I would move them to first grade."

"Chambry and who else?"

"Lily Jones. Bringing that little girl into town was a stroke of genius."

"It was logical. You know, Gator is extremely intelligent. He wasn't given opportunity. He failed grades simply because he missed too many days, not because he didn't have the grades. Ask Mamaw. She taught him."

"Sherry's smart, too. Mac, what do you think would happen if I offered an adult education class once a week?"

"You'd have takers, but don't overextend yourself. You're one person."

Sunny laughed and rubbed her forehead. "I go home at night, make a sandwich or stick something in the microwave, take a hot bath, pop in an old tearjerker, and fall asleep on the sofa. I think I can offer a night."

"You sound depressed, Sunny. That's not you." He leaned back comfortably in his chair behind his desk.

"Naa. Maybe a little lonely."

"That's what you get for watching tearjerkers alone."

"Are you volunteering to watch one with me?"

"Sure. You got popcorn?"

"I do."

"I'll watch a tearjerker with you, if you watch an action flick with me. Do you have any of those?" Mac leaned forward with his elbows resting on his desk.

"My tastes are varied." Sunny crossed her legs, kicking her foot subtly. "I have all kinds. I have a membership in a DVD club."

"Hm." He stroked his chin in thought. "We should find a way to play them on a big screen. We could have our own little theater."

"We could probably do that. Let me work on it. Back to my errand. Do I have permission to test the boys Monday?"

"Absolutely. Do you need me to sign something?"

"Yeah." Sunny handed Mac the permission forms from her binder. He signed them and gave them back.

"Thanks," Sunny said with a smile. "Now, I'm going to talk to Gator."

"He'll be ecstatic."

Sunny knocked on the Joneses' door. She smiled as she waited for an answer. Sherry had brought the wooden plaque that said "The Joneses" from their old house and hung it beside the door.

When Gator saw Sunny, he immediately worried. "Is somebody in trouble? Please come in."

"No, Mr. Jones. Your children are delightful, but I would like to talk to you about Lily."

"If she ain't in trouble, what's to talk about?"

Sunny laughed. "I'm not one of those teachers who only communicates with parents when there's bad news."

"So, this is good news, then?"

"Yes. I'd like to test her for gifted. I think she's very intelligent. I'd like to see if she should go to first grade without kindergarten."

Gator knitted his eyebrows. "Miss Bankston, I like the idea o' my daughter bein' special, but if'n you test her, can you test Fox and Rooster, too? I don't want them to feel left out like I always did."

More reality of Possum Holler's past hit Sunny as she felt the hurt in Gator's voice. "Of course, I can test them, but even if they don't fall in the gifted range, they're quite smart. I don't think they should skip a grade though."

"I understand. You should know that Rooster showed Lily ever'thing he studied last year."

"Commendable, but the fact that she grasped it from him is outstanding."

"Yes, test all of 'em. Stay for supper so we can tell Sherry."

Sunny sniffed the aroma and her stomach rumbled. "I'll stay on one condition," she said.

"What's that?"

"Call me Sunny."

"That'd make me equal to Mac and Tipper."

"You already are, but it would make me your friend."

Gator nodded. "Sunny it is, and we're Gator and Sherry."

"I'd like that."

Sunny tested all five children on Monday. Every one of them fell in the ninetieth percentile, and Sunny placed them in gifted. However, as she predicted, both Lily and Chambry fell in the ninety-fifth percentile or higher. Since she had their parents' permission, Sunny bumped them to first grade. She felt certain Chambry could have skipped to second, but, for the age factor, she would wait for him to skip another grade. She did, however, pay Mac another visit.

"Are you stalking me, Miss Bankston?" Mac joked.

Sunny blushed deep crimson. "N-n-no," she stammered. "I just wanted to share the test results with you."

"Burst my bubble, why don't you?" the doctor continued to tease.

"Mac, stop it."

"Oh, all right. Come into my office."

They sat down, and he asked, "How smart is my kid, I mean, are my kids?"

"Abner scored a hundred twenty-five on the IQ test. He's been moved to gifted. Chambry, on the other hand, you won't believe."

"Do tell."

"One sixty-three."

"Oh, my God!"

"I only bumped him one grade because he's so young. Next year, we might need to go another."

"I guess I should call Felicia with this. She'll be thrilled. How about Lily, or can you tell me that?"

"I'm not supposed to, but you're her doctor. One forty-eight, and both Fox and Rooster scored almost a hundred thirty."

"It's amazing what a change in environment can bring out in a kid, isn't it?"

"Parents, too. I'm finally on a first-name basis with Gator and Sherry."

"Good. Oh, I have a surprise for you. You can institute your movie night Friday."

"What? How?"

"You'll be receiving a seventy-two-inch flat-screen television delivered to the school Thursday. It has built-in VHS and DVD players. The men delivering it have been instructed to install it in the school cafeteria."

The bell for the door opening chimed. Sunny pointed. Mac waved it off. "Jess can handle it. You may also expect a dozen computers next week with additional phone lines, so you can have internet. It'll have to be dialup way out here, but it's better than nothing."

"How?" Sunny asked in total disbelief.

"Gifts from Norton Entertainment."

"Ron?"

"I called about testing Chambry, and he felt his stepson and others needed these advantages."

Sunny squealed. She leaned across the desk and threw her arms around Mac's neck. "This is wonderful!"

Mac hugged her back and wondered for a moment if he smelled her scented hanky because she smelled so good.

Sunny pushed back. "Silly me. I lost all sense of decorum."

"Well." Mac grinned. "Maybe you should hug Chambry. After all, he's the bright kid."

36
Movie Night

Sunny got the word out: Possum Holler would have movie night on Fridays, but she racked her brain about what to show for the debut. The television was delivered, installed, and working by Thursday night. Sunny stuck in *Braveheart* to test the set-up. She flipped off the light to give a real theater effect.

As she sat down with a sandwich, someone knocked at the cafeteria door. Sunny unlocked the door and cracked it. Hands holding a bag of rippled potato chips, a container of sour cream and onion dip, a bag of chocolate-covered peanuts, and two one-liter colas popped through. "I brought concessions," Mac's voice said on the other side of the door.

Sunny laughed and opened the door. "I have a turkey sandwich we can share."

"Sounds great. I thought you'd test it. I put the boys to bed a little early and took a chance. What are we watching?"

"*Braveheart*. I guess it's both action and tear-jerker."

"What's the debut?"

"I don't know yet."

In the dimness from only the blue screen, Mac pulled a chair near Sunny's. She passed her sandwich toward him.

"No, thanks," he said shaking his head. "I had supper with the boys. I'll open the snacks though. One sandwich is hardly a meal."

"It's enough, but who told you I like chips and onion dip?"

"Nobody. I'm psychic."

"Uh-hum."

"I like 'em," the doctor confessed.

"Good, just so you share. Have you seen this?"

"Yes. It's terrific. But it's been a while. Hit play."

Sunny hit the play button on the remote control. They watched the movie while they devoured chips, dip, and candy. At the end of the movie, Sunny turned the light on. "Oh, my gosh!" she exclaimed. "We ate all of that."

"So?"

"Not healthy, doctor."

"Just don't do it all the time. Besides, I had to have something to do with my hands and mouth."

"What does that mean?"

"Well," Mac said after putting the food wrappers in the trash can and Sunny's getting the DVD, "if I hadn't had things to keep me busy, I might've done this." He took her face in his hands and kissed her softy.

She looked totally stunned but spoke not a word. Mac shrugged. "Well, you didn't slap me. You didn't respond, but you didn't slap me."

"I-I-I wasn't expecting that."

"Dare I try again?"

"Walk me home. It's late and dark."

Sunny locked the door. With only a sliver of a moon, the night was black. Walking toward Sunny's house, Mac fumbled in the dark and found her hand. She didn't pull it away. They didn't talk until they got to her door.

"Mac," Sunny said softly. "I haven't dated in a very long time."

"Did someone break your heart?"

"Not exactly. I'm not ready to talk to you about that."

"All right. I won't push. I like you, Sunny. Think about it. There could be something there."

"Maybe."

"Good night." He let go of her hand and started to leave.

"You didn't try again."

He stopped and smiled in the dark. "I'll walk you home tomorrow night. Good night." Mac walked home.

Sunny touched her fingers to her lips and sighed. *I wish you had tried again.*

The next morning at school, Chambry Reardon knocked on Sunny's office door. "Come in," she called.

The child opened the door.

"Good morning, Chambry," she said cheerily.

"Good morning." The boy came in. "I have a note from my daddy. He threatened to tan my hide if I opened it and read it."

"Has he ever spanked you?"

"No, ma'am, but I don't wanna tempt him. Here's the note, unopened."

"Thank you, Chambry. Go to class."

Sunny opened the note. It was completely innocent, simply saying:

> *Star Wars* saga. That'll give you six Fridays. Thursdays could be more personal and on a smaller screen. I'll take care of popcorn tonight, and I'll make sure you get home safely.
>
> Mac

Sunny laughed. "*Star Wars* it is."

Before time for the movie to start, Mac rolled in an old-fashioned popcorn machine, complete with red-and-white-striped bags. Then, he brought in three coolers of iced soft drinks.

Sunny laughed. "You've thought of everything." She recognized the machine from Harvest Fest.

He held up a finger. "The movie's free, or you'd be breaking the law. Popcorn is a quarter, and drinks are fifty cents. All concessions proceeds will go to purchase books for our fledgling little library."

"What a wonderful idea!"

"Let me get to popping. Here, put up my sign." He handed her a poster Chambry and Abner had made for the concessions stand.

She taped the sign beside the popcorn popper, and Mac started the popcorn. Half an hour later, the first patron arrived. Within an hour, the room was packed with children sitting on the floor and adults taking the chairs. Almost everybody had a drink and popcorn. On the first movie night, they raised over a hundred dollars for books.

When Sunny stood to welcome everyone, she noticed even the Richter family had come into town and she prayed no one would say anything to offend them. Since there would be no alcohol at movie night, they shouldn't get out of hand at all. She nodded at Alain who nodded back.

Sunny spoke excitedly. "Ladies and gentlemen, thank you for the huge turnout. I'm excited to initiate Possum Holler Movie Night. Over the next six weeks we'll watch the movies in the *Star Wars* saga. I think you'll really enjoy them. I don't have anything else to say except, Mac, hit the lights, and, Leo, start the movie. Have fun."

Many of the residents of Possum Holler had never even heard of *Star Wars*, but they sat back and enjoyed themselves immensely.

The cafeteria clean, Sunny got ready to go. Mac popped back in. "You've finished cleaning."

"They didn't leave much mess."

"I tucked the boys in and got back as quickly as I could."

"It's okay."

"Next time, wait for me to help."

"Thank you, kind sir." She curtsied in a silly manner.

"Are you ready to go?"

"Yes."

Sunny locked the door. She felt in the dark for Mac's hand before they ever turned to leave. The man cradled it firmly, yet gently, in his. They walked leisurely to Sunny's door.

"Are you in a hurry to get home?" Sunny asked.

"No."

"Would you like some coffee or anything?"

"Sunny, you're trembling. Why are you so afraid?"

"It's a really long story I'm not ready to tell."

"Who hurt you?" The gentle surgeon's hands comfortingly put strands of hair behind the woman's ear. "Who made you want to hide in a place like Possum Holler?"

"I like Possum Holler. I feel safe here. It's been a long time since I felt safe."

"I won't hurt you, Sunny, and I won't let anybody else hurt you."

"You already saved me once."

"Is that it? You were in love with your principal, and he died."

"A small part."

"I'm sorry I couldn't save him. He was gone before he ever got to me. Still, I'm glad I was there for you. I'd like to kiss you good night."

"I wish you would."

Mac cupped Sunny's face in his hands and found her mouth in the dark. He kissed her softly without any further intent. This time, Sunny responded and was loath to let Mac go home, but he slipped away from her with a whispered, "Good night."

She giggled behind her closed door and thought about the soft tickle of Mac's facial hair.

37

Teacher, Teach Me

Gator believed business matters should never be discussed in church; thus, he waited until Monday afternoon when he rushed back from tending his hogs to catch Sunny as she left the school. And although they were on a first-name basis, Gator was old-fashioned enough not to visit her alone at her house. She was, after all, single, and he was a married man. Gator realized Sunny always left the school last after she walked through and made sure all was secure before she locked the building.

As Sunny started to turn the key in the door, Gator walked up. "Good evening, Sunny."

"Hello, Gator. How are you?"

"Jest fine, but I'd like to talk to you 'bout somethin'."

"One of the children?"

"No, ma'am. Me. Can we talk inside? It's kindly private."

"Of course. Come into my office." Knowing Gator would feel uncomfortable meeting with her alone behind closed doors, Sunny left her office door open. "What do you have on your mind, Gator?" She indicated a chair in front of her desk as she sat in her office chair.

Gator sat down politely. "Mac reminded me there's a test you can take so it's like you graduated from high school. I'd like to take that test. Sunny, can you teach me the things I need to know?"

"Wow! I told Mac I'd like to offer an adult education class, but I haven't said so yet. The test you're talking about is the high-school equivalency test. Yes, Gator, I can teach you what you need to know. How far did you get in school?"

"I passed to seventh grade, but I's already sixteen. It was jest hard to get there in the winter, and I missed so many days, I'd fail ever time, 'cept when Miss Langston, Mrs. Tomlin, I mean, and Miss Stone lied about the absences. I always had good grades. I can read, and I'm real good at ciphering. I have to be so's I don't git cheated at market."

"I understand. The test will check you on reading comprehension and language mechanics. That's being able to write with correct grammar."

"My grammar's awful. I know that."

"I can teach you to speak with good grammar, too. You'll have to practice. The test also has a math portion and social studies portion."

"Social studies? You mean history and geography?"

"Yes. I understand being able to read maps and charts is really important."

"I can do that."

"I know you can. Then, there's a science section and a writing section in which you have to use those language mechanics on paper."

"You can teach it to me, right?"

"I can. The first thing we need to do is for you to take some placement tests for me. They will let me know what you already know, so we'll know where to start."

"When?"

"Each placement test will take about an hour. I would suggest taking two at a time. You can take a couple tonight if you want to."

"I cain't 'cause I ain't told Sherry I'd be late for supper."

"Do you think Sherry would like to take the class, too?"

"It'd be real hard for both of us at the same time. Maybe when I get done, she can."

"Okay. How about two tomorrow evening and three Wednesday evening? The writing part is in with the language mechanics. It takes a little longer to complete. Then, we could start classes next Monday, say from six until nine. You can have supper and then come. We'll have class every Monday until you're ready. It won't happen in a day or two." She placed both her hands flat on her desk. "I have one request of you. Ask me, using correct grammar and pronunciation. I know you can; you've been lazy about it."

"Yes, ma'am. I guess I've been very lazy. It didn't seem to matter. It does now because I don't want my very smart kids to be ashamed of me."

Sunny teared up as she spoke. "Gator, I wish little rich kids could have a father like you. You know, people can be impoverished in more ways than money. Your family is rich in love. That's very important."

"Thank you, ma'am. Here goes. Sunny, will you please teach me the things I need to know to take and pass the high-school equivalency test?"

"Wow! You're going to make my job easy. Yes, Gator, I'll teach you and anyone else who might want to do it. I'll see you tomorrow at six. We'll take the English with writing and reading placement tests."

"I'll see you then."

Sunny's weeks took on a new routine. Monday evenings she tutored Gator, always with the door open. Thursdays she and Mac watched a movie on her couch. Mac never made sexual advances toward her. He would put his arm around her during a serious movie or pelt her with popcorn during a comedy before he would softly kiss her good night and go home.

Fridays had become movie night. They finished the third installment in the *Star Wars* saga. Mac took his boys home and came back to help Sunny clean. The job didn't take long because the moviegoers put their trash in the receptacle by the door on their way out.

"All clean again," said Mac, putting the mop in the bucket outside the door. "It's turning cold. Where's your sweater?"

"I didn't need it earlier," laughed Sunny.

She shivered as a night breeze blew.

"Let's get you home." Mac put his arm around her as they walked.

On her front porch, he kissed her as always and turned to leave. "Mac," said Sunny. "Would you like to come in for a while?"

"Change our routine?"

"Variety is the spice of life."

Mac sighed. "And do what?"

"I don't know. We could watch another movie. Tomorrow's Saturday. We can stay up later."

He stepped back onto the porch. She shuddered. "Do you have any pie?" he asked. "I'd love some dessert."

"We can make hot, fresh brownies."

"Brownies are good." Mac pushed the door open.

Sunny went into the kitchen and pulled a box of brownie mix from her cupboard, her date trailing behind her. Mac put his hand over hers. "Sunny, I don't want any brownies. Breakfast, I would take."

"Oh," she said nervously. "Breakfast. Um. I don't know about breakfast." Tears smarted her eyes.

He took both her hands in his. "Sh. Don't cry. Why are you so afraid?"

She pulled away from him. "This was a bad idea." She turned her back to him and leaned over her sink. "Maybe you should go home."

Mac turned Sunny around. "I don't have to have breakfast. This is enough." He kissed her deeply and pulled her into an embrace. She shook as if having a seizure, and he felt silent tears on his chest. He soothed her hair and kissed the top of her head. "I wish you would talk to me."

"I can't," she sniffled. "I just can't."

"All right. If you want me to go. Good night." Mac left through Sunny's back door. It disturbed him to leave her like that for he had never seen her so sad.

Mac got up early and went into the woods to gather a bouquet of wild fall flowers. He brought them home and tied a ribbon around them. When his three boys came to breakfast, he said, "I have a pre-breakfast errand for y'all."

"What, Daddy?" Chambry asked.

He handed the flowers and a note to Chambry. "Deliver these to Sunny."

"Did you have a fight?"

"No, but maybe you should give me some pointers."

"Did you kiss her?"

"Yes, and she cried."

Chambry, Abner, and Zeke all three looked at Mac with arched brows and clenched jaws.

Flustered, Mac said, "Don't look at me like that. Just deliver the flowers and the note. *Please.*"

The three boys walked to Sunny's and knocked. When she opened the door, she wore frumpy sweatpants and a baggy sweat shirt from her university.

"Good morning, Miss Bankston," said the three boys together as if they had rehearsed it.

"Are you all right?" asked Chambry.

"I didn't sleep well last night," she answered.

"Neither did Daddy. He sent us to deliver these." Chambry handed Sunny chrysanthemums, cat tails, black-eyed Susans, and twigs with fall leaves while Abner handed her the note, and Zeke spontaneously threw his arms around her hips, his head barely coming to her hip bone.

Sunny rubbed the little boy's head. "Thank you. Have you had breakfast yet?"

"No ma'am, and Daddy's not even cooking." Chambry wrinkled his nose. "I think it's gonna be cold cereal from a box."

Sunny laughed. "Zeke and Abner, come in with me. Chambry, get your daddy. Tell him Sunny's breakfast buffet is open."

"Yes, ma'am."

She put the flowers in a vase on her dinette set and discreetly opened the note that read:

*I'm sorry. I didn't mean to make you cry.
Please forgive me.*

Mac

Sunny wiped tears from her cheeks. Zeke put his arms around her legs again and said, "Don't cwy. I wuv you."

She almost sobbed but took a deep breath. "I'm all right. I need to change clothes. Then, I'm going make us a great big breakfast. I'll be back in a minute." She kissed Zeke on the head and Abner on the cheek. "I love you, too."

Sunny washed her face, put on a pale blue sweater with a pair of jeans, and pulled her hair back in a ponytail. She hurried back to the kitchen and got out eggs, sausage, grits, flour, and sugar.

"Okay. Everybody has to help," she instructed Zeke and Abner. "Abner, I think you can crack the eggs just fine. Zeke, what can I get you to do?"

The little boy shrugged his shoulders as the front door opened and Mac called, "Sunny?"

"We're in the kitchen," she answered.

Mac and Chambry came in. "Welcome." Looking like the flower child she had been brought up to be, she smiled, walked over and kissed Chambry on the head and Mac on the lips. "It wasn't your fault," she whispered. "I'm just not ready yet."

"Okay," said Mac.

"Now, Mac, fry the sausage. Abner crack those eggs."

"How many?"

"Ten, and then add a little salt and pepper and a splash of milk. Can you do that?"

"Yes, ma'am."

"Then whisk them with this." She handed Abner a whisk.

"Chambry," she said as she put water in a pot and added salt and butter, "when this water boils, add seven scoops of grits, turn the fire all the way down, and put the lid on. Come here, Zeke."

She set Zeke on the counter. "I want you to take this cup and this bowl." She handed Zeke the cup and the bowl. Then she set the flour and sugar beside him. "Now, use that cup and put two cups of flour and one cup of sugar in the bowl." The teacher showed the three-year-old the numbers using her fingers. "If you make a mess, it's okay."

With everybody working, they sat down to sausage, scrambled eggs, grits, and pancakes forty-five minutes later. After they cleaned up the kitchen, Mac said, "I have to go into the city to pick up some medical supplies. Would you like to go with me? We could have dinner at a real sit-down restaurant."

"What about the boys?"

"Afternoon with Uncle Tipper."

Sunny nodded. "Okay. You get the boys settled, and I'll get completely dressed. We'll leave in an hour."

They spent the afternoon in the city and had dinner at a Japanese steakhouse. When Mac delivered Sunny to her front door, he kissed her soundly and said good night.

Monday evening, Gator came for his tutoring session. Sunny seemed bubbly. "Good evening, Gator."

"Sunny."

"I want you to take a practice math test tonight. It's similar to the one you'll have to take. I think you have the math skills, and we need to focus on the other areas. This test will tell me for sure."

"All right."

"You have to use the computer."

"You showed me how to do that."

"Okay." Sunny gave Gator instructions on how to load the test. When he was ready, she set a timer. "You have an hour and forty-five minutes. Begin."

While Gator took the test, Sunny read the book, *Christy*, because Mac had suggested it. After an hour, Gator said, "Sunny, I'm finished."

"Are you sure?"

"Yes. Math is easy."

Sunny clicked a few buttons and scored the test." Excellent!" she exclaimed. "Math must be easy for you. You missed one."

"Which one?" asked Gator in agitation.

"Number twenty-eight."

He looked at the question. "Oh! I forgot the negative sign."

"Gator, you did great."

"Am I ready to take the test?"

"The math portion, but since you'll have to go into the city, you'll need to take it all at once. It'll take all day. It costs forty dollars."

"So, I need to study the other things harder."

"Yes. You might be ready in January."

"That's my goal." Gator looked at the clock on the wall. "We have an hour. What should we study?"

Sunny realized they would not be leaving early. She laughed and retrieved some grammar work sheets. "Let's see what you remember about language mechanics, and your homework will be to write a narrative essay about the scariest experience you've ever had."

"Homework?"

"Yep."

"All right." Gator completed the two work sheets and handed them to Sunny. He commented, "I don't remember many of my teachers being as nice or as pretty as you. Mac's lucky."

"What?"

"Sunny, it's obvious you and Mac have an attraction. Don't fight it. Mac's a good man."

"I'll remember that, Gator." She looked over the sheets. "Great work. You didn't miss any. Next week you get more advanced. It's time to go."

"Thanks, Sunny. I feel like a new man."

"You sound like a new man."

"I was lazy."

She escorted him to the door. "I have to shut everything down."

"Good night, Sunny." He gave her friendly squeeze around the shoulders.

"Good night, Gator. Give Sherry my best."

Gator went home and Sunny shut down the computer and made sure everything was secure.

Mac had a late evening patient with a severe case of indigestion the man thought might be a heart attack. The doctor gave the elder Farmer Maddox Zantac and provided him a sample to take home. Mac locked his pharmaceutical pantry.

As Sunny locked the schoolhouse door, she felt hands slip around her and grab her breasts. The pungent odor of sweat and liquor stifled her. She screamed as a bearded face grazed her neck and a stupored voice growled in her ear, "Teacher, teach me them thingsh you been teachin' Mac and Gator."

38
Hands Off!

The man popped his hand over Sunny's mouth and slurred, "Sh! I ain't gonna hurt ya! Ain't no reashon to shcream 'lesh I make ya feel real good. I jesht want a l'il o' what ya been givin' other men in Posshum Holler. Ain't I ash good ash Gator Jonesh and Mac Reardon? You been mighty cozhy with them lately. I thought you wash better'n that."

"Get your hands off her!" snarled Dr. Reardon as he charged across the road and leveled Sunny's assailant with a shoulder to the man's midsection. Mac straddled Alain Richter and pounded him across the face. "You stupid…moronic…inbred…vermin! If you ever touch Sunny again, I will kill you," the healer raged with all oaths to do no harm forgotten.

The commotion brought out other townspeople. Tipper pulled Mac off Alain, and Constable Hill jerked Alain up by the scruff of the neck.

"Mac! Settle down!" Tipper hollered. "You're gonna kill the idiot! You know he's just drunk!"

"That's right! I *am* gonna kill him."

Constable Hill demanded, "What happened?"

Sunny sank to the ground in a heap and gasped for breath as she sobbed.

Leo ran up in his pajamas, clearly ready for bed.

"Tipper, let go of me!" Mac hollered.

"Only if you promise not to hit Alain again."

"I don't care about the loathsome, despicable son-of-a-bitch! He's the kind that gives us hillbillies a bad name! His momma's his sister, and his sister's his daughter! He makes a good argument for abortion!"

"MacKenzie Reardon!" snapped Leo. "You don't mean those things."

"Yes, I do!" Jamming a finger into the drunk man's chest, the doctor bellowed, "If you ever touch her again, I'll kill you! I swear it, Alain Richter!" Mac knelt by Sunny and tried to hug her.

Momentarily, Sunny screamed and slapped at Mac before she slipped into his arms and continued to sob.

Constable Hill said assertively, "Miss Bankston, please tell me what happened."

Sunny continued to sob into Mac's chest. She choked, "Mac, oh, God! Mac, he raped me."

"I ain't raped that womarn!" yelled Alain Richter. "I jesht wanted shome o' what she givesh Mac and Gator. She ain't got no problem with them. I sheen Mac shlobberin' all over her and goin' in her houshe and not comin' out and the way she'sh holed up in the shchool with a married man!"

"What?" yelled Mac and Gator simultaneously since Gator had run back to the school.

"Sunny," Mac said firmly. "Look at me. What did Alain Richter do to you just now?"

She gasped for air. Finally, she stammered, "H-h-he grabbed me and put his hands on my breasts and said he wanted me to teach him what I've been teaching you and Gator. Mac, I didn't do anything wrong."

"No, you didn't. Alain is just a retarded, good-for-nothing drunkard. Maybe if he had a little of what you've been giving Gator, he wouldn't be that way."

Mac turned to Alain. "You idiot! She's been teaching Gator so he can get his high school equivalence. As for me, yeah! You *all* need to know I'm courting Sunny, but she has done nothing immoral. Why would you even think that?"

"I sheen you go in after the movie, and you didn't come out!"

"I left through the back door. Why were you watching her?"

Alain started to cry. "Caushe she'sh beautiful and kind and good like Amy."

Constable Hill asked, "Miss Bankston, what do you want me to do with this fool? He's so drunk he can hardly stand up, but that don't excuse him."

Sunny looked at Mac. "Lock him up and let him sleep it off. Mac, he's pathetic; but make sure he knows to keep his hands off me, or Mac will kill him. Mac, please take me home."

"Okay. Tipper, will you put my boys to bed?"

"Sure. You take care of Sunny."

Tipper put a hand on Alain's shoulder. "Alain, go sleep it off. I'll talk to you later."

Mac picked Sunny up and carried her home. He set her on her couch. "Are you hurt?" he asked gently.

"No, just scared."

"Do you have chamomile?"

"In the cupboard."

"I'll make you some."

"Mac, I need a bath. I can still smell him."

"Not too hot. Sunny, you didn't do anything wrong. If you're gone too long, I'll come after you."

Sunny ran a bubble bath and slipped in up to her neck. After lying in the water for a while, she ducked her head under the water and held her breath as long as she could. When she came up for air, Mac stood over her. She gasped.

"I told you I'd come after you," he chided. "It's been half an hour. You're water-logged. Did you use the whole bottle of bubble bath?"

"I think so. I can still smell him though." Sunny reached out her hand and touched Mac's knuckles. "Don't do surgery any time soon."

"I'm fine. I've always been a scrapper. I'll put some ice on my hand while you drink your tea." He took the big white towel from the rack over the tub and held it open. "Come on."

"I can get out by myself."

"I won't look."

Sunny snorted. "Why would you want to?"

"Okay. I'll look."

"What?"

"Sunny, you're beautiful. I want to look. I want to touch. But I'm a gentleman. I'll wait for you. Now, come on." Mac wrapped the towel around her. "Do you want PJs?"

"I can dress myself."

"Yes, I know. Come get your tea. We need to talk."

Sunny came into the living room in her frumpy sweat suit.

"Comfy?" asked Mac.

"I feel safe in it."

"That's good. Come here. Sit by me." He patted the sofa, handing her a cup of chamomile tea as she sat beside him. He put his arm around her, and she laid her head on his shoulder. He rested his other hand on a washcloth filled with ice. He kissed the top of her head. "Talk to me, Sunny. Who raped you?"

She cried silently. "I don't know. Tonight, it all rushed to the surface, all the fear, all the anger. Alain Richter did *not* rape me."

"Tell me what happened."

Sunny breathed hard. "It's been nine years, but I still have nightmares. I was a freshman in college. Like most freshmen, I just had to experience the Greek scene. I was pledging a sorority, and we went to a fraternity party. I wasn't even drinking. All I had was Coke."

A deep, ragged breath escaped the woman's chest as Mac gently caressed her arm. "I remember dancing with several guys, just having a good time. I remember eating cheese and crackers.

"I woke up the next morning in my dorm room. I was bleeding, and I was in so much pain. Twelve hours before, I had been a virgin."

Sunny shivered, and Mac held her more tightly. "I went to a rape crisis center because I didn't know what to do. They took me to the hospital and filed a police report. The rape kit revealed nothing except I had been raped. The rapist used a condom. I was bruised, but there was no DNA. They did blood work. I had been drugged. They called it GHB, Georgia Home Boy."

Sunny cried quietly for a few minutes, and Mac didn't interrupt her. "Mac, I have no idea who did it. There were seventy plus suspects. I couldn't go to class. I was scared to death. I transferred to another university.

"The lady at the rape crisis center was really nice. She's the one who introduced me to Jesus. She wrote me throughout college and in Chicago. I've gotten one letter here."

He kissed her hair. "Go on. You need to get it all out."

"Mac, I've tried to put it all behind me. When I started teaching, I met Perry."

"Perry?"

"My principal."

"Oh, yes."

"I felt so safe with him. Yes, I fell in love with him, and, then"—She cried a little harder—"I never told him I loved him, and he was gone. I didn't even get to tell him good-bye. I wasn't able to go to the funeral, and they flew his body back to Detroit for burial. I felt so alone. I couldn't stay there without Perry.

"So, I came here. Did I hide here? Maybe in the beginning, but I belong here. Mac, I don't want to leave."

"I don't want you to leave."

"Mac, I've never been with a man by choice. Perry and I were not sleeping together. It never went beyond kissing and snuggling. I never told *him* about this. I'm so scared nobody will ever want me."

"Sunny, how can you think that? You're special. Please don't leave. Don't let tonight scare you away. I want you on so many levels."

She snuggled closer to him. "Is this level all right for now?"

"Yes. You know what I think?"

"What?"

"It doesn't count. You didn't want him. You don't even know who it was. It doesn't count."

Her tears spent, Sunny chuckled. "That's what Felicia said."

"She knows?"

"She and Jess. That's all. I never even told my parents. Felicia said it didn't count. She said it had been so long, it would be like the first time."

"Well, she's kind of right. It'll…"

"What?"

Mac grunted.

"It'll what, Mac? Hurt?"

"Well, yes, maybe a little."

"Felicia also said you're gentle."

"Sunny, I won't hurt you in any way. I already told everybody outside I'm courting you. That means—hands off! You're mine."

"So, you don't see me as somehow tarnished?"

"No. You're shiny and new. Sunny, the only woman I've ever been with was Felicia."

"I know that."

"How?"

"Your sense of morality."

They were quiet for a moment. Mac stroked her back and arm in comfort. Finally, he broke the silence. "Sunny, we're talking as if we are gonna do something."

She pushed herself up, damp red hair trailing across his chest and looked him in the eye. "Are we?"

He pushed her wet hair back, smiled softly, and nodded. "Eventually."

Mac kissed Sunny softly and tenderly.

39
Nuptials

Mac did spend the night at Sunny's, but it was completely innocent. He got up early to get home to make breakfast. Sunny started to get up. "No, ma'am!" Mac said firmly. "You will take today off."

"I can't! The kids need me."

"Not today. This is your doctor speaking. You need a day off."

"Mac, if I stay busy, I don't think."

"Think! Think about me." He tapped his chest. "Ah! Go help Jess. The wedding is Saturday."

"Mac!"

"Sunny!"

"Humph!" She crossed her arms over her chest.

"You're stubborn," Mac said with a smirk playing around his lips.

"So are you."

"I'll sedate you." The threat from the doctor did not sound ominous.

"You wouldn't dare." Sunny set her jaw.

"Oh! No! Please? Take today off. Please?"

"You play dirty—like sending the boys to plead your case."

"Will you take today off, *please*?"

"Yes, because my *doctor* said so."

Mac took Sunny in his arms. "I'll be back tonight.

"Bring the boys. I'll make supper."

"Some date!" he exclaimed, feigning indignation.

"Yes, it will be." She grinned. "I get to be surrounded by four handsome men."

Mac laughed. "What's for supper?"

"Your favorite."

"What time?"

"Six."

"We'll be here." He kissed her and left to take care of his three sons.

Mac tried to sneak into his house, but three boys met him and bombarded him with questions. "Where have you been...What happened to Miss Bankston...Is she all right...Did you hurt her?"

"Whoa!" Mac said assertively, holding his hand up like a shield. "One of the Richter brothers assaulted Miss Bankston. She's all right, but she's taking today off from school. I stayed with her last night because she was very shaken up. You three may see her later at supper."

"Was he drunk?" asked Abner.

"Yes, he was." Mac nodded with a deep frown on his face.

"Daddy, is Miss Bankston your girlfriend now?" asked Chambry.

Mac's frown quickly turned upward. "Yes. Is that all right?"

"Yes, sir. I told you to kiss her on New Year's Eve."

"Yes, you did." He mussed his son's hair. "I'm glad I listened to you."

"Daddy." Zeke reached up for Mac. Mac picked him up. "I wuv her."

"She loves you."

"Daddy," said Abner quietly. "Do you love her?"

"Time for breakfast."

Sunny visited with Jessica. Jessica laughed. "My wedding's not going be huge. You're my maid of honor; Mac's Tipper's best man. We'll have a Possum Holler celebration before we go to Miami for our honeymoon. Tipper's never been to the beach."

"Are Felicia and Ron coming in?"

"Yes, and bringing the twins. Just wait until she finds out what Mac did last night."

"Last night, oh, Jess."

"Want to talk about it? Want to talk about Alain?"

Sunny sat with her legs pretzel style in the middle of Jessica's bed. She held one of the throw pillows against her. "Why did he do that? He didn't want me."

"Tipper talked to him in jail. Sunny, Alain has always been in love with Amy. Her mother broke them up when they were still teenagers. That poor man has been through hell."

"I've heard his father murdered his mother and then committed suicide. Alain found the bodies."

"No, he *saw* the whole thing."

"Oh. Traumatic. How old?"

"Fourteen. Then, he dropped out of school to be the head of his family."

Distaste dripping from her tongued, Sunny asked, "Did that include sleeping with his sisters?"

"Unfortunately. Tipper says Alain prayed last night."

"Repented?"

"Yes."

"I'll believe that when I see the evidence."

"Can you forgive him?"

"I have to. He didn't really hurt me, but it just brought everything back, the rape and Perry." She brushed unwanted tears from her cheeks. "It all finally had to come out."

"Mac certainly came to your rescue."

"Yeah." She twisted a tassel on the corner of the pillow.

"Wait until Felicia hears this story."

"Don't tell her."

"Why? She wants you and Mac to be together."

Sunny picked at the piping of the cushion. "It's a little awkward."

"Don't let it be," the nurse in Jessica comforted.

"Jess, I told Mac about what happened to me, and we talked about Perry, too."

"Good."

"He completely understood my feelings for Perry and my desolation at his loss."

"Of course, he did. What about?"

Sunny laughed softly. "He agrees with Felicia. He said it didn't count."

"See. You're meant to be."

"Did you tell Tipper?" She eased the cushion to her lap.

"That I'm a virgin?"

Sunny nodded.

"Yes. He said he would've been disappointed if I hadn't been. He's really old-fashion even if he did make a mistake with Amy."

"He's sweet and unspoiled."

"So is Mac."

"To a point." Sunny sighed. "Jess, Mac scares me."

"Why?"

"Because he's everything I ever wanted in a man."

"That's bad?" Jessica finished her makeup and stood at the end of the bed with her hands on the footboard.

Sunny shivered, but not from the coolness of the room. "What if I lose him, too?"

"Don't think like that. Is he worth the risk?"

"What if I'm not good enough?"

"Hogwash!"

"I'm so scared." She held the pillow closer to her chest.

"Stop fighting it. Let it happen." Jessica sat on the bed and pulled her long legs into the same position as Sunny.

"All of it?" Sunny asked tentatively.

"Did Mac tell you he wants to sleep with you?"

"He asked to stay for breakfast the night Alain Richter thought he stayed."

"Whoa! But he didn't."

"Because I wasn't ready. How will I know I'm ready?"

"You'll know. Honestly, I've been ready for Tipper since this time last year. He never seriously asked."

"You only have four more days."

"Then a lifetime."

Mac and his boys knocked on Sunny's door promptly at six. Mac held up two bottles in his hands. "Pinot Noir for us. Grape juice for them."

"How thoughtful."

"Maybe I just want to ply you with wine."

"No, not so. Not you."

"No, never." He kissed her with the boys watching.

Sunny had, indeed, made spaghetti, Caesar salad, garlic bread, and brownies. Smiling in delight, the sprite-like woman sat back and watched her little group of men devour the meal.

"They're growing," Mac said with a smirk on his face.

"Let me guess. They'll need a bedtime snack."

"Yes. I think they're Hobbits—second breakfast. Then, there's the Taco Bell theme—fourth meal."

Sunny looked at the boys. "Have you boys ever had tacos?"

"I have," volunteered Chambry.

"What about you two?"

"No, ma'am," said Abner. "What are they?"

"Delicious. What about nachos?"

"No, ma'am."

"Tomorrow night is Mexican night."

Mac said, "Sunny?"

"Oh, hush! You enjoy my company. If you're courting me, all my men get supper."

Zeke got out of his chair and climbed onto Sunny's lap. He said, "I want nacos." He looked up at her with his big blue eyes.

"And you shall have them," Sunny said as she kissed Zeke's nose.

Sunny made nachos and tacos, along with refried beans and Spanish rice, the next evening for the Reardon men. She could hardly believe three little boys could eat so much. The week continued as normal. Mac and Sunny watched a comedy on Thursday. Ron and Felicia arrived Friday afternoon and enjoyed *A New Hope* with the rest of Possum Holler.

Saturday dawned clear and cool. The mid-morning wedding of Jessica Langston and Tipper Campbell was honest and true. Their vows were simple. The celebration following sent the couple off with love.

40

A Waltz

The celebration for Tipper and Jessica was just that—a celebration. It was not a reception. Everyone in Possum Holler knew both of them. There were few guests from outside. Ron and Felicia did not count as outsiders anymore. The residents did not look upon Felicia with derision. They could see Mac still cared for her, but she was not Mac's, and, perhaps, never had been. She belonged with Ron.

On the other hand, Tipper had had a wife, but the most of residents of Possum Holler had written her off as dead to them. She had done the unthinkable—deserted her family. When the people saw Tipper and Jessica together, they knew this was a match made in Heaven. Jessica would never leave them, just as her father would never leave them.

The people of Possum Holler catered the event. For a marriage feast, they brought out their best. The table sported thinly sliced ham and turkey, fresh baked yeast rolls, chicken salad, chunks of cheese, fruit, bread-and-butter pickles, roasted pecans, and a cake topped with a bride and groom figurine. White linen covered the tables, and the ladies put out the best dishes they had to offer. Even if they did not match, each lady gave her best.

For once, Tipper was not one of the musicians. A string quartet, of a sort, played music for the revelers. The musicians played a banjo, a fiddle, a bass fiddle and a washboard for rhythm. Tipper spun his bride in a simple white satin, long-sleeved, scoop-necked, fitted bodice, with an A-line skirt wedding dress around the area cleared for dancing before the rest of the company joined in the merrymaking.

They ate and danced and drank and celebrated a love that was real and true and pure. To the amazement of the crowd, Alain Richter called several square dances and offered a tune on the harmonica. Mac toasted Tipper and Jessica with expensive French champagne, a gift from Ron.

At last, the music slowed. The groom held his bride close to his heart in a wedding waltz. He whispered, "I love you, Jess. I am so honored to have found you."

Jessica looked Tipper in the eye and ran a finger along his clean-shaven jaw. "It is I who has been blessed to have found you. I love you so much, Tipper."

"Is it time to leave yet? I can't wait to make love to you."

"Would you like to help me change clothes for our flight?"

"Mrs. Campbell, are you suggesting we not wait for Miami?"

Jessica blushed. "Everyone here would know what we were doing. It's the middle of the afternoon."

"I can wait until Miami, but it *is* time to go. Throw that bouquet. Make sure Sunny catches it."

"You have to throw my garter first."

"Are you gonna show off your thigh?"

"How daring!" She clapped a hand over her slightly-revealed cleavage.

"I think I *will* help you change clothes."

Tipper got the crowd's attention. "It's that time, guys and gals! Gather 'round! Gents, don't look too hard at my gorgeous wife's sexy thighs! But I have to throw this garter. Now, there's a catch. I expect my best man to snag this. If he doesn't, I'll be very disappointed. Okay, now. I'm not gonna look."

Jessica put her foot on a chair, and Tipper snaked her dress to just above the garter. He slipped the garter off, and to the wedding guests' delight, kissed Jessica's thigh. Tipper turned his back and tossed the garter over his shoulder.

"Get out of my way!" shouted Mac jokingly. However, he did snatch the garter from the air. Tipper turned around, and Mac waved the garter triumphantly.

Jessica got ready to toss her bouquet. She took note of where Sunny stood and aimed deliberately. Jessica did not need to aim; Sunny had every intention of snatching that bunch of flowers, which she did.

Felicia gave Sunny a questioning look. Sunny shrugged. With deliberation and purpose, she walked to Mac and slipped her hand into his.

Tipper and Jessica disappeared into the Tomlins' house long enough to change clothes. They came out and got into Jessica's car with Tipper at the steering wheel. The car had the traditional cans tied to it and "Just Married" on the back-window pane. They drove out of Possum Holler to applause and cheers.

After the clean-up, the guests headed home. Mac sent his boys to his house with Felicia and Ron. As darkness fell, he took Sunny's hand. "Shall I walk you home?"

"Yes, but don't you want to change clothes?"

"I'm fine except for this." Mac loosened his tie.

"I'm fine, too, except for these." Sunny held up her foot in heels. "Take me home so I can take them off."

They walked down the road toward her house. On the porch, Mac pulled Sunny into his arms. "Waltz with me."

"There's no music."

"Yes, there is. Don't you hear it?" Mac began to waltz in perfect rhythm as if hearing music. Sunny followed and laughed in delight as Mac picked up speed and lifted her in the air.

He set her down and kissed her passionately. He kissed her neck and moved his hand across her breasts. Sunny gasped. Mac kissed her again and softly nibbled her lip.

"Mac," breathed Sunny.

"I want to stay for breakfast."

"Mac, everybody would know. They would think badly of me."

"Will you ever let me stay?"

"Eventually." She placed both hands on his chest.

"Sunny, I don't wanna go."

"I don't want you to go, but you have guests. Go home."

"One more waltz."

"No. If I waltz with you again, I won't send you home."

41

Tear-Jerker

Sunny joined Mac's family and guests for Sunday breakfast.
Felicia cornered her by dragging her to help find proper church
clothes. "Talk," she demanded, shutting the bedroom door. "It's
been four months since you came to New York as *friends*."

"Since New York some things have happened."

"Explain."

"It's really Ron's fault."

"How?"

"He donated all that electronic equipment to the school. We
have movie night every Friday now. Mac helped me initiate the
movies. He came and watched *Braveheart* with me as a trial run.
He brought snacks, my favorites. He kissed me. I guess that was
our first official date."

"What happened before that?" Felicia dressed as she talked.

Sunny sat on the bed. "As you know, everybody has been
throwing us together on all sorts of occasions, you included.
Before school started back, I went to hide out and relax at my
favorite spot by the creek. It's kind of hidden, but it turns out to
be Mac and the boys' favorite fishing hole. They showed up with
fishing poles and a picnic. All four of them stripped down to
their underwear and went swimming. They manipulated me into
swimming with them and picnicking with them."

"What did you swim in?"

Her face burning, Sunny said, "I took off my shorts, but I
kept my tank top on over everything else."

"Chicken. Your underwear is not as revealing as most
bikinis."

Sunny sputtered, "Th-th-that's what Mac said to goad me into
getting in. We had fun, though.

"Then, Mac and I started watching a movie together every Thursday. On the third movie night, Mac walked me home as usual, but he came in. Felicia, he asked to stay for breakfast."

"Mac?" She paused with one stocking leg half on and looked at her friend, slack-jawed.

Sunny nodded. "He didn't. I'm scared to death."

"Of Mac?" She finished pulling on her pantyhose. "There's not a mean bone in that man's body."

"Have you ever seen him angry?"

"Does he get angry? I've seen him mildly irritated."

"Oh, he gets angry." Sunny nodded, her blue eyes stretched wide. "I thought he was going to kill Alain Richter last Monday."

"What happened?"

"Apparently, Alain has been watching me."

"A stalker in Possum Holler?"

"He's not a stalker. He's pathetic."

"Alain Richter? He's the ZZ Top wannabe with the gorgeous green eyes, right?"

Sunny laughed. "Only you would notice his eyes, but yes. They rarely come to town, but they've been coming for movie night."

"What did Mac do and why?" Felicia pulled out her makeup case. She applied makeup as Sunny related the story.

"You know I've been tutoring Gator Jones to take his high-school equivalency test. After he left the school, Alain accosted me at the door as I locked up. He was completely intoxicated. He insinuated I've been having sex with both Mac and Gator, and he wanted some. Mac must've heard me scream. Suddenly, Alain lay on the ground, and Mac straddled him, beating the stew out of him. Tipper had to pull him off. Mac told Alain if he ever touched me again, he'd kill him. Felicia, Mac *meant* it."

"Mac?" Felicia said again in dismay.

"He took me home. I told him about what happened in college and about losing Perry. Felicia, he stayed the night, but he just held me. However, last night, he asked to stay again."

"Wow," breathed Felicia. "He's in love with you."

"Can you say, 'Rebound'?"

"No, that's not in Mac's character. I'm shocked he wants to make love to you without a wedding band. You know, *he* was the virgin on our wedding night."

"Felicia, I don't know what to do."

"Do you love him? Be honest."

Sunny sighed. "I think I do."

"Then, what's stopping you?"

"The social mores of Possum Holler."

"Then, the next time he asks, tell him you need a piece of gold."

"Marriage?"

"Either that, or damn public opinion. Sunny, you and Mac work."

"Felicia, I don't want Mac to ask to stay for breakfast. I want him to tell me he loves me."

"Tell him so. Tell him you have no intention of being his booty call."

"I don't think that's his intention."

Felicia sat on the bed and patted beside her for Sunny to scoot closer. Felicia took Sunny's hand when she could reach her. "Not consciously. Let's face it. I hurt him. I wish I had never married Mac. I like him, and I'm sorry I hurt him. I was so immature. I was totally infatuated with the idea of this hillbilly with aspirations rising to a place of prominence in his community. I thought it was such a wonderful idea to come here and help the downtrodden. It would make a good movie." She grinned. "I think Mac was just as infatuated by the idea a real city girl would be attracted to him. He still saw himself as inferior." She tilted her head to the side. "Sunny, Mac is gorgeous. What's not to like in appearance? He's incredibly intelligent, and he's loving, kind, and compassionate. However, I was not in love with the man. I was in love with the notion. All it took was two minutes in Ron's presence for me to abandon that idea, though I tried to make it work. I love Ron with all my heart. Mac accepts that, and we're still friends. I could never hate him. He just wasn't the right man for me. Nonetheless, he's probably a little gun shy. However, he *is* a man, a man with needs. You have to let him know you don't want a relationship without a future. Be honest."

Sunny laughed. "I told Mac once I went home at night and watched a tear-jerker. Our story could be a good tear-jerker. Mac told me to read a book called *Christy*. I did. It's about a young teacher who goes to Appalachia. She's torn between the minister and the doctor, a homegrown healer like Mac. The doctor tells Christy he loves her, and his words bring her back from the brink of death. Why would Mac tell me to read that book? It's not exactly a manly story."

Felicia squeezed Sunny's hand. "Because the homegrown healer is too scared to tell the young teacher he loves her. He thought you would catch the symbolism."

Mac knocked on the bedroom door and opened it as the two women talked. "It's time for church. Is everything all right in here?"

"Just fine," assured Felicia. "Just fine."

When Mac and company entered the sanctuary with the babies, in the absence of a nursery, they were shocked to see the three back pews on the right side of the church filled with Richters. More shocking was even with twenty-six adults and children, no stench emanated from them. They appeared to be wearing clean gingham dresses or clean flannel shirts and overalls or jeans, depending on gender. However, all the men still looked as if they were members of the band ZZ Top with their long, frizzled beards, albeit clean beards. Even so, Mac steered his company as far away from them as he could.

Leo's sermon dealt with forgiving your fellow man. Jesus's disciples had asked how many times they should forgive their brother. Jesus had replied, "Seventy times seven."

Leo explained Jesus's words did not mean four hundred ninety times, but as often as asked. He went on to encourage the congregation to forgive any offense to which they were still harboring hard feelings. He reminded the worshippers "The

Lord's Prayer" asked for "forgiveness as you forgive." He ended his sermon by asking, "How are you forgiving others today?"

At the weekly altar call, every Richter walked up front to the astonishment and amazement of all the other worshippers. Leo and Alain talked a while before Leo stopped the music.

Behind the pulpit, Preacher Tomlin said, "Alain Richter has something he would like to say to the congregation. Alain..." Leo indicated his spot.

Alain stood beside Leo and spoke. "The first thing I gotta say is to apologize to Miss Bankston for the other night. I'm real sorry. I ask your forgiveness." Alain made eye contact with Sunny. She noted he did have beautiful green eyes, like emeralds sparkling with mist, and he was not speaking as badly as she had remembered. She wondered what she had missed before about this man.

Alain turned toward Gator. "Gator, I was a fool for even thinkin' you would do somethin' with another womarn. I know better'n anybody how much you love Sherry. I'm sorry.

"Mac, you still done wrong." He pivoted to face Mac. "You made Miss Bankston look bad, and that was wrong; but I shoulda known she was a better womarn than that."

Alain continued, "Second, thing is to ask forgiveness from all of y'all. I've been harborin' some real anger and resentment toward most o' y'all. Because o' that, we been livin' in our own little world, 'cause I was tryin' to keep my family from experiencin' the cruelty I've felt. I confess we been doin' things that were illegal and immoral. That's all stoppin'. We ain't drinkin' heavy no more. We ain't takin' our kin to use as wives no more." He shook his head for emphasis. "What's done is done; so, I'm askin' y'all to forgive us and to accept us for who we are without judgin' or bein' cruel, especially to the children. Just know, we're gonna be new people. I do wanna tell y'all that contrary to rumor, we ain't murderers or rapists and we ain't got no kids other than the ones you see here."

Alain took time to let his words sink in. Sunny listened intently, feeling this man had put every person in the sanctuary in his or her place. Alain Richter was not a fool. He had been seriously hurt, just as Jessica had said.

Alain spoke some more. "Miss Bankston, come tomorra, all these kids five and older will be in school. You put 'em where they need to be. You teach 'em." Alain looked toward Lauren. "Mrs. Tomlin, I commit 'em to your safekeepin'. Miss Bankston, I know you been teachin' Gator. All of us grownups want to be in yo adult education. We ain't stupid. We ain't morons, and we ain't retarded, unlike what Dr. Mac thinks."

Alain glared at Mac. It was evident he still struggled with some anger over Mac's words. "Next thing is, we come to Jesus. Preacher Tomlin is one man I respect. He ain't *never* judged me, and we've talked many times over the years. I just hadn't come to the place to admit I was a sinner that could be forgiven. No, that took Tipper Campbell talkin' straight up to me, but without judgin'. Y'all best git used to seein' us, 'cause we gonna be back there on them three pews ever week from now on."

Alain took a deep breath. Letting go of his pride was taking a great deal of effort. "Next thing is I want y'all to remember we farmers. We ain't got no runnin' water and no electricity, but we gonna be clean and groomed. There's a dozen fam'lies like us that ain't got the things we need to be as good as the rest o' y'all. There's another half a dozen that's jest got water, but no electricity. They didn't even pave the road all the way out to us, but that ain't gonna stop us from gettin' here.

"Last, 'cause it's a l'il bit of a grudge I gotta git off'n my heart. MacKenzie Reardon, *I...AIN'T...VERMIN!* I ain't no good reason to kill an unborn baby. What you said really hurt." Alain's voice choked. "We were friends; we were musketeers. You said you come back to Possum Holler to help people, and I guess you have. Still, you best be rememberin' you might be jest like me if'n yo fam'ly hadn't died and Preacher Tomlin ain't took you in. Yo old homestead ain't but two miles closer in than my place. You done told yo wife, ex-wife, we *used to be* friends. You didn't even introduce me to her, but I met her when she was dealin' with some guilt of her own 'cause she told me she was a disgrace like me. It ain't so. She's a fine lady that was jest confused 'bout where she should be. We ain't useless neither. Who do you think grows the fruit Tipper uses? Now, he's payin' good, and our crops have been real good lately. We always worked hard even if we wudn't livin' quite right. 'Cause of Tipper, we got new lives. Mac, I miss you."

Alain had to turn away to compose himself. Leo rubbed the man's back soothingly. Alain turned around. "I guess I'd like to conclude by thankin' Tipper, but he ain't here. He's on his honeymoon with a fine womarn who's gonna make him real happy. Mac, you got another chance with a fine womarn now if'n you jest open yo eyes. Don't make it look like she's yo whore. That's jest wrong. Don't go out her back door no more. If you love her, marry her."

Alain turned to Leo. "I guess, I'm done, Preacher Tomlin. I mighta said too much." Alain rejoined his family.

Leo looked over the congregation and saw many tear-stained faces. Alain's sermon had been more powerful than his. Leo made eye contact with Mac who dropped his head from Leo's piercing gaze. Preacher Tomlin said, "The Richters will be at the front of the church after the service. Please welcome them to the fold. Next Sunday, we'll have a creek-bank service if it's not too cold. This entire family wishes to be baptized. Let's dismiss by repeating 'The Lord's Prayer.' Take to heart what you're saying."

The congregation repeated "The Lord's Prayer" and filed past the Richters on their way to spread dinner for which the new church members had brought a washtub filled with ripe apples.

Mac waited until the crowd had drifted out before he went forward. He looked Alain in the eye. "I'm sorry. The things I said were cruel. I miss you, too. Alain, has anybody said anything about Sunny? She's never done anything but kiss me good night."

"I forgive you. You had ever right to be mad, 'specially since you courtin' her. I ain't heard nothin', but I don't come to town often. 'Sides, folks wudn't talkin' to me, but don't put no slight on that wonderful lady's character. She might be an outsider, but her heart's one o' us."

"I know. I've known since Chicago. Thank you."

Mac offered Alain his hand, but the two men embraced each other. They held onto each other a long moment. Mac whispered, "My son told me to make up with you months ago. He told me to ask Sunny out. I think I have a wise son."

Sunny waited even longer than Mac before she greeted the Richters. "Mr. Richter." She extended her hand.

"Miss Bankston. I reckon you should call us by our first names if'n you wanna git the right one."

She laughed. "That's a good idea, but if I do, then, I'm Sunny. Will you introduce everyone please? Even though I've been to your place, I've never met everybody. I do know Fay, and I've met Matthew."

Alain nodded. "I'll go down the line. You know Fay. Meet Robert Lee, Calvin, Gloria, Glenda, Joel, Arlene, Aaron, Oscar, Simon, Yvonne, Debbie, and Polly. We got four boys, Matthew, as you know is the oldest; Mark; Luke; and John. The eight girls are Mary, Suzy, Nettie, Zelma, Robin, Stormie, Autumn, and Summer."

Sunny laughed again. "The last three are all weather like me."

Alain laughed. "I suppose so."

Sunny said, "Nice to meet everybody. Can you have the children at school by seven tomorrow?"

"Yes'm."

"I'll need to test them. How old is Matthew?"

"He's the oldest. He's seventeen."

"Yes." She bit her bottom lip. "It might be best for him to join the adult education."

"No. I want him to git a diploma. He wants a diploma."

Sunny realized instantly Alain might not be the father of all the children, but he was the patriarch, and he could be stubborn. She could also tell Matthew *was* his son, and he was proud of the boy.

Sunny chose her words carefully. "I understand, but I'm concerned about how far behind he might be."

"He ain't behind. If anything, he might be ahead."

"How?"

"Miss Bankston, I ain't stupid, and we ain't ignorant. I guess, I need to sound better, but I'm smart. I been home schoolin'. We been orderin' books and study packets."

"Really?"

The man nodded. "*Life Pac* study packets for language, science, and social studies. We used Saxon math 'cause it was more challengin'."

"Saxon?" she said in disbelief.

"Yes, ma'am."

"What level is Matthew?"

"Calculus."

"No way."

"You seem surprised."

"I am." She hugged her Bible to her chest. "Forgive me for being judgmental about this. I'm seriously impressed. All right. I'll test everybody. How about you adults?"

"We can all read and do math."

"Are you as good as Gator?"

He stroked his beard. "At math?"

"Yes." She nodded as the smaller children began to fidget.

"Better."

"Will you come Monday night so I can test you? We might need to wait until the next session in January for everyone else. Will that be acceptable to you?"

"Yes."

"Sherry Jones and Miss Ina want to join the adult education class in January, too. That will be a lot of people. I might need help."

"Mrs. Tomlin would be excellent."

"Yes, she would. Let's get this testing done tomorrow. I'm hungry now; let's eat. Alain, you're forgiven. I look forward to getting to know all of you."

"Likewise."

Sunny's week fell to its normal routine after Felicia and Ron left Monday morning. She tested all the Richter children and was absolutely astounded. Matthew Richter was ready for college. She could not believe how articulate he was even if he did drop his Gs when he spoke. The senior class would have six graduating members.

Mark and Mary placed in tenth and eighth grade, respectively, and were right on target developmentally and educationally. Mark was actually advanced in math, and Sunny placed him in accelerated courses.

Stormie, Autumn, and Summer were under five, Summer only an infant. Sunny tested the younger children to find they, too, were on target. She developed a great deal of respect in a short time for Alain Richter.

When Gator came Monday night, Sunny had him take some more practice tests. She felt he was ready, so she scheduled him to take his official test the second Saturday in January. While Gator took some practice tests, Sunny tested Alain. She went ahead and gave him the same practice test in math she had given Gator since Alain claimed to be better at math than Gator. A small part of her wanted to prove him wrong, but he was better. He complained the test was too easy. Therefore, she allowed him to take the tests Gator was taking. Her jaw fell open. Never had she seen a person score perfectly in all areas. She looked at Alain and asked, "Did you cheat?"

"No, ma'am." Alain looked a little hurt.

"I was teasing," said Sunny hurriedly. "Alain, I'm going to schedule you to take the test with Gator. There's no need for you to waste your time with the classes. Your siblings might be the same, but I'm not ready to test them. I'll just have fifteen students in the spring. Lauren will help. If they show promise like you, I'll schedule them for March. Let's wait and see."

"Thank you, Sunny. When will the results be back?"

"Not until March, I'm sure. They're slow with it. Alain, I do want you to come every Monday for oral communications and computer training. It's not on the test, but I want you to speak like you should. I think you've been lazier than Gator. You'll have to use a computer to take the tests."

Alain nodded. "I have been lazy. It'll take practice to stop soundin' stupid."

"You sound like a stereotypical hillbilly, which you are *not*. Your writing is beautiful. You're poetic."

He blushed. "I write my thoughts and feelin's, feelings." Alain worked hard to pronounce the word correctly.

"I'd love to read some of it."

"What if you don't like it?"

"Chicken?"

"A little."

"Nobody likes every kind of writing. Let me read it. You choose which pieces. I'll be honest with you."

"Okay, Sunny, I'll do that."

Gator waited for Alain to leave. The two men sounded like schoolboys as they jabbered about being ready to take the high-school equivalency test. Sunny could not help but laugh. Lauren Tomlin had said Alain Richter was an undiscovered genius. Perhaps, she was right.

Tuesdays and Wednesdays became a Reardon family thing for Sunny and Mac. Sunny prepared supper on Tuesdays while Mac cooked on Wednesdays. Thursdays remained Mac and Sunny's private movie night while Fridays stayed community movie night. They finished the *Star Wars* saga, and Sunny had to decide what to show next. Mac suggested, "Show some historical movies."

"Such as?"

"*Braveheart, The Patriot, Saving Private Ryan, The Last of the Mohicans.*"

"Very violent for kids."

"But fairly accurate, with liberties. Don't show *Friday the Thirteenth* or the like. Go with epics and classics like *Gone with the Wind* and *The Ten Commandments*. War violence won't bother these people. Gratuitous sex *will* bother these people. Chopping people up for the sake of chopping people up is a no-no. Language?" He shrugged. "I'm not sure. Some of these people, women especially, have never heard the 'F' word. Warn them it'll have language and go from there."

"What about fantasy or witchcraft?"

"It will probably be fine. Thinking about *Harry Potter*?"

"Yeah."

"*Wizard of Oz* first, and maybe *The Lord of the Rings*. I would like those at home, too. And sex within the right context will be okay, just don't make it explicit or X-rated."

"What about extra-marital or premarital sex?"

"Tastefully done within the context of love will fly. Give 'em a tear-jerker."

"Well, how about one tonight? Are you ready to let me soak your shoulder?"

"If my shirt gets wet, I might have to take it off."

"Mac, are you hinting you want to have sex with me?"

Mac flipped his hands up in mock surrender. "Forget I said anything."

"Come on. Get huffy. MacKenzie Reardon, what is courting me supposed to lead to? Is that what you're looking for? If that's *all* you're looking for, you can get out right now. I'm not your whore!"

"Damn! Temper, temper. Do you really want me to leave? Just sex? No. Would I like to carry you up those stairs to your bed right now? Well, right now, no. Two minutes ago? Yes. Turn on the damned movie. You sit at that end of the couch, and I'll sit at this one." Mac scooted to the other end of the couch. "I won't even hold your hand. That might lead to touching and kissing and, oh, let me keep my phrasing parallel, fucking."

Sunny picked up the stack of coasters on the end table and threw them at Mac, hitting him in multiple places before she pressed play. Mac started back to the other end of the couch but plopped down with a huff and folded his arms across his chest.

As Richard Gere and Louis Gossett, Jr. screamed at each other in the rain in an *Officer and a Gentleman*, Sunny boohooed.

Mac snapped, "Good grief! What makes this a tear-jerker right now?"

Sunny sniffled. "Are you *kidding*? When Mayo hollers, 'Don't you do it! Don't! You...I got nowhere else to go! I got nowhere else to go...I got nothin' else,' I just want to hug him and give him someplace to go."

Mac scowled, picked up the glass of water in front of him, poured it over his head, and hollered, "I got nowhere else to go!"

Sunny started giggling behind her hand.

Mac hollered again, "For God sake! Hug me and give me someplace else to go."

Sunny really started laughing. Mac continued, "I know how it ends. Mayo swoops Paula into his arms and carries her out of the factory. Would you like me to swoop you into my arms and carry you anywhere?"

Through chuckles Sunny said, "The altar would be nice."

"The altar?"

"Never mind. Come here so I can hug you and give you someplace to go."

Mac moved beside Sunny. He kissed her, and she slipped her arms around his neck. He whispered, "Into your arms is a very nice place to go."

42
A Picnic

Mid-Saturday morning, Mac knocked on Sunny's door. He received no answer. The door was not locked, so he went in. "Sunny?" he called. No one was in the kitchen. He became anxious, so anxious he went upstairs to her bedroom.

He opened the door to where Sunny slept soundly. He sat on the side of her bed and shook her gently. "Sunny!"

"What?" She jolted awake and sat up.

"Don't do that to me ever again!" exclaimed Mac, a hand to his chest.

"Do what? What are you doing here? How did you get in?"

"The door was unlocked. I thought something was wrong with you when you didn't answer. I came to take you on a picnic."

"What time is it?"

"After ten."

"I was sleeping." She fell back onto her pillow. "You interrupted the most awesome dream."

"Do you always sleep so late on Saturday?"

"Sometimes. I thought I locked my door."

He leaned forward and kissed her. "I'm finally in your bedroom. I'm even technically in your bed."

She argued, "No, you're *on* my bed. You would have to be under the covers to be in my bed."

He grinned, rolled over Sunny, and slipped under the covers. "Now?"

She laughed. "Take off your boots."

"Are you just trying to delay progress?" Mac took off his shoes. "Now what?" he asked, propping his head on his elbow.

Sunny wiggled close to Mac. "Good morning. Did you make coffee? I'm not nice until I've had coffee."

"You're being very nice. What do you sleep in?" Mac peeked under the covers. He laughed. "Cute. I should've known it wouldn't be skimpy. If I bought you something extremely sexy and naughty, would you wear it?"

"Under the right circumstances."

"And those would be?"

"Hm. Let me see how fast I can make you jump out of my bed. Sunny Reardon has a nice ring to it."

"Does it?" Mac ran his hand up Sunny's thigh and under her flannel night shirt with a teddy bear on it and hooked his thumb under the elastic of the leg of her panties. "And everything that entails?"

She kissed him sensuously and then pushed back. "The last time I checked, my name was Sunny Bankston. What was that about a picnic?"

"Oh, lady, you are killing me." Mac moved his hand further inside Sunny's underwear. She shivered at his touch. "Are you sure you want a picnic right now?" he breathed as he kissed Sunny and moved his fingers to feel her moistness.

She whispered, "The picnic was your idea, Dr. Reardon. Where are you taking me?"

Mac withdrew his hand and rolled onto his back. "So far into the woods nobody can hear you scream."

"I'm not afraid of you."

"I don't think you really want me to stop what I was doing. What if I try again on our picnic?"

"I guess we'll have to see. Let's go. Out! I have to get dressed." Sunny bounded out of bed. "Make me a cup of coffee."

"Oh!" groaned Mac, but he put his boots back on.

Sunny got to the kitchen and a waiting cup of coffee. "Cream and sugar, the way you like it," said Mac.

"Merci." Sunny drank her coffee. "Now, I'm ready to face the day."

He held out his hand. "Come on. We have a little hike."

"Your fishing hole?"

"Farther up the mountain, but I might go fishing."

"The fish might bite with the right bait."

"A wedding band?"

"A prelude."

Mac picked up the picnic basket. They walked hand in hand up the mountain beside the stream to The Musketeer Clubhouse.

"What is this place?" asked Sunny, smiling at the sturdy little dwelling and listening to the soothing roar of the falls.

"This is the clubhouse Tipper, Gator, Alain, and I built one summer. We rafted the creek. It was Alain's fourteenth birthday, one week before his whole life shattered."

"You and he really were friends?"

"Yes. We were musketeers, the four of us. You know, Tipper was almost my brother. My pa died the night before he was to marry Tipper's ma. Gator and I are actually first cousins. Alain was always just a little on the fringe, but he was a part of us. I think he kept lots of secrets for lots of people. He had to grow up way too fast. He was abused frequently." He shook his head and grimaced. "I saw the bruises and the scars. His broken arm. Gator's pa sort of nipped that when he threatened to kill Alain's pa. Sunny, Alain's youngest sibling is also Gator's, but most people don't know that."

"I noticed she does look a bit like Gator. Possum Holler would make a great soap opera."

"Yeah. Miss Ina and Pa had a child, too. Very few people know that. Sunny, I think it's Sherry."

"She does look a lot like Miss Ina, but isn't she Gator's age?"

"So, they say."

"Mac, when you talk about your people, you make me feel…"

"Horny?" Mac winked.

"MacKenzie Reardon! Stop that!"

Mac caressed Sunny's cheek and kissed her. "Wanna go skinny dipping?"

"It's too cold for swimming."

"It's not too cold to make out."

"Make out?" Sunny teased. "You're willing to stop there?"

"Yes, Miss Bankston."

"Feed me. I'm starving."

Mac took Sunny's hand. "Come in here." He led her inside the clubhouse where he spread the clean blanket over the pine straw bed that had been his and laid out the picnic he had prepared by himself: fried chicken, potato salad, apple turnovers, and a bottle of peach moonshine.

"Did you cook this yourself?" asked Sunny

"You know I did. I'd do anything for you."

"Anything?"

"Anything."

"Mac." She caressed his cheek. "Pour me a drink."

They ate in relative silence as a million thoughts flew through their heads.

Sunny thought: *Can't you say you love me? Do you love me? Oh, Mac, I do love you, but I'm so scared. I couldn't bear to lose you. Please tell me what to do.*

Mac's thoughts were just as reticent. *Sunny Reardon? Would she marry me? Does she love me? Can she? Can I? Do I? Oh, my God! Sunny, I'm scared to death. Please tell me what to do.*

After three glasses of Tipper's moonshine, Sunny lay back on the blanket and giggled. "Are you trying to incapacitate me, Dr. Reardon?"

"No," Mac replied seriously. "I like reciprocal sex."

"Mac, I was joking. I am intoxicated, though."

"I would never take advantage of you."

"I know that. I thought you wanted to make out."

"Sunny, I…"

She put her finger to his lips. "Sh. Kiss me. Don't say anything you're not ready to say. Kiss me now. Touch me. Go fishing. This fish is ready to nibble, just not ready to bite."

"Sunny." Mac kissed her hungrily. "Oh, God! Sunny, how I want you! How I need you!"

43

Hayride

The Halloween celebration in Possum Holler had little to do with ghosts or goblins or ghouls or monsters or witches or vampires or werewolves, although the children dressed in homemade costumes and frolicked at Harvest Fest. The celebration had absolutely nothing to do with death, but with the bounty and yield of the earth, much like the ancient Celts would have celebrated.

The people had a festival filled with food, fun, and fellowship. There was the dunking booth, a favorite among any who spent even an hour in Possum Holler's small jail for both Constable Norman Hill and Mayor Royce Dent took turns risking a plunge into the water. A baseball to throw cost twenty-five cents. The prize, the knowledge of victory.

There was the fishing booth where patrons fished for small bags of fudge, divinity, peanut brittle, and other confections made by the women of Possum Holler. The cost to rent a fishing pole, twenty-five cents.

The horseshoe tournament always had a good turnout. The cost to enter the tournament was twenty-five cents. The prize for the winner was to have the person's name and date engraved on a brass horseshoe hanging at the entrance to the course. Many had won over the years, among them MacKenzie Reardon, Tipper Campbell, and Gator Jones.

Every family who came contributed a cake, pie, or other baked sweet for the cake walk in which the head of the house promenaded around the circle where the sweets were displayed while the music played. The hope was to stop in front of something the person's own family did not bring.

There were team races: a three-legged race, a potato sack relay, and an egg toss (All participants prayed not to crack the egg, which would most likely be rotten.). There were normal track and field events, dashes and relays. For each event a person entered, the fee was twenty-five cents. There were blue, red, and white ribbons for first, second, and third place.

There were music and dancing, of course. There were roasted corn, potatoes, chestnuts, and peanuts. With Jessica's arrival, there were wieners, sausages, and marshmallows to roast over the bonfire. The cost of a skewer, an ear of butter-drenched corn, a potato, or a bag of nuts, twenty-five cents.

Sunny had instituted a scavenger hunt. The prizes to be found consisted of books, crayons, markers, paints, coloring books, and other educational items. The cost of a hunting map and clues to the treasure chest from which a person could take one item, twenty-five cents.

For the first time in nearly twenty years, the entire Richter family came in. They brought with them three wash tubs, and bushels of apples. With their bounty, they proposed a new booth, apple bobbing. The price for a chance to bob was twenty-five cents, and the prize was the juicy, delicious apple. The Richter women also brought candy and caramel apples to add to the fishing booth.

Another new booth was Tipper's Shots. Each shot, naturally, cost twenty-five cents. In addition, Tipper and Alain had concocted a cider-sipping contest with the price of a straw for the jug being twenty-five cents.

The festivities commenced in the late afternoon, and after dark, the hayrides began. Three of the local farmers provided real wagons pulled by mules. No flatbed trucks were used. Each wagon held twenty-four riders. The course, winding around the outskirts of town beneath ancient oaks almost barren of leaves and tall sweet pines, was about seven miles and took about half an hour. The cost of a seat was, as always, twenty-five cents. Every quarter collected would be given to a Possum Holler charity. This year, the recipient would be the hospital. The only other two charitable organizations in Possum Holler were the church and the school, which had received the proceeds the year before since Mac had been unable to attend Harvest Fest. Sunny had used the funds to buy the first books in the school library.

She had also visited the county library when they had their used book sale and finagled books for free.

After one of each flavor of Tipper's shots, Mac grabbed Sunny's hand. They had already danced several times. "Time for a hayride," he gloated.

"Mac!" Sunny laughed.

He handed the old man, Farmer Maddox, who had driven Ina and Ander years before ten dollars. "Every seat is taken," he said with a mischievous grin. "Keep the rest, drive slowly, and don't turn around. I'll be smooching with my girl."

"Mac!" Sunny blushed.

Farmer Maddox laughed and spit a stream of tobacco juice near the mule's back hoof. "Like father like son."

Mac hauled Sunny into the wagon and said, "Drive." Turning back to Sunny, he pulled her down into the hay, threw a blanket over them, and said, "Stop arguing."

"Make me."

"Mm. The lady wants to fight." He kissed her after teasing, "This'll shut you up."

The thirty-minute hayride took forty-five minutes. Mac and Sunny were, indeed, smooching.

"You've had too much to drink," whispered Sunny.

"How much did you have?" asked Mac, moving his hand under Sunny's sweater.

"Enough to wish there was no driver."

"Did you enjoy our picnic?"

"Very much."

"My darling, that was just a prelude."

"To what?"

"Mm. I *will* make love to you."

Sunny touched Mac through his jeans. He moaned, "Do you want me to kill the driver?"

"No, I can think of better things for you to do with your hands."

Sometime later, Famer Maddox said discreetly, "Mac, you decent? We comin' back into town."

"We've never been indecent. We've only been smooching."

"Mac, you ain't the first or the last. Don't mind me, but you might want to think about puttin' a weddin' ring on that sweet girl's hand. Might git to do more'n smooch."

Sunny giggled. "Wisdom of age."

Mac lifted Sunny from the wagon to teasing whoops and hollers and cat calls.

"Oh, my God!" said Sunny. "What must they think?"

"The same thing Farmer Maddox thinks. Perhaps, I should do some serious thinking."

"Did you enjoy our hayride?"

"Very much."

"My darling, that was only a prelude."

"To what?"

"What could be." She gave him a Mona Lisa smile.

Tipper's voice broke the tête-a-tête. "Mac! You and Sunny are holding up the cider-sipping contest. You signed y'all up. You already paid the entry fee. Get in the cafeteria and prepare to lose to Jess and me."

"Bring it on!" laughed Mac as he and Sunny meandered to the school cafeteria. Sunny picked straw from her hair.

"Oh, leave it," whispered Mac. "I think it's sexy."

"It's itchy. Don't even think about a straw bed in your serious thinking."

"Yes, ma'am. Let's go beat Tipper at this cider-sipping contest. At least this year I'm fighting to beat him, not save his life. Do you realize it has been one year?"

"A very wild ride."

44

Sippin' Cider through a Straw

Tipper and Alain's new contest appeared to be well-received. All around the cafeteria on tables sat gallon jugs of Alain Richter's apple cider. Tipper had a new business contract with Alain to brew and bottle his hard cider at Tipper's Bottling. Betsy had designed another label, slogan, and ad, "Feel Richer with Richter's." The label resembled a dollar with an apple for the face.

Each jug held a single straw. At each jug sat a couple. Jessica waited for Tipper, and a jug waited for Mac and Sunny.

Alain stood up and said, "Okay, couples, take your seats. These are the rules for sippin' cider through a straw. As you can see, there ain't but one straw. This is a race. We all will be singin' 'Sippin' Cider through a Straw.' That's a whole gallon. The couple that sips the most by the end of the song wins a jug of Tipper's apple moonshine 'cause y'all will be sick of cider, maybe sick *on* cider."

The spectators laughed at Alain's little joke, and he continued the rules. "This ain't apple juice. This is hard cider. Now, you can't sip alone. You gotta do it as a couple. If your lips slip off, you gotta kiss your partner. If you've had a lovers' spat, this is a good way to make up. If you ain't got sense to know your partner's your lover, you're gonna find out. And if you walk out after a gallon of my cider, you need to go home and make love to your partner."

There was more laughter. Alain said, "Couples, you got two minutes to discuss strategy. The clock is tickin', so talk fast."

"Dr. Reardon, how do we do this?" asked Sunny.

"Well, I propose slipping a bunch of times and letting Tipper win."

"No way! I'm too competitive."

"Okay." Mac grinned slyly. "You put the straw in your mouth, and I'll practice mouth-to-mouth resuscitation on you."

"You have no intention of sipping cider, do you?"

"I'll sip some. I promise."

"You had better. I want to win."

"Okay! Time's up!" called Alain.

The Richters all picked up some kind of instrument. Alain announced, "You start on the first chord."

Throughout the song there was much kissing and numerous fits of coughing. Mac deliberately pushed the straw out of Sunny's mouth several times, and he refused to peck for a kiss because hecklers pointed out peckers with derision by shouting, "That ain't a kiss! Disqualified!"

The song began with antiphonal phrasing of the anonymous ditty by the males echoed by the females and so did the competition:

The purtiest girl (The purtiest girl)
I ever did saw (I ever did saw)
Was sippin' ci...der through a straw.
(Was sippin' ci...der through a straw.)
The purtiest girl I ever did saw-aw-aw
Was sippin' cider...through...a... straw.

I says to her (I says to her)
"Whatcha doin' that for ("Whatcha doin that for),
Asippin' ci...der through a straw?"
(Asippin' ci...der through a straw?")
I says to her, "Whatcha doin' that for-er-er,
Asippin' cider... through...a...straw?"

She says to me (She says to me)
"Why, don't you know ("Why don't you know)
That sippin' ci...der's on the go?"
(That sippin' ci...der's on the go?")
She says to me, "Why don't you know-ow-ow
That sippin' cider's...on... the...go?"

I told that gal (I told that gal)
I didn't see how (I didn't see how)
She sipped that ci...der through a straw.
(She sipped that ci...der through a straw.)
I told that gal I didn't see how-ow-ow
She sipped that cider...through...a...straw.

Then she said to me, (Then she said to me,)
"I'll show you how (I'll show you how)
I sip my ci...der through a straw."
(I sip my ci...der through a straw.")
Then she said to me, "I'll show you how-ow-ow
I sip my cider...through...a...straw."

Then cheek to cheek (Then cheek to cheek)
And jaw to jaw (And jaw to jaw)
We sipped that ci...der through a straw.
(We sipped that ci...der through a straw.)
Then cheek to cheek and jaw to jaw-aw-aw
We sipped that cider...through...a...straw.

And from time to time (And from time to time)
That straw did slip, (That straw did slip,)
So, I sipped ci...der from her lip.
(So, I sipped ci...der from her lip.)
And from time to time that straw did sli-i-ip,
So, I sipped cider...from...her...lip

That's how I met (That's how I met)
My mother-in-law, (My mother-in-law)
By sippin' ci...der through a straw.
(By sippin' ci...der through a straw.)
That's how I met my mother-in-law-aw-aw,
By sippin' cider...through...a...straw.

Now seventeen kids (Now seventeen kids)

All call me "Pa" (All call me "Pa")
As they sip ci...der through a straw.
(As they sip ci...der through a straw.)
Now seventeen kids all call me "Pa-a-a"
As they sip cider...through...a...straw.

The moral of (The moral of)
This little tale (This little tale)
Is sip ci...der from a pail.
(Is sip ci...der from a pail.)
The moral of this little ta-a-ale
Is sip cider...from...a...pail

The crowd clapped in rapid succession six times to the rhythm of the music.

The purtiest girl (The purtiest girl)
I ever did saw (I ever did saw)
Still sips her ci...der through a straw.
(Still sips her ci...der through a straw.)
The purtiest girl I ever did saw-aw-aw
Still sips cider...through...a...straw.

So, cheek to cheek (So, cheek to cheek)
And jaw to jaw (And jaw to jaw)
We'll sip our ci...der through a straw.
(We'll sip our ci...der through a straw.)
So, cheek to cheek and jaw to jaw-aw-aw
We'll sip our cider...through...a...straw.

And I will make (And I will make)
That straw to slip (That straw to slip)
To sip ci...der from her lip.
(To sip ci...der from her lip.)
And I will make that straw to sli-i-ip
To sip cider...from...her...lip.

"Whew!" Alain trilled. "Stop sippin'! Mac! Yo, Mac! I'm sure she ain't got no more cider on her lips!"

"No," said Mac. "Our jug is empty, but her lips still taste good."

"Empty?" yelled Tipper. "No way!"

"Check it yourself. Alain, are you the judge?"

"I am."

"Check it."

Alain picked up Mac and Sunny's jug. "I'll be! It's empty to the last drop!"

"Tipper!" Mac chortled. "Give me my bottle. I've already got my prize."

"Mac, you're drunk," laughed Tipper.

"Yep. Sunny just had to win." Mac pulled Sunny up by her hand. "Come on, Sunshine! It's time to take you home." Mac pulled her to him and kissed her. He looked specifically at Alain and then at the rest of the crowd. "I might not leave."

"Only because he's too drunk to walk home safely," laughed Sunny. "Maybe I should walk you home."

"I won't let you leave if you do. I love you, Sunny. Please don't ever leave me."

She caressed his cheek and kissed his lips. "I have no place else to go."

Mac scooped Sunny into his arms and carried her out of the cider sipping contest to a round of applause. "What are you doing?" she asked.

"It's not a factory, but it's the best I've got."

"Mac, I only wanted those three words."

"I love you. I love you, Sunny."

"I love you, Mac, forever."

He carried her directly to her bed. "I'm staying for breakfast. I am *not* leaving," he said determinedly.

Sunny shook her head. "I don't want you to leave." She pulled him to her. "Just tell me you love me again."

"Sunny, I love you. I think I've loved you since the first time I saw you. My heart skipped a beat that day in Chicago. You fit me. You are *everything* I've ever wanted. God! I love you. I love you so much."

"Show me."

Mac and Sunny melted into each other.

45

No Need for Mistletoe

The next school day, Sunny flitted around the school like a butterfly fresh from its cocoon. Everybody knew Mac had spent the night with her, but she did not care. She was happier than she could ever remember being.

On the other hand, Mac could not be found. Jessica said he came in and told her to hold down the fort, and he'd be back. He did not say where he was going.

He got back in time to make supper for the boys. At the table, they all glared at him. "What did I do?" he asked.

"Well, Daddy, today Miss Bankston acted like a giddy girl. She walked around all day, humming 'Sippin' Cider through a Straw.'" Chambry folded his arms across his chest. "You better not do something to bring her down."

Abner followed up. "Miss Bankston is a very sweet lady. I like it when she ruffles my hair and kisses my head." He folded his arms across his chest. "Don't you hurt her."

Zeke, in his usual fashion, climbed onto Mac's lap. "I want her to be my momma." He folded his arms across his chest. "Humph!"

Mac hugged him close and whispered so the other two couldn't hear, "I'll see what I can do, but it's our secret." Zeke looped his arms around Mac's neck.

At eight, Mac put the boys to bed and walked to the school. He walked in the front door and overheard Sunny instructing Gator and Alain. "Neither of you needs class anymore for your upcoming test. You're ready. I am so proud of you. Gator, you've mastered the computer and keyboards. Your speech in nearly perfect. I'm kicking you out. Alain, I want you to keep coming for a few more weeks to get the keyboarding and computer skills needed for today's world. Next week I also want you to make that speech and I want to talk to you about the pieces you brought for me to read."

Alain asked, "Are we finished for tonight?"

"Yes."

"Then, if you don't mind, I need to leave. Matthew needs a little help with the science fair thing."

"Are you cheating?" teased Sunny.

"No, of course not. He just needs help cuttin' all the pieces. He's already measured them; all I'll be doin' is usin' a saw."

"Take off!" laughed Sunny.

Alain walked out and started to speak to Mac, but the doctor put a finger to his lips. Alain nodded a silent understanding, and they shook hands quietly before Alain went home.

Gator continued to talk to Sunny. "Sunny, thank you for all you've done. Are you all right?"

"Yes. I've never been happier."

"You love him, don't you?"

"Mac?"

Gator nodded.

"Yes, Gator, I do."

"Mac's a good man. You fit him."

"That's what he said."

"Just know if he hurts you, he'll have to deal with this entire town."

"It's nice to know I'm wanted here."

Mac knocked on the door facing. "Am I interrupting?"

"Not really," said Sunny. "I've pushed Gator out of the nest. Alain will be next. He already left."

"I saw him. Gator, if you're ready, you won't mind me stealing Sunny, will you?"

Gator gave Mac a look. "In a minute. I'd like to talk to *you* first. Sunny, would you let Mac and me talk in here alone for a minute? Why don't you make sure everything else is locked up?"

"Well, all right," Sunny said hesitantly as she left to make her final rounds of the evening.

"What's on your mind, Gator?" asked Mac nonchalantly.

"Did you use one of those rubber things?"

"What?"

"Did you use a condom?" Gator closed the door.

"I don't see it's your business."

"Are you protecting her?" The doctor's first cousin folded his arms across his chest. "You lectured me about protecting my wife. Sunny's not your wife."

"Not yet."

"That shows promise. Mac, do you remember grade school? Do you remember The Musketeers—you, Tipper, me, and I made you include Alain? You had read that book, and you said that was us. Well, we sort of split up and went our separate ways, but we're back together. I want to be honest with you the way we used to be."

"Okay."

"Sunny is a terrific lady. If I wasn't married, I'd give you a run for your money." He held up a hand. "Don't take that wrong. I love Sherry. I've never wanted another woman since I met her, not really even one before. I'm glad you showed me the error of my ways."

"That's good to hear, Gator. Where are you going with this?"

"Do you know how I met Sherry or where she even came from?"

"No."

"Not many people do. They just know I went to the city and brought her home. I'm gonna tell you a story, a love story.

"You had already gone to college. Mac, by the way, how old do you think Sherry is?"

"I don't know. Y'all have been married eleven years, right?"

"Yep."

"I guess she's about your age."

"Nope. She just turned twenty-three in August."

The expression on Mac's face showed he knew more than Gator thought. "August? Twenty-three? You can't be serious."

"Let me tell you the story."

Gator sat on Sunny's desk with one foot touching the floor and his arms crossed over his chest. He pointed to the chair for Mac, and the doctor sat. "I actually took a trip into the city with

Alain for his twenty-first birthday. Now, there are a lot of good things in the city. On the other hand, there are a lot of ugly things in the city.

"The Richter boys took me to one of those ugly things—a house of ill-repute. I know we have Fester, but this place was protected and sanctioned by law enforcement. The women paraded around in nothing or next to nothing, even the waitresses. Alain, Robert Lee, and Calvin all hooked up with one woman or another. Those women didn't care so long as they earned a few dollars."

"What place?" asked Mac.

"It was called Jacqui's Gentlemen's Club. There were no gentlemen on the premises. I was mortified and repulsed. Then, I saw this pretty girl sittin' in the bay window. She looked like a deer caught in spotlights. She looked like a female Tipper. She was obviously terrified, but I just had to talk to her.

"I introduced myself, and she laughed at my name. She asked me if I bit. I looked at her face in the light. She had a black eye. Impulsively, I reached out to touch her." Gator reached his hand out just as he had that night, as if Sherry were sitting in front of him. "She flinched, and I asked what had happened. She had said no. She didn't want to.

"I asked what she was doin' there, and she said she had nowhere else to go. I asked her how old she was. She replied she was almost thirteen. This beautiful twelve-year-old girl was being forced into prostitution. I asked where here ma and pa were. Jacqui was her ma, her adopted ma. She didn't know anything about her pa. Sherry said she was adopted like several other girls, so Jacqui had a full, fresh stable. I asked her name. It was Sherry Fields."

"Oh, my God!" gasped Mac.

Gator held up his hand. Mac became quiet. "Suddenly, I was a musketeer." He spread both hands in a wide, arching motion, finally resting his hands by his hips on the desktop. "Sherry was a damsel in distress. I remembered to fight for right and justice. I asked her to run away with me. As we talked, Jacqui came over, and I paid the wench to take Sherry upstairs.

"We talked some more, and later, Alain caused a commotion so Sherry could sneak out. Fester was still a municipal judge. We lied about her age, and he married us.

"A week or so later, a fellow came lookin' for her. He tracked the Richter brothers because Jacqui thought I was one of them, and Alain's commotion had been suspicious. Alain threatened to kill the man, but that didn't stop him from lookin'. He talked to the town gossip and found out where I lived.

"The fool came to my place. I guess I must be Talmage Jones's son. Mac, I shot the bastard. Alain and I made sure his body will never be found. You know, Gators don't leave no evidence." A wry grin crossed the storyteller's face. "I even went back to Wilmington and threatened to kill Jacqui if she ever came lookin' again."

Mac's hand had covered his mouth. It amazed him the only thing that could set Gator off into a frenzy of violence was a threat to Sherry.

Gator continued. "I guess over the years I've been too harsh, too demanding sometimes. I love her. I would die for her. I killed for her. I wanted to kill you when you said I raped her. I would never deliberately hurt her. You were right though. Mac, Sherry was this little girl being forced into horrible things. She had her first cycle three months after we married. I waited until she was ready to come to me. I never forced her. We were married almost a year before she came to me.

"Yes, Sherry would've been a whore if I'd left her there, but she's *never* been my whore. We were both virgins. She's my love, my life."

Gator laughed. "I even felt bad about kissing her under the mistletoe that first Christmas, so the second Christmas when we had no need for mistletoe was extraordinary.

"Mac, maybe I'm stickin' my nose in, but I'm your friend and your family. If you love Sunny, marry her. Don't make her your whore. She loves you."

"I do love her, Gator." Mac reached into his pocket and brought out a box with an engagement ring. "This is where I disappeared to today and why I want to steal Sunny."

Gator nodded. "I didn't need to tell you the story."

"Yes, you did. I needed to hear it. It makes me believe in love. You know your secret is safe with me, but, Gator, I think I know who her ma is. I could do some tests to know for sure."

The first cousin smiled. "We know. Sherry's your sister, Mac. Miss Ina isn't ready for the world to know, but we know."

The doctor closed his eyes to keep tears from escaping.

Gator put a hand on Mac's shoulder. "Get your woman and propose in the moonlight."

"Thanks, Gator. You know, if you told Constable Hill what happened, he'd report a trespasser being shot."

"No evidence now. I have to live with what I did, but I'd do it again to protect Sherry. I love her more than my own life."

Mac smiled and nodded. "I do understand."

Sunny sat on the bench in the hall when the two men came out. "Is everything all right?" she asked, remembering the fight between the two men.

"Yeah," said Mac as the cousins clasped hands and emotionally embraced. "Gator was reminding me we're family and about some musketeers."

"Oh, I see."

"Are you ready to go home?"

"Yeah. Gator, I would like to read one more essay. I'd love to hear your take on the musketeers."

"Mac tell you about us?"

"A little. He showed me the clubhouse. Why don't you write your memory of the rafting experience? I read Alain's. I'd like to compare the two. He's an amazing man just like you. I just have to get ready for the rest of the Richters."

"Sherry, too."

"And Miss Ina. I'll have a full class. I'll *need* Lauren's help."

Mac put his arm around Sunny. "Gator is an inspiration."

"I agree."

"Night all," said Gator as he practically skipped home.

Mac kissed Sunny's forehead. "Let me walk you home. I have to keep my Sunshine safe."

They walked languidly along, just listening to the night sounds—crickets with long interludes between chirps since it was colder, a hoot owl, the baying of someone's hound. Finally, Sunny broke the silence. "Are you staying?" she asked as they walked.

"It depends."

"On what?"

"Your answer to a question."

"So, ask it," Sunny said as they stepped onto her porch and she stepped two steps higher than Mac and put her arms around him.

Mac kissed this little sprite of a woman. "Um. You taste good. I love you."

"I love you, too, Dr. Reardon."

"Enough to spend your life with me?" Mac knelt on one knee.

"Oh, my God!" breathed Sunny excitedly.

"Sunny Bankston, I love you with all my being. I want to spend my life showing you. Will you be my wife?" Mac opened the box to reveal a wedding set in yellow gold with the engagement ring being a half carat diamond-shaped solitaire. The two wedding rings were yellow gold with diamonds all around.

"Oh," breathed Sunny.

"Will you be my wife?" Mac asked again. "Zeke really wants you to be his momma."

Tears smarted Sunny's eyes, and her hand trembled as she held it out for Mac to slip the ring on. "Yes, Mac, I'll marry you. Sunny Reardon has a nice ring to it."

Mac slipped the ring onto her finger. It was a perfect fit. He sealed it with a kiss. He stood and took her in his arms.

"When?" asked Sunny

"Soon. I'd like to have no need for mistletoe."

"Two weeks. I want Felicia to come. Actually, I'd like her to be my matron of honor. Is that too weird?"

"It actually works. How about having Jessica and Sherry as bridesmaids?"

"I have two sisters, too. I'm going to drag my family to Possum Holler." She bumped his shoulders with the heels of her hands. "Get ready for weird."

"Okay. I guess Tipper has to be my best man."

"That's okay. We'll just have a little fruit-basket-turn-over."

"So, then, I'll have Ron and Gator and your brother. I need one more."

Sunny started chuckling. "What's so funny?" asked Mac.

"Ask Alain Richter."

"Seriously?"

"Seriously. He did force your hand."

"Okay."

"I have to get to planning." She danced a little jitterbug on the steps.

"Not tonight."

"Are you staying?"

"Yes. I'll get up very early to go home."

"In two weeks, you can carry me across *your* threshold."

"I won't forget. Grandma Newton would haunt me. Do you want me to go home and wait?"

"No."

46
Weird

Felicia answered her phone cheerfully. "Hey, Sunny! Not so sunny here. It's already snowing. What about there?"

"Beautiful fall foliage, frosty nights, sweater days. Since Halloween, my nights have been warmer—hot, actually. That's why I called. Are you up to being my matron of honor?"

"Oh, my God! You're sleeping with him. He asked you to marry him. Yes! When's the wedding?"

"Two weeks from Saturday."

"Are you pregnant?"

"No!" She switched the phone to her other ear.

"Okay. That's Mac. He wants to make an honest woman of you."

"He said he'd like no need for mistletoe."

"I told you he was in love with you."

"I know. Felicia, will you bring bridesmaids' dresses?"

"How many? Sizes? Colors? Wow! We have a lot to plan. Need tuxes, too?"

"Yes. This is going to be a cultural affair."

"Okay. First, colors. What do you want?"

"The fall colors are so gorgeous here. I'd like a fall theme."

"So, crimson, rust, and gold? Chrysanthemums?"

"Yes, and cat tails and black-eye-Susans if there are still any."

"Pretty and different. We'll gather them on Friday and arrange them."

"They're actually the flowers Mac gave me."

Felicia squealed into the phone. "How sweet! This is so much fun! How many attendants?"

"You, Jess, Sherry, Skye, and Starr. I'll get my sister-in-law, Pearl, to man the guest register, and Laurie will be our flower girl. I have my wedding dress. I've had it a long time. How about I email you particulars?"

"Okay. That takes care of your women. You trust me with style and colors, right?"

"Yes."

"Wait, your mother."

"Uh, no. I wouldn't even attempt to get my mother a dress. She can pick her own. She's a little odd. I wouldn't be surprised if she wore black slacks with a tie-dyed blouse and smoked a blunt before the wedding."

"Sunny?"

"Just get ready for weird."

"All right. The men. No tails, I'm sure."

"No, mid-morning wedding so we can celebrate and take a little honeymoon."

"Where?"

"Mac won't tell me. 'It's a surprise, but pack warmly,' is all he says."

"It'll be good and unusual."

"I envision an igloo in Alaska."

They both laughed. "Okay," Felicia said still chuckling. "Men and sizes. Let's go with just black."

"Agreed."

"Let's use ascots, and I'll match ascots with dresses. Give me pairs."

"Of course, Tipper's best man. You have his measurements from the trip to New York, and you have Mac's and Ron's. Pair Ron with Jess. Keep Sherry and Gator together. Put Starr with my brother, River. She's not a tolerant as Skye and might not be able to stand the last guy, Alain Richter."

"Are you serious?"

"Yep. Get River a boys' eighteen."

"He's that small?"

"Yes. So is my dad. My two brothers-in-law, Vince and Toby, will be ushers. Little Zeke, our ring bearer, is a four-T.

"I'd like cute little dresses for Callie and Betsy. They can pass out birdseed bags."

"All right. I promise nothing will be inappropriate for Possum Holler."

"Except my mother."

Felicia laughed. "Is she that bad?"

"Just wait. Of course, things are changing here, slowly, but changing. Don't worry about music. I'll use recorded music for the wedding. We know what to expect for our reception."

"Yes, we do."

"Well, I had better make sure the ladies know my mother is a strict vegetarian and to have lots of veggies."

"You have me worried."

She blew out a breath over the line. "No, it'll be okay, I hope."

"It'll be spectacular. May I do one thing just to goad Mac?"

"What?"

"Hang mistletoe all around."

Sunny hooted. "Yes."

Sunny's next call went to her parents. "Here goes," she sighed as she dialed.

"Hello," said Angus Bankston.

"Dad, it's Sunny."

"What's wrong?"

"Nothing. I need you here in two weeks to give the bride away."

"Who's stealing my baby?"

"Mac Reardon."

"The doctor?"

"Yes."

"Do you love him?"

"Very much, Dad."

"He love you?"

"Yes."

"We'll be there."

"I have your tux taken care of. Tell Mom the colors are crimson, rust, and gold. Rust will look beautiful on her, but no excessive cleavage."

"You're afraid she'll embarrass you."

"Dad, she's so far left I don't see her on my periphery." She released a long compunctious sigh.

"I'll temper her a little, Sunny."

"Dad, bring your own tofu."

"Do they at least have fruit and vegetables?"

"Lots."

"Then, we'll live. I can't wait to meet your doctor. I love you, baby."

"I love you, too, Dad."

Felicia and Ron arrived a week before the wedding, as did Sunny's family. Not even Mac was prepared for Eudora Bankston. Mac confided in Tipper as they got back from an overnight camping trip Tipper, Gator, and Alain conspired, "She's got a loose screw."

"She looks like Sunny."

"That's where the similarity ends. That woman is nuts."

Tipper chortled and began to sing. "That's how I met…My mother-in-law…By sippin' ci…der through a straw…"

"Oh, shut up!" laughed Mac. "I won't be living with her and not visiting very often. How many times have they been here since Sunny came?"

"This is the first."

"How many times has Sunny gone home?"

"Once."

"Whew!" Mac wiped his brow in mock relief.

"Her father's nice."

"Not quite as strange, but strange enough. How did Sunny turn out normal?"

"Is Sunny normal?" asked Tipper with a smirk. "What woman in her right mind chooses to move to Possum Holler?"

"You're right. She's not normal; she's extraordinary."

"Yep, like Jess."

"We are lucky men, aren't we, Tipper?"

"Absolutely, even if it did take a second try."

Felicia moved the wedding plans along despite Eudora's strangeness. She walked in at the end of Mac and Tipper's conversation. "She's having LSD flashbacks," said Felicia as she plopped into a chair.

Both Mac and Tipper laughed. "What happened?" asked Mac.

"We were putting up ribbon and the vases for flowers. Now, the bows are shiny gold satin, but she wanted to add something glittery and whimsical, perhaps, hanging bubbles." She rubbed her temple. "Sunny said no, and they started arguing. Sunny got mad and said she wasn't going to have any of her mother's drug-induced fantasies. Eudora ran out in tears. Skye and Starr diffused the situation. We are going to get soap bubbles for the children to blow as the bride and groom leave, as well as the bird seed bags."

"That's not so bad," said Mac.

"No," agreed Felicia. "It's cute and sweet and very childlike. Sunny says her mother took a 'trip' to Neverland and never came back."

Mac laughed. "Well, that explains it. I'm going to hug Sunny. I think I'll intrude on supper. Feed the boys, Felicia."

"Gladly. Mac, expect pouting. Sunny might serve souse."

"To vegetarians?"

"She's pissed."

"I've experienced her temper." He rubbed his cheek at the memory of coasters flying his direction. "Gotcha."

Mac knocked twice and walked in. "Hello?"

"Mac!" squealed Sunny and left the dining table. She leapt into his arms and bawled.

"Sh," he whispered. "Two more days. You can handle it. I love you. Invite me for supper. I'll put her in her place if you want me to."

"She just makes me so mad."

"Did you serve souse?"

"Yes, just to sicken her."

"Sunny!"

"Oh, there's coleslaw, cinnamon apples, and glazed carrots. I'm not totally mean."

"You're not mean at all. Feed me."

Sunny and Mac walked back into the dining room hand in hand.

"Hello, Mac," said Eudora with a little smile that looked just like Sunny's.

"Hello, Mom," said Mac as he planted a kiss on her cheek. "I'm starving. What's good?"

"Everything except the dead pig."

"I disagree. The dead pig is tasty." Mac snagged a piece of souse and grabbed a plate from the cabinet. He served himself and sat in Sunny's chair. He patted his leg for her to sit on his lap since there were no more dining chairs.

Supper continued as River declared, "I think the souse is great, but I'm not a vegetarian anymore. Suck it up, Mom. Eat your veggies."

"I tried it," said Angus. "Not my cup of tea, but it's fine as far as fat goes."

"It is fatty," agreed Mac. "That's why I eat it in moderation. On the other hand, I could eat the whole bowl of Sunny's coleslaw. It's the best I've ever had."

Eudora smiled broadly. "It's my recipe."

"Is it?" He arched his brows in mock surprise. "Thank you for teaching Sunny to make it."

Skye and Starr had to bite their lips not to laugh. River did laugh. Skye's and Starr's husbands and River's wife hid their faces. Angus left the table to get another glass of juice.

Eudora said, "You're a charmer, aren't you, Dr. Reardon?"

Mac shook his head. "I only wish to charm one person, my Sunshine."

Angus sat back down. "It seems you've succeeded in that," he said. "I've never seen Sunny so happy."

"She makes me just as happy," assured Mac. "I love her, and I'll do everything in my power to make her happy."

"Good enough for me," Angus approved.

Mac caressed Sunny's arm. "Baby, what do you have we can watch as a family tonight?"

"Oh," said Sunny. "I didn't think we'd have a movie tonight. Tomorrow night we have *Grease*."

"That'll be fun, but Thursday is *our* movie night."

"Why don't you drive into the city for a real movie?" suggested River. He whispered in Mac's ear, "Get her away from Mom before one of them ends up dead."

Mac said, "Would y'all mind if I take Sunny on our last date before we get married?"

"It's a great idea." Angus nodded vigorously.

Mac playfully popped Sunny's behind. "Let's go, baby."

Sunny stalled, "The dishes."

"We've got the dishes," said Skye. "Go!"

Mac pulled her through the house.

"Where are we going?" Sunny asked as she and Mac stepped onto the front porch.

"Away from here."

"Thank you," came out as a rushed whisper. "I love my mother, but she grates on my last nerve. She's so flighty"—She waved her hands like bird taking wing—"and she wants everything her way. We were always encouraged to find our own path, but when we stepped off *her* path, she was always ready to prod us back onto the Yellow Brick Road. Dad just ignores her."

"That's a task."

"They've been married forty years. They met at Woodstock. River is a love child. He was conceived during Santana's concert. Mom was six months pregnant when she tracked Dad down. There are about three years between each birth until me. There are six years between Skye and me. I guess they really do love each other."

"They do. And they understand each other."

Sunny put her arms around Mac's waist. "Are we actually driving into the city?"

"Too far."

"I agree. So, what are going do?"

"Feel like fishing?"

"It's cold."

"I'll warm you up."

"MacKenzie Reardon!" She playfully popped his arm.

"I'll build a fire."

"Let's go."

Friday was uneventful except a few moviegoers were disappointed Sandy lowered her standards for Danny rather than Danny raising his standards for Sandy. They concluded it was proof of what a woman will do for the man she loves. Their conversation turned immediately to the wedding the next day.

Tipper dragged Mac away. "I've got to get you away from her before midnight." Tipper passed Mac to Ron. "Don't let him out of your sight. He might try to sneak in her window. Mac, Grandma Newton is watching. You know, she always thought you belonged with Sunny."

"I suspected. She adored Sunny. I promise I won't see Sunny until she walks down the aisle."

Tipper glanced at the watch he allowed himself the luxury of buying. "Twelve hours. That's all that's left. I'll see you at nine A.M. Good night."

Mac walked into his kitchen the next morning and rubbed his eyes. Felicia set a quiche on the table. "Real men eat quiche," she joked.

"It's delicious," agreed Mac. "What's with all the mistletoe? It's in every doorway."

"No need for mistletoe?" Felicia teased.

"Oh! Come on!"

"You'll see it all day."

"That's fine. Others may use it."

Mac, Ron, and the boys got dressed. Felicia had made a run to the city for two more little tuxedos and bottles of soap bubbles. She had decided Callie and Betsy could pass out birdseed bags while Chambry and Abner passed out soap bubbles. She bought only red and yellow bottles. She wanted to strangle Eudora, but it gave two boys who were feeling left out something to do. Perhaps Gran Eudora was a blessing in disguise.

Tipper showed up fully dressed at nine as promised. All the men met in one of the Sunday school rooms. Felicia came in to make sure everyone was dressed properly. She pursed her lips and audaciously stroked Alain's chin.

Perceptively, he said, "You don't like my beard, do you?"

"It's scruffy and scraggly, and you look like a member of ZZ Top."

"I ain't shavin' it off." He lapsed back into his comfort zone briefly.

"Will you let me shape it?"

"Mac, what's she gonna do?"

"Felicia, let it go," said Mac with a chuckle.

Felicia shrugged. "Fine, but you'd be better looking and look a lot younger."

Alain knitted his brows together. "You think?"

"I think," said Felicia decisively.

Alain stroked his beard. "I've had it a mighty long time. I started it when I was sixteen."

Felicia waved it off. "We don't have time now anyway," she said. Sarcastically she added, "I guess it defines you."

"What do you mean by that?"

"It tells people who you are."

Alain scowled. "Felicia, do you mean when outsiders see me like this, they automatically think bad things?"

Knowing she had won a major battle, Felicia nodded innocently and stretched her blue eyes wide. "I'm afraid so, Alain. It's not fair, but it's a fact."

"Yeah, I know." Alain nodded. "When Sunny's ma saw me, she screamed."

It was Felicia's turn to scowl. "In that case, keep it," she said maliciously.

Alain laughed. "Felecia, after the wedding, I'll let you shave it and give me a haircut."

"It's not necessary, Alain."

"But I wanna make a good impression on folks. That's why I've been doing Sunny's adult education. I'm not an ignorant fool or a disgrace anymore."

Felicia smiled at Alain. She really liked him. "Then, come by Mac's on Monday. Ron will be there, and we'll get Miss Ina to give you the works. You can always let it grow back if you don't like it." Felicia left to take care of the bride's attendants.

The wedding music began. Felicia had matched the design of Sunny's wedding dress, but kept the attendant's dresses street length, just to the knee. They were all velvet with satin waistbands. The dresses had scalloped necks and puffed sleeves to the elbow with satin trim around the end of the sleeve. The bodice was fitted to the waist, and the skirt formed a bell, except for Pearl's, which was pleated for her protruding abdomen. The ladies wore matching patent-leather, three-inch, heeled pumps. Felicia chose a gold dress while the other attendants were outfitted in russet. The little girls' dresses were the same in crimson.

Sunny's dress was an exact replica but came to her ankles and had a double waistband and trim at the hem. It was white. Sunny wore a white wide-brimmed straw hat with a satin band and matching patent leather pumps.

All the ladies carried bouquets of bronze, crimson, and yellow chrysanthemums and miniature yellow rosebuds. Sunny's was larger. The men wore yellow rosebud boutonnières. Each man's ascot matched his female counterpart's satin waistband. The men without females to escort wore black ascots. Lauren Tomlin wore a simple bronze-colored linen skirt and blazer with a cream-colored silk blouse and bronze-colored low-heeled pumps.

This was a wedding where the guests might have noticed the mother of the bride more than the bride. Eudora wore a dress reminiscent of a 1920s flapper in crimson. The fringe struck her at the knee. The neckline curved tastefully to show only the top of a full bosom. The fringe ringing the front of the neck downplayed the low neckline. She wore four-inch-heeled crimson pumps and a shiny gold headband and shawl. Mac sighed when Vince escorted her in.

Tipper whispered, "It could've been worse."

"How?"

"It could have been a miniskirt."

Mac tried not to laugh. Luckily, Mattie Boone, the teacher manning the music, started the wedding march. The attendants were lovely. Zeke was adorable as he regally carried the pillow holding the wedding rings down the aisle. Laurie came behind him and scattered crimson, yellow, and bronze chrysanthemum petals.

When the bridal chorus began, Mac bounced with excitement. Sunny floated on her father's arm. Even Eudora's getup could not detract from her genuine beauty. Sunny stopped and gave her mother a yellow rose and a kiss, symbolic of leaving her home.

Leo smiled lovingly as Angus stopped beside Mac. "Who gives this woman to be married?" he asked.

"Her mother and I," replied Angus. He kissed Sunny and laid her hand in Mac's. Angus sat beside his flamboyant wife.

Leo asked, "Dr. MacKenzie Reardon, will you have this woman to be your wife?"

"I will," Mac answered joyfully.

"Sunny Bankston, will you have this man to be your husband?"

As she nodded, Sunny replied, "I will."

Leo addressed the guests. "Dear family and friends, as you heard this man and this woman express the desire to become husband and wife, I ask you now to bear witness to their commitment as they exchange vows before you and God. If there is anyone here who can show just cause that these two should not be joined, speak now or forever hold your peace."

Hearing no objection, Leo continued. "MacKenzie Reardon, because of your love for this woman, you have expressed the desire to become her husband. Do you wish now to vow before God your love and fidelity to her?"

"I do."

"Then, repeat after me: 'I, MacKenzie Reardon, take you, Sunny Bankston, to be my wife to have and to hold from this day forward or better, for worse; for richer, for poorer; in sickness, and in health; to love and to cherish as long as we both shall live.'"

Mac repeated each phrase with confidence

Leo turned to Sunny. "Sunny Bankston, because of your love for this man, you have expressed the desire to become his wife. Do you wish now to vow before God your love and fidelity to him?"

"I do."

"Then, repeat after me." Leo gave the same vows and Sunny recited them joyfully. "MacKenzie and Sunny, do you have rings to exchange?"

"Yes," Mac answered.

Leo motioned Zeke to him, and he took the rings from the pillow. Leo held up a ring. "The ring is a symbol of marriage. Notice its shape. It is an unbroken circle. Traditionally, wedding rings have been made of gold, a precious metal from ancient times. It is purified by fire and formed into this perfect circle. Its shape symbolizes unending commitment. Its purity symbolizes fidelity.

"MacKenzie, Sunny, once you place this ring on the other's finger, you will seal your commitment to each other."

Leo handed Mac Sunny's ring. "Place this ring on Sunny's finger and repeat after me: 'With this ring, I pledge to be faithful to you all the days of my life.'"

Mac slipped the ring on Sunny's finger and said, "'With this ring, I pledge to be faithful to you all the days of my life.'"

Leo handed Mac's ring to Sunny. "Place this ring on MacKenzie's finger and repeat after me. 'With this ring, I pledge to be faithful to you all the days of my life.'"

Sunny slid Mac's ring into place. "'With this ring, I pledge to be faithful to you all the days of my life.'"

"MacKenzie and Sunny, as you vowed before God and these witnesses and demonstrated by the giving and receiving of rings your commitment to be married, I pronounce you husband and wife. Mac, kiss your bride. You have no need for the mistletoe hanging above you."

Mac laughed as he glanced up, and then kissed Sunny soundly.

Leo declared, "Ladies and gentlemen, it is my great honor and pleasure to present to you Dr. and Mrs. MacKenzie Reardon. You are invited to join them in a celebration of their union outside."

The wedding celebration lasted for several hours before the tossing of the garter and bouquet. Mac really did blindly shoot the garter over his shoulder. To everyone's amazement, including the recipient, the garter fell into Alain Richter's hand.

Sunny flicked her bouquet over her shoulder, not caring where it landed. It fell into the lap of Mattie Boone, the thirty-year-old widowed mother of three who had come to teach in Possum Holler after her husband had been killed in Iraq.

Mac laughed at the cans and balloons and streamers and "just married" sign on his car when he and Sunny returned from changing clothes. The soap bubbles turned out to be delightful and whimsical.

Sunny and Mac landed in Banff, Alberta, Canada. "It's freezing here," said Sunny.

Mac kissed his new bride below her ear. "I'll keep you warm, and I don't need mistletoe."

They were taken to an ice cavern. Inside was anything a five-star hotel would have had, including a natural hot spring. The "room" was chilly, but the bed was king-size and furnished with fur covers. There were food and beverages, alcoholic and non-alcoholic, including a fruit and cheese basket and a bottle of champagne. There was a full bath with warm terrycloth robes. Mac carried Sunny through the entrance. She was astonished.

The taxi driver placed their baggage on the luggage stand by the bed. "I'll be back in four days, Dr. Reardon, unless you call before that. Your itinerary and travel arrangements for your stay and excursions are on the nightstand. Congratulations and best wishes." Mac handed the man a tip from behind Sunny's shoulders.

Mac still held Sunny in his arms as the man left. "What first, Mrs. Reardon?"

"You have a one-track mind, Dr. Reardon."

The husband smirked. "Then, I guess the question is, 'Where'?"

"Put me down. I have to use the bathroom."

Mac put Sunny down and stepped outside just to take in the view while Sunny went into the bathroom. It was frigid, but majestic. Crystal clean marshmallow snow peaks jutted into radiant, blinding azure sky. A few cotton-candy clouds hovered around the peaks. All reflected in the deep, dark indigo of the mountain lake. He came back in to find Sunny in the hot spring.

She gave him the come-hither finger. "I thought we'd start in the hot spring."

"Excellent choice," said Mac, undressing as quickly as he could.

47

How Do You Heal a Broken Heart?

Tipper's New Year's Eve party was becoming a tradition. This celebration took place in his new house, and there were more guests. In addition to the ones the year before, Alain Richter with the Richter clan; Dr. Rockford, Mac's new resident who seemed taken with Glenda Richter; and Mattie Boone with her three children came.

Mac poured himself a glass of his favorite peach moonshine and slipped outside into the falling snow to ponder all the secrets and changes that had spurred Possum Holler forward. Momentarily, Tipper joined him. "Too crowded?" he asked.

"No. I was just thinking. You know, it's been exactly one year since I first kissed Sunny. I gave her a peck so Chambry would hush. I miss him tonight."

"He's with Felicia. Unfortunately, that's the nature of divorce when both parents want time with their children. At least Chambry's mother wants to be with him."

"Let's talk about your matchmaking schemes. It's funny. All of you knew I belonged with Sunny long before either of us did." He sipped the whiskey. "Are you playing matchmaker again?"

"What do you mean?"

Mac jerked his head toward the people inside. "Alain and Mattie."

"They did catch the wedding paraphernalia."

Mac took another swig of his moonshine. "That doesn't mean they'll marry each other."

"He certainly has made a change in his physical appearance."

"Felicia's influence."

"I can't believe he shaved the beard. He does look younger. Did you notice the capped teeth? Felicia must've really got into his head."

"Yeah. She's good at that. It's so nice to see Miss Ina happy. Having found Sherry has made her at least ninety-nine percent complete. Why don't you match her up with someone?"

"Who? Pa Dent, I mean, Royce?"

"Could be."

"No. I caught him looking at Fay Richter."

"Seriously?"

Tipper nodded slowly.

"What does Alain think about that?" Mac asked.

"I haven't talked to him yet."

"Are you sure you're Tipper Campbell?"

"Lots of things have changed. Secrets are becoming fewer."

As Tipper and Mac talked, Gator joined them. "Congratulations, Tipper. Jess told Sherry. Sherry told me."

"Told you what?" asked Mac.

"She's pregnant." Tipper smiled broadly.

"When were you gonna tell me?"

"I was getting there."

"How many do you plan to have with her?"

"Maybe three. We'll see."

"Congratulations."

"Thanks."

"I'm not having anymore," declared Gator. "My quiver is *full*."

"Well, to be honest, I want a boy," said Tipper. "I guess that's egotistical, huh?"

"Natural," said Mac. "We all want to carry on our name."

"You have Chambry."

"Yeah." Mac sighed. Possum Holler still had lots of secrets. "Sunny and I just signed the papers to legally adopt Abner and Zeke. Their last name is now Reardon."

"I bet Zeke is ecstatic. He wanted Sunny to be his momma." Tipper laughed.

"He's overjoyed," affirmed Mac.

"So," teased Gator, "when are you and Sunny gonna have some?"

"The end of July."

"Explain," Tipper and Gator said simultaneously.

"For Christmas, Sunny gave me a book of baby names. It seems I put the cart a little before the horse. We made a love child, a little trick-and-treat on Halloween."

Tipper and Gator broke into song. "Now seventeen kids (Now seventeen kids)...All call me 'Pa'... (All call me 'Pa'...)"

Mac guffawed. "I promise there will *not* be seventeen kids."

"Well, what do you want?" asked Tipper.

"I don't care so long as it's normal and healthy and Sunny is all right."

Gator goaded, "I asked you if you used a condom."

"You did. I should've taken my own advice. But I'm happy. I'm happier than I can ever remember."

"I know what you mean," agreed Tipper.

"How about you, Gator?" asked Mac.

"I've always been happy with Sherry. I think I'm happy to have the musketeers back together."

"Yeah," said Tipper. "I notice one musketeer is not outside in the snow."

Mac looked inside. "Alain..."

"He's changed so much. He was always one of us, just a little on the margine."

"He has changed, but something's still missing. Tipper he's not talking to Mattie."

"I see that." Tipper sighed. "I remember the day he said was the happiest day of his life."

"Rafting?" Gator chimed in with a lifted eyebrow.

"Yeah."

Mac observed, "That's a sad commentary on what Possum Holler was like. Not only has Alain changed, but Possum Holler has changed. Is that good or bad?"

"It's good," assured Gator. "So long as we hold to our faith, modernization is good."

"And give back," said Tipper. "I have loads of plans for the future. My heart was broken. Jess, my business, my friends have helped it heal. I want to help Possum Holler heal."

"Yeah," agreed Mac. He looked at his watch. "It's getting close. I'd like to propose a toast."

"Let's get back inside," said Tipper.

As midnight grew near Tipper filled glasses with champagne. He gave both Jessica and Sunny the children's sparkling cider, Alain's newest addition to his apple beverages. "Congratulations," he whispered to Sunny.

"You, too."

Mac raised his glass. "A toast and an announcement. First, to Sunny and Jessica as first-time mothers. That takes care of the announcement. Now, to Grandma Newton. We miss you, and we acknowledge you always knew what was best for us. To broken hearts being healed and bright futures for all of us."

Tipper counted down the seconds and glasses clinked at midnight. Mac took Sunny in his arms and kissed her passionately. In her arms, Dr. MacKenzie Reardon knew the way to heal a broken heart was true love. "Happy New Year, my love," he whispered.

"I love you, Dr. MacKenzie Reardon. You are a true homegrown healer."

Epilogue

The tall sandy-haired man with sparkling blue eyes and his best friend who was the local doctor with chestnut hair and hazel eyes reviewed the blueprints with the blonde-haired, blue-eyed female architect.

"Fantastic concept, Tipper," said the woman. "Does this look like what you had in mind?"

"Exactly, Felicia. Mac, what do you think?"

"We won't recognize Possum Holler. Chambry will get his restaurant."

Tipper laughed. "I'm happy to have a sign with Possum Holler on it."

"The new and improved Possum Holler," bragged Felicia.

"When do we start building?" asked Mac

"After the spring rains," said Felicia. "Nobody in Possum Holler will ever be without running water and electricity again."

Original Completion Date
February 16, 2010

About the Author

Like many of her characters, Janet is a history buff and loves anything of historical significance from old cars to old cemeteries. Get to know Janet and you'll see why she's been critically acclaimed at the Faulkner Wisdom Competition and why her writing continues to receive 4 and 5-star reviews, as well as winning awards—It could be that readers see so much of her in her characters: mother, educator, author, editor, native Mississippian, graduate of the University of Southern Mississippi and Belhaven University, and a person who has overcome great obstacles and still holds on to her faith.

http://www.janettaylorperry.com/
http://janettaylor-perry.blogspot.com/
https://authorcentral.amazon.com/gp/profile
https://www.facebook.com/Author-Janet-Taylor-Perry-299698950061301/
janettaylorperry@gmail.com
https://www.facebook.com/janettaylorperrybooks/
Instagram: @janettaylorperry & @jtaylorperry
Twitter: Janet Taylor-Perry— @mom5kidz421
Goodreads:
https://www.goodreads.com/author/show/7376480.Janet_Taylor_Perry
Pinterest: https://www.pinterest.com/mumzy25/
YouTube: https://bit.ly/30hJsYg

Hillbilly Hijinks continue in *Mountain Moonshine*

An only child of a widowed mother, Tipper Campbell is anything but ordinary. Among a people lost in the late twentieth century in the backwoods, Appalachian town of Possum Holler, West Virginia, Tipper has a plan—He is going to be an entrepreneur.

His business? Moonshine whiskey. His goal? Put Possum Holler on the map.

But all his good intentions take a turn for the unknown when his childhood love, Amy Dent, deserts him and their three daughters, leaving him without a clue what he did to drive her away. When he discovers the sad truth, can his spirit survive? Will a new, unexpected love heal his broken heart? Can Tipper stay his course and make his way to Easy Street? Will his dreams come to fruition?

The second installment in the *Hillbilly Hijinks* series, *Mountain Moonshine* follows Tipper Campbell, but his three friends MacKenzie Reardon, Gator Jones, and Alain Richter stay in stride with him as these four young men determine the future of Possum Holler.

.